TILTSTONE,
FIRE AND BRIMSTONE

TILTSTONE, FIRE AND BRIMSTONE

Part Two of
THE TILTSTONE TRILOGY

by

DONOVAN LEAMAN

For my Family
Past and Present
Dreamers of Dreams
Those Born to be Teachers and Storytellers
And Janis, My Unforgettable Tower of Strength

First published in 2005 by
Scotforth Books
Carnegie House
Chatsworth Road
Lancaster

British Library Cataloguing-in-Publication data

A catalogue record for this book is available from the British Library

ISBN 1-904244-41-6

Printed and bound by Alden Press, Oxford

Contents

Acknowledgements

In gratitude I thank all those readers of Tiltstone who asked for further information on the Stone. You have waited for three years and I salute your patience.

My good friend, Jackie Warden, who manages to decipher my pencilled manuscript and persuade her computer to accept it on disk. You turn my loopy scrawl into brilliant clarity.

Lesley Evans, proof-reader supreme, who so punctiliously not only put my punctuation in its proper place but also found time where necessary to iron out my Latin, French and German. I know that had I included more than one word of Latvian you would have checked that also.

Scotforth Books, in particular Anna Goddard and Lucy Day, whose enthusiastic commitment to their Fine Art has produced a book, pleasing to handle and lovely to look at.

Above all, Carol, my wife, who has known for some years now that, when I fail to respond to her queries and comments, I am incommunicado, lost in the far reaches of my imagination in mythical Yowesdale. "My broken dreams are yours to mend".

Genesis: Tiltstone (In the beginning was the stone)

An Extract from Part One of the *Tiltstone Trilogy*

Daniel was born in Tupshorne in the autumn of 1934, the son of James Greensward a prosperous agricultural engineer whose forebears had been blacksmiths. His mother Emily, the daughter of a railway engineer from York, had been a teacher of mathematics prior to her marriage. On the occasion of his christening in St Michael the Archangel, the vicar at the time, the Reverend Raphael Manley asked the reason for the boy's middle name, "Tiltstone". Mrs Greensward provided the answer. Her great grandfather Joseph North was born in a village near Darlington in 1821, the only child of very loving but very strict parents who truly believed in such sayings as 'Spare the rod and spoil the child', 'Children should be seen and not heard', and 'Whom the Lord loveth he chasteneth' (Paul's letter to the Hebrews). When young Joseph was about eight years old, so it was told, he quite unintentionally managed to break a pane of glass in the conservatory by kicking at a loose pebble which flew in the wrong direction. This so incensed his father that by way of punishment Joseph was shut in the cellar overnight and only let out at breakfast time the next morning. He never forgot the horror of being in total darkness with no means of escape and in some ironic way such an experience was to shape his whole life. He grew up to become a famous architect, noted for his designs of fine mansions, all of which, from the earliest plans had light and airy basements with provision for at least two windows where no child could be confined in blackness. Then one of his most influential, not to say wealthy, patrons insisted on having a house built without any natural light reaching the cellars. Joseph refused the commission and explained to his client the reason why he would not exclude light from any house which carried his name as the architect. An argument ensued between the two stubborn men, the upshot of which was that the patron told the architect that a personal problem dating back to childhood was no concern of his and if Joseph wished to design the mansion and earn his fee - and he as the potential owner still wanted Joseph to design it - then surely he could work out an alternative way of escaping from a dark cellar other than by the door, which once a child had been incarcerated was locked behind him. In brief, Joseph was ordered to use his ingenuity. His architect's fees for such a commission would be considerable and he recognised that his reputation within the Profession demanded of him that he should maintain a certain lifestyle in keeping with that reputation. He needed the money! He thought back in time, with much anxiety, to when he was that young lad in the cellar - no key to open the lock from his side of the door and perhaps the door was bolted anyway - no axe on hand to chop his way out and no form of light to work by. Then an old saying, surely of biblical origin, suddenly pierced the fog of his contemplation. "You only need to look upwards for inspiration". In a black cellar it is no use looking up because you cannot see anything, but you know the ceiling is there and if you can touch the ceiling then a means of escape should be within the reach of an architect. For an eight year old boy to reach the ceiling, there must be some kind of mounting block in place which can be located in the darkness. The mounting block could be built into the foundations. The ceiling had to move. He had the answer to his problem. At the drawing board, he designed a stone ceiling slab for the cellar which served as a floor slab in whichever room was above the cellar. This slab was mounted on an iron spindle allowing it to oscillate on its axis just enough to allow a body to climb out from the cellar. The slab would be secured in place in the cellar by a simple but substantial latch or catch, operable only in the cellar, and when the prisoner had passed into the room above then the stone would automatically resume its place with the latch re engaging. There would be no provision made for moving the slab from the room above by anyone wanting to enter the cellar, except by the usual door and steps down into the 'dungeon'.

Joseph North called the device his Tiltstone and he incorporated it into all his buildings from that time on, whether or not the cellars were lit by natural light or as black as night. In much the same way that the famous landscape gardener Lancelot Brown became known as Lancelot 'Capability' Brown because he would look at a landscape, weigh it up and state that it had 'capabilities', Joseph became known as Joseph 'Tiltstone' North.

"So, vicar, James and I decided to have him baptized Daniel Tiltstone Greensward just in case there might be a touch of genius in there somewhere. Don't worry, vicar, we won't lock him in the cellar to test the theory."

Live Animal Characters

(in order of appearance)

1. John Smith.
   An unusual tramp.

2. Baggins.
   John Smith's black labrador bitch.

3. Janis Kalējs.
   A Latvian farmer's boy, aged fifteen.

4. Zigrids Kalējs.
   Blacksmith. Uncle of Janis.

5. Arvids Kalējs.
   Farmer. Father of Janis.

6. Otilija Kalējs.
   Mother of Janis.

7. Scharfschütze Lutz (Ludwig Kaltmann).
   German sniper. Olympic gold medal marksman – Berlin 1936.

8. Heinrich Bormann (Heino).
   SS trooper.

9. Karl-Heinz Schultz-Steffen (Kalle).
   SS trooper.

10. Eleanore Bormann.
    Widow of Heino.

11. Else Bormann.   ) children of Heino and

12. Wolfgang Bormann.) Eleanore.

13. "Old Tom" Howard.
    Lincolnshire Farmer.

14. Donald Farrison.
    Lincolnshire blacksmith.

15. "Mrs Tom" Howard.
    Wife of "Old Tom".

16. "Young Tom" Howard.
    Son of "Old Tom".

17. George Griggs.
    Cricket club groundsman.

18. Max Herrick.
    Schoolmaster. Head of English. Cricket coach.

19. Daniel Tiltstone Greensward (Damnit).
    Director, Rolls Royce research.

20. Colin Blunden.
    Motor research engineer.

21. Miss Smithers.
    Secretary to Mr D. T. Greensward.

22. Henry Holland.
    Owner of agricultural machinery company "Agri-Presto".

23. Albert Prince.
    Master locksmith. Mentor of Daniel Greensward.

24. Aidan Ferrers.
    Cumbrian blacksmith.

25. Miss Athene Hope.
    Artist of Preston.

26. Merlin Swift.
    Agricultural machinery dealer of Co. Durham.

27. Miss Wanda Smiley.
    A bank, farming advisor – and fiancée of Merlin Swift.

28. Mr Nathaniel Ross.
    Consultant physician.

29. Benbo Beaumont.
    A Grassington lad.

30. Bilbo Beaumont a.k.a. "Stupid".
    Benbo's exceeding handsome black labrador dog.

31. Jolyon Walker.
    Outdoor clothing specialist – The Jolly Walker of Leyburn
    (Walkies).

32. The Reverend Jacob Drake (Jake).
    Vicar of Saint Michael the Archangel, Tupshorne (Retired).

33. Miss Bindle.
    Jake's black labrador bitch.

34. Ermintrude.
    Daniel Greensward's black labrador bitch.

35. Sprottle (Sprot).
    Hairy lurcher bitch. Owner – Douglas Swann (Nigeria).

36. Lorna Swann. (Not an Ugly Duckling).
    Caretaker of Sprot and mother of Douglas.

37. Martha Drake.
    Wife of Jake.

38. Bert "The Bells" Alderwood.
    A bellringer at Church of St Michael the Archangel.

39. Harold Palmer from Preston.
    The leader of a group of ramblers.

40. Nathan Fraser.
    The veterinarian of Yowesdale.

41. Timothy Welsh.
    Churchwarden of St Michael the Archangel.

42. Ken "Chop" Stickles.
    Firefighter of the Tupshorne Brigade.

43. Violet Rose.
    Church treasurer.

44. Henry Stint.
    Solicitor of Tupshorne.

45. Freda "The Flowers" Alderwood.
    Leader of St Michael's Floral Display Team and Church Hall Co-ordinator.

46. Rowena Herrick.
    Wife of Max.

47. Mr Beaumont of Grassington.
    Father of Benbo.

48. Muriel Welsh.
    Wife of Timothy.

49. Baggins' seven puppies.
    Rauch (Daniel's wedding gift to Lorna). A bitch.
    Nosh (sold to Harold Palmer). The only dog.
    Butty.
    Tiffin (Tiff).
    Collation (Coll).
    Snackerooley (Snack).
    Beautybaggins (originally Elevenses. Lev).

50. Douglas Swann.
    Lorna's son. An oilman, working in Nigeria. Owner of Sprot.

51. Dr Rachel Rosenbaum (Daughter of Mr Nathaniel Ross).
    Douglas Swann's fiancée. Hospital doctor in Lagos.

52. William "Tell" Taylor. (a.k.a. "Sweetie").
    Preparatory school contemporary of Jake and Daniel.

53. Bronwen Belinda Taylor (Bel).
    Tell's wife.

54. Miss Stephanie Potts (Spotty).
    Church organist and Director of Music .

55. The Reverend Julia of Cambridge.
    Officiant with Jake on the occasion of Daniel's marriage.

Important Inanimate Characters

A random selection

1. A Luger revolver.

2. The SS Training Manual (The "Isaac" Chapter).

3. A lawnmower.

4. A water jug.

5. Schnapps.

6. A bowie knife.

7. Ferrers. An outsize shovel.

8. "Aphrodite" perfume.

9. Pregnant. A massively capacious rucksack.

10. Moll. A C90 Honda motorbike.

11. Tottie. Damnit's ancient Toyota car.

12. Trollop. Damnit's new Toyota RAV4. A wedding gift.

13. Bethdan. A narrow boat berthed at Skipton.

14. Ghosts.

15. The Tiltstone.

16. The Almighty Insurance Company which underpins everything!

PART 1

CHAPTER I

Fata Viam Invenient

IT WAS AUTUMN IN THE YEAR nineteen ninety-nine when in his seventy-fourth year, a giant of a man by the name of John Smith started out to walk home alone, with only his dog for company, across the Pennine range from Preston, Lancashire, eastwards towards the rising sun. His name was foreign to him and English was not his native language. In fact, English was his fourth language after Latvian, Russian and German, but his sense of humour was pure and sometimes irreverent English. His command of written and spoken English, acquired as a resident in England for over fifty years, was well nigh perfect; even if occasionally his peculiar accent left much to be desired and revealed traces of his true origins. A born raconteur supreme, surprisingly well versed in Shakespeare and the Authorized Version of the Holy Bible, from which works he had a penchant for quoting, only very rarely was he lost for words. A man's man, without family of his own, this huge gentle man, rather like the Pied Piper of Hamelin of German folklore, held a fascination for children who were captivated by his colourful fairytales, and there was about him an aura of integrity and almost tangible security which was powerfully reassuring to any anxious mother who watched so carefully as she sensed the magnetic attraction he held for any imaginative and adventurous youngster. Nobody seemed concerned that he derived so much obvious pleasure from smoking his hand-rolled cigarettes – a lifelong habit he had acquired at an early age during his army service in the early nineteen forties.

Into an enormous rucksack, carried high on his back, was crammed the paraphernalia he deemed vital to his survival in the wild. An inventory of the contents included the basic minimum requirements for a man to keep warm in the cold, cool in the heat, dry in the wet, fed, watered and clean. Cooking and eating utensils, rabbit snares, dog food and a bottle of fine schnapps were to be found in an auxiliary sack, suspended beneath the master back pack. The topmost item in the main sack was always the first thing to be unpacked – it was the biggest, most sweet smelling bar of soap he could find – and at the bottom, carefully wrapped in a heavy gauge polythene bag, were secreted his last will and testament, a letter in a woman's handwriting, postmarked Hamburg, Germany, and a loaded Luger revolver.

A neutral observer, watching from below the brow of a hill for a man approaching from the far side, would have gasped in disbelief at the sheer size of a hiker as big as John Smith with his backpack, appearing on the horizon. Yet his first sighting, if the weather was dry, would not have been the apex of the rucksack which reached up above John's head, but a strange pole, split into a Y at the top and closed by a wooden bar. At a distance, what resembled some simple type of telecommunications aerial was the Y handle of a massive iron-bladed shovel, firmly strapped to the outside of the rucksack and stretching up to three feet above the hiker's head. In damp weather conditions, the same observer would have witnessed a different, more alarming sight – a tall, slender, white Red Indian tepee perhaps reminiscent of the Klu Klux Klan, seeming to glide over the terrain like a strangely modified hovercraft. Ever the practical man, in his concern to stay dry whatever the elements rained down on him, John had invented, for his own use, the first ultracape, and before leaving Preston on his long homeward walk, had persuaded a firm of tentmakers to sew for him a tailored dunce's cap of such size that when suspended from the very top of his shovel handle, it would just reach his toe caps and, apart from a small viewing window, cover him completely. The material he chose was white, waterproof and breathable. John Smith was neither poor nor needy but on his broad back he carried the harsh experience of a whole lifetime and in his heart he nursed the nagging guilt of responsibility for one tragic accident which had occurred getting on for sixty years earlier when he was only a boy of sixteen. His black dog knew nothing of her master's teenage years.

CHAPTER II

Vestigia ... Nulla Retrorsum

J ANIS KALĒJS HAD BEEN A NORMAL, carefree farmer's boy with a keen interest in the rather primitive examples of farm machinery scattered around the farmyard of his boyhood. In those days, before the outbreak of the Second World War, horses provided most of the power required for the heavy work essential to so many farming activities as well as such down to earth tasks as hauling the bier at a funeral. Truly a nature boy, he had an uncanny understanding of horses which, allied to his bent for machinery, often took him into the forge of the local blacksmith, his uncle Zigrids Kalējs, where he learned much about the craft of working with metal which stayed with him all his life. Growing up in Latvia in the early 1940s was, for the native population, a constant struggle for the normal freedoms of thought and speech which went unrecognized by its communist masters from Mother Russia who in 1939 had made a secret pact with Germany, assigning the little country to Soviet control, until 1941 when Germany, in the typically brutal fashion of the Nazi regime, reneged on the agreement, invading the Baltic states and subduing not only Latvia but Estonia and Lithuania as well.

Born in nineteen twenty-six, Janis had celebrated his fifteenth birthday in 1941. Physically mature beyond his years, at over two metres in height he towered over his father, Arvids, who remarked of his handsome young son, 'He doesn't know his own strength'.

With forty percent of the country being wooded, he had grown up with all the folklore, myths and legends which had been spawned over hundreds of years by the enchanted land, and encouraged by his mother he could tell a good tale to anyone who cared to listen. His head may have been filled with fairytales but his hands bore the calluses of toil on the farm and in the smithy, and sadly it came as no surprise to Ottilija, his mother, when together with his father and the rest of the able-bodied men in their village, Janis was rounded up, lined up against a wall and invited to represent *Das Vaterland* in its quest for *Lebensraum*. The three German soldiers in charge of the "selection panel" were of an arrogantly cheerful disposition born of the knowledge that in their hands lay the power of life and death – they each brandished a Luger automatic pistol. While weaving pretty patterns in the air with their pistols, the persuasive trio pointed out to the potential world conquerors standing before them, silent and frightened, the several benefits of joining a winning team. There would be no requirement for them to be able to read or write and, that being the case, no official papers would need scrutinizing and signing. Regular balanced meals would be provided as well as a smart uniform. If any one of them was to be assigned to a particularly dirty and distasteful task, a plentiful supply of schnapps would be available before, during and after the execution of said unpleasant job. But, of course, the prime reason for throwing in their lot with that of the Third Reich would be the exquisite pleasure and satisfaction of ridding their homeland of their loathsome Russian overlords. And when all the fighting was finished, in a few months time, and peace once more was reigning supreme they could have their own country back again. Such was the will and promise of *Der Führer!* Uncle Zigrids Kalējs, standing next to Janis, understood every word of the good news which, had he believed it, would have meant a necessary dereliction of his duty to the rural community, particularly having in mind his equine clients. He stepped forward out of the pathetic line and in halting German said, 'I am sorry. I can't do it. My horses nee …' His last sentence remained unfinished with the 'duh' and the 'me' floating on the air, unspoken. A single rifle shot rang out and the blacksmith collapsed at Janis' feet, a neat bullet-hole drilled in his forehead. The German sniper, ensconced at the upper window of a cottage across the street, adjusted the telescopic sight on his rifle by a minute fraction. Perhaps his hasty snap-shot had been a trifle snatched because the bullet was intended for the bridge of his target's nose.

Even the swaggering members of the recruiting panel were shocked by the lethal intervention into their customary spiel of a trigger-happy sniper intent on a spot of sitting-target practice. The summary execution served only to foreshorten the pleasure which they derived from persuading non-combatants to join them in the nobly idealistic fight against the might of Stalin's Soviet Union.

The trembling line of invitees, already struck dumb with fear, was shocked rigid by the crack of the rifle shot followed by the immediate dropping of the blacksmith, and the whole tragic scene seemed to freeze into the stillness of a photographic pose, while the men and their tormentors slowly came to grips with the enormity of their situation, with the sniper overseeing and controlling their every move. The silence in the street was palpable. The senior officer of the German recruiting party was the first to speak. He spoke firmly and very quietly. 'Do not step out of your line. Stay calm. Stay still. Breathe deeply. Do not panic. Lutz, *der Scharfschütze*, is not acting under orders and will be disciplined for this outrage in due time.' He paused. 'Now, ever so slowly, raise your hands above your heads and when I tell you, turn to your right and in single file shuffle round the corner out of the line of fire and we will continue our delicate negotiations. Leave the body where it lies.'

In vain, Janis' father begged for his son's liberty. How, in any kind of a civilized world, could a mere lad of only fifteen years be expected to fight alongside grown men? His pleas fell on deaf ears, being curtly answered with the incontrovertible evidence that if Janis was big enough then he was old enough. Father and son were separated, never to meet again in life and Janis was destined never to see again the land of his birth. Within a matter of days his medical checks revealed that his blood group was A rhesus positive and he was immediately drafted into the SS with his blood group tattooed onto the soft flesh on the underside of his left upper arm. And he enjoyed every moment of his initiation rites as if he was taking centre stage in a grim Brothers Grimm fairytale. He found that deep within himself, he had the sinister power to forget his family and his background as if they had never existed. Neither innocent nor naïve, as a son of the soil he possessed an earthy sense of adolescent humour which appealed to his more mature comrades who treated him with the good-natured affection reserved for a kid brother. In the same way that he had learned to speak Russian while living under the Russian yoke, so he quickly picked up German, a new language which was vital to his survival if he was to understand and obey orders. The many stories and jokes told by his fellows Janis was able to add to his store of myths and when he had the opportunity to re-tell some of their yarns, his own embellishments together with his Latvian accent and sometimes imprecise German grammar ensured an attentive audience, ready for a laugh and welcoming a little escapism from the rigours of army life and its suffocating discipline. Janis realized fairly quickly that it was as much his physique as well as his blood group which had determined his drafting into the fighting arm of the SS – the *Waffen Schutzstaffel*, Nazi Germany's elite corps. In later years, he found it hard to believe that some of his fellow countrymen had been conscripted into the *Allgemeine* SS and so were responsible for some of the atrocities perpetrated under orders of their Nazi commanders. It was then that he understood the importance of the recruiting officer's words referring to the "plentiful supply of schnapps" available to those given a "dirty and distasteful task" to carry out. The schnapps, with which they were so liberally plied, was always of the lowest quality, sometimes contaminated, but always guaranteed to damage the brain, sooner or later. In time, he was to share the nightmares of at least one of those permanently mentally scarred by the memories of what he had done, wrapped in a red mist of alcohol – fuelled horror. To hear a grown man crying and screaming in his sleep in the middle of the night when he is sharing your quarters was an experience never to be forgotten.

CHAPTER III

Graviora Manent

SERVICE IN THE *Waffen* SS laid down the discipline which governed Janis' life as he matured into precocious manhood. Not necessary for him were the brain-washing techniques and propaganda common to the Hitler Youth Movement. His was a personal fight against Soviet Russia and Stalin, his original slave master, and he believed that Germany would finally deliver him safely home to a free Latvia. Sadly for him his comrades in arms, more cynical and battle-hardened than he, made no attempt to disillusion the personable young Balt, preferring to keep quiet lest they should witness the shattering of their storyteller's idealistic dreams. The ethos of the SS was encompassed in their motto *"Ordnung muss sein"* – Order Must Prevail – and discipline was the keystone in the edifice of the elite fighting corps. Instilled in them was the arrogant notion that no other fighting force of long renown would wish to tangle with the mighty SS and it was to come as an unbelievably bitter blow that when their iron discipline finally cracked they would be reduced to a pathetic rabble as that hollow edifice collapsed. They were persuaded that, until proved otherwise, they were superhuman to the point that even in their barrack room horseplay, which served as a safety valve in the straightjacket of martial life, the physical competition between one man and another was full-blooded and no punches were pulled for fear of being classed as second best or faint-hearted. Yet Janis was strangely different and from the start, perhaps because of his youth, his elders were more gentle with him when they indulged in bodily contact games until after some months the inevitable happened and, momentarily, one of the "old hands" forgot about the age difference and Janis was hurt. Retaliation was swift. An angry Janis picked the man up as if he were a dead calf and flung him through a window. It made no difference that the window was on the ground floor or that the glass was smashed into so many pieces. What amazed those men who rushed outside to check on the state of health of the human missile was not the absence of blood or the broken neck but the distance the corpse had travelled after bursting through the window. Janis sat on a chair awaiting the return of the man who had caused him pain and marvelled that he had reacted with such frightening speed and brutality in a manner that demonstrated the raw power he possessed, developed on the farm and at the anvil. When he was told that the man was dead he could not believe that such a thing had happened, continuing to sit on the chair in a state of severe shock until a comforting little thought crept into his mind and he remembered his uncle, the blacksmith. He was filled with genuine remorse and regret for what he had done in the flash heat of the moment but he could not blot out from his mind the wishful thought that the dead man should have been Lutz, the *Scharfschütze*. His display of such formidable, uncontrolled strength went unpunished, noted in SS records as an unfortunate accident occurring during a training exercise. From that moment on, however, nobody volunteered to join in an amicable rough house with *Janis der Jähzorn* (The hot-tempered one) and a legend was born out of a game that went sadly wrong.

CHAPTER IV

Frangas, non Flectes

IN THE SUMMER OF NINETEEN FORTY-TWO the mighty German VIth Army under the command of Colonel-General Friedrich von Paulus was ordered into the Soviet Union, charged with the task of seizing the oil fields in Azerbaijan and the accompanying oil refineries at the state capital Baku on the Caspian sea. This was to prove a rash move by Hitler but progress was rapid and the advance of the crack troops appeared to be unstoppable, smashing through all the Russian lines of defence until they approached the city of Stalingrad. Once Stalingrad was overrun, so it was said, there would be no major obstacle on the road to Baku. Joseph Stalin decided that the city once called Tsaritsyn but now named after himself would prove its pedigree by being the immovable object at which the German onslaught would reach its terminus and ordered in Marshal Georgi Zhukov, the defender of Moscow in 1941. The bitter winter weather of December and January, allied with the fanaticism of Russian fighters willing to fight to the death, resulted in the slaughter of nearly three hundred thousand Germans alone. Zhukov succeeded in surrounding twenty-one German divisions and after two months of the most bloody warfare, von Paulus along with the exhausted remnants of his much vaunted army, reduced to shooting their horses for food, was forced to surrender on the 31st January 1943.

Later that same year Zhukov went on to lift the siege of Leningrad, a siege which had lasted since the Autumn of 1941. The nine hundred days of siege there eventually came to an end in January 1944 after a death toll estimated at one and a half million people, the majority of the dead being Russians. In the most horrific circumstances the Russian defenders and civilian population of Leningrad, under siege and starving to death, resorted to eating their own dead to survive. Occasionally, unattended children would disappear, as cannibalism became a sure way of stifling the pangs of hunger for those determined to stay alive.

On April 20th 1945, Zhukov was to be found in Berlin at the head of his victorious army.

Janis fought at Stalingrad – just one young man of so many in the last grand and ultimately futile offensive which was intended to smash the indomitable courage of the besieged city and for the first time since leaving Latvia he came across his father. The Russians had partially repulsed an earlier attack before dropping back to regroup once more, and his detachment, arriving fresh from recent training manoeuvres, was ordered in to press home any advantage which may have been gained in spite of the temporary setback. Janis' group made swift progress sweeping through the agricultural landscape of the country-side outside the suburbs of Stalingrad, hindered only by an occasional pocket of Russian resistance. The desolate terrain, however rural, bore the wounds of bitter warfare, pock-marked by bomb craters and lit-tered with burnt-out farmhouses. Not a single roof was to be found intact, nor any domesticated animal. Moving quickly along a frozen muddy cart track, deeply rutted by the passage of heavy battle tanks, all of a sudden he stumbled over a crumpled body lying face down across his path. After carefully turning the corpse over, the shock of seeing what he knew to be his father's face, partially disfigured by shrapnel, broke his shell of absolute discipline. Lying down close to the body, he looked questioningly into the sightless eyes as if gazing into a clouded double crystal ball. The cloud darkened into a red mist, which as he lay in the mud, closer to his father than he had been since he was a tiny child, gradually cleared to a bright and lucid vision.

In his vision, he saw a gravestone engraved with the names of his mother, Ottilija, and her infant son Willams – both dying in childbirth. To think he might have had a baby brother, and when the German army took him away he didn't even know his mother was pregnant. It seemed obvious to him that, without German interven-tion, both he and his father would have been at home and his mother and little brother would be alive. Such a double tragedy had nothing to do with Russia and everything to do with Hitler. A shad-owy figure of a person unknown to him came into the picture and a voice told him in his native language that he was destined never to see Latvia again but rather like the Flying Dutchman of legend be condemned to wander in perpetuity.

The sound of an exploding mortar bomb, not far away, broke his reverie and he gently lowered the eyelids to cover his father's sunken, staring eyes. Alert now and ready to assess the situation in the most practical manner he realized that his father's clothing, even if better or warmer than his own, would not fit his own so much larger frame but the boots would suit him well. It had always been a source of amused friction between father and son that they shared an identical size in footwear and it was an acknowledged fact that Russian boots were in a class of their own, especially in a hard winter, when compared with their German counterpart. So it followed that one of the best reasons for killing a Russian was the hope that his boots might fit you and Janis' father was wearing Russian boots!

In haste Janis searched his father's pockets and person for anything of value, acquiring in the process letters, a personal wallet, an identity disc, a gold ring and the massive clasp-knife which he had always associated with his father for as long as he could remember.

Half an hour later, he had managed to haul and sometimes, for a short distance, to carry the body to a deserted ruined farmstead. Searching for a digging implement, eventually he found a heavy long-handled iron shovel and set to work to dig a grave in a corner of a little paddock where under the remnants of an old hayrick the earth was not frozen solid. The battlefield seemed to become distant as, laboriously, he dug out the hole centimetre by centimetre until he was about one and a half metres down. Dusk was creeping up on him and so absorbed was he in his task that he was unaware of the stealthy approach of another man. The man spoke.

'What are you doing Kalējs?' It was his senior officer.

Janis was startled. 'I am burying a body, *Herr Hauptmann*', he replied in halting German.

'Such action is against the rules. You know, that after removing identification, all bodies are left for the Russians to bury. The SS do not bother with trifles. Why have you decided to disobey strict orders?'

Janis searched his German vocabulary for the right words to answer the question.

'I think you will understand, *Herr Hauptmann*, that I must bury this body. He was Arvids, my father. I have had no contact with him until now, since we were taken away from our village by the SS recruiting party. I cannot and will not leave him to the Russians. They may mutilate the corpse and I could not bear the thought of that.'

'I understand no such thing, Kalējs, except that you are flouting orders. I do not care who it is you think that you must bury. It would be the same if it was Herr Hitler himself. Orders are orders and that is that! You can fill the hole again – now.'

'*Herr Hauptmann*, you know I have a dangerous reputation with the nickname *"Der Jähzorn"*. Do not try to stop me burying my father. For me it is a matter of family honour.' His German was becoming stronger with every second.

'Are you threatening me with your reputation – earned in an accident? To hell with your family honour. The SS is your family.

'No, *Herr Hauptmann*, I am not threatening, just telling you straight, that I will not obey this particular order and you are not strong enough to force me to do so against my will.'

'Then you will do it at pistol point', said the officer, menacingly, indicating the Luger revolver resting in its holster.

Sheer rage flooded through Janis as he tightened his grasp on the handle of the shovel. He was still standing in the partly-dug grave while his senior officer was back from the edge, about one metre away from him.

'If you think that you can frighten me,' he replied, slowly lifting the shovel up, out, and to the side of the grave, 'by brandishing that revolver over me, then listen to me very carefully. If you touch it, I promise you this. You will not be left to the Russian gravediggers but as a personal favour I will bury you here along with my father and I will keep him in one piece while I will tear you limb from limb with my bare hands. And if you shoot me, an unarmed soldier, you had better bury me here with my father, regardless of any stupid orders, to cover up your crime.'

His fury subsided quickly as he realised he had gone too far, and he ended up by tempering his brutal statement with an escape clause. 'So may I suggest that you leave me alone to do what I have to do and return to our lines as if we had not met in such highly charged circumstances – that is unless you wish to stay while I say a prayer over the grave'. He smiled grimly. 'I take no pleasure in killing.'

Despite Janis' final proffering of an olive branch, the officer was not to be appeased. The spoken threat of being torn to pieces by a young Latvian yokel masquerading as an SS trooper, and the sheer calculated insolence was more than he could stomach and in his fury he made the fatal mistake of moving his right hand towards the butt of the revolver. As the Luger cleared the holster, the heavy shovel in

Janis' fierce two-handed grip scythed through the air and smashed with tremendous force into the knees of the officer standing above him. A pistol shot, intended for Janis' chest, went wildly adrift, passing through the material of Janis' right trouser leg and scoring deeply the inner side of the calf muscle before the officer crashed forwards into the grave, his shattered legs no longer able to support his weight. One more clumping blow to the head from the shovel was enough to provide another body for burial. The light was failing fast and Janis, because of shortage of time, contrary to his promise refrained from dismembering the second corpse. After relieving the body of any valuables, identification papers and the Luger, he quickly buried both bodies in a grave which, had he been able to work uninterrupted would have been appreciably deeper. He smoothed off the burial mound and covered it with hay before saying a brief prayer and begging forgiveness of God for the deed which he had just been forced to carry out. His wounded leg was beginning to stiffen up and his final thoughts, before he dragged himself away from the scene and crawled back to his lines later that night, were of a sniper's bullet executing his Uncle Zigrids.

"Alles in Ordnung und Ordnung muss sein!"

During the debriefing which followed the withdrawal by his unit, Janis handed in the officer's belongings stating that in some hand-to-hand fighting he had seen him struck down and killed with a shovel. His statement made interesting listening as he proceeded to elaborate on how he had seen the officer attempt to draw and fire the revolver in the same moment as the enemy swung the shovel. He explained that the resulting wild shot had hit <u>him</u> after ricocheting off a rock a few yards away and that accounted for his own damaged leg. The Russian soldier had dropped the shovel and disappeared into the murk as if by magic.

'After retrieving the Luger and his identification, I thought of bringing back the shovel as a trophy but in the circumstances decided that it was too heavy to crawl with unless I could somehow strap it to my back so I left it behind, knowing that it would be needed by the gravediggers. They must be running out of weapons, I suppose, to be reduced to fighting with shovels. That one was heavier than any I ever made when I worked for my Uncle Zigrids, the blacksmith – it needed a Titan to lift it! I even thought of using it to bury him, but remembered, "Orders are orders".'

CHAPTER V

Horribile Dictu

H E TOOK HIS FATHER'S *Namensschild* and secreted it in the hem of his greatcoat before examining the pitiful contents of the wallet. He kept only three items, a photograph of his mother and father, Ottilija and Arvids, happy and smiling, on their wedding day in 1925, another photograph of himself with his parents and Uncle Zigrids, the blacksmith, standing outside the smithy door, and finally the black-bordered letter informing his father of the death of his beloved wife and baby boy a mere seven months after the visit of the recruiting party. For a moment he considered keeping the dilapidated old wallet as a sentimental memento of his father but decided that such a course would be stupid – he already had the heavy clasp knife – so he tucked the letter and photographs into his own comparatively new wallet and at the next opportunity burned the old wallet. The sight of the dying embers reminded him of the smithy furnace and served to rekindle in him all those thoughts of home he had, so he thought, so successfully suppressed, so strenuously obliterated since his recruitment, and within a short time he retreated into a shell of his own invention where his comrades could not reach him as he hid the seed of any guilt that he felt.

Janis' memories of the battle for Stalingrad were never to be erased by the passage of time. He found it very difficult to come to terms with the fact that he had served under von Paulus in the VIth Army which had managed to seize nine-tenths of the city and yet failed to capture the whole. He remembered fighting his way with his comrades into the massive "Tractor Factory" and marvelling at the machinery which had been producing battle tanks. How could he forget the cold, dead furnaces of the "Red October" steel plant; death traps occupied by Soviet machine gunners who knew their only exit was to certain death. His youth saved him as he battled to the point of total exhaustion and he was evacuated to recuperate with Army Group A before the VIth Army was itself encircled within Stalingrad. The besiegers became the besieged and when von

Paulus, newly promoted General Field-Marshal, finally surrendered, Janis was not among the ninety-odd thousand starving and typhus-stricken German prisoners, only five thousand of whom were destined to return to *das Vaterland*. Many, many years later when histories of the Second World War were written, Janis was able to read, in English, that of the nearly two hundred thousand dead bodies recovered from within the city for reburial, three-quarters were men of the German VIth Army. His own father's grave in the countryside outside Stalingrad was neither registered nor marked in any way, but Janis could remember the precise location!

It was ironic, that in the absence of the recuperating Janis, the beleaguered VIth Army, short of total annihilation, fought so doggedly up until its capitulation that Colonel-General Yeremenko's armies, understrength on account of the priority for men needed to retake Stalingrad, were unable to prevent the escape of Army Group A as it retreated from the Caucasus through Rostov-on-Don in late January, 1943. Janis lived to tell the tale – just one more wounded man in the estimated one and a half million war casualties in the German armies at Stalingrad: the remainder were either wounded, dead, missing or captured. Hitler had failed them all. With the crushing defeat of the German VIth Army at Stalingrad, the tide of battle had turned by the end of January 1943. It was as if the mighty Russian bear had been fighting in a dream, only to wake up to reality, growl, bare its teeth and sharpen its claws before launching a ferocious counter attack. By March the surviving German forces had been beaten back to the river Donets and such a reversal of military fortunes marked a turning point of the Second World War.

The Russian commanders had remembered the lesson of "The Scorched Earth Policy" carried out in the face of Napoleon's advance on Moscow in 1812 when as the defending armies fell back so they destroyed food crops and almost anything which might have been of use to the aggressors. The same policy prevailed as they had retreated to Stalingrad in the Autumn of 1942 so that when the Germans, starved of vital supplies from the Fatherland, were finally driven back, there was nothing to be gleaned from the corn which had never reached harvest time. The retreating Germans of Army Group A were reduced to eating roots, rats and worms to stay alive. Shelter was never easy to find as the winter bore down on them mercilessly. Sometimes a half-demolished building, even a wall or a mercifully dry ditch was the only protection against the elements.

Janis survived. His earlier upbringing guaranteed that if he set out to snare a rabbit, catch a bird or even find some wild honey he would succeed more often than his comrades and he made the long, painful journey "home" to Germany, a sadder but infinitely wiser young man. After the battle and retreat from Stalingrad the rest of his war service seemed tame and almost uneventful by comparison.

CHAPTER VI

Quieta non Movere

FORCED ONCE MORE to fight the Russians on their first inexorable push towards Berlin, Janis took a sniper's bullet which passed through the flesh of his left forearm and he was ordered back to Hamburg to rest and recuperate. He pushed to the back of his mind the memory of house-to-house, hand-to-hand fighting he had experienced in the very heart of the city of Stalingrad.

Before his involvement in the ill-fated campaign to capture Stalingrad, he had made tentative enquiries through the regular SS channels in an attempt to locate the family of the fellow soldier whom he had killed accidentally in the barracks rough house. The authorities were downright unhelpful, even obstructive, believing that everything to do with fighting in a war should be separated from what was happening on the home front. All manner of excuses were put forward as reasons why they were unable to divulge the address of the unfortunate widow and Janis had become increasingly frustrated in his quest for information on her whereabouts. Somehow, somewhere in the innermost recesses of his subconscious rested the nagging sense of guilt which, however hard he tried, he was unable to erase. Eventually, to the great relief of those who chose to withhold the information he was seeking, he let the matter drop – or so it appeared. His apparent lack of persistence was motivated by a sudden insight, born of his naturally optimistic attitude to life in general, that sooner or later somebody would come up with a lead that would provide the answers to his enquiries, – and he was right. The trail had gone cold and then the day came when he was introduced to a new face in camp who laughingly said that he had heard from camp gossip that Janis was rather reverentially referred to as *"Der Jähzorn"*, but no-one would tell him how he had acquired the nickname. Resisting the urge to grab the newcomer by the throat to give credence and substance to his reputation, Janis smiled and took him to one side before explaining the whole sorry tragic accident which had given rise to the legend of his awesome strength and temper.

'You will notice when a similar scenario crops up that I never get involved in the horseplay', he said. 'I used to really enjoy the fooling around, the masculine sense of fun behind it all, but after that dreadful happening I quickly realized that, when I participated or even looked as if I was about to join in the fray, everyone kept their distance and the friendly brawl would quickly peter out. So now I let the others get on with it and they never bother with me or badger me to join in. It's better that way, you know. Although I'm only a comparative youngster I can understand that in single-handed unarmed combat at least, they are all afraid of me and feel safer allowing me to keep my own counsel. Now you know the full story. If I'm hurt it seems that I react violently; otherwise I'm just a farmer's boy waiting to return to his farm and not a soldier at all!'

His listener eyed Janis warily. 'Did you say the soldier's name was Heinrich Bormann?', he asked.

'Yes. That's right', replied Janis. 'Sad. I quite liked him although I knew precious little about him really.'

'How well can you describe him – height, build, colour?'

'I still see him in my dreams, quite vividly at times. Not surprising I suppose after what I did to him. He was just above my shoulder in height, weighed about eighty kilos. Dark hair – not black – but close cropped like all of us, and he had grey-blue eyes. I heard someone say that he had been quite a sportsman in his youth. He was certainly well-muscled without being too muscular. I think he was in his mid-twenties.'

'That's just amazing', said the newcomer. 'He has to be the Heino I knew at school. He was three years my senior – Victor Ludorum on the athletics ground. We juniors all aspired to throw the javelin like Heino. The Bormann I remember would have been very surprised to have been treated as a human projectile.' The topic of conversation changed. 'You seem to have remarkably good German for a Latvian conscript. I presume you must have learnt it at school. Can you read and understand it as well as you speak it?'

'I get by', replied Janis. 'My mother is a fine linguist, perhaps because she is part Russian, and I am a quick learner particularly when it comes to the basic essentials such as money matters, food and drink. Military commands I picked up in less than no time, as you might imagine. Russian is really my second language, either drummed into me by my mother or gleaned from story books. Like a young sheep dog, I enjoy being taught new tricks, and words of command I can anticipate as second nature. It may sound stupid to you, but I am rather looking forward to barking at the Russian soldiers when we meet some! Would you care to learn a few choice phrases? They roll off the tongue very easily and sound most impressive'.

'I don't think so, thank you. I even get tongue tied with German which is hardly surprising with a name like mine Karl-Heinz Schultz-Steffen. I answer to Kalle!'

Janis saw his chance and seized it eagerly. 'If you were at school with Heinrich, where exactly was that? We just knew he was from the Hamburg Land and presumed it was the city itself.'

'Hamburg is a massive city – we lived in one of the south western suburbs, almost on the river, the Elbe you know.'

'I envy you', said Janis, 'having somewhere to go on leave. I am not supposed to return to Latvia until we've wiped out the Reds. I wonder if, when I do get some leave, and I've had none yet, I might visit your family, take some news or messages from you – or something of that sort. I've had to write off my own family completely for the time being. The "recruiting" party that grabbed me and my father said this war would not last long. How long is long?'

'That's not a bad idea,' said Kalle. 'I should tell you now, that I don't have a beautiful sister waiting at home! I don't suppose we are likely to be given leave at the same time but if so, maybe you could come home with me for a break and see a German family at close quarters. Whatever happens, I will give you my home address in case you get the chance to visit on your own. To face reality for just a moment, I hope if you do meet my folks that you will not be the bearer of bad news. Forgive me – I am not as optimistic as you obviously are and must continue to be. Let me write the details in your pocket book.'

Janis now had in his possession the information which the authorities had denied him and he calculated that if he could, in the course of his next leave, visit Kalle's family, he would, with a bit of covert investigation, manage to track down Heinrich Bormann's at the same time.

In preparation for the major offensive eastwards towards Stalingrad most of Janis' detachment were allowed brief leave and he went to Hamburg with the sole intention of locating the Bormann family once he had carried any news on behalf of Kalle. Discreet enquiries at the post office resulted in him finding his way to a small ground-floor apartment, two hundred or so metres from the banks of the Elbe. He was totally unprepared for the sight which greeted him when the door was opened in response to his gentle rapping on the knocker. A tall blonde woman, with a little girl clinging to her apron, stood in the doorway and the apron, capacious as it was, could not disguise the fact that the young mother was heavily pregnant. For a moment, Janis was rendered speechless and then began to blurt out his first words of self-introduction in Latvian. His carefully rehearsed little speech had deserted his memory and when he finally managed a few words in German his foreign accent thickened inexplicably and seemed to obscure the meaning of what he was trying to say. The woman, on the other hand, was totally in command of the situation having taken in, at a glance, the SS uniform and the youth of its wearer, however large he was. She smiled easily and invited him to begin his story again – but more slowly! He explained that he was a comrade of her late husband and that he had taken upon himself the rather awkward task of expressing his sympathy in person, once he had succeeded in finding out the correct address. Eleanore Bormann, impressed with the earnestness of her young visitor, invited him into her home.

'You are the first of his pals to come and visit me. I thought perhaps they were too shy as if they did not know what to say – lost for words so to speak. But here you are, a non-German, to make amends for their understandable neglect.'

'Has no SS officer been to see you?', said Janis, puzzled.

'No. After the initial hurt, and thinking they did not care, I persuaded myself that they were simply too busy with the war effort to come and visit just one more war widow. At least I have his medal and citation for outstanding bravery on the battlefield where he ...' She swallowed a sob, and lifted the hem of her apron to her face. 'They are on the little table over there by the window.'

Janis stayed until his leave was up and would have wished to stay for ever were it not for the realization that the true circumstances of Heino's death must always remain obscured by the medal lying in its place of honour on the table. When the time came for him to return to his unit, he left in haste and steeled himself not to give a backward glance. The significance of his parting words were lost on Eleanore. 'Ask me no questions now or ever. Wherever I go from here I will always send you some money from time to time to help bring up the children. That, I promise for as long as I live, which could be only a matter of days or for many years. Only God knows.' He kissed Eleanore and Else, her little girl, before walking away into the ominous future, already a man in his seventeenth year.

He had never intended to return to Hamburg to see Eleanore, but when he was ordered there after the retreat from Stalingrad to allow his wounded forearm to heal, he was unable to resist the urge to find out how she was coping with a baby which must surely have arrived not long after their first meeting. He was dismayed to discover that her apartment block had been destroyed by British bombers during a night-time raid, targeting the Hamburg docks and the Mittelland canal which connected the three great rivers, Elbe, Rhein and Weser. Ever the optimist, he listened to a little voice coming from nowhere which said, "She is alive." In the same way that he had found Eleanore Bormann in the first instance by enquiring at the post office, he was able to ascertain that a week before the air raid she had moved into the countryside between Hamburg and Lüneburg, taking with her Else and a baby boy she had named Wolfgang. Yet he was not destined to meet her again.

CHAPTER VII

Spero Meliora

THE REST OF JANIS' war passed by in a whirl and without for-
getting the bitter defeat of Stalingrad and the extreme privation
which ensued, he seemed to lead a charmed life, a born survivor. He
saw service in France, Belgium and Holland before being summoned to one of the Führer's Breeding Camps where his impeccable
Aryan credentials of blonde hair, blue eyes and a tattoo that proclaimed him to be full of genuine A rhesus + blood guaranteed him
a place at stud. Such Nazi eugenics, however exciting, were not to
be a part of his life story. It was February 1945 and in response to
the arrival of the Russian army on the German border, intent on seizing Berlin ahead of the Allies, his battle-hardened, battle-weary unit
was swiftly reformed to be thrown into the path of the advance in
a last ditch attempt to stem the Red tide and once again turn the
course of the war. By now Janis had come to the conclusion that
death was just around the corner. His one-time dream of returning
home to a free Latvia was shattered. The victorious Russian hordes
were sure to find out that he had fought at Stalingrad where so
many thousands of Russians and Germans were buried and shoot
him out of hand as an easy reprisal, or merely cut his throat so saving a bullet. Should he be captured by the Russians while fighting
for Germany he now expected the same fate. He had never found it
difficult to embrace the warrior lifestyle of the *Waffen SS* just as long
as he could still believe in the prospect of a free Latvia. For some
time he had been hearing stories about the barbaric treatment meted
out to Jews and Gypsies, rumours of cruel medical experiments carried out on women and children and even the wholesale obliteration
of defenceless beings. Even the suggestion that all these tales were
Russian propaganda did not ring true because every true German
knew that the Russian army was capable of perpetrating any con-
ceivable atrocity in the thirst for savage revenge. The idea of
becoming a deserter crossed his mind only to be quickly dismissed
when he calculated that the penalty would be summary execution if

he were caught before he could distance himself from the field of battle, far enough to play the part of a deranged shell-shocked refugee. Matters came to a head within hours of his boarding the troop train scheduled to take the weary reinforcements to the eastern battle front when, in common with his comrades, he was checking the cleanliness and efficiency of his bolt-action rifle. In a sudden flash of inspiration, tempered by a chilling fear of self-mutilation, he slotted a round of ammunition into the breach and, as if in the haste and heat of battle, rammed the bolt home. The lightly-oiled mechanism worked perfectly. Just as he was on the point of activating the safety catch he changed his mind and in so doing brought his war to an end. As the troop-train entered a tunnel Janis could be seen polishing vigorously the inside surface of his rifle's trigger guard, the muzzle firmly tucked under the biceps of his left arm and the butt jammed tight between his boots on the floor. In the darkness, a shot rang out followed by a cry of pain and an agonized groan while the rifle toppled over, falling across the thighs of the soldier on the opposite bench. As the train emerged from the tunnel into the light of day, an ashen-faced Janis sat with his right hand clutching his left upper arm, just below the shoulder, in a desperate attempt to apply a tourniquet above the bleeding hole in his biceps, a wound complicated by fibres from his clothing being driven into the flesh by the force of the bullet which had passed clean through the muscle before becoming embedded in the roof of the railway carriage. In his unorthodox method of anchoring his rifle, he had made sure that the loss of an unknown amount of muscle would not be accompanied by a shattered humerus. At the next railway station the train halted to allow a medical orderly to dress the wound and Janis was abandoned on the platform, a rather pathetic and forlorn figure, to make his own way back to whatever the future had in store for him. The medical orderly was kind to the young giant who could so easily have killed himself in such a freak accident, providing him with extra dressings and bandages for when a change was required and rustling up enough food to last two days. The commanding officer on the troop-train signed the necessary certificate of "temporary medical discharge", countersigned by the medic, so allowing Janis safe passage within Germany without the possible stigma of being branded a deserter. An innate kind of wariness within him dictated that he should not hurry his return journey. All transport networks were in a state of chaos with many bridges and river crossings having been targeted by the Allied bombing offensive so he decided to find his way westwards in much the same way as he had been forced to backtrack from Stalingrad, except that this time he was wounded and moving through and over friendly terrain. Slowly he moved from village to village, from farm to farm where, with his farming background, he knew he could count on the true kindness of his own kind. His bullet wound was dangerously inflamed and beginning to fester, so much so that within two days he was feverish almost to the point of delirium and he asked a farmer's wife to examine the damaged arm. She bathed the wound with extreme care and tenderness, picking out with tweezers most of the shreds of material which were responsible for the inflammation, before applying a generous poultice of honey and grated cheese rind. When she had finished off the unorthodox wound dressing with a light bandage, she smiled at him and promised that within a week he would be healing rapidly and when the time came for another change of dressing he would even enjoy licking the wound clean as would any healthy young animal. Janis laughed and in thanking her for her gentle care said that the unusual poultice had reminded him of a time when he had impaled himself on a set of rusty harrows in the farmyard. On that occasion his mother had plastered the wounds with honey and sour milk. Tapping his right buttock, he remarked that no "healthy young boy" could reach that particular area to lick it clean!

Even as a child, he had always been a good healer where grazes and even serious cuts were concerned and so it came as no real surprise to find that, as the farmer's wife had predicted, a week later the wound was beginning to close with the early formation of scar tissues in the immediate areas where the bullet had entered and exited the flesh. It was not easy to inspect the wound site under the biceps where the material fibres had made such a damaging impact and when eventually he was able to carry out a reasonably careful examination he was amused to discover that the tattoo of his blood group had been obliterated, and wondered if such an accident could be described as bad luck or good fortune.

Days and weeks passed by as he meandered his way towards the setting sun, unaware that as he was gradually clearing the future Soviet sphere of influence in east Germany so he was drawing closer to the Western Allies. Eventually, after crossing the Elbe and the Mittelland canal, he decided to steer clear of Hamburg and to try to reach Bremen on the Weser, which route brought him very near to Lüneburg. He had no idea, as he was ferried across the canal on the last day of April 1945, that on the fourth day of May more than a million German soldiers would surrender to Field Marshal Montgomery and lay down their arms on Lüneburg Heath but he was there when it happened. He managed to persuade his captors to allow him to keep his father's heavy clasp knife by explaining its importance to him as the only memento of his father whom he had buried at Stalingrad, and in so doing learned his first two, very important words in the English language. 'Please' and 'Thanks' were to open many doors for him as he went out through the German army door, closing it firmly behind him.

CHAPTER VIII

Coelum non Animum Mutant qui Transmare Currunt

THE END OF THE WAR in Europe gave rise to a flood of refugees and a record high tide of human misery. By May 1945 there were as many as forty million people washed up and left stranded far from their true homelands, unsure as to whether they could ever return to their native country. The new German Federal Republic offered a home to any German who could find a way home but the victorious Western Allies found themselves burdened with over eleven million "displaced persons", referred to as D.Ps, of many nationalities other than German. Ten of the eleven million D.Ps either elected to return home, or were forcibly repatriated against their will and better judgement.

Half of that ten million returned to states under Soviet rule to be enslaved, imprisoned or put to death, stigmatized and contaminated by life and living in Nazi Germany. More than a million people remained for the Western Allies to "place" in the free non-communist world in the earnest hope that they would be enabled to put down fresh roots in yet another foreign land and perhaps find some happiness in the years of life still left to them.

One of that million was Janis Kalējs, who, still a young man only nineteen years of age, but a true army veteran, found himself working on a large farm near Boston, the county town of Parts of Holland, Lincolnshire. After several weeks of settling in to his new job and fresh surroundings he was able to appreciate the strange irony of the fact that, as he had been crossing the North Sea to a new life in an alien country, shiploads of German ex-prisoners of war were travelling home in the opposite direction to an unknown, uncertain future in the land of their birth.

The farming fraternity, into which he had been pitchforked, realized that the misfortunes of war had deprived most cruelly the still fresh-faced warrior of four years of adolescence, and showed him much kindness and understanding; so much so that he could see the benefits and possibilities for any ex-prisoner of war in Britain who, given the chance, might have chosen to stay rather than to return to a war-ravaged Germany.

To begin with, his living quarters comprised an old caravan, sited in a convenient corner of the farmyard, which became his private world. Conditions inside the caravan were basic but not primitive and although the lack of proper insulation made it difficult to keep comfortably warm in winter, the roof was watertight and the interior was dry. Janis contented himself with the thoughts that such conditions were infinitely preferably to some of the chicken coops and deserted pig styes he had occupied during the retreat from Stalingrad and that in four years nothing much had changed – whichever country he had landed in, he was still a farm lad, quite prepared to muck in and muck out! He was paid the basic agricultural wage, which was generously supplemented by lunch and tea provided in the farmhouse itself, where he was also invited to use the family bathroom three nights a week if he so wished. There was no lock on the bathroom door.

On the first occasion that he used the bathroom, he ran a hot bath, stripped naked, then examined his face closely in the big wall mirror and smiled at himself. For one fleeting moment the face that smiled back at him was that of his mother, and although he put it down to his own imagination he thought that he heard her say 'Janis, my son, only you have survived to tell the tale. So tell it, like I taught you and always give it life'. He stood back and took stock of what he saw of himself, before the condensed steam from the bath clouded his vision. Staring back at him was a handsome farmer's boy bearing several scars of war but only one of them earned in the heat of battle. Not yet having reached his prime, he could recognize a horseman who had come to live and work on a farm where horses were important: a metal worker with some essential experience both in the blacksmith's forge of his early teenage years and with the inevitable contact with the machinery of transport and warfare during his years of service with the SS: and in spite of his war wounds which had healed so remarkably well, a powerfully strong man but with unseen blood on his hands and undeserved guilt on his mind.

For a few years after the end of the Second World War life on a farm was uncomplicated without being simple. True horsepower was a vital component of the agricultural labour scene until the advent and rapid development of the modern farm tractor, coupled together with the application by Harry Ferguson of the science of hydraulics to tractor mounted implements, gradually resulted in the retirement of most of the magnificent draught horses. "Old" Tom Howard, the farmer, was not slow to recognize the value of his young "displaced person" on a farm which used both horses and tractors, and without exploiting Janis, intentionally involved him in the care of both, to the point that when a horse needed the attentions of a farrier he would be sent with the animal to the forge of his friend, the blacksmith, with a written request that he be allowed to assist, only if convenient, in any treatment procedure. In such a manner did Janis find Donald Farrison a substitute Uncle Zigrids!

He took every opportunity to learn English, and special government-sponsored evening classes were arranged to hasten the learning process. Many of the students were D. Ps of other nationalities – Poles, Ukrainians and Estonians among them. It was perhaps inevitable that in such a motley company of men the swapping of tales of war experiences swamped the desire to learn one more language. Even the class tutor on occasion was forced to listen, open-mouthed, to a highly unlikely story, truth stranger than fiction, delivered in the most atrociously broken English. In later life he would recall with regret the fact that he never had the sense to record so many fantastic tales in the vein of Jaroslav Hazek's book "The Good Soldier Svejk".

One day Janis, in an uncharacteristic moment of naiveté, asked "Young" Tom, the farmer's fourteen year old son, if he thought he could help to improve his English in some way other than attending the evening classes, so full of red herrings. The lad was stumped for an answer on the spot but showing remarkably good sense for a youngster passed the question to his school teacher the next day.

'Can he read?' asked the teacher, as yet not knowing that Janis already spoke three languages.

'He somehow manages to read the Daily Express, sir', replied Tom, 'But I really don't know if he can understand what he's reading. I don't think he's slow on the uptake but he certainly reads very slowly'.

'Well, Tom, if he can manage the Express, however slowly, he'll speed up – I don't doubt that. I'll give you a proper answer tomorrow'.

Next day he presented Tom with two books, one a copy of the "King James Bible", the other "The Complete Works of William Shakespeare". 'Give these to your D. P. with my compliments, Tom. If he doesn't already own a Latvian/English dictionary, I think he should be able to acquire one through the fledgling society "Latvians of England" based somewhere in Herefordshire. He probably has the proper address to contact. If he can read and make sense of those two books – and he may need help, you know – then he'll more than qualify as an honorary Englishman. When he recognizes and knows the difference between "interment" and "internment", "prophet" and "profit", "satin" and "Satan", he'll be able to tell a good story.'

'He manages that already, sir' answered Tom, grinning broadly. 'Would you like to hear his hair-raising account of the battle for Stalingrad?'

In time, Janis read, re-read and read yet again both books. Many passages he learned by heart, especially the famous soliloquies of Shakespeare which he could declaim with intense dramatic feeling, over-riding any shortcomings in his accent or his pronunciation. All the biblical tales and dramatic plots went into his memory, so serving to enhance his future reputation as a storyteller. Life was beginning to look up for Janis until the fierce Winter of early 1947 took a hand in his future.

CHAPTER IX

Vade Retro me, Satana

IN MID-FEBRUARY there was an outbreak of influenza in the Boston area. "Old" Tom and "Young" Tom went down with the disease in the first wave and were followed two weeks later by Janis. Mrs Tom, already tired with nursing her two men, realized that trying to take proper care of Janis, living in the caravan in the most bitter winter weather anyone could remember, was one call too many on her precious time and her physical resources. So it was with "Old" Tom's approval that Janis was installed in a spare bedroom in the farmhouse. The young giant was laid low with the virulence of the strain of influenza but Mrs Tom nursed him through it like one of her own and when he was restored to health, ready to return to his caravan, it was "Young" Tom who prevailed upon his parents to gently insist that Janis should remain living in the house with the family.

Integration into the social life of the community was far from easy for a young foreigner, who through the loss of his adolescent years to war service in the SS had been deprived of any normal teenage high jinks, which so often work as a preparation for the social relationships of manhood. The Howard family did their best to bring him "out", including him in the village dances and film shows, but they never managed to persuade him to join them in their church pew.

Evening classes, while not always furthering his knowledge of any particular subject, were important in that he was brought into contact with various teachers, a few of whom at least were able to pass on some of their social graces to an eager student. He joined the Boston Amateur Dramatic Society as a backstage boy and quickly became a star as a scene-shifter! Donald Farrison, the blacksmith, was the stage manager as well as the prompter for the various performances of the club and it was he who opened up a new social outlet for Janis by suggesting half in jest that he ought to take up cricket. He had witnessed Janis' unerring accuracy when working at the anvil with a heavy hammer and it was perhaps a happy coincidence that "Old" Tom was a keen cricketer and "Young" Tom entertained thoughts of playing for England some day. To the great surprise of all concerned Janis embraced the sport with a passion and zeal comparable to that of Saul of Tarsus, following his conversion to Christianity after being temporarily blinded on the road to Damascus. Much of the subtlety of the game eluded him, perhaps because he did not possess the particular kind of patience of waiting for something to happen. The manner of his batting was his strong point but his style would have made a cricket coach weep. Janis was still immensely strong in spite of his war wounds which had left him with a left arm only a little weaker than the right. Consequently, when he really connected with the ball it was despatched to his left hand side with considerable velocity, usually into the air and over the boundary. Any cricket team for which he was chosen had to give notice to any other club in the same league, with a river passing by the ground, that they should provide at least one "off-the-pitch" ball-boy, equipped with a long-handled fishing net when their Latvian fieldgun was at the wicket. In the social context, even more important than the camaraderie of sporting competition was the stage afforded the spinner of yarns after the match, when Janis could command a corner of any clubhouse rather like a court jester – but never the fool!

Donald Farrison, happy with horses and agricultural implements, was also a shrewd businessman and judge of character. The smithy employed three men, including himself, and the demand for their services was such that they were truly overworked catering to the demands of a thriving farming community, beginning to prosper as the industry picked itself up off the floor of the austerity of the war years. The arrival on the scene of Janis, already part-trained, seemed like a gift from the gods. The smithy premises were just about large enough to accommodate a fourth man even if the last one in would need to bow his head to avoid the beamed ceiling. He carefully calculated that there was too much work for three men to complete satisfactorily, with a backlog building up which showed no sign of easing. Hardly had he decided that the answer to his problems had arrived from Latvia via Germany when he was jolted back to the reality that he could never poach from the labour force of his friend, Tom Howard. Donald knew the true story of Janis' uncle Zigrids and in the same moment that he realized that Janis could not work for him he was suddenly touched by Zigrids' spirit. He was moved to act on behalf of the young man even if it meant that both Tom and himself would be the losers.

It was early July 1947 when Tom was approached by Donald with the suggestion that Janis should apply for British citizenship by naturalization and that the pair of them should be his referees when it came to completing the documentation. Tom answered by wishing that he had thought of the idea first.

'Too late', laughed Donald. 'I've found out how to go about it from my solicitor!'

In the evening, that same day, Janis had just stepped out of the bath when the bathroom door, unlocked as usual, opened quietly. Mrs Tom stood in the doorway. Janis snatched his towel from the towel rail to cover himself, acutely embarrassed.

'I'm sorry Janis. I didn't realize there was anyone in here', she said, and unhurriedly withdrew.

Janis knew as soon as she began her second sentence that her timing was perfect and she had waited, listening, for the precise moment. His time on the Howard farm must come to an end – even moving back into the caravan was not an option if a potential catastrophe was to be avoided.

The next morning Tom and Donald put the proposition to Janis that he should become British and that they would be very pleased to be his sponsors. He understood the thrust of their suggestion immediately but was so taken by surprise that he replied in his native tongue before all three of them fell about with laughter.

'My first words of English', he said.

'Please. Thank you'. He paused. 'How long do I wait?'

'It can take two years – no more,' said Donald, 'But my solicitor thinks it could be as little as a year for a young man like yourself'.

'Then I change my name too,' stated Janis. 'For a long time I think of this – since I meet Janice at a village dance. A lovely girl!' He grinned. 'And I am a big boy!'

'Good Heavens', said Tom. 'You are in a hurry. What name do you wish to change to?'

'*Kein Problem!*' replied Janis. 'Sorry! No problem. John Smith. Janis – John. Kalējs – Smith. John Smith is a very English name, I think. If I am Janis Bulla now, I would be John Bull next. Very, very

English! What you think about "Winston Churchill" perhaps?' They all laughed.

Within fifteen months, in September 1948, John Smith of England was registered but he no longer worked on the Lincolnshire farm of Tom Howard.

It was shortly after his bathroom encounter with Mrs Tom and the putting in train of his naturalization that Janis decided to tell "Old" Tom that he felt he was more engineer than farmer and that, with great regret, he would be leaving immediately after harvest. Tom was, understandably, very sorry to see him go but having witnessed from Janis' early days on the farm how much "at home" he appeared to be in the smithy, made no serious attempt to persuade him to stay. Quite how Donald Farrison would deal with the situation, knowing that a potential blacksmith was about to become available, Tom was not sure. He was well aware of Donald's overstretched labour force but found it hard to believe that when it came to the point he would not snap up such an obvious candidate to complete a quartet of forgemasters.

Once Janis had decided to leave the farm he thought long and hard about his next move. He knew how overworked the blacksmiths were and sensed by the same token how his pair of hands would be a welcome asset on a permanent basis. Regardless of Donald's close friendship with Tom, he felt bound in the first instance to risk asking him about the chance of a job. Donald was ready for him with the wisdom and judgement of a favourite uncle. He chose his words very carefully.

'I'm sure you know the several meanings of the words "loyalty" and "respect", Janis. They are very important parts of true friendship and Tom and I are old friends. He would be very upset if I should take you on. You, yourself must have wondered if it would be right or wrong to approach me. But you <u>were</u> right to ask and I am right to say no. I'm not altogether sure in my own mind about your reason or reasons for leaving the farm and trying to become an engineer. I won't ask. One thing is certain – you will make a fine engineer, out of my league. I have been expecting this situation to arise sooner or later and have carried out some research on your behalf. A world class firm of agricultural machinery manufacturers in Suffolk runs as good an apprentice scheme as anywhere in the country and it so happens that the managing director and I are on good business terms. If you can knuckle down and endure four years as an apprentice then I don't think I can point you in a better direction.' He smiled at Janis. 'And what's more, the company sports its own cricket club.'

CHAPTER X

Nunc Dimitis

IN THE HOWARD FAMILY, Young Tom was the person who missed John Smith the most. In terms of their experience of life there was a vast, never to be bridged, gulf between them. Tom could only read about the horrors of war or listen to tales about it as retailed by John who carried the scars of conflict. Yet in terms of age, with only five years difference between them, they could have been brothers. As suggested by Tom's English teacher, he had been of considerable help to Janis when trying to make sense of Shakespeare and the Bible, with the occasional intervention by Mrs Tom when they came across a passage which had to be unravelled before either of them could understand it. It was inevitable that a little of the story teller's flair rubbed off on Young Tom with the unexpected bonus of firing him with a love of Shakespeare, off and on stage – a passion which was not lost on Donald Farrison, stage manager of the local amateur dramatic society.

One of Janis' accomplishments, under careful instruction from his father, Arvids, was the ability to take a small piece of an ash tree, flush with Spring sap, and using his heavy clasp knife produce a simple whistle with a difference. The difference was that by careful, delicate tapping of the bark it became loose and free of the hard wood beneath. This allowed the craftsman to produce a whistle with a slide, not unlike a miniature trombone, giving a range of notes covering at least two octaves, depending on the expertise of the instrumentalist – truly woodwind with a difference! Janis produced several such whistles for Young Tom and before leaving his life on the farm made him a present of the clasp knife which he had carried with him since Stalingrad. But of all the many war stories that he shared with Tom he stopped short of mentioning the second body in the grave of his father. And only in the historical records of the SS was there any mention of the untimely, accidental death of Heinrich Bormann, and the record lied.

CHAPTER XI

Usus est Optimus Magister

TIME PASSED. The apprenticeship scheme, so highly commended by Donald Farrison, proved to be a triumph in the case of John Smith to the extent that he remained with the firm of agricultural machinery manufacturers for a further five years after the completion of his four year term as an apprentice. He would probably have stayed much longer if he had not chanced to overhear a conversation between two senior managers for whom he had great respect. In the mid nineteen-fifties, most men and women who considered themselves to be settled in a steady job expected to remain in that job for their working lives. Only much later in the century did it become commonplace, acceptable and even expected that the working man might have more than one career, often involving several moves around the British Isles and even overseas. In the case of the senior managers they were arguing but agreeing, rather sagely and with much nodding of their heads, that five years in one job was enough for any man. John failed to pick up on the remainder of the conversation, in which the two men argued the undoubted merits of changing departments within such a sizeable organisation as theirs, if a suitable vacancy were to occur. Looking back on his own experience of life since being "persuaded" to join the German army, he seemed to be growing older in stretches of four to five years. Perhaps he was predestined to follow such a five year pattern and if that was to be the case he would give the notion a helping hand. Without mentioning his theory of predestination, he decided to ask the advice, once again, of Donald Farrison with whom he had always remained in contact since leaving the Lincolnshire farm some nine years earlier. The outcome of their discussion was that within six months John had moved from the agricultural machinery manufacturer in East Anglia to an internationally famous firm of tractor manufacturers in the Midlands, to a position with considerably greater responsibilities. He took with him his cricket bat!

In 1961 John attained the ripe old age of thirty-five and carried out a re-appraisal of his received philosophy of "five years in one job is enough for any man". His firm's cricket team had won the area league for the second year in succession and although he had been unable to play in several of the matches, he enjoyed such good fortune when batting in those games in which he did manage to participate, that for the first and only time in his cricketing career he topped the club's batting averages. At the same time it seemed reasonable to admit to himself that he really enjoyed the tractor business – certainly enough to extend his allotted timespan there by another few years if the firm still valued his services!

Then in the early Spring of 1962 George Griggs, the groundsman responsible for the care and preparation of the cricket field, very much an honorary appointment filled by an enthusiastic volunteer who expected no pecuniary reward over and above the minimal expenses incurred during the season, suffered a minor stroke which resulted in him being demoted to the position of assistant scorer as soon as he regained full control of the regulation issue pencil and rubber. John stepped into the breach immediately he heard the sad news. Although, as a volunteer, he had no right to lay down any conditions under which he would fill the post, he decided that in this case it would be polite to stipulate that he would act only under the direction and supervision of George Griggs whensoever George felt fit enough to issue orders. In the same moment that he elected to step into the groundsman's boots, in typical Kalējs fashion he decided to bring his own playing days to an end. The club had a fine crop of young cricketers coming on and it was not in John's nature to overstay his welcome in any circumstance. Having topped the batting averages, truly he would be bowing out at the top and there was always a chance that, if anyone had to cry off for some reason, he might be asked to fill the vacancy on the team sheet. For just that situation he always kept his cricket bag packed, ready for action, and his trusty willow well-oiled. It had not escaped John's notice that George's other keen interest was in helping to coach the club juniors and after a rather formal approach to the committee, requesting that he be permitted to assist the coaching staff –

especially with regard to the youngsters, he found himself practising in the cricket nets with the club colts who were of an age at which he himself had already killed two men. Of these particularly chilling facts of his personal *curriculum vitae* he never breathed a word to anyone!

CHAPTER XII

Docendo Discimus

ONE OF THE OTHER MEN with a cricket coaching remit that Summer of 1962 was the newly appointed head of the department of English at the local secondary school – Max Herrick by name. He was intrigued greatly by John's ability to captivate people of all ages with his genius for story-telling. The execrable accent which had characterized his early years in England had mellowed and given way to a strangely endearing form of delivery that seemed to lend an extra dimension to any tale he cared to tell – however far-fetched – and even young children appeared to have no trouble in understanding what he had to say, often proudly mimicking the narrator even to his face. John's peculiar accent allied with the occasional strong Black Country accent of the Midlands, which the children were quite capable of stressing, caused much merriment among parents and adult listeners alike. But to Max the most extraordinary thing about John was the enthusiasm which he was able to kindle in his audience with his use of words and language, and when in full flow no-one ever interrupted him. Max recognized a teacher *manqué* and was inspired to invite John to take over his classroom from time to time somewhat in the manner of a peripatetic. The effect on the pupils was nothing short of electric as the story-teller produced the key which opened the door into their own imaginations and wildest dreams.

At the start of his school visiting John never had any intention of asking for payment for his time. He expected nothing, being just happy to have an audience. Then, following his third session, Max realized that his imported story-teller was neglecting his work to entertain his English classes and offered to reimburse him from school funds for his loss of earnings at the tractor-makers. John refused to accept more than a cup of tea and a biscuit in the masters' common room and then proceeded to rationalize the whole arrangement, making four morning appearances a term at the school, with the approval of his employers, who nevertheless could not overlook the opportunity to dock his pay accordingly! Max was quick to fall in with the scheme if only because it suited John to play it that way. However, after John's final appearance of the term he was tricked, in the most kindly way, into attending the last school assembly, on which grand formal occasion he was presented with a bottle of the finest Schnapps, a large packet of his favourite handrolling tobacco and a presentation copy of Aesop's Fables. Max had found the best possible way to express his appreciation of John's classroom presence.

CHAPTER XIII

Virtute Fortuna Comes

FOLLOWING HIS EARLIER YEARS as an apprentice John had realized the value of formal training in his field of engineering, taking every opportunity to increase his knowledge, understanding and feel for "metal on the move". Many a fine pocket handkerchief, in his hands, became an oily rag. If there was any engineering qualification within his reach he grabbed it with both hands with the result that by the end of his ten year stint with the tractor-maker he was a valued member of staff and an important cog in the machinery of production. Now forty years old, he took stock of his situation, making inventory of his lifestyle with regard only to his strengths. Any weaknesses he chose to ignore as irrelevant. He was searching for ten positive reasons why, after so long in the same firm, he should not be seeking for an excuse to move on. He found nine and listed them in random order, as follows:

1 Settled as an Englishman, but well known in expatriate Latvian circles.
2 Successful at earning a living.
3 Popular without seeking popularity.
4 Happy, backstage as a stage-hand (and occasional spear-bearer!).
5 Happy on stage as a raconteur.
6 Satisfied with salary.
7 Still cricket-crazy even as a part-time groundsman and coach.
8 Healthy and young at heart.
9 Open to innovative ideas and initiatives.

A possible tenth reason, however hard he tried to find it, eluded him until, finally, he came to terms with the one reason he lacked but for which he still craved – fulfilment. Quite inexplicably, with his life seemingly on an even keel, he felt that he had yet to realize his full potential. Perhaps, at forty, he ought to be satisfied with what he had achieved, stifle any further ambitions and truly settle for a quiet life. He decided to decide that he was "fulfilled" after all, to continue just as he was and to carry on building tractors. Hardly had the decision been made, when he had a letter from Donald Farrison. Donald had always retained great affection for his "adopted" nephew since he had first pointed John in the direction of an apprenticeship in agricultural engineering in 1947 and had followed his subsequent successful progress with pleasure and a certain amount of justifiable pride.

A week before the arrival of Donald's letter John had been at a riotous get-together of the West Midlands Latvian Community Club. It was late in the evening when the Schnapps was beginning to talk, tongues were loosening and undercurrents of a few deadly sins were surfacing. An unexpected wave of envy threatened to spoil Janis' night. One of his compatriots buttonholed him, speaking in his native tongue.

'Well, Mr English Kalējs, I thought our super engineer would have done better by now than making tractors. If you were really any good you'd be at Rolls Royce, surely.' He laughed. 'Perhaps John Smith doesn't sound English enough when he opens his stupid Latvian mouth!'

John had enjoyed his fair share of the now empty crate of Schnapps and was more in mellow mood than feeling belligerent, but the insult penetrated his natural *bonhomie*. He reacted with surprising speed. He grabbed hold of his unfortunate tormentor by his earlobes, pinching them viciously between his thumbnails and index fingers. Earlobes are one of the least sensitive areas of the human body until they are twisted. Janis twisted the lobes and blood appeared under his thumbnails as the skin burst under the pressure. The atmosphere had turned sour as Janis spoke, glaring into the now frightened eyes of his thumb-pinned victim.

'Say that again – preferably in English please – and I will tear out your tongue. But you can't, can you? It's time you learned some English and to take your drink, before your tongue drops you in it again.' He released his grip and the man reached for a handkerchief to dab at his injured ears. The other club members nearest to the pair stepped forward in a belated effort to part them but Janis had already stepped back, regretting that out of one stupid, alcohol-fuelled remark he had brewed up a storm in a teacup. He was neither inclined nor minded to apologise for his savage retaliatory action. The incident served to remind him that not far beneath the civilized veneer of his gentle outward appearance could still be found the rage required to throw a man through a window. He found it reassuring that, to have insulted him so openly, his fellow Latvian could have had no knowledge of his reputation as *"Janis der Jähzorn"*. His secret seemed to be safely buried with Heino Bormann, now over twenty years dead, and Janis reflected on the possible fact that perhaps all the SS men who had witnessed Heino's unfortunate death were themselves killed in battle, vanished in Russia or dead from natural causes. Ever the optimist, he was still loth to presume that they were all dead but at the same time he remembered that they were native Germans and if they survived they would still be living there – one or two of them perhaps with their own dark secrets to hide.

After the unpleasant incident at the Latvian Club Donald Farrison's letter came as more of a shock than a surprise. As he unfolded the letter, a scrap of a newspaper cutting fell to the floor. For a moment he was undecided whether to read the cutting or the letter first but, as he bent down to pick up the scrap of newsprint, he could not avoid catching sight of the heading of the item which was in bold black capital letters. He read "ROLLS ROYCE"; then he read the remainder which was advertising a vacancy in the research department of their motor engineering company. Donald's accompanying letter was brief and written in haste. It read:

'My dear John,

It is just five days since I returned from a short holiday in Devon and in catching up with the pile of mail which awaited me I neglected to study my regular engineering magazine – until now.

You have, at the most, only eight days to reply to the enclosed advert. It may be that you will never own a Rolls Royce in real life, but I have had a recurrent dream, over several weeks, in which you are behind the wheel of what is, patently, a new model! Surely a good omen.

Perhaps you never thought of R. R. yourself but my subconscious must have had you in mind. I think you should apply. I think you are well qualified, widely experienced and certainly up to the job. I say "Do it"! They can only say "yes" or "no".

I don't suppose they would be interested in a reference from
me ... who remains ever,
> Your biased "Uncle" Donald.

P. S. I'm not sure, but they may run a cricket team within some
kind of leisure complex.

John wrote off for an application form immediately and returned
it to Rolls, within the closing deadline of eight days from receipt of
Donald's letter, by driving up to Cheshire to deliver it by hand. He
was not prepared to let his form be delayed in the post and,
although he had visited Chester on more than one occasion as a
sightseer, he had never played cricket in the county, so he seized the
opportunity to take the road A51 between the RR headquarters, at
Crewe, and Chester – roughly west north west – and found himself
driving through hunting country, close to the Shropshire Union
Canal. He was reminded of crossing the Mitelland canal five days
before he was disarmed on Lüneburg Heath.

Leaving the A51 he came across a pretty hamlet where he was
forced to drive very slowly when approaching several hunters
returning to their stables on the outskirts of the village. Next to the
stables, which belonged to the local manor, he found what he was
looking for – a cricket field.

CHAPTER XIV

In Tempore Opportuno

WITHIN TWO MONTHS John was a new member on the staff of the firm which built the world's finest motor car – Rolls Royce.

It was several months later, in the early Summer of 1967, that John thought to ask a colleague if there was any significance attached to the symbol on the car's bonnet.

'It's a representation of the Spirit of Ecstasy', was the reply. 'She really looks as if she's enjoying herself!'

Returning home that same evening, he thought to look up in his well-thumbed dictionary the definition of "ecstasy". He understood it to be a superlative of joy or rapture. From then on, whenever he came across a Rolls Royce, whether in factory or car park, he would give the Spirit of Ecstasy a friendly polish with his sleeve. Such a silly little habit became his personal equivalent of "touching wood" to avoid bad luck and over the years many a snooty chauffeur was to give him an old-fashioned look on seeing him touching up "Ecstasy"!

Donald Farrison's dream had come true and John's instincts told him that if he was still in search of fulfilment he would now be chasing his own shadow. After several weeks of living in lodgings in Nantwich, almost a twin town with Crewe, and scrutinizing the "Properties to let" columns in the regional newspapers, the Gods truly smiled on him when a cottage came vacant in Reedgrave, the tiny rural village off the A51 where he had been led to the cricket field by the horses returning from their exercise. He felt as if he had succeeded in turning back the clock to when he was a boy, to a time when horses were everywhere – even if they had been heavy horses then – when in a smoke-blackened forge, redolent with horsedung and hoof-parings and ringing with the sounds of hammers on the anvil, there had been a blacksmith at work

The cricket club welcomed a new member who was so happy to be an assistant groundsman as well as servicing the mowers when required. One particular corner of the club site was heavily over-grown with coarse grass, brambles and nettles to the point that even a farm tractor-mounted mower found the going almost too rough to cope with. A boundary scored in that corner usually resulted in lost time searching for the ball, nettled hands when picking it up and frayed tempers for the fielding side in general. John borrowed an old scythe, which hadn't been used for years, from the blacksmith, unearthed a whetstone from the outhouse of his cottage and put a sharp edge on the blade. He had not forgotten how they used scythes in a gang of reapers to cut the corn in the fields of his child-hood. The rough place was made plain in time for the start of the 1967 season!

The cricket ground was close to the Shropshire Union Canal but not so close that John, even in his prime, could have landed a six in it. Nevertheless, in the small amount of coaching which he was able to undertake, he was always urging the batsmen to have a crack. He delighted his usual audience in the pavilion with his stories of other teams he had played against in his Suffolk days, who were required to have a long-handled fishing net when he was batting if there happened to be a river running by the ground. Of course, nobody believed him until the day of an away match against Ashton-on-Mersey, when Reedgrave were a man short because the pregnant wife of a middle-order batsman elected to go into labour. Bagman for the day, John was pressed into service – how fortunate he always took his own cricket bag to away matches, just in case – and landed four sixes in the River Mersey, where a long-handled fishing net was regulation fielding equipment because, if a man was to fall in, his next fielding position would be a hospital bed staring down the bar-rel of a stomach pump! Reedgrave won the match, John obliged by buying drinks all round and for a few minutes knew how Samson must have felt, when with his strength restored he pulled down the temple of Dagon at Gaza so killing himself and about three thou-sand Philistines. "What a way to go", thought John, wondering how he himself had never encountered a personal Delilah.

He quickly found out how easy it was to get from Crewe to the Lancashire County Cricket ground at Old Trafford and when oppor-tunity arose would spend many happy hours there.

John's appearance as a dynamic story-teller in school surround-ings came to an end when he moved from the Midlands but he soon attached himself to an amateur dramatic society in Chester as a backstage strongman. He was the proudest man in Cheshire when one production by the society contained a small role for a foreigner who sounded genuinely foreign and he was invited to play the part. He polished up his gutturals for all he was worth to produce an accent, referred to in the programme as suitably sinister!

In 1968 he felt so well settled, happy in his work and content in his village life, that he finally felt the moment might have arrived when he could invite Eleanore Bormann and her family to venture over to England for a holiday. Her children were both in their late twenties and married. Ever since his first meeting with Eleanore John had kept his promise to always send money to her as long as he managed to stay alive, and, just as he had bade her to ask no questions, so she never did.

John had vowed never to return to continental Europe of his own volition, unless Latvia became free of oppression and the heavy hand of Soviet Russia. His holidays would find him, over the years, in any continent but Europe and many of the footpaths and bridle-tracks of the British Isles had felt his heavy footfall. Walking and trekking, whether alone or in an organized group, he had been to the Andes and Zanzibar as well as most of the alphabet of the atlas in between but he loved the English Lake District best of all.

When invited to come to England, Eleanore climbed on to her high horse and announced that she had no intention of crossing the Channel until Janis had first visited her in Hamburg. In over twenty-five years of corresponding with each other and exchanging photographs of children and events this was the first occasion on which they were unable to resolve a stalemate. Neither would give way on the issue, and in an apparently amicable way agreed to differ. Yet, deep down, John felt hurt and in a fit of pique even contemplated ceasing to send money to her, before realizing what a childish act it would be. Eleanore, for her part, thought of refusing to accept any further money from him until, on reflection, she could see how hurt he would be and hurt was the last thing she would wish him. The stand-off between them was forgotten and John suggested that maybe they should meet again on neutral ground – Morocco! "Perhaps, sometime", was Eleanore's reply and the subject never arose again.

CHAPTER XV

Totus Teres Atque Rotundus

IN 1974 ROLLS ROYCE created a new, senior post in the motor engineering research department, luring back to Britain from Ford, America, a forty year-old specialist called Daniel Tiltstone Greensward, known to his friends as Damnit, to become an executive director with a seat at the boardroom table.

Earlier that same year, "Uncle" Donald Farrison had died, quite unexpectedly, following a fall on to the stone floor of the smithy which resulted in a badly broken femur. The limb was repaired to the satisfaction of the orthopaedic surgeon but, quite out of the blue, Donald went down with pneumonia and, unusually for those days, with well-proven antibiotics on hand, he was never to recover. John wept openly at Donald's funeral, knowing in his heart of hearts that, at long last, he felt free to grieve for Uncle Zigrids, his parents and the brother he had never seen, baby Willams. After the funeral Old Tom Howard, by now in his seventies, invited John back to the farmhouse for a meal before he set off to drive home to Cheshire. Young Tom, still a youthful forty-two, proudly produced the clasp knife which John had given him twenty-eight years earlier. The Solingen steel blade was as sharp as the day John had left the farm. Mrs Tom clucked happily like a mother hen over a chick which has returned to the shelter of her wing.

John had wandered round the farmyard before joining the family at table. He felt a slight sense of disappointment that his caravan had disappeared! Over the meal the conversation never flagged. Old Tom enquired of John, apart from the absent caravan, what he missed most in the yard.

John replied, 'Horses. And I bet you miss them too!'

'That's a safe bet', said Tom. 'We never got rid of a single one, you know. They lived out their lives here and they are all buried here. I can't remember now how many years have gone by since Bill Boy, the last one, died, but we still live off their legacy in the Autumn when we go picking mushrooms in the paddocks where they used to gallop free. I suppose I'm just a sentimental old softie at heart because each year at mushroom time I am reminded to take a nostalgic trip down memory lane and spend a couple of days at a village in north Norfolk where they still use Shire horses on several farms. You should go sometime yourself – the farmers welcome visitors especially heavy-horse men like yourself. You'd not be in the way, I'm sure of that, and the horses always recognize a kindred spirit. God alone knows how! It would not surprise me if they turn the whole situation into a tourist attraction sooner or later. To be near those marvellous animals for a few hours a year still lifts my spirits – I wish I knew why. Your "Uncle" Donald accompanied me on more than one occasion. He always insisted on taking his leather apron with him "just in case" his services might be needed – sadly, they never were and now they never will be.'

'I'm not quite so deprived', John said. 'Where I am in Cheshire is keen hunting country and, per head of population, the Pony Club probably has the highest membership in England. My cottage is only a few minutes walk from the busy village smithy so you will understand that I really feel at home.' He chuckled. 'What's more, I'm close enough to the cricket field to need a protective screen in front of my greenhouse!'

Mrs Tom entered the conversation with a probing half-question. 'I don't know how you've remained a bachelor all these years, John. I seem to remember that when we first took you along with us to the local hop, the sight of you quickened more than one feminine pulse.'

John flushed slightly before he answered her. She had either forgotten their confrontation in the bathroom doorway or she was reminding him of it now, in an oblique manner. One thing did appear certain though: she had no idea that he had left the Howard farm out of respect for her husband Tom, and in so doing had preserved his respect for her also. Then, smiling, he said, 'I don't seem to have found the right lady with whom to share my bath towel. I have had my moments though. The trouble is that the really attractive women – well, desirable in my eyes – invariably turn out to be married. If my parents were still alive I fear I would be a sore disappointment to them.'

She smiled at him in tacit acceptance of the veiled compliment which had remained unspoken for nearly twenty-seven years. Quite clearly, her memory was sound.

John could not resist a barbed comment, harmlessly directed towards Old Tom. 'You must realize what a lucky man you are Tom – happily married for what must be well over forty years. Who knows, if Mrs Tom had been your daughter I might still be driving around the farm for you. When I saw that lovely new combine harvester parked in the corner where "my" caravan used to be, it seemed to say to me, "fancy a test drive?".

It was Mrs Tom's turn to flush slightly as she turned to Tom and said, 'To think you always wanted a daughter, Tom. Would John have passed a son-in-law exam?'

They all laughed together at the very thought, and not much later John took his leave to drive back to Reedgrave. They vowed to remain in touch, as if, in the absence of "Uncle" Donald, the Howards would fill the empty chair at John's table of life.

CHAPTER XVI

Ignis Aurum Probat, Miseria Fortes Viros

JOHN SMITH HAD NEVER encountered Daniel Greensward but, as soon as the public announcement was made of his appointment to the post of director of engineering research, he made it his business to find out all he could about the man before his eventual arrival at the Crewe works. He found it a comparatively easy task to check out Daniel's engineering pedigree from his early days as a Cambridge graduate with a first class honours degree in General Engineering, to a Ford employee working at the forefront of motor technology. The name Greensward cropped up with maddening frequency in the reports of the magazine "International Engineer". Gossip among the Rolls men suggested that Daimler Benz in Germany had wanted him at their Stuttgart headquarters and he had rebuffed their overtures after discovering the frequency of *Sauerkraut und Leberknödel* on the staff canteen menu. Apparently, Daniel's command of the German language was so very rudimentary that he was unable to translate "Roast beef and Yorkshire pudding" for the benefit of *der Küchenchef*. It was also rumoured that his appreciation of German beer nearly won the day for the Mercedes team.

John delved deeper into Daniel's past, only with some difficulty. He seemed to have established a reputation as a self-contained bachelor, undemonstrative and boringly level-headed. Then came the first major breakthrough – he played cricket! John didn't need to know any more – the man was human after all and would know the difference between engine oil and raw linseed oil! Finally John uncovered the most important fact of all, Damnit Greensward came of a long line of blacksmiths. Now that "Uncle" Donald Farrison had gone to join Uncle Zigrids at the great anvil in the sky, could it be that he was about to encounter "Uncle" Damnit? On further consideration, after calculating that he was eight years older than Daniel and for those eight years he had been a Rolls employee, perhaps it was time for a rôle reversal; "Uncle" John sounded rather good, he thought.

John stayed at Rolls for seven more years. Along with Colin Blunden, he became Daniel Greensward's most trusted aide. Although no longer an active cricketer, Daniel was easily persuaded to become a non-playing member of the Reedgrave club, happy to help in coaching the juniors and maintaining the ground as an occasional assistant to John – the only time he ever deferred to him.

In John's original search of Damnit's unpublished *curriculum vitae* he had overlooked one salient fact – he had, in his prime, been a finer rugby player than a cricketer. The first time they met, that particular oversight was swiftly remedied. As they shook hands on being introduced, Daniel took a step backwards and looked up at the huge man standing in front of him.

'Ye Gods!' he said. 'Desperate Dan to the life! What on earth do they feed you on, cow pie and Guinness?'

John laughed, before answering in his most execrable, pronounced heaviest foreign accent, reserved for special occasions. *'Vee Schmidts are rhised an volf's milch, rhinedeer fleisch, sauerkraut und schnapps. Ven Ik bin "desperät", Ik kann eet rats und vorms!'*

It was Daniel's turn to laugh. 'I've done my homework before coming here and you may be surprised how much I know about the personnel in this department, but no-one told me anything about a resident giant.'

'Has your personnel check thrown up the story that I can lift the front end of a "mini" with one hand and grease its nipples with a grease gun in the other?', said John. 'I have not done so for some years, since my doctor pointed out that my left arm was several inches longer than my right.'

'Pull the other one', said Daniel. 'I am well aware of your reputation as a story-teller and that one is as tall a tale as I've come across. I hear that you're something of a cricket fanatic – or have been! Right?'

'Right! But now I'm not far short of fifty I'm more use pulling the heavy roller than wielding a cricket bat. I do a little bit of coaching of the juniors once in a while and when the opportunity arises I go and watch any match at Old Trafford. I too have done some homework in advance of your arrival. We all have. You also have been a cricketer. Do you still play? No, I don't suppose you do – having just come back from years in America. Reedgrave, the village where I live, has a smashing little club – though I say it myself – and if you think your playing days are really behind you, I tell you now, you look to me like a potential assistant groundsman, if you don't object to being told what to do by your humble servant – sir!'

Daniel smiled, acknowledging with an easy grace, the good-humoured acceptance of his seniority in the Rolls hierarchy. 'Your detective work failed to throw up the fact that rugby was my number one sport. I always enjoyed playing in the mud, even as a child. When I look at the size of you, I'm surprised no one grabbed you as a potential rugby player. I suppose it depended on where you first came to rest after the war.

'It was a farm in Lincolnshire', said John. 'The farmer and his friend, the local blacksmith, introduced me to the beloved summer game. Donald Farrison, the smith, I still regard as a courtesy uncle and a wonderful man'.

'All blacksmiths are wonderful men, John. I come of a long line of them, you know! Did your research reveal that bit of my ancestry?'

'No', replied John, quickly crossing his fingers behind his back. 'Neither did it tell me why you're called "Damnit". Would you care to explain that?'

'When I was about eight years old, I swore at my head master. I had lied to him and tried to justify the lie by adding "Damnit", to reinforce what I was saying. The name has stuck from that day to this. Are you blessed with a nickname? I presume at some stage of your life you've been called "Atlas", or the Latvian equivalent of "Tiny" '.

John's brow furrowed slightly as he pondered the question for a few moments before he gave a half answer covered by a smoke-screen of evasion. 'You are bound to find out, sooner or later, if you don't already know that I was an SS storm trooper. I earned a nickname among my barrack room mates that was hardly complimentary and I have no intention of resurrecting it now or ever. When my war finished on Lüneburg Heath, I threw away my Iron Cross and with it my nickname. Consider that particular subject closed, twenty-eight years ago.'

Daniel was taken aback by the vehemence behind John's reply and changed tack immediately, albeit only slightly. 'An Iron Cross, you say? Germany's highest award for bravery. If my mental arithmetic is as good as it used to be, you must have been very young when that was pinned on you. Mind you, I'm told that, as the end of the war approached, everybody collected an Iron Cross.'

Hardly had the words left his mouth than Daniel wished he had bitten his tongue, as John's face flushed with displeasure at the mild insult. As a man noted for his diplomacy and consideration in all situations, in a few tactless moments he had succeeded in causing offence to a member of staff, until now a stranger. He hadn't dropped a brick of such magnitude since earning his sobriquet of "Damnit". He apologised as quickly and heartily as he could.

'I'm sorry John. That was a stupid remark to make. I wasn't there, so what do I know about such things? Are you able to talk about it or is it one story excluded from your repertoire?'

Conciliation was in the air.

The fire of John's anger burnt out in a flash as he realized that in an unguarded moment he had blurted out the truth about the only episode in his war service in which he took any pride but had never mentioned to anyone since his surrender. His carefully concealed self-esteem had been disturbed by Daniel's thoughtless remark which only served to remind him that he had not always been a killer. He summoned a rather half-hearted smile which strengthened as he answered Daniel's gentle enquiry.

'Yes, on both counts', he replied. 'I never talk or tell about it and why I let it slip now is a mystery and along with my nickname it will remain so! But you may as well know the truth since I mentioned the fact, however unintentional it may have been in the first place – and you will kindly not raise the subject again with me or anyone else, please. I was only sixteen when I fought at the siege of Stalingrad. The savagery of those few months was unimaginable unless you were there. For a farmer's boy like me to end up shooting and eating the horses to keep us alive was perhaps the ultimate horror. Even now I find it hard to believe that after hand-to-hand fighting of unparalleled ferocity we penetrated to the heart of the city yet failed to take it. How someone of my size never attracted even a stray Russian bullet as we fought from house to house was a miracle. I was awarded my Iron Cross for bringing out two of our wounded men while under intensive enemy fire. Such rescue missions were not unusual, especially among the brotherhood of the *Waffen SS*, but only I carried or dragged two at a time back to some sort of safety. Had I known then that Germany was destined to be defeated and that I would be unable to return home to "Soviet" Latvia, I might have left them to die. And now, it all seems like a bad dream. I've said too much – I really did not mean to lift the curtain on my soul.'

'Thanks for the glimpse', said Daniel. 'You'll never hear me talk about medals again unless it's in connection with excellence in engineering.'

In the years that followed, John, with his stories, some fabled but the great majority true, lifted the veil of silence which he had so purposefully imposed on his war service with the SS. Damnit listened, in some wonderment, often spellbound, to every tale: told with such vivid imagery that he could not distinguish fact from fiction – nor, in all honesty, did he wish to in case the spell might have been broken. He quickly realized however that the master raconteur, so genial with his fellow men, must inevitably in the course of fighting a brutal war have sent many of them to meet their maker earlier than expected. After all, he had been trained to kill from the moment he was conscripted into the SS. The iron fist of the storm trooper never appeared other than clothed in a velvet glove and John never talked about killing anyone! For his part, Daniel thought it inadvisable to enquire how many notches might have been found on John's rifle. Truly, discretion in such a matter was the better part of valour, especially after John's sharp reaction to his tactless slur concerning those who earned their Iron Cross in the heat of battle. Yet it seemed so fitting that a man so skilled in the field of engineering should win a medal for valour on the field of battle. How many other warriors had discarded their hard-won fancy bits of metal, and with them their pride, on the heathland of Lüneburg? Judging by John's tale, which he had no reason to question, a man with a metal detector operating on that site of the Allied triumph and German surrender would probably unearth so many medals, which, if they could talk would reveal enough stories of barbarity, heroism and humanity, which when related would last until the Day of Judgement. However much blood John might have spilt in the service of the Third Reich, there was some comfort to be found in the fact that his own Cross of Iron was awarded for saving life with no thought for his own safety.

Time passed. Daniel and John passed through the potential mine-field of mere acquaintanceship in the workplace to the firm ground of mutual respect and friendship. They both knew when to call a spade, a spade!

Without doubt, John was the most down-to-earth, practical man Daniel had ever encountered in his whole life thus far, and a prime example of his practicality provided Daniel – not known for his own powers as an anecdotist – with a tale to cap most of John's yarns. At the end of his first week as research chief Damnit summoned his staff to his office with a view to outlining his thoughts and policy for the future and soliciting their critical opinions on such matters. It was a time in the twentieth century when a ban on smoking tobacco in an office situation was almost unheard of, unless the principal occupant of the office was strongly anti-smoking. Daniel was quite open-minded on the subject, remembering with nostalgic affection his own father's enjoyment of a choice cigar, even if he himself hadn't smoked since childhood! As usual, John lit up one of his own hand-rolled cigarettes and it wasn't that which set the waste paper bin alight but the partly burnt tobacco from the pipe of the colleague sitting next to him, who thought it was dead before tapping it out on the inside of the metal bin. John smelled the alien smoke of smouldering paper before anyone else and leapt into action. The teacups on the table were empty except for the dregs. He ascertained that information in a flash; then without a second thought unzipped the fly of his trousers and doused the fire in the most natural way known to man. The lady secretary, taking notes, didn't even have time to avert her eyes and the meeting terminated abruptly as hilarity held the floor. 'Where on earth did you learn to pull a trick like that?' snorted Damnit, rocking with laughter.

'From the Bible', replied John, with mock solemnity.

'Not my version of it!'

'Yes. Every version in whatever translation you like.'

'This, I must hear,' said Daniel.

'Well', replied John, 'you know the story about Abraham sacrificing Isaac, and the angel calling a halt to the proceedings before things got out of control. Then old Abe turned round to find a most unlucky ram stuck in a bush – poor thing. The rest is history.

He called the place Jehovah-Jireh: "the Lord will provide". Anyhow, in the SS manual we called it the "Isaac chapter", in the "Self-sufficiency" section. Being interpreted, the "Isaac" said that when you are in serious trouble, look around and then grab the nearest thing to hand! Any complaints?'

'Yes', laughed Damnit. 'Find some air-freshener-*schnell*. One of my few but useful German words. "*Ordnung muss sein*", you know, Fireman John! With regard to the "Isaac" you talk about – I wonder what your Latin is like. A few words of Latin I was taught as a lad sound like a candidate for an "Isaac". "*Aequam servare mentem*" means "*Panic not!*" I think you and I are going to get along just fine as my American friends would say – as soon as I can put up a "No Smoking" sign in my office. I can't risk you setting fire to anything for fear of a repeat performance. Miss Smithers' face was a picture!'

CHAPTER XVII

Vitam Regit Fortuna Non Sapientia

JOHN REMAINED AT ROLLS for a further seven years after the advent of Damnit Greensward, taking his length of service to fifteen years. He looked back on that time with great satisfaction and some introspection which suggested a hint of smugness. The mystical lucky number seven of the ancients appeared to have showered good fortune on him after bending under the wayward whims of the Fates since leaving Latvia. The year was 1981 and he hadn't felt the good earth of his homeland on the palms of his hands for forty years. All of a sudden, he wondered who might be farming his land; who was shoeing the horses? Powerfully nostalgic memories came flooding into his head, giving him cause to question if he was losing his mind. Then he re-asserted control of his thought processes with the over-riding admission that England had been good to him all along the line. If happiness was to be measured in standard of living, being valued and appreciated in one's profession, having a varied spectrum of leisure activities throughout any given year, then he was happy. The future was bright with a double capital R – at least until his retirement.

In the Spring of that year he went on a solo walking holiday based in Kirkby Stephen, a busy market town in Cumbria. From there he was able to go hiking in any one of the three counties, Durham and North Yorkshire as well as Cumbria itself. One day, choosing to walk in Ravenstonedale, only a few miles out of Kirkby Stephen, he got wind of a burning horse's hoof and tracing the source of the unmistakable stench to the local blacksmith's forge, he went in for a chat and a mug of tea! For the remainder of his holiday he walked no further than the forge, becoming an honorary Cumbrian blacksmith and champion tea-drinker in the space of four days. The blacksmith took to him as if he had found a long lost cousin and John felt that after such a long time in an alien land he had the sensation of putting down just a little root. The joy of working with horses trumped everything. While driving home to Reedgrave down the M6, and feeling peckish, John decided to leave the motorway at Junction 32 and make for Preston in the hope of finding a restaurant to his liking for a bite of lunch, rather than patronizing a service station café. It turned out to be a poor decision in one way, but once again his life's deck of cards dealt him a "joker". He was following, not too closely, a wagon toting a loaded skip, full of demolition waste. With a stream of traffic approaching from the other direction and a high kerb on his nearside, there was no way of taking evasive action when a plank of wood became dislodged from the top of the skip, which had no restraining net, and fell on to the road. The plank was not without nails! The offside front tyre punctured immediately it hit the plank, which swivelled as it passed under the car and another nail lodged in the nearside rear tyre. John pulled up as quickly and safely as he could in the circumstances, and found himself on the forecourt parking area of Agri-Presto, a tractor and farm machinery dealer. With only the obligatory spare wheel available and two damaged tyres to replace, it was pointless for John himself to change the wheel and he was only too pleased to let the mechanics on site sort out both tyres on the spot, even if it meant a longer wait while a brand new tyre had to be fetched from a tyre dealer to replace one damaged beyond repair. Business was quiet at the time and he found himself talking to the managing director owner, Henry Holland, over a cup of coffee. Lunch was forgotten! It took less than a minute for the company owner to cotton on to the fact that a highly experienced engineer had literally landed on his doorstep, although he was not particularly impressed by any Rolls Royce connection. They discussed the complexity of the modern tractor like two boys inspecting a new range of toys! When the time came for John to settle the bill, the owner passed it to him together with a verbal bombshell.

'I realise that with an unusual accent like yours, even with the name of John Smith, you can't possibly be English except by naturalization. No matter! I may not understand your every word – that would take weeks – but talking with you for only a brief time, it's obvious you're in the wrong job. You never should have left the agricultural scene. I'm ready to retire, and until now hadn't the faintest idea what to do with my business. I know now all right! Buy it, and I'll knock the cost of the tyre repairs off the price!'

John had always taken delight and not a little pride in his acquired knowledge of English words, especially any outrageous or onomatopoeic examples with which he might ornament his tales. His vivid stories for children depended on the sort of elaboration that he was able to give them. "Flabbergasted" was one of his favourites – an adjective which has to be experienced to really understand the meaning. He laughed off Henry's offer and the further protestations of sincerity which followed. Only when Henry flatly refused to take any money for the repair bill did he realize that he was in deadly earnest. John tipped the mechanics as generously as he dared, before driving away, already acknowledging deep down inside himself that something seismic was stirring. Henry's passing thought, as cheerfully he waved John on his way, was "He'll be back – sooner or later, he'll be back." He had noticed that in the moment John sensed the offer was genuine, his eyes had narrowed and his ears had tightened closer to his skull – sure signs that the bait had been taken. In the time it would take John to reach home, Henry calmly expected that hook, line and sinker would have disappeared as well. Now that he had as good as sold his business to a casual passer-by, he would have all the time in the world to devote to his favourite leisure pastime – sea-fishing.

Rejoining the M6 at Junction 31, John drove steadily and very thoughtfully only as far as the service station at Charnock Richard where he indulged in a late lunch. In the excitement of the afternoon his appetite had deserted him but he decided that it would be wise to eat something *en route* rather than waiting until he reached home and it would be an opportunity to debate with himself the motion, "This house considers that a man who works for himself must be a fool"!

Although the debate had no set time limit, it was only as John was slowing down, approaching the speed restriction sign on the outskirts of Reedgrave, that as chairman he put the proposition to the vote. The motion was carried *nemine contradicente*. That was the vote of the head which decided that acquiring his own business was an avoidable mistake. The unspoken secondary motion was then put to the heart – "This house considers that a man who never made a mistake, never made anything". As if the heart could speak, so it voted, "Yes" *una voce*. It was time to make – something. The following Monday, on his return to work, John recounted to Damnit the whole story of his week away, culminating in the extraordinary events at the Holland company. Even though he had already made up his mind to go he felt that he owed it to Daniel to give him the chance to comment on the matter and even to try to talk him out of the move. The bonds of friendship demanded such consideration on his part but he was stunned by the unexpected avenue by which Daniel chose to approach the situation, making not the slightest attempt to suggest that RR could not possibly do without him.

Daniel was not without intuition, detecting at the outset, from John's demeanour and unconcealed excitement, that he was anticipating a very lively leaving do!

His head was clamouring at him, "Persuade him to stay"; yet when he spoke his mind, it was from the heart.

He grinned at John. 'Quit while you're ahead, I say. At the least it saves someone the task of telling you, by way of a warning, that this is now a young man's job! Not my words, I assure you. We've been good friends, almost from our first meeting seven years ago. Not all that long, but long enough to know that if I was going into battle, I'd want you with me – preferably in front – shields don't come much bigger. I have asked myself, more than once, what I would have become, or what would have become of me if I had followed my dad into his agri-machinery business instead of diverting into automobile engineering. I shall never know now what it feels like to be my own boss. So you can do that bit for me and tell me what a big mistake I made!' He laughed. 'Give me the chap's 'phone number. If you don't act quickly I might just give him a ring!'

It was John's turn to laugh. 'A good friend, you said! I think if I was leading you into battle, I'd carry my shield behind me. Mind you, I'm a big-hearted fellow. When you feel like turning back your family clock, just give me a ring. It'll be the same Holland number. Work that one out. If you can?'

Damnit turned practical. 'How will you finance the deal, John? You're comfortably off – that I do know – but can you afford it? You may need a sympathetic bank manager to provide some financial backing. Seek good advice – it's worth paying for – and I can put you in touch, if you like, with a financial wizard whom I trust. May I suggest that <u>we</u> look at the firm's books together? I think I could be most useful or helpful in that respect. Mustn't be misled by an excess of shiny new machinery in the showroom! By the way, you made no mention of a cricket club nearby. Better check that out before you do anything rash, my lad. Good groundsmen don't grow on trees! One small thing that may have slipped your mind – Rolls Royce will require three months notice. At least that will give you a breathing space to set up the deal properly. Any holiday entitlement you might have could reduce that three month period – you'll need to check that out with personnel.'

John suddenly looked pensive. 'You don't think I might be a bit long in the tooth for such a dramatic change, do you, Damnit? After all, I am fifty-five?'

'Fifty-five years young by my reckoning', said Daniel. 'Businesswise, as regards sales technique or techniques, you'll be something of a novice: a situation easily remedied if you have a keen, experienced sales rep. If your Mr Holland is so eager to sell you his business, he should be perfectly happy to give you a run-down of his staff, complete with its strengths and weaknesses. One thing's for sure – your vast experience over so many years, beginning with your apprenticeship, means that the mechanics won't get away with anything remotely slipshod. They'll soon work that out! As the thrusting young men of today might say, "Go for it". Now there's a thought, "Old man"; if you don't go for it, perhaps you might just pass the Holland number to this "young man". Oh dear! Now I'm repeating myself. Maybe old age is creeping up on me.'

John laughed. 'Fat chance! Young man! You're all car, but I'm only fifteen years car and the other nineteen years farm. But to be serious now. I would be grateful for any advice which you think would be useful, beginning with your suggestion of looking at the books together. Oh, by the way – unless I'm very much mistaken, I think Henry Holland has already decided that I've swallowed his bait, hook, line and sinker. What he doesn't know is that the SS trained me to spit it all out again if need be and I have a wise friend watching me! Thank you.'

CHAPTER XVIII

Aere Perennius

THE SALE OF AGRI-PRESTO to a peculiar sounding Englishman went through eventually with no more than the average number of hiccups along the way. John encountered no problems with funding the purchase and any frustration he felt in the months before he completed the deal were all to do with his enquiries of the local authority planning department about the possibilities of expanding the business on an adjoining field, a field which looked more like a bomb site. The kind of expansion that John had in mind was the creation of a National Blacksmiths' Museum complete with obligatory "Spreading Chestnut Tree" of Henry Longfellow's famous poem "The Village Blacksmith". Five years later, in 1986, the museum was declared open by the Minister for Agriculture but John Smith was nowhere to be seen until the Right Honourable Gentleman began to quote from Longfellow:

> "Under a spreading chestnut tree
> The Village smithy stands;
> The smith, a mighty man is he,
> With large and sinewy hands;
> And the muscles of his brawny arms
> Are strong as iron bands."

A specimen tree had been planted at enormous expense some time earlier, the previous winter, and as the speaker reached the words "mighty man", a huge man, leather-aproned and carrying a mock anvil, walked from the back and through the assembled crowd to stand, centre stage, under the chestnut. John Smith, curator, had arrived.

Daniel Greensward had been party to all John's arrangements and machinations since his original offer of advice had been received so gratefully and gracefully. Yet it came as a rather un-nerving surprise when the concept of a blacksmith's museum was first mooted. When John had approached the planners about usage of the adjoining waste land, no mention was made of creating an educational tourist attraction and when he raised the subject two years after the acquisition of Agri-Presto it became obvious that it had been in his mind from the outset. Damnit felt slightly aggrieved that this was one confidence that John must have been unable to share with him, until with a little further introspection he realized that his disappointment was based on nothing more than petty jealousy. His own background and ancestry were rooted in the family forge; why on earth hadn't he dreamed up such a splendid notion instead of leaving it to an immigrant Latvian farmer's boy! Then it was that he understood that John had come to know him well enough to read his mind – when it suited him – and recognized in the project the tiny seed of jealousy, best left buried until disturbed and reaching the light of day in due course. The next time he went to Cambridge to visit his old friend and mentor, Albert Prince, the Master Locksmith, he expressed his misgivings about being left in the dark concerning the idea of a museum devoted to the arts and crafts of a blacksmith. Albert looked at him sagely over his spectacles which were perched on the end of his nose and laughed.

'I never forget, and neither should you Daniel, why your middle name is "Tiltstone". You are never in the dark for long. It's perfectly obvious, to me at least, that you're dying to be invited to the party – envy doesn't enter into the equation. Let me see now! It's 1983, I'm sixty-four, you're forty-nine, your foreign friend must be about fifty-seven or thereabouts if your dates are to be believed. He'll need all the help he can get if he's going to make a proper job of it. If it's to be a "National" establishment it will attract public funding even if the initiative is private in the first place. It seems to me that Rolls Royce ought to have some involvement, somehow, whether it be as a potential sponsor or as a provider of any metal-working knowledge they possess. How about asking your board to second you to Agri-Presto for a few months? They won't miss you I'm sure! One last thing. Tell John Smith from me – do not forget to pay tribute to Vulcan, the Roman God of Fire and Forge. Such an acknowledgement should protect the museum from thunderbolts thrown by a disaffected smith!'

'Right', said Damnit. 'I'll take it from here and see how we go. I suspect that if my father had been alive, he'd have said much the same except for the bit about Vulcan. He must have felt some sense of disappointment when I went into automobile engineering rather than following in his footsteps as an agricultural machinery dealer, although he never said anything about the matter except to give me his blessing. If John allows me to assist in this museum project of his, I think I might qualify for a second paternal benediction! What say you?'

'What I say will have no bearing on the outcome of this particular undertaking. I always thought you'd make a finer locksmith than a carmaker and you proved me wrong', said Albert. 'I wasn't all that disappointed – just a bit! However, to show my personal approval of John's plans I'll let the museum – and I'm sure it's going to happen – I'll let the museum have some of the ancient locks in my collection. I have several duplicates that I can spare, without depleting the range which I have been accumulating over the years. I might even leave the lot to you, if you're good!'

Damnit roared with laughter. 'There's no point in me being good. You'll outlive me – wait and see. Longevity is the second name in your family tree, you once told me, while my ancestors rarely made three score and ten before being returned to Mother Earth.'

'Wait and see indeed', said Albert. 'But while we're waiting we may as well live a bit before we also become museum pieces.'

And so it all came to pass as Albert had suggested rather than predicted. If a museum could be likened to a jigsaw puzzle, it contained many thousands of pieces – all pointless until the final piece was in place. John's masterstroke, the vital piece of the jigsaw puzzle which brought the whole museum to life, was to persuade Aidan Ferrers, his working blacksmith friend from Cumbria (the champion tea-drinker), to occupy the forge every Wednesday. The fire was lit, the bellows were squeezed and the building rang to the glorious sound of hammers on the anvil. The ghost of Uncle Zigrids was not far away and in the entrance hall, courtesy of the top student of the local College of Art, hung a huge portrait of Vulcan, Roman God of Fire and Forge. It was no coincidence that the mythical figure, as interpreted by the artist, was portrayed as lame and ugly: that was the description of the Greek God Hephaistos, recognized by the Romans as Vulcan, and such was her shame at his appearance that Hera, his mother, threw him down from Mount Olympus. Yet in spite of the obvious physical shortcomings of the principal subject, the painting itself exuded an aura of immense power. The picture dominated the foyer to such an extent that the initial question from every first-time visitor was, "Who on earth is that?" and the second question, "If he's supposed to be the Divine Smith working in the hellish heat given off by that open furnace, with his craftman's implements in easy reach, why is he working with clay instead of metal?" A decorative bronze plaque beneath the painting gave the answers:

VULCAN, ANCIENT ROMAN GOD OF FIRE AND FORGE, CREATES THE FIRST WOMAN, PANDORA, OUT OF SOIL.
Athene Hope – artist.

When Athene was commissioned to produce a canvas of Vulcan at work in his smithy, she had demanded and been given *carte blanche* in its execution and total secrecy with discretion until the unveiling, as part of the museum's opening ceremony. It seemed only right and proper that as the official artist, named after the Goddess of Wisdom, she should pay tribute to the Athene who breathed life into Vulcan's exquisitely shaped lump of clay, giving rise to Pandora. Quite deliberately, she chose to overlook what horrors were unleashed on the world when Pandora opened her box, being content in the knowledge that, at the bottom of the box, remained "Hope".

Within two years John had relinquished his post of museum curator when he recognized that Agri-Presto needed his undivided attention. It was something of a wrench to give up his "baby" even if it was an undertaking with charitable status. Even so, the museum was still next door to Agri-Presto, he remained on its board of trustees and he enjoyed the company of his successor as curator, enough to take a long lunch break with him every Wednesday, the day when his friend the Cumbrian blacksmith brought fire, smoke and din to shatter the gentle peace of an otherwise sedate building.

Following his purchase of Agri-Presto in 1981, for two years John commuted from his cricket club-side cottage in Reedgrave. There were a few occasions when pressure of work or severe weather conditions on the motorway necessitated his remaining at his company headquarters overnight. The first time it happened, he booked into a hotel in Preston but subsequently he decided to doss down in his office with a sleeping-bag and a blow-up mattress. With toilet and canteen facilities available to him at the far side of the main building, and an electric shower, he wanted for nothing. In fact, he rather enjoyed the impromptu nature of such events until the time came, just before Christmas 1983, when at the A-P Christmas party he exceeded his self-imposed ration of Schnapps. It was a lunchtime affair before the firm closed down for Christmas. Fortunately, he was not too drunk to realize that he was not sober enough to drive home and was all set to sleep things off in his office after the party had broken up when suddenly he remembered that he was to be "playing" Father Christmas at the Reedgrave Cricket Club Christmas party that same evening. He could not possibly let the side down. Copious quantities of strong black coffee and a very expensive taxiride home enabled him to fulfil his engagement in the club's Santa's Grotto, and sobered him up enough to make him realize it was time to move to somewhere nearer his business. Immediately on negotiating the social perils of New Year, 1984, he met the problem, head-on, and by April that same year he was settled comfortably in a self-contained flat on the outskirts of Lytham – a few miles and a few minutes drive from A-P.

The move from rural Cheshire to the Lancashire coast put geographical distance between John and Damnit. Their meetings, such as they were, became limited to cricket matches at Blackpool, Southport and Old Trafford, just so long as they, between them, remembered to liaise on time and place. Their lines of communication began to develop faults, but without ever breaking down completely. The happy harmony, developed during their days of working together, became just an echo borne on the wind with a reprise from time to time when one or the other made a concerted effort to meet for no other reason than to rake over the coals of social fires, which had burned so fiercely when they had worked together and lived only a few miles apart. They both knew what was happening as friendship turned into mere acquaintanceship and it saddened them.

CHAPTER XIX

Siste Viator

IT WAS IN JULY, 1989, three years after the opening of the museum that a new director on the Rolls board thought it appropriate to review all company sponsorships, past and present. He was unaware of Daniel Greensward's contribution to the establishment ticking over so sweetly next to Agri-Presto not far from Junction 32 on the M6 motorway. Daniel seized the opportunity to recall his involvement in the setting up of the museum and his long-standing connection with John Smith, once a Rolls employee, and was delighted to be given the brief to carry out an appraisal of how the museum was progressing.

Although John was no longer the principal curator, he was still a museum trustee with a high enough level of responsibility to suggest that all the ten trustees might convene on a date mutually convenient to them all. So it was that following a courtesy telephone call from Damnit the first Wednesday in August was chosen as a suitable date for a meeting. With the approval of the trustees, Colin Blunden, Damnit's "chief of staff" in the research department, accompanied him to Preston. John had great respect for Colin, stemming from his own years at Rolls Royce; yet Colin was surprised when John took him to one side, rather furtively, just after lunch.

John came straight to the point. "Is Damnit all right, Colin?'

'So far as I'm aware,' replied Colin. 'Why do you ask?'

'Well, it's a fair while since I've seen him face to face, although we have spoken on the phone recently, in the process of setting up today's get-together. He looks a bit "drawn" to me. Are you over-working him? Perhaps he's short on exercise in his leisure time. Today, he doesn't strike me as the human spark plug I used to know and love! Now there's a point! He's not in love or anything silly, is he? I understand that can be extremely stressful.'

Colin snorted. 'Not him! I'd be the first to know. Mind you, we both know our Damnit well enough to be aware of his relationship to a clam when he doesn't want you to know about something. No, even on second thoughts I still don't think he's bathing more than three times a week or investing in any expensive aftershave lotion! Seeing him every day, of course, I am probably oblivious to any subtle change in his appearance or social attitudes. There could be some stress involved – we're heavily committed to a research problem at this moment – the sort of tangle you were good at tackling. We think we can see our way clear fairly shortly, but in the meantime there are a few hurdles to be overcome. Actually, coming here today could be what we both need – a stimulating break, however brief. And Daniel always used to say, a day out with you at a cricket match was like a breath of fresh air or a tonic. Now that you mention it, I will keep a weather eye on him and if I find anything to report, I'll get in touch.' Exactly one week later, even to the hour, Colin rang Daniel's office, absolutely certain that he would be present and awaiting his call relating to some data on the research problem currently exercising their minds. Daniel failed to answer the telephone and Colin, sensing that something was seriously amiss, rushed over to his chief's office just in time to summon medical help for the man, collapsed over the telephone but deaf to its insistent ringing. There was little doubt that in some bizarre fashion, almost a paradox, an unanswered 'phone call had saved Damnit's life as the medical team were in time to prevent a second, potentially fatal, cardiac arrest succeeding the first minor heart attack.

Colin Blunden kept his word to John and, as soon as he was assured that Daniel would survive, rang him with the news of what had happened. John took no pleasure at all in saying "I told you so".

Daniel's working life was finished and on strict medical advice he took early retirement, selling his luxurious flat in Chester and returning to his roots in Yowesdale, North Yorkshire, where he bought a bungalow which he shared with his sister, Bethan, who had been widowed earlier in the same year he had suffered his heart attack. Spring 1990 saw the pair comfortably installed in the little market town of their childhood. The heart consultant responsible for monitoring Daniel's progress and rehabilitation assured him from the start that he would make a full recovery – if he would follow his advice and be sensible. No doubt a man of his reputation and experience would be an obvious target for headhunters fishing the seas of engineering for personnel to fill non-executive advisory posts, but the cardiologist suggested that if he could manage to ignore the blandishments and appeals to his vanity he should live well into the twenty-first century. "Keep active and keep eating – SENSIBLY" were the orders to be obeyed. Daniel laughed at the orders which reminded him of instructions to a dog owner but he followed them unquestioningly.

John made himself as useful and supportive as he could to Damnit during the time before the move from Chester to Tupshorne, within the constraints of his own responsibilities to Agri-Presto. The bonds of true friendship appeared to have been strained or stretched but never broken since John had left Rolls, and having discovered that fact following the heart attack, they were not surprised when they resumed their previous distant relationship, separated now by the Pennines, but meeting once or twice a year to walk the high hills together, with Ermintrude Daniel's black bitch labrador retriever; and once in a while but always on a Wednesday, Damnit would drive over to the museum to lunch with John and Aidan and feast on the sight and sounds of the blacksmith at work in the forge. The ringing of hammers on the anvil was like music to the soul, declared Daniel. John was not too sure about that – there were times, usually when a class of apprentice blacksmiths were at work, the acrid smoke and clangour re-awakened painful memories of battle tanks crashing and burning out at the siege of Stalingrad.

CHAPTER XX

Otium cum Digniate

JOHN WAS SIXTY-NINE when he decided to retire from business while he was still enjoying robust health. The year was 1995 and he had been his own boss for fourteen years of unbroken success and steadily climbing profits derived from organic growth of his company. He was lunching at the museum as usual – it was a warm, sunny Wednesday in May and the "spreading chestnut tree" was in full bloom, smothered in a profusion of white candles. It had been an unwritten rule over the years that he and Aidan, the blacksmith, never discussed business unless days of constant wet weather put a serious dampener on affairs. The farming fraternity know well that you cannot sign a wet cheque book. Suddenly, Aidan said, 'And now about business!'

'You know we don't do "business", you and I', growled John. 'Don't spoil things now.'

'I'm serious', replied Aidan. 'For several weeks you, my friend, have lingered long over your lunch here. Something's up which you are oblivious to because you're too close to whatever it is. As an onlooker, I think I have identified what this unseen problem might be. Agri-Presto is becoming Agri-*Rallentando*.'

'Kindly explain', said John, a trifle acidly.

'You know that in music Agri-Presto would translate, freely maybe, as Farm-Quick or, better still, Farm-Fast.'

'I never knew that. I always presumed the Presto bit had its "n" bitten off! Do carry on.'

'Well, it looks to me as if it's now rallentando – slowing down. And don't blame the weather. Your business has matured and if you intend to grow any bigger, either you will have to diversify into something like a plant-hire business, using your accumulated capital – or you'll have to buy out one of your competitors. Personally speaking, John, at your age I don't think you need the extra hassle. You've made it all work like a well-oiled machine and in terms of personal finance and security you yourself have "made it". I reckon it's high time to pack up before you crack up. Do you need me to tell you, "you can't go on for ever"? That's what's expected of black-smiths!'

'You don't pull your punches, do you, Aidan? I think you may have hit me below the belt while the ref was looking at the time-keeper! You could just be right in your analysis. So what do you suggest I do about the matter?'

'Me?' smiled Aidan. 'I wouldn't have a clue but Damnit would. Give him a ring before he drops off his perch. Let him rack his brilliant brain on your behalf!'

'I'll think about it first', said John. 'Then, I might contact Damnit. You wouldn't know this, but a good few years ago now he paid me one of the greatest compliments of my life. He said he would follow me into battle – he felt that safe in my company. Shortly after that statement, I learned that as a young schoolboy he had earned the reputation of being a "safe pair of hands in any situation", – some words his head teacher had written on his school report so I was led to believe. Whatever, he's a great man in my book. You already know that, in the first place, he advised me to seize the opportunity to buy Agri-Presto, so if I decide to sell out, you can be sure I'll pass the problem back into his safe hands. After all, life is no more than a game of cricket as my "uncle" Donald used to say. He was a cricketing blacksmith – but you know that already as well. In the meantime, I trust you will keep this chat under your hat.'

That same evening John rang Damnit in Tupshorne. 'It's time for "walkies" again. How about meeting up in Clitheroe before consulting the witches' shades on Pendle Hill?'

'When exactly do you have in mind, John?'

'Saturday. Three days time. Short notice but the weather looks promising. Can you make it? Bring Ermin of course. I'm sure you both need the exercise. By the way "walkies" means "talkies" as well!'

'Sorry. No can do this time. It's not the actual timing – I turned my ankle when walking in Wensleydale yesterday and it's strapped up. I expect I'll live. It may be mended by Saturday but not fit to do a decent walk. Hang on a moment – such urgency on your part would indicate there's a hidden agenda somewhere. Am I right?'

'Sort of', said John, crossing his fingers behind his back and chuckling to himself. 'Item one on the agenda. The owner of Agri-Presto is contemplating expanding his business.'

'You're a prize idiot, John. At your age you must be going round the bend. Strikes me, you need a padded cell not a walk. We'd better get our heads together before you do something daft. What's Latvian for "daft"? I wonder. If me walking this coming Saturday is out, then how about us meeting in Skipton? I've no problem driving. There's a pub you may know it – the Hammer and Tongs, close to the canal basin where Bethan and I berth our narrow boat. You've never met my sister, Bethan, have you? Maybe I'd better bring her along as well – she'll talk some horse-sense into you. On second thoughts, I'll leave her to walk Ermin. Shall we say half twelve? Item one on the agenda: Yorkshire beef hotpot and a quart of Black Sheep Bitter – on your expense account. That should set us up for a *tête à tête*.'

'You're on', said John. 'I've not seen the narrow boat although you have mentioned it before. Maybe you could introduce us.'

'Sure', replied Daniel. 'She's called the Bethdan. We can adjourn there after lunch and hold a floating conference!'

By the time John met up with Damnit at the Hammer and Tongs, he already knew that Agri-Presto was about to become another part of his past. How best to dispose of his business, the final fourteen years of his working life, was the poser he was going to drop into Daniel's lap.

After the introductory niceties of deciding who would foot the drinks bill, they retired to a table in the darkest corner of the bar, where Daniel immediately broached the subject of the possible expansion of Agri-Presto. John cut him short, bluntly stating that since their brief telephone conversation three days earlier he had done a complete *volte- face* and now wanted out completely. He was not daft, after all! Damnit was amused. 'I thought, the other night, you were set on bidding for a tractor manufacturer. Precisely what has caused you to see the light? You've never had an attack of cold feet since Stalingrad.'

'Well, since we spoke the other evening I've been to the bank – on routine business you understand – and almost fell over the manager. Anyhow, once I'd set him back on his feet again, he invited me into his office saying that my bumping into him like that had saved the bank a 'phone call. It seems that one of my accounts was a bit, "top-heavy" was the term he used. We sorted the matter out quickly enough and as we were shaking hands on parting, he suddenly said that he presumed I had made a will. I'm afraid I was unpardonably rude and just replied that that was my business, and went. But I haven't, Damnit, and I know I should have.'

Daniel listened carefully. 'Carry on – I'm just about with you.'

'I've no dependants, no relatives, no one to follow me, no one to leave my "fortune" to. So there is no point in getting bigger and richer. Time to go! This old nag is going to sell out and put himself out to grass. You're here to tell me how to do it, please, and point me in the direction of some decent pasture.'

'I'm glad you asked me. This could be your lucky day. Only last week, I heard on the north-east grapevine that the agricultural machinery firm that bought my dad's business back in the late fifties, when dad could see I wasn't going to succeed him, is looking to expand once more. The word is that an acquisition doesn't necessarily have to be east of the Pennines. Let's see if I can broker a deal in that direction first of all. It's inevitable that I'll need to familiarise myself with your books, as the two of us did before you bought A-P. Any objection to that?'

'None whatsoever. It worked then, when I was such an inexperienced business man. You told me then to get sound financial advice when I was buying, and not to rely entirely on your rather biased opinions in my support. Now I am selling, I only need you, Daniel – and a valuer, of course, to put a price on A-P.' He grinned at Daniel. 'As my broker, you will command a generous fee. Name it!'

'A new heavy roller for my cricket club will do for a start', replied Damnit, with a matching grin. 'But this question of your last will and testament is of equal importance with selling A-P. Strange that we're both bachelors – very comfortably off with no family. Only you can decide what to do with, or rather what should happen to your wealth after you die. I can't help you there. Get yourself a good solicitor – he or she will sort you out; decide whether you're to be cremated wearing purple pyjamas, brass knobs on your coffin, ashes scattered on Blackpool sands – all that sort of thing. And when you have sold A-P, you'll need some very special financial advice on investing the money in which you will find yourself wallowing. You may feel the urge to move to a more convenient area that will provide you with the stimulation you will need as you find time on your hands. Maybe your Reedgrave cottage by the cricket club's come vacant! Think it over. Meanwhile, I'll contact Swifts who bought my dad's business – in fact, I'll drop in and see them face to face first thing tomorrow. This particular bull of yours needs taking by the horns. O.K.?'

'O.K.', replied John. 'So when I've forked out for your lunch, can I go aboard your narrow boat? If I like the feel of it – you never know, I might decide to get one myself and berth it on the Shropshire Union Canal where it passes Reedgrave; that's if I have to move home.'

Damnit opened his mouth to speak then shut it again quickly, but not before John had noticed the movement.

'Were you about to say something?' he asked, seeing a look of consternation flitting across Daniel's face, only to be replaced by one of pained seriousness.

'Yes and no', replied Daniel. 'it was just when you said "move home", I had a strange flashback of imagining you back home in Latvia. Please don't be offended, but do you ever dream of home, as it once was or as it might be now? Do you ever contemplate returning?'

'Not even in my wildest dreams, Damnit. Never. Never. Never. I can't.' And he broke down in tears.

CHAPTER XXI

Occasionem Cognosce

VERY MUCH IN THE SAME manner that Henry Holland had offered Agri-Presto to John Smith, so did Daniel on behalf of John sell A-P to Swifts of County Durham. The direct approach had never been more direct!

Although Daniel had not been party to his father's sale of Greenswards to Swifts Farm Machinery in the 1950s, he was acquainted with the family who still owned the branch of the Swift empire operating in Tupshorne. Merlin Swift, the present managing director, and grandson of Derek who had bought out James Greensward, was a frequent and regular visitor to Tupshorne, not only on account of his business interests there but also because he was romantically entangled with a young lady whose office in the local bank carried a sign on the door with the title "Dales Farming Business Adviser".

The morning of the day after his meeting with John Daniel marched into the bank, surprising the counter staff, quite accustomed to his requests for a word with Walter Sheepshanks, his bank manager and friend, with a wish to have audience of Wanda Smiley, the Farming Adviser. 'Won't keep her many shakes, if she's in', said Daniel.

Wanda invited him to take a seat when he was ushered into her office. 'No, no! I've only got a very quick question for you, my dear', said Daniel. 'Where's your little falcon friend today? Anywhere near? I need a quiet word in his shell-like! Like, not on the 'phone.'

She laughed. 'Am I my fiancé's keeper, Mr Greensward? I am not generally privy to his business diary but today is an exception. He told me he would be closeted with the accountants for the best part of the morning. Would you like me to give him a ring and check his next movements for you? All part of the service, you know.'

'I'd be most grateful,' said Daniel. 'I have a quite splendid business proposition to put to him – not a matter of life and death, you understand, but in terms of the blacksmith's forge, I really want to strike while the iron is hot.'

A single telephone call was all that was needed to bring Daniel into Merlin's office at two o'clock that same afternoon. The two men exchanged a respectfully firm handshake before a tray of tea and biscuits arrived within two minutes of them sitting down.

'So, Damnit,' began Merlin, 'I am intrigued. What affair of state brings you to my Durham HQ at such short notice? Surely you're not coming out of retirement and wanting to buy your dad's business back – no, your wisdom in maturity rules that out. Besides, it's not for sale as long as Wanda retains her office at the bank. Something's up!'

'Your grandad used to breed Labradors at the time he bought Greenswards, so my father told me. He also said that if he loved labs he was bound to be a sound, reliable chap. Do you keep up that family tradition?'

'I do. But what has that to do with your visit?'

'Just re-assuring myself that, all being well, you might be a sound chip off the old reliable block! They say that dog-owners take on at least some of the characteristics of the breed they favour. My own labrador has a stomach for anything, tasty morsel or more often choice carrion. I come to tempt you with a rich meaty chunk of business. Word has reached me that Swifts have found enough choice mud to be in a position to contemplate building onto their nest. Is that right?'

Merlin chuckled. 'At least it isn't an ugly rumour Daniel. I'm surprised the news item has taken so long to reach you.'

'It's a while since I heard about it but at the time I had no reason to be excited. Now I am. I've come to offer you – no, sell you – a business.'

'I had no idea you had a business to sell,' queried Merlin, somewhat mystified.

'Not mine,' replied Daniel. 'It belongs to a particular friend of mine whom I hold in great esteem. He has entrusted me with the task of selling it on his behalf. If I succeed, and I will, given time, there's a heavy roller deal for my cricket club as commission for me from him. Should you also value my services as intermediary, a gang-mower for the outfield would not come amiss!'

'All right, Damnit! Enough beating about the bush. Shoot! This labrador is ready to retrieve – whatever the game. What's the business? Where's the business? Whose is the business? Can Swift's afford it?'

Daniel then explained everything about the proposed deal and the nature of the man for whom he was acting. Each of Merlin's questions received a straight, honest answer. There was nothing to hide or to be hidden from the potential buyer, except for the matter of the valuation of the company, which in due course would be provided by an independent valuer. Only then would he know if Swifts were in a financially strong enough position to extend a grasping hand over the Pennines to Preston.

The opportunity for Swifts to spread their wings over the Pennines and swallow a similar trading company to their own proved to be too good to miss. Merlin, a keen club cricketer, could not believe his ears when eventually he met the massive immigrant, still with his execrable foreign accent, to be told that he had declared his own innings closed and it was time for the other team to bat. John had always been able to charm the birds from the trees and Daniel was amused to see Merlin fall under the spell of the master storyteller. There was a little token haggling over the valuation in relation to the asking price, but in six months, almost to the hour when Damnit rang Merlin from Wanda's office, the deal was done. Seller and purchaser were happy and the facilitating agent could hardly wait to ride the roller and mow the outfield to test match venue standards.

Shortly afterwards, John moved to a modern flat in a new building development between Lytham and the museum which he had founded. The local cricket club was but a cricket ball's throw away and he prepared himself for walking holidays in Wales by trying to teach himself to speak Welsh. He failed. His mastery of Latvian, Russian, German and English was powerless when confronted by the intricacies of Celtic pronunciation and he had to content himself with the excuse that at the age of sixty-nine, hiking in Wales was quite enough without having to converse with the natives!

John had never had a dog of his own, even as a farmer's boy, and when Damnit told him of Merlin Swift's interest in labrador retriever breeding he reduced the asking price for Agri-Presto by the value of one black bitch puppy to be supplied from the next whelping of Merlin's brood bitch. He would have liked to have acquired

Damnit's Ermintrude, a constant companion on their joint walks, but when invited she invariably refused the offer – only giving it consideration when she was "in the doghouse"!

Early in his own retirement John suddenly realised how much he missed his time in the classroom as a dramatic raconteur when he was building tractors in the Midlands, before his time at Rolls. Now, with time on his hands, he tracked down Max Herrick – not by enquiring after him at the school where, although retired many years, he had been head of English, but by visiting the cricket club where they had been coaching members together. Max was delighted to hear the voice from the past which had so enlivened his department all that time ago. After several hours of hectic conversation and many cups of tea John finally took his leave, armed with a letter of reference and a bit of advice from Max to the effect that, if he wanted to appear on television, it was not too late even at sixty-nine to have some elocution lessons. The advice was heeded and for the next few years John became a "peripatetic" storyteller, visiting schools throughout the Fylde and making rare "cameo" appearances on TV Northwest. His reputation was made when in 1998 he was voted in at number one in the TV Northwest competition "Who would you most like as a special guest at your dinner table?" Such is the power of television! And Baggins went with him everywhere that a dog was allowed to go and sometimes to places where she was not supposed to be.

Occasionally he would meet Damnit at county or even test cricket matches and once in a while, on a Wednesday, he would invite him to join him for lunch at the museum. Baggins and Ermintrude became firm friends, regardless of the difference in their age.

John had never ceased to send gifts of money to Eleanore Bormann every month of every year since he had first come to live in England and, as he had first bade her, she never questioned why. Both of her children were married with children of their own and by nineteen ninety-five Wolfgang was himself a grandfather. Eleanore was a great-grandmother – twice over. She had never remarried and at one stage during the early years of their correspondence John had summoned up the temerity to gently enquire why. He found it hard to understand that the lovely young woman that he remembered so well should remain a widow. Eleanore pointed out that German men with suitable matrimonial qualifications were in very short supply after the collapse of the Third *Reich* and sadly, eligible young men of her own age were disinclined to overlook the presence of two little children, whatever the attractions of their widowed mother. John never raised the question again but was content to follow her family fortunes in letters and occasional photographs.

So after settling in his new flat, John following Damnit's advice rationalized his financial affairs and with the help of a solicitor specializing in such matters made his will. John felt that, at last, the voyage of his life's sailing ship had entered calmer waters, he was on an even keel with a gentle breeze to propel him into the autumnal sunset of his years. Then in the Spring of 1999, without any prior warning, his craft was torpedoed and holed below the waterline. A letter arrived from Frau Eleanore Bormann.

CHAPTER XXII

Dux Femina Facti

JOHN LOOKED AT THE outside of the letter in his hand with growing trepidation, bordering on panic. The envelope was black-bordered with the name and address typewritten where he was accustomed to seeing Eleanore's characteristic, neat script. His customary vivid, fertile imagination was jolted into action as he turned the envelope over, appalled by its bristling formality. On the back, again in type, he read "Abs: Frau E. Bormann". So she was alive! Then the black border must betoken another death in the family which he had carried in his heart since he took his leave of Eleanore in 1942 before his disastrous involvement at Stalingrad. Suddenly, he found himself praying aloud that Eleanore's little great-grandchildren were safe and well. Why should he pray now, when he had managed so well without a god since leaving Latvia in 1941? And yet, still he prayed, waiting for an answer. He slit open the envelope – all his fears were realized and his unspoken questions as Eleanore addressed him in the first line of her letter. She began *Janis der Jähzorn*. So, after fifty-seven years the truth was out. The black-bordered envelope was Eleanore's way of announcing the death of their strange friendship. The blood seemed to drain from his face, turning to ice in his veins and causing him to stay rooted to the spot where he was standing, as if turned to stone. The letter fell to the floor.

For a few fleeting moments which seemed like an eternity John felt as if he was in a state of suspended animation rather like the Sleeping Beauty of one of his often quoted fairy-tales, except that he was no beauty and this was no fairy-tale scenario. Hardly had the letter touched the floor than John was aware of a searing pain behind his eyes and a dull ache in the pit of his stomach where his sympathetic nervous system took the full force of the blow that Eleanore had delivered in three simple words. Beginning to breathe more deeply as the shock waves receded, he eventually recovered enough composure to bend down and retrieve the letter before sitting down in an easy chair to study it in its awful entirety. Eleanore was brief, brutal and unforgiving. She wrote:

Janis der Jähzorn! (Immediately, he realizes that the game is up.) *Muss ich weiterschreiben? Ich glaube schon.*

Es ist vielleicht etwas tragisch für alle Betroffene, dass ich nach 58 Jahren einem ehemaligen SS Offizier begegnet bin, der ganz zufällig während einer harmlosen Diskussion über den Krieg meinen Heino erwähnte, bevor er wusste, dass ich Frau Eleanore Bormann bin. Die Geschichte war raus!

Jetzt verstehe ich, warum Sie (mit den besten Absichten) mir die Wahrheit nicht sagen konnten, da Sie meine Erinnerungen an meinen tapferen Mann nicht verderben wollten, und ich verstehe auch, warum Sie meine ganze Familie all die Jahre unterstützt haben in dem Sie verlangt haben "keine Fragen stellen".

Ich kann das Geld nicht zurückgeben – so viel habe ich auch nicht.

Dies ist der letzte von mir geschriebene Brief, den Sie erhalten werden. Ich schreibe in Trauer. Trotz der Umständen danke ich Ihnen. Seien von Gott gesegnet.

Hiermit nehme ich Abschied, Janis der Jähzorn.

Lettland ist frei. Sie sind von Stalingrad zu Fuss heimgekehrt. Sie sind 1945 von der russischen Frontlinie zur Lüneburger Heide gegangen. Jetzt schlage ich vor, Sie gehen heim, nach Lettland – da das noch möglich ist – oder sind Sie Engländer geworden?

Betrachten Sie mich als tot. Schreiben Sie mir nie wieder.

Eleanore Else Bormann.

Janis, der Jähzorn!

Need I write further? I think I must.

It is perhaps most unfortunate, for all concerned, that after fifty-eight years I have encountered a former SS officer who, quite accidentally, in the course of a harmless conversation remembered my Heino in a wartime anecdote before he realized that I was Frau Eleanore Bormann. The cat was out of the bag!

Now I understand why you, with the best of intentions, could not tell me the truth, spoiling my memories of my valorous husband, and why you have supported my family all these years, demanding of me, "No questions".

I cannot go on like this now; nor can I return the money – so much I do not have anyway.

This is the last letter you will receive from me. I write with sadness.

Thank you, despite the circumstances.

Truly, may God bless you!

Goodbye, *Janis, der Jähzorn*.

Latvia is free. You walked back from Stalingrad. You walked to Lüneburg Heath from the Russian battlefront in 1945. Now may I suggest you start walking home to Latvia – while you still can – or have you really become an Englishman?

Think of me as dead and never write to me again.

Eleanore Else Bormann.

John sat motionless in the chair following with his eyes the sweep-hand on his wrist-watch as it traced its unerring path in a circle from which there was no escape. Time passed. Just how long he remained in his self-imposed trance went unrecorded – it didn't matter – but gradually he became attuned to the strong, steady beat of his heart, which gave him the vital pause to summon his memory to account and it threw up the "Isaac" of his SS training manual. He had had no recourse to the fundamentals of the "Isaac" since his fire-extinguishing heroics in Damnit's office all those years ago, and now it failed him. Nothing and no-one had prepared him for such a personal trauma as this. He was truly on his own and only the depth of his character would enable him to climb out of the pit into which he had fallen after fifty-seven years. The training manual had offered no guidance of any kind to the ram so unfortunately caught in the thicket at Jehovah-jireh. No! It was up to John Smith to re-write the "Isaac" and redefine it as the "Ram's Restitution"!

CHAPTER XXIII

Fortiter in re,
Suaviter in Modo

THE DAY FOLLOWING the arrival of the fateful letter John addressed himself to his future. It seemed to him that with careful self-examination allied with a certain amount of introspection he was in good shape both mentally and physically. He was confident that his powers of judgement were unimpaired as he settled on the strategy to be played out over the next six months. He was never to know that the excruciating pain behind his eyes that he had experienced on reading Eleanore's letter had left a minute but permanent scar as if his brain had been touched by a red-hot soldering iron and one of his vital thought processes had been snapped. All his plans appeared so eminently sensible as he wrote a detailed letter to Daniel explaining his future movements but the information never made much sense to Daniel when he read it. Was it just strange or was John attempting to be humorous when he began the letter "Esteemed Sir"? Damnit remembered with astonishing clarity his first ever encounter with John when, having offered him the post of unpaid assistant cricket club groundsman under his senior instruction, John had called him "Sir" in acknowledgement only that he was his boss at Rolls.

"Esteemed Sir", John began,
   "You may recall that, when we discussed together the sale of my Agri-Presto business some four years ago, I became distressed when you so kindly enquired if I would return to Latvia one day. My answer was "never". I have changed my mind. I have received a letter from Frau Bormann in Hamburg. You will have heard me mention her name in conversation before now. She suggests that now may be an appropriate time for me to go home and I have decided to follow her advice, even though I have no idea what awaits me there. Apart from the sea-crossing,

I shall walk it! So much of my leisure time over the years has been spent trekking or walking the world – excepting continental Europe – and now I shall wend my way back home without regard to any timetable.

As I do not expect to come back again, any animal quarantine laws in current operation will not apply to Baggins and she will accompany me on my journey."

Daniel had only just become accustomed to the strange, stilted formality of the letter from his old friend when suddenly John changed his tone, reverting to his usual chatty approach to letter writing. Alarm bells sounded in Daniel's head at this point. Such behaviour in correspondence was undeniably out of character for John and gave rise to concern. For a moment he wondered if John had a screw working loose or if he was in danger of losing a marble: he dismissed the idea as quickly as it had arisen, deciding that John had written, pen in one hand and schnapps bottle in the other. He read further.

"With luck, I should sell my flat by Christmas at the very latest. When I bought it, I was convinced that it was a quality dwelling in a quality area which would be easy to sell if I ever needed or wanted to move on. That gives me about nine months to once again put all my affairs in proper order, re-write my will etc.

I am looking forward to meandering my way through a land which I have grown to love to the land which I had chosen to forget. How I go about it may surprise even you but I intend to leave nothing to chance when it comes to equipment for the long walk.

You know that more by accident than design I seem to have managed to keep remarkably fit since I retired. I suppose strenuous walking on a regular basis has been the key to that. Perhaps I ought to take up serious long distance swimming as well now, and make arrangements to swim the North Sea. Mind you, it would be a bit too far for Baggins and she's not too keen on salt water, even with her webbed feet, so we'll have to settle for the ferry. You will be relieved to know that before I set out I shall be having a rigorous medical, only to reinforce my personal conviction that even at seventy-three it'll be a doddle – as they say!

Mind you – I did contemplate travelling on horseback. I do know that a good horse is still appreciated where I am going. Perhaps I should keep a light-hearted diary – a kind of travelogue – about my peregrinations. A lovely word that! Look it up. In its archaic form, a peregrine was a traveller in a foreign land. Such a word could so easily be applied to yours truly. You would understand that such a diary would be entitled "Baggins and Me", rather than "One Man and His Dog" which has been overdone on television; and Baggins wouldn't dream of chasing sheep even if she was paid! As a story, I wonder if "Baggins and Me" could have a fairy-tale ending. I wonder. Now I am getting maudlin and I see the bottom of my bottle of schnapps approaching.

I will keep in touch and let you know how my plans are coming to fruition. We might manage a cricket match tryst – or two – this Summer, with luck, but don't count on it. And I want to spend as much time as I can at the museum, where I am still a sort of curator emeritus. I think Aidan may be thinking of handing over his Wednesdays to a younger man. He's been there every Wednesday, barring bad weather and infrequent holidays, since the place opened thirteen years ago. If he does pack it in, I'll just have to go up to Cumbria for Wednesday lunch once in a while. Could this be my own "Journey of a lifetime"?"

The mood of the letter changed once more and amiability was replaced by a certain *froideur*. Daniel had a vision of John addressing the tragic situation of an empty bottle before continuing his epistle in more serious vein.

"I am minded to return to my real name – perhaps on leaving English soil. England has been good to John Smith but the land of my birth surely would frown on such a foreign name as a stranger arrives from out of the blue. Presumably there will be a fair number of "leftover" Russians in some areas of Latvia, married into the community and with families. Who knows? I could even bump into a Stalingrad veteran who missed an unmissable target – me. I have two regrets from my war service which may surprise you. I am sorry that I never met face to face the German sniper who executed my Uncle Zigrids or the unknown Russian who shot my father. I would have taken pleasure in killing them both in cold blood, slowly. Not that I normally bear a grudge, but I would have enjoyed carving them into little pieces with my father's heavy clasp-knife except that I gave the knife away to the young son of the farmer for whom I first worked when I came to England. If it be true that revenge is a dish best eaten cold, then after over half a century my plateful would be disgustingly mouldy and I should prefer to heed Juvenal who stated, "Indeed, revenge is ever the pleasure of a mean, weak, small mind". I find comfort in the certain knowledge that, however small minded I may be, *Scharfschütze Lutz* at least and maybe my father's killer are rotting in hell! Perhaps I also have a hot future after "shuffling off this mortal coil". God only knows."

Tupshorne has been pencilled in as a likely watering hole along my route, so you can safely expect this bad penny to turn up in due course but don't count on advance warning of my advent. I shall not need a bed.

I have just read what I have written so far. You must think I'm off my rocker, Damnit – esteemed sir, indeed! I'm not inclined to begin it all again. Just take the strange bits with a pinch of salt, and humour your old friend. And yes! I do know the proposed travelogue should be "Baggins and I". Yours 'til the wheels fall off.

John."

Daniel took several deep breaths before re-reading the letter and seeking to reassure himself that the schnapps had been speaking through John's pen in those passages which appeared alien to John's usual composure. Then he penned a brief reply which ran as follows:

"Honourable Sir,

Your message is received and fully understood by your correspondent who detects, within the meaning as a whole, the several idiosyncrasies of old age combined with more than a shower of schnapps!

But to be honest, even serious, John, I am not altogether surprised about your decision to return to Latvia. Precisely how Frau Bormann persuaded you to go back, I don't expect I shall ever know unless you yourself choose to tell me. There is so much in your past that may be termed "a closed book" which you, long ago, decided to keep from prying eyes and I, as you know, have always respected your unspoken wishes in that regard. As far as I am concerned, you can take your secrets to the grave with you, leaving me none the wiser. I am reminded of a German prisoner of war whom I met at the end of the war, who when asked for his opinion on important matters of international relations at that time, invariably replied that it was, "No mine business". So if you are seeking my opinion about your plans, all you will get from me is, "No mine business"!

Let me offer you a few tips, on a well-meant, take it or leave it basis.

You may find yourself with some unwelcome bedfellows in your "peregrinations", so take some flea powder for both you and Baggins. There may be times when you will need each other's bodily warmth without the presence of jumpers! I remember you telling me a hilarious tale about the lice of Stalingrad – except that it was only funny for those who weren't there.

Take some water-sterilizing tablets. I've never subscribed to your view that all running water is potable. I know from our walking experiences together that you will be following the water-courses through the hills. There must come a time when the water you are drinking so blithely has come tumbling over a rotten sheep carcass not all that far upstream. Drinking it may not affect Baggins, but it could be the death of you and what would happen to her then? She'll be after the sheep once she has eaten you!

I've said enough for now. If I think of any more vital tips I'll be in touch. In the meantime I wish you well with the sale of your flat – the housing market is pretty buoyant at the moment if one is to believe our local estate agent. One thing is certain – if you are taking to the road and without a fixed abode you'll end up with a lot of cash in the bank. How you get that back to Latvia with you could be an interesting exercise, never mind clarifying your pension arrangements. Better you than me, old friend! Again, you'll need a clued-up financial advisor and that will involve you in making another will. Problems, problems! I have no doubt that you will triumph over any obstacles, pecuniary or otherwise.

I'm very tempted to offer to join you on the leg of your walk from Tupshorne to the Newcastle ferry terminal. Baggins would enjoy Ermin's company – or maybe it would be the other way round considering E's advanced age. There's an excuse for me in case I can't stand the pace any longer!

Meanwhile, keep your powder dry and I'll expect you when I see you.

Yours 'til you blow a gasket.

Damnit."

John read Daniel's letter, smiling with satisfaction at the warmth of approval which ran like an unbroken thread from beginning to end. As for Daniel's half-baked suggestion of joining him on the final leg, he had no means of knowing the self-imposed punishing conditions which would prevail as he sought to carry the enormous burden of his long-term personal guilt back to the Europe of his childhood.

His smile faded as he looked into the future, the road that inevitably would lead to a dead end. Then he looked down at Baggins lying at his feet and smiled again. All would be well.

CHAPTER XXIV

In Omnia Paratus

JOHN DELIBERATELY REFRAINED from making any kind of move in his plans until he had received a reply to the letter he had written to Damnit. He had a wait of two weeks, at the end of which period of time he was becoming fractious and impatient. How could he have known that Daniel was on a ten-day malt whisky distillery trail based on Speyside? He attempted several times to write to Eleanore, only to consign his efforts to the waste-paper bin as he acknowledged in his heart of hearts that any letters that he might now write would end up in a German *Papierkorb* – unopened and unread. She had once confided in him that when she was a little girl, her mother, at times of confrontation, would call her, "*Kleines Mädchen Starsinn*" – "Little Miss Obstinacy"! He was wasting his time.

Daniel's letter of approval gave him the green light to proceed, albeit with caution. His first move was to sell his flat, which although furnished with every modern luxury and set in beautiful surroundings, held no sentimental value for him. It represented no more than its constituent parts, bricks and mortar carefully put together to provide something to live in for the time being and he was astounded to learn from the estate agent, whom he had instructed to sell the property, that in a mere four years its value had almost doubled. Regardless of the asking price, his des. res. sold inside two weeks and within six weeks he was living in rented accommodation not far from Agri-Presto and feeling as rich as Crœsus.

The speed of the move so surprised him that his other plans were thrown into disarray for a short time. He realized how serious a situation he had landed in when he missed the opening cricket match of the season at Old Trafford!

Once the money from the sale of his flat was safely banked John visited his solicitor with whose advice and assistance he had drawn up his previous will and testament. Together they fed the original document and the copy of it, which John had retained, into the office paper-shredder. He would have preferred to burn the papers in the presence of the solicitor, as a form of catharsis, but the smoke-alarm would have spoiled the spirituality of the occasion. The paper-shredder made a very efficient job with the minimum of fuss and the maximum lack of the personal touch. If fire was a quill pen; a shredder was a ballpoint pen.

The first will, now in little strips, had been an uncomplicated document in both wording and dispensation. The second will was even more simple, particularly with regard to the list of beneficiaries which John reduced from over a dozen to fewer than the fingers of one hand but it differed from the first in one major aspect. First time round he had no dependants – now he had the beautiful Baggins, his beloved black bitch labrador, the most important beneficiary of all. He had always spoken to her in Latvian and she would be deaf to any command in another language, so she would be his problem child. What would become of Baggins if he himself never reached Latvian soil? It was his solicitor, not John, who raised the point. John invoked the "Isaac" of his SS training manual and explained that his dog would look around and find a new master.

'You mean *"Jehovah-jireh"* – The Lord will provide', said the solicitor with a touch of sarcasm.

'I haven't the slightest doubt on that score,' replied John. 'Baggins adores men! But as you have raised such a delicate subject, I will give the Lord a hand, just in case. As of today, I'll teach her English and by mid-Summer she'll be bilingual. Don't presume to bet against it – my Baggins is "Bright and Beautiful", as in the hymn the children used to sing at a school where, once upon a time, I told stories.'

The solicitor was intrigued by John's reference to the Isaac chapter of the SS training manual because he had never heard of such a book. His initial reaction was to presume that John was pulling his leg and just to humour his client he went along with the idea, introducing into the conversation which ensued, a hint of scepticism. John was quick to detect the faint air of mockery, bringing his solicitor down to earth with a bump by quoting in German (with English translation) from the "Despatches" chapter which, with brutal brevity among other things, described five easy ways to kill a man without spilling any blood. Two of the recommended methods involved blinding the opponent first. When the solicitor looked directly into John's eyes he then understood that he was hearing the pitiless truth, and was unable to suppress a shudder.

'Don't worry yourself about it', said John, with a teasing grin. 'It was all good, clean fun, you know. Rest assured, there was no chapter concerning "Torture" – like "Ten foolproof ways to extract the truth". The revised edition with a chapter on "Bloodcurdling" never reached the printers, so I understand.'

'Point made and taken', replied his solicitor. 'Even the prospect of an injection of antibiotics terrifies me, I'm sorry to say, and the very thought of giving any of my precious blood makes mine run cold. Pathetic, I know!'

'Just as well to know your shortcomings, I suppose', said John. 'All solicitors are the same, I expect, and the Blood Transfusion Service probably have it stated in their Manual that "You can't get blood out of a stone"!'

'That reminds me,' replied the solicitor, 'Did I tell you that my fees went up by ten percent only yesterday, and two minutes ago by a further two and a half percent.'

'Do you understand, "*Haben Sie ab*"?' enquired John.

'Could it be something like, "Get lost"?.' smiled the solicitor.

'Spot on', said John. 'One hundred percent!'

They shook hands.

Now that he had put his monetary affairs in order, John applied his mind to self-preservation. Not long after making his will he arranged to visit a leading tent manufacturer who specialized in the production of tents and equipment for use in extremes of climate. A detailed discussion with the managing director resulted in John buying a generous remnant of a recently introduced fabric. The M. D. reckoned that such a tent material was going to revolutionize the camping scene, being waterproof, breathable and, most important of all, ultra-light-weight. He was amazed when John explained that he wanted the fabric for the purpose of tailoring a cape to fit his own massive human frame – not a tent at all.

'Let us do that for you', offered the expert.

'That's very kind of you,' said John, 'but it's a bit more complicated than your average cape. It will have to cover an enormous framed back-pack which I am going to ask you to custom-build for me – sorry, I failed to mention that before. So far as I know, the most capacious pack available is, including its auxiliary, the 120 litre model. I need 150 litres at least. By the way, I am expecting to pay over the odds for anything out of the ordinary. Most of my life, apart from my days in the SS, I have had to pay extra for clothes to fit me – and I can afford something special like this to be truly made to measure. I had expected to employ a local seamstress to make up the cape for me but, if you are prepared to do it, I can be certain that the seams will be properly sealed, and no doubt your machines and machinists are set up to cope with a range of materials and the correct threads. I had better explain why this will be a cape like no other, to cope with a situation that you would never dream of! Have you a tape-measure handy, by any chance? Or would you rather wheel me down to your draughtsman's office? You see, my ultra-cape will need to be about nine feet long when I bring it into use and the whole ensemble will make me look like the greatest Grand Wizard of the Klu Klux Klan ever seen on earth.'

'I get the gist', nodded the tentman. 'It's the drawing office for you – right now. Your project will give the team something novel to get their teeth into!' He looked at his watch. 'Hey up! It's baggin time – let's talk it out a bit further over that cup of tea and a biscuit – or a coffee if you'd prefer it.'

'Thanks for reminding me', said John. 'My dog Baggins is in the car. I'd better let her out for a quick stretch before much longer. I'll do it now, while the kettle boils. By the way, this super-cape which you are going to rustle up for me is intended to protect Baggins as well.

'Maybe we should construct a doggy-cape for her, personally, while we're about it. Matching materials – his and hers! Could be a lucrative side line for a tent maker. On second thoughts though …!'

Both men laughed at the idea.

'She'd make a real supermodel', said John. 'Quite the queen of the dogwalk, in fact. I'll go and ask her what she thinks of your brainwave!'

John's conception of a gigantic backpack, covered by a sort of mini-tent cape, intrigued the tent maker to the extent that he supervised personally the whole scheme from drawing board to the finished products. It was essential that the manufacturer should be entirely in tune with John's thoughts about the design of the cape, in particular the way in which it was to be suspended from the handle of a shovel lashed to the pack.

'I presume that this special long-handled shovel will be made of the lightest alloy you can lay your hands on. Otherwise you will need very heavy-duty straps to attach it to your pack', queried the specialist.

'Extra heavy-duty, please', replied John. 'For reasons which I cannot divulge, I must not compromise on the weight and strength of the shovel even if it's the death of me. I suppose it would have the potential to be, "The last straw that breaks the camel's back," in which case you might say that we all have a cross to bear and I'll carry this one to the grave.'

'Amen to that!' was the answer. 'Grave or not, it's a bit too deep for me. However, I'll need the precise dimensions of the handle so we can attain a really snug fit of the apex of the cape on to the cross-piece of the handle. Can you let me have it next time you come, or at your final fitting when we can tailor the garment absolutely precisely – while you wait?'

'You must be joking', chuckled John. 'It's not even made yet! I have to consult my blacksmith friend at the National Museum – I'm depending on him and his expertise to help me manufacture it with my own fair hands. I take your point, though, about the snug fit of cape on handle. I thought a big crocodile-clip might have done the job but your idea is very much better and won't damage the fabric. I'll bring the finished article at the eleventh hour and settle up at the same time.'

When eventually John arrived, shovel in hand, for his final fitting, the tent maker was appalled at the weight of the implement. 'The shovel straps on the pack are the strongest available but, just in case, I'll have the workshop add another – and – it's just struck me this second, we'll sew on a reinforced envelope that will accommodate the bottom three inches of the blade; then it can't slip. Cracked it! You won't need the extra strap after all.'

John left two hours later, having settled the bill, but not before he had been photographed together with the entire workforce at the tent makers. The giant cape dominated the picture. The fabric was of the purest white from apex to base, relieved only by a transparent "porthole" at head height which allowed the wearer to see the way ahead. John's head was clearly visible on the photograph, with the "porthole" open, but only on closer inspection would the viewer notice the head of a black dog, peeping out from under the skirt of the cape. Baggins, although too shy to be a supermodel, was alive to the unique excitement of the occasion and, overcome with the curiosity more typical of a cat, put her head out to catch the moment in a flash!

CHAPTER XXV

Ligonem Ligonem Vocat

THE EPISODE WITH THE tent manufacturer had turned John's plans upside down. It had been his original intention to leave the forging of his mighty shovel until the very last moment – the vital, final brushstroke in the complicated picture of his equipment. In hindsight, it was so obvious that the backpack fixing would have to be tailored to fit the shovel and not, *vice-versa.* He realized that he was in too much of a hurry to complete his preparations and foolish in making no allowance for possible hitches. Ever the optimist, he viewed his journey in the simplest of terms, expecting no complications. Quite suddenly he grasped the irony of the situation – the shovel had been a problem in his life ever since Stalingrad; it was never going to leave him in peace.

He had decided, in the first instance, to begin his long walk in late September 1999, giving his landlord six months notice of his quitting the flat. The period of notice he now extended to the end of November before taking himself off for a two-week break in Cumbria – the grand opportunity to fashion the shovel of his nightmares.

Turning up at Aidan Ferrers' forge, out of the blue, he surprised the blacksmith with his singular request to make a humble shovel, but one of Heraklean proportions. They discussed the precise dimensions over many a mug of tea. Aidan could not understand why John would want to make his own heavy iron spade when modern metal alloys and advanced plastics were available, weighing a fraction of the unique prototype which John had in mind.

'John, I've known you long enough not to call you a fool and now you give me reason to call you stupid. You're not making sense. Let me suggest a compromise as follows'.

'No. I won't compromise. Like Margaret Thatcher, I'm not for turning.'

'It seems to me you're bent on some form of masochism. Why won't you listen? As I see it, or perhaps as I understand it from the tale you tell me, every single item in your backpack is going to be as light as possible – alloy this, spun fibre that. An implement such as you describe, made of iron, and strapped to your pack will destabilize the whole shebang.'

'What's a shebang?' queried John, innocently, but with a twinkle in his eye! Is it the same as "the whole bang shoot", old boy?'

'A shebang? Well, in this context, it's a, it's a sort of contrived situation – a bit like a house of cards which, if you don't play your cards or place your cards right, falls down.'

'I get you,' smiled John. 'It all goes "shebang" when it collapses. I prithee, do carry on!'

'If it were my shovel, I would want the weight in the blade – a bit like the tip of a javelin or a tadpole in that respect – the business end. Think sledge-hammer, John: a weight on the end of a lovely, smooth wooden handle. I've got a choice bit of hickory which has been waiting for just such a commission as this. It isn't light – well, lighter than iron – but it's warm and sensuous to the touch. With a bit of a turn at the lathe, I reckon I could match it to your grip – personalize it like; then every time you lifted it you would remember me. Tell your friend the Bard, I prithee, "Hickory for remembrance – not rosemary". I read "Hamlet" at school. I was Polonius!'

'And it shows,' said John. 'I didn't meet Shakespeare until I was about twenty. He found me a nice part as a spear-bearer. Big man – big spear. You can see why I can't settle for less when it comes to size of shovel. But you're right of course. Life is a compromise, a kind of balance, and I can see now that my backpack must not be allowed to interfere with my walking equilibrium. Bring on the hickory!'

'Praise the Lord! Some commonsense at last,' said Adrian. 'Let's refine the design of the blade. I know you've got something special in mind so we may as well brew up, sit down and draw up a blueprint for the John Smith Supershovel.'

'That's fine by me,' said John, 'But the brand in this case will read "Janis Kalējs". I'll etch that on to the blade. You wouldn't allow me to burn it into your prized piece of hickory now, would you?'

The end product of their endeavours, more than anything else, resembled a sugar-shovel at about eighteen times arithmetical magnification, with very shallow turned-up edges at the sides, and the leading edge protruding about two and a half inches beyond the shallow concave bowl of the blade. And those extra inches were of hardened steel, with the tip as sharp as a screwdriver rather than a chisel. The long hickory-wood handle was in proportion to the blade, rich brown in colour, heavily oiled with linseed and deeply inserted into the socket shaft of the metal blade which was polished to a mirror finish. Overall, the strange tool measured six feet, from metal cutting edge to the tip of the comfortable wooden handle, sculpted to the firm grip of its inventor.

Weighing up the finished article, both men heaved a mutual sigh of self-satisfied relief. Then suddenly, Adrian said 'You've gone and forgotten to name the thing!'

'Not me,' answered John. 'It had been my original intention to make it all on my own – my own idea, all my own work, you know. Now I know that I couldn't have done it alone. You have done the lion's share of the hammering, shaping, turning, smoothing and polishing. This shovel is going to be my salvation and henceforth I shall call it "Ferrers", after you.'

'I hate to raise the matter, John, but what on earth are you going to <u>actually</u> do with it? I've never thought to ask 'til now. You certainly can't take it to a football match – it's a lethal weapon. I'm reminded of the legend of Colonel Jim Bowie and his famous, eponymous knife. It is said of him, that before he was finally overwhelmed at the Battle of the Alamo, he killed thirty men with that knife. Must have buried himself in dead Mexican bodies before they eventually spitted him.'

'Don't worry on that score', said John. 'Ferrers is going to be a force for good – that is unless I need to defend myself. In fact, I think he will open many a door for me – given the opportunity.'

'Well, when you've finished with him, send him back to me and I'll put Ferrers on the museum wall, for old times sake.'

'I might just do that', replied John. 'I expect he'll have a few tales to tell by the time you get to hang him. By the way, have I told you that my little walk home is scheduled to start at the Museum? I do hope you will come to wave me off and what's more, I'll turn it into a party – get some media coverage for the Museum while we're at it. I know how you love having your picture taken!'

'With such a charming invite, I wouldn't miss the occasion for all the mugs of tea we've drunk together since you wandered in here all those years ago ... nineteen ... The time day turned into night as you blocked the doorframe with your own bulk. Unforgettable!

A sudden cloud flitted across John's usually sunny face – a shadow which was not lost on Adrian.

'What's up, John? Have we missed out on something? You're troubled!'

'It's nothing really. It's just that, in a flash, I glimpsed the future. I was looking into a classical "burning fiery furnace" of biblical proportions, holding Ferrers in my hands but he was glowing red-hot – too hot for even me to handle. I don't think I've a gift for clairvoyance, but, just in case, let's create a twin shovel for you and you can call it Janis. It won't need to be quite so big for a little lad like you – well, it can't be anyway because the hickory off-cut isn't long enough to produce a handle to match that of Ferrers.'

He was trying to make light of one of those moments when it is said, "I feel as if someone has just trodden over my grave." Yet that very moment had been so vivid that on glancing at his hands he was surprised not to see blisters appearing on the palms. Maybe his imagination was over-reacting. Maybe.

CHAPTER XXVI

Quid Faciendum?

N OW THAT MAN, backpack and shovel were perfectly matched
for size and proportion, John began to question if he had over-
estimated his physical ability to heft the burden that he had planned
to carry and so, throughout the Summer and Autumn, for the first
time in his life he visited the nearest fitness club under a weight-
training regime while he gradually accumulated the contents of the
backpack, destined to deliver the necessities of life on the tramp. So
successful was he in the selection of items, a choice based on the cri-
terion of weight alone, that in the end he realized that although his
weight-training had been a waste of time and money, he did feel
extremely fit and ready to keep his promise to Damnit to have a
proper medical examination before taking to the road.

His own doctor arranged an appointment on a private basis for
him to visit a physician for a major check-up from top to toe. The
doctor explained, with a chuckle, that he was not qualified in the
Geriatric Discipline and the ministrations of a consultant were called
for to examine heart, lights and liver, and brain function if that could
be detected at the age of seventy-three!

The physician, Mr Nathaniel Ross, carried out the examination
with extreme rigour and vigour, to the point that John was surprised
not to be taken apart at the seams and stitched up again.

'You've knocked about a bit, haven't you, since you first saw the
light!' remarked the specialist. 'Judging by some interesting scars on
different parts of your anatomy, you're no stranger to lead poison-
ing – and I don't suppose it's the sort you might get from a badly
shot pheasant.'

John could not resist rising to the bait.

'When I fought with the SS at Stalingrad', he began and then he
clammed up, regretting his indiscretion.

'Sorry!' said his examiner, sensing that however old the wound
might have been there was still some tenderness present, 'I didn't
mean to pry.'

'That's all right,' said John. 'It's something I never talk about normally. You, of course, already know that bullet scars go further than skin deep – not everybody understands that sometimes the scar extends to the mind. Enough said! I don't know if you understand the German saying *jetzt geht es um die Wurst*, now we get to the sausage, or this is the moment of truth.'

'Oh yes,' laughed Mr Ross. 'It's the nearest the Germans get to saying, "The cat's let out of the bag". Do I assume or presume that you might know the cat in question refers to the cat-o'-nine-tails, an unpleasant instrument of punishment used in the sailing ships of old? You've certainly taken some punishment yourself in your time.' Then, without a smile, he added, 'I expect your SS discipline introduced you to some pretty dreadful and barbaric methods of retribution which would, in comparison, make the cat-o'-nine-tails little more than a toy. As you say – enough said!'

While John was getting dressed again, the physician was checking through his preliminary notes before speaking.

'Several of the subjects of enquiry in my report, such as your E.CG, will need more accurate evaluation before my final inventory of your state of health. Would you like me to send my findings to your own GP, or would you prefer to see me again to discuss matters?'

'You're a very busy man and I've taken up too much of your time already. I might even dare to say "wasted your time". No. Send the report to my GP and I'll take it from there. Thank you very much.'

He smiled at the consultant. 'You may be interested to know that I haven't had such a thorough medical since I was branded by the SS in 1941. At fifteen, that was quite an ordeal – quite unforgettable in fact.'

'That's interesting. My careful examination of your skin failed to find the brand. Presumably you had it removed surgically. Now I am curious!'

'So you might well be', replied John. 'The truth is that the freak rifle shot which produced that unsightly scar on my left upper arm blew the brand to kingdom come! Wasn't I a lucky boy, and its obliteration never cost me a penny – which is more than I can say for your examination! Do you want paying now?'

'Good Gracious, No! My secretary will bill you at the month end. Just at this moment, against my better judgement, I feel inclined to treat you as a deserving cause and not call you to account. You must know as well as I, that for your age you are in remarkably good shape – certainly from the outside. Your GP will comment further on my report when you next arrange to see him. Good luck with your walk home, whenever it takes place. Two bits of advice for you, for what they're worth. Keep a diary – it could be a best seller – and fit yourself up with the finest walking footwear, regardless of cost. But that's a superfluous recommendation for you. From hearing you talk of walking the Andes, and the healthy state of your feet, you must be a footwear specialist in your own right. I'm intrigued with your idea of reassuming your original name on returning home. Perhaps I might do the same one day but I know only England as my home. I'm somewhat relieved that we have never met before. As you miraculously survived Stalingrad when little more than a boy, somehow by another miracle, as a baby still with his mother, I survived *Buchenwald*. Ross is so much easier for the English to pronounce than *Rosenbaum. Shalom aleichem!*'

Two weeks later John visited his doctor's surgery, ostensibly to enquire about Mr Ross's report.

'Do take a seat, John. I won't keep you many shakes while I just put a final remark on my last customer's notes.'

'No,' said John, abruptly. 'I'm not stopping. Is that Mr Ross's letter by chance by your telephone? It looks unopened to me.'

'Yes. That's right,' answered the doctor. 'I was intending to go through its contents with you – that's if you can spare the time!'

'I can't,' said John, leaning across the doctor's desk and seizing the envelope. 'I don't want to know and I don't care to know what's in it. Next patient please! That has to be your fastest consultation ever – and you'll never know what Mr Ross had to say. I'm not one to waste your time. *Shalom!*' With which final remark he left the room, the mystified doctor looking over his spectacles at his departing broad back and wondering about John's state of mind – not Mr Ross's specialized field at all.

John's whole way of life was turned upside down during the Summer and early Autumn of 1999, so preoccupied was he with his plans and preparations to go on a long walk, knowing he would never come back.

At Damnit's invitation the two of them took in the Scarborough Cricket Festival, combining the supremely relaxing event with some strenuous walks in the North York Moors National Park accompanied by Ermintrude and young Baggins. The boisterous Baggins wondered if Ermin was slowing up more than a little towards the late afternoon and was totally baffled that when John shouted out the new-fangled commands he had been teaching her for the last few months Ermin obeyed them without question. The two black bitches seemed to enjoy working as a pair until John lapsed into Latvian, at which point Ermin would immediately heel up to Daniel, leaving Baggins to do as she was bid, alone.

Just following Bonfire Night Daniel wrote to John to tell him that Ermintrude had lost the earthly scent and was on the heavenly trail. John understood the metaphors immediately and wrote his final fairy-story based on the idea of "The Quest for the Celestial Bone", sending it to Daniel with his sympathy and looking forward to seeing him at his leaving party to be thrown on Wednesday, 24th November 1999.

Mr Ross's advice that he should keep a diary of his homeward walk touched a chord in John. He had no intention whatsoever to record his meanderings for others to follow at a later date. He had a fundamental belief that unless a diary recorded absolutely every detail of daily life, however intimate in thought or action, it would be a waste of time, effort and materials and he could not countenance carrying such an extra weight on his back. It was then that Max Herrick came to mind and he wrote to him with the news of his impending late November departure, suggesting that he might enjoy the farewell party. Max replied immediately to the effect that he would not dream of missing the send-off and he expected that the *schnapps* would be flowing like water. The postscript to his reply caught John on the hop! Max had decided to visit himself on John, without any invitation, to record as many of John's stories and fairy-tales as he possibly could in the course of a week and he was quite prepared to sleep on the floor in that time waiting for the oracle to utter. And so it came about that as the notion of a diary was dismissed, so the riches of John's imagination were harvested by Max Herrick who first heard him telling tales in a cricket pavilion during the Summer of 1962. Eventually Max, after a sojourn of two weeks in John's flat, knew that he would have to be satisfied with the stories which he gleaned during that period, while acknowledging the frustration of being able to record only an unquantifiable fraction of the whole of John's repertoire. Many of John's tales seemed, to Max at least, to have a basis in reality but he was never able with any certainty to differentiate between truth and fiction – such was the power of the narrator to convince the sceptical. When it came to their final evening together, before Max was due to return home to his wife, Rowena, John in his cups suddenly announced that there was just one final true story which he felt Max should know about and it related to his time at the Siege of Stalingrad – an incident which he had never mentioned since the day it happened. The *schnapps* bottle was empty by the time John started the tale of how he stumbled on the body of his father, *Arvids*, and after two intro-ductory sentences he went promptly to sleep. Max was never to learn the secret of the shovel. Not for the first time in his life, at breakfast time the following morning John was to be found bending over the kitchen sink, a bottle of *schnapps* in each hand with the spirit running away into the drain. In vain, did Max try to remon-strate with him to persuade him to keep the *schnapps* for another day but John was adamant. On such occasions, full of repentance and just a smidgeon of self-loathing, but never self-pity, he would trot out his favourite quotation specially tailored for his fall from grace. "When God wants to punish a man, He takes away his senses." As Euripides would have said when visiting Rome, *"QUOS DEUS VULT PERDERE, PRIUS DEMENTAT."*

It was to be two years before Max Herrick was able to publish "John Smith – Storymaster-Supreme", (as recounted to Max Herrick), and he never ceased to wonder if John's unrecounted final adventure story, the culmination of a *schnapps*-sodden evening, would have been truly the honest truth or truly a brilliant figment of the raconteur's ever fevered imagination. After all, so many of John's genuine fairy-tales had the ring of truth.

CHAPTER XXVII

Ut Fata Trahunt

WEDNESDAY, 24TH NOVEMBER 1999 came and went. John's farewell feast turned out to be one of the strangest social events ever witnessed in the British Isles, never mind in Lancashire. Quite a number of the four hundred or so people who were privileged to attend could not remember very much about the party when asked about it the following day.

The National Blacksmiths' Museum, at John's behest, was *en Fête* for the occasion. He masterminded the whole operation from start to finish and in drawing up his guest list, as well as summoning work colleagues dating back to his earliest days in England through to his former staff at Agri-Presto, he also included friends from the worlds of cricket, amateur dramatics and teaching. Then he remembered to invite the members of the West Midlands Latvian Community Club together with their families – at which point he arranged to have a bottle bank installed in the Museum car park, the greater part of which was covered by a vast marquee. Overflow car parking facilities were provided by the farmer who owned the neighbouring farmland, as well as any space available at the Agri-Presto site, courtesy of Merlin Swift.

The catering company responsible for the restaurant at the Museum was delighted to be asked to provide a banquet, rather akin to a wedding breakfast, for such a gathering even though it meant having to double their staffing levels for the unique occasion. John's choice of menu favoured English cuisine almost exclusively, the only exception of note being the presence of *sauerkraut* as an optional vegetable in deference to the expectations of his Latvian guests, whose other expectation of plentiful *schnapps* was also to be taken into account – hence the need for a bottle bank.

Thoughtful as ever for any of his guests who might have been prevented from attending the party for reasons financial, John arranged and paid for any transport or overnight accommodation for those who responded to his sensitive enquiry about such matters. The only aspect of the whole operation over which John felt he had no control was the provision of post-party taxis and this he delegated to Merlin Swift, happy and confident in the knowledge that as long as Merlin was reasonably sober, he could manage such a problem, should it arise, and settle up with him somehow at a later date.

The official, printed invitation card stated, "12 noon for 1 o'clock luncheon" for those who were so favoured. Some later-recalled acquaintances were summoned by telephone to attend what was for many the party of a lifetime. In full the invitation read

---

John Smith of Latvia and England
requests the pleasure of your company
at a Grand Farewell Luncheon
to be dished up at
The National Blacksmiths' Museum
on Wednesday 24th November 1999,
12 noon for 1 o'clock luncheon.
Please, no parting shots or personal gifts
but any contribution to the Museum Endowment Fund
would be gratefully received.
Dress Casual.
R. S. V. P. to John Smith
c/o The National Blacksmiths' Museum

John's appeal for donations to the Museum benefited the fund by over ten thousand pounds, the greater part of which was given anonymously.

Aidan Ferrers, meanwhile, had decided to bring to an end his own practical commitment to the Museum at about the same time as the farewell party, which gave John the opportunity or rather the idea of having a few guests of honour to occupy a top dining table in his company and at least during the meal to share the limelight which inevitably was bound to fall on himself as host. At the top of his list of special guests was Old Tom Howard who at the age of ninety-five was still of a lively mind but beset by the physical frailties of his long innings and the passing of Mrs Tom two years earlier, just after reaching their platinum wedding anniversary. In the event,

Old Tom decided that a feast such as he envisaged could be one blow-out too much and Young Tom, at the tender age of sixty-seven and already invited to sit at the top table, was deputed to represent his father and challenged to eat enough for two.

The farewell luncheon turned into a mildly riotous and raucous affair, a celebration of a brotherhood, formed over more than half a century, amid an atmosphere of tangible and mutual goodwill generated primarily by the remarkable man who had finally gathered the members together before leaving on his last journey of discovery to the land of his childhood – Latvia.

It had not been John's intention to have any speeches, with the exception of his own words of welcome before the company sat down to dine. However, as the meal progressed and the number of bottles of various alcoholic beverages imbibed increased, so did the levels of sobriety decrease and as coffee was being brought to the tables a Latvian jumped up onto his table and roared, loud enough to be heard over the general chatter and hubbub of the throng, in Latvian and English, a toast to the host. One toast followed another in rapid succession from different tables and different guests. Short snappy sentences – sometimes slurred – were the order of the day. *Schnapps* was having its say! John sat powerless, in smiling bemusement for over half an hour as his guests jumped up or stood up, toasted his health and happiness, then sat down again only to be called to be upstanding once more within a matter of seconds.

At half past three, the only truly sober person at the party called a halt. John, armed with his first glass of *schnapps*, stood up and in so doing succeeded in stunning the runaway assembly into silence. He had no need to climb on to a table to make his presence felt as he looked down from his great height on the seated assembly. He thanked them all for making the effort to attend, for their gifts to the Museum and most of all for their gift of friendship down the years. Then in a moment of uncharacteristic acknowledgement of his own human spirituality which caused Damnit some surprise, he raised his glass in an all-embracing toast that God might bless them all, before leaving the marquee – rather like a bride leaving her wedding breakfast – to change into a more informal rig-out.

After John had been absent for a quarter of an hour, Daniel sensed that the curtain had come down on the last act and there would be no curtain call. Reasonably sober on account of his need to monitor the state of his heart, he hurried out of the marquee, making for the main entrance to the Museum just in time to intercept a big man, toting a massive backpack topped by a giant shovel, taking a black dog for a walk before he disappeared in the fading light. He called out, almost in anguish, 'John. John. Wait. I need to say goodbye.'

John stopped and turned to face Damnit. 'I'm sorry, Daniel. I suddenly realized that I couldn't bear the thought of shaking all those hands. It seemed better to quietly leave you all wondering while I made my exit and I couldn't make any exceptions. You will understand that, I'm sure.'

'No, I'm not so sure. Never mind the magnificent meal and soliciting gifts of money for the Museum – I've got a little something for you, not giftwrapped but guaranteed to warm the cockles.' He handed over a half-bottle of *schnapps*. 'I would have made it a full litre but respected your need for a bearable burden.'

'That's very thoughtful of you, Daniel. It's a funny thing, but you weren't to know that the top item in the sack is a litre of *schnapps* in a plastic bottle. That doesn't mean to say I will refuse another bottle – half or otherwise. Thank you.'

Damnit looked at Baggins. 'Take good care of him for me, Beautygirl. He's a good man.' He fondled her ears gently.

'Don't patronize me, Damnit,' growled John. 'I'm quite aware that that remark was aimed at me, not at Baggins. I thought you knew me better. There will be times on our trek when we will share the same dish, but she will always have the first helping. She comes first.'

'*Touché*,' replied Daniel, wincing slightly. 'That wasn't very subtle of me, was it? But I'm glad you got the thrust of my comment. Off you go. There's no point in prolonging the agony of saying farewell. You will know perfectly well the words of Shakespeare, "Parting is such sweet sorrow". He didn't know what he was talking about. I find the experience a downright pain. Next encounter in North Yorkshire – time unspecified. Good luck, old lad. Keep warm, the pair of you.'

'Same to you, Daniel. And it's time you found another dog. Mustn't hang about or the other guests will be chasing me. Look after yourself.'

The two men shook hands in a firm double-fisted grip before John turned away and walked out through the gateway without a backward glance. Daniel stood still and watched man and dog as they were swallowed up in the gloom. He wasn't altogether sure but he fancied that at the very last moment Baggins turned round to have one final look at him. It was beginning to drizzle with rain as he returned to the marquee to tell everyone that the giant bird had flown, too upset to say goodbye, and it crossed his mind that there was a chance he would never see John again.

A flash of lightning imposed its brilliance on the subdued lighting of the marquee, to be followed shortly by a distant rumble of thunder. "I don't like it," thought Daniel, not looking for omens, "sounds like the god Vulcan is flexing his muscles and coming to work at the National Blacksmiths' Museum."

The storm began to build.

Not very far away John located the tumbledown barn that he had earmarked weeks earlier for his first night on the tramp. He and Baggins sat down together under the white cape, backs to the crumbling wall of the barn, warm and dry, and waited for the rain to pass over. Then out came the doggie bag. Supper was served.

CHAPTER XXVIII

Permitte Divis Cetera

JOHN AND BAGGINS walked and walked, and time passed. The man had no time schedule to govern his daily movements, no strict route to be followed. Whenever possible he would keep to what he called his "green roads", – grass tracks, bridle-paths and old drove roads. He sought out the water-courses where they were to be found; rills, becks and streams were vital if he and Baggins needed to quench their thirst and keep clean.

Apart from an occasional visit to a chemist, food shop, off-licence, public toilet or bank, he set out with the firm intention of never permitting himself to enter a building of any kind with the sole exception of ruins which might afford some shelter against the winter weather. Many a night Baggins proved to be a valuable source of warmth as, in the lee of a hedge or tree, the pair dossed down under the huge cape, oblivious to most of the weather, fair or foul.

In the last few weeks before leaving the Museum on his long walk John had given very careful consideration to how he would arrange his days when he was not on the trail and he mapped out for himself a strange existence.

Wherever his inexorable path eastwards led him, he looked out for any sizeable village, generally proclaimed by a church spire, and made his way there by as direct a route as he could manage, leaving his chosen way to cross any obstacle in his path between him and the spire. Being a farmer's boy he always kept to the field margins, but there were occasions when, confronted by a less than understanding landowner, he had to resort to his foreign charm, explaining in his most exquisitely polished broken English that he was late for church. Other landowners, having caught sight of him and Baggins at a distance and keen to see them off the property, as they drew nearer had to come to terms with the size of the intruder and on coming face to face would be quite happy to pass the time of day discussing anything other than thoughts of trespass, and be beguiled by the beautiful black Baggins. They always parted company on good terms, and "yes", man and dog would be welcome to come back when convenient and catch as many rabbits as they could find. Once in a while farmer and tramp would hit it off from the first exchange of greetings, giving John the opportunity, to the astonishment of the listener, to air his vast knowledge of farm machinery, tractors and, given enough time, the world's finest motor car. Invariably offers of hospitality were politely declined but, in the rare event that he allowed himself the luxury of a cup of tea and a piece of cake, John steadfastly refused to enter the farmhouse. What Baggins thought of this arrangement was never recorded and she appeared to be content with a share of the cake, preferably a rich fruit cake.

Once he had established the position of the church, John's next objective was to locate the parish priest who, on account of several parishes in sparsely populated rural areas being lumped together and sharing the ministrations of one priest-in-charge, was not always to be found in the vicarage next the church. Gentle enquiry would eventually reveal the whereabouts of the priest, who on first meeting with John would be taken aback by the question, 'Do you need any graves digging, Father? If you do, then I am the man sent by God to do the job with Ferrers here, my trusty shovel.' This introductory *spiel* would be delivered with a beatific smile, accompanied by the wagging tail of Baggins. Before a priest could answer, John would press on. 'I may be in this area for some time – I'm not sure how long – and you can expect to contact me on the village green, in the market place or wherever the hub of the community exists should my specialist services be required. And I come free of charge.'

Only once during his months of hiking did he turn up in the right place at the right time when the local sexton was *hors de combat*, suffering with a "bad back" – inevitably the first time in his life since childhood afflictions he had been unable to work.

'Truly a case of, "Cometh the hour, cometh the man",' observed the lucky vicar, as John unslung Ferrers from his backpack. 'No doubt an emergency service such as this comes at a price. I hope it is affordable.'

John teased him. 'Well, Father, if you can't afford to pay the piper maybe you'd like the personal use of Ferrers here – my trusty shovel. If you know the correct magic words of command he is able to work unassisted – a sort of abracadabra job. Mind you, the cost of the spell is greater than if you should employ me to dig the appropriate hole in the hallowed ground. Perhaps Baggins here could help if necessary. She is an acknowledged expert in the field of bone interment – if you get my drift.' He paused for a moment. 'I had you going there for a moment, Father. Actually, even you with your belief in the supernatural may not believe this, but I dig for nothing except perhaps a square meal and a quart of ale. Oh! And something a bit special for my four-legged friend here – she's rather partial to chicken with rice. It makes a change from fresh rabbit.'

The vicar beamed at him. 'Consider it done – whoever you are.'

'Just call me John, and, as already introduced, this is Baggins,' said John.

'You will eat with my family of course,' ventured the vicar. 'Would you care to have the use of our bathroom? We even have a choice of two.'

'Why? I don't smell, do I? I pride myself on my personal hygiene whatever I may look like on the outside,' answered John, only mildly offended.

'Good Heavens, no,' replied the vicar. 'I was only offering what comfort and hospitality I could. You're bound to work up a good sweat, watching – Ferrers I think you said – doing the hard work. The bath is there if you need it, also the automatic clothes washing-machine if it helps.'

John smiled down at him. 'That is most kind of you, Father, but I never go indoors at all, except perhaps to do a vital bit of shop-ping, the chemist, even the bank. Sometimes, given the right opportunity, I stand at a shop door and shout out what I want; at other times, shop hygiene rules permitting, I send Baggins in with a list of my requirements and she can even pick out my favourite hand-rolling tobacco if offered a choice of six. At least she knows I'm not off my rocker. Having said that, she doesn't read washing-machine instructions and I would appreciate the chance to wash a few clothes if you would care to push or pull the right knobs.'

This particular encounter with a priest, blessed with a sense of humour akin to his own, was one of the high spots of John's mean-derings across Northern England. It was his habit that, having established whether or not his grave-digging services were to be called upon, his next move would be to find the village green or market place, sit down either on the grass or on a seat if one were available and wait for the local children to come and talk to Baggins. As her master, he was well qualified to reply on her behalf and in so doing introduce himself as the supreme storyteller. Depending on how long he chose to remain in any locality, he could rely on the company of Baggins to provide the magnet which would attract an increasing number of young listeners as each day passed. Eventually the children would drag their parents along to meet and listen to the charismatic tramp who had arrived, almost as if from another planet.

The vicar who offered the use of the vicarage washing facilities recognized in John the manifestations of a troubled spirit and in the short time of his sojourn in the parish did his utmost to salve the unseen wounds which John revealed to no man. Allowing for John's antipathy to any home comforts which might be afforded by a human dwelling, vicarage or otherwise, he inveigled him into eating the meals, provided by his wife, in the dilapidated greenhouse which was in some danger of collapsing, by the simple ruse of decreeing that the whole family would lunch in there – whatever the weather – and if John wished to have audience of the three "vicarage kids", they would all risk the consequences of falling panes of glass. John was nobody's fool and in his heart of hearts was amused to see how the vicar was prepared to sacrifice his whole family in the prosecution of his Christian duty to provide comfort and succour to such an obvious unfortunate as himself, and he was content to go along with the charade until his spirit urged him to move further down his unplanned trail. It was a Monday morning when John sought out the vicar for the last time and told him he was off, thanking him for all his many kindnesses and asking him to say goodbye to the rest of the family on his behalf. Before a final shaking of hands, they sat down in the draughty greenhouse and John explained how much he had enjoyed being the willing subject of the application of the "Isaac" chapter of the SS Training Manual. 'What on earth do you mean?' asked the vicar, puzzled.

'Do you really need me to tell you the strange story of Abraham's attempted sacrifice of Isaac in accordance with God's wishes? You used your whole family to lure me into the greenhouse and it worked. Without any regret I bent my own self-imposed rules and humoured you in doing so. Anyhow, the "Isaac" was all about using whatever was nearest at hand to dig yourself out of a hole. God provided the ram caught in a thicket as a replacement sacrifice in Isaac's stead. You sought to bring me into your family circle for however brief a time I would be here. As a family you were quite irresistible. Now you will read that bible story and see it in a different light. Baggins is the bait on the end of my fishing line – black labradors always seem to attract humans of all ages – anyone, be they child or adult, enjoys meeting my dog and she is my conduit into the society of my choosing.'

They rose from their rickety chairs and John laid a gentle arm across the shoulders of the vicar. He smiled. 'You've got everything a man could wish for, you know. Lovely wife, three grand kids and your God. Just short of one thing I reckon, but I won't part with Baggins!'

Without ceremony they parted company and without any sanctimoniousness the vicar said 'Goodbye, John. May God bless you.' And he meant it.

It was inevitable that most of his approaches of a "grave" nature to the parish priests he encountered along his way were rebuffed – matters of that ilk being already in the hands of the funeral director and his or her staff. But there were instances when the priest took the trouble to ring the firm responsible just on the off-chance that the gravedigging team was understrength and John was able to be of service, especially when there was more than one burial in the locality within a short timespan. In lieu of any payment which may have been owing to him for such labours, John asked merely for a donation to be made to the RSPCA.

As the weeks went by, John found himself undertaking other tasks which he thought might be useful were he to offer his services. Sprucing up graveyards, once in a while, gave him the opportunity to display his skill with a scythe if one was available. Little rural cricket clubs benefited from his interest if by chance his path passed by the ground and some out of season maintenance seemed called for, either on the pitch or in the machinery shed.

The time came when he learned not to refuse a ready made meal when it was plonked before him. He had been carrying out a check on the tractor hydraulics at a farm not far from Skipton when, about half past twelve, the farmer's twelve year old daughter brought him a steaming dish of Yorkshire hotpot. Up until then, he had always made it plain that a cup of tea and a slice of cake, no more, was acceptable. He was just about to open his mouth to ask the girl to take the plate back to the farmhouse kitchen when she forestalled him by saying 'Mam told me to bring you this. She said, "Tell that daft beggar out there to get this down him. He'll see sense if you quote him – Never look a gift horse in the mouth". I think that means that you shouldn't question where it's come from.'

John guffawed. 'Your mum is very subtle in her approach. How can I deny her? Come and sit here while I eat and I'll tell you all about gift horses. It's a story of teeth – nothing to do with the siege of Troy.'

Such enforced feeding happened shortly before John's Isaac encounter with the vicar. It took a farmer's wife to give him a square meal and a vicar's family to lure him into the dangerous shelter of a greenhouse.

By February 2000 a grapevine had sprung up, planted and nurtured by the numerous parish priests who had been approached by the potential gravedigging storyteller. The short telephone message warned of the advent of John the Narrator and Baggins. Vicars, farmers, cricket clubs and, most of all, children were alerted to the possibility of a massive presence appearing over the western horizon.

At ten o'clock on Christmas Eve 1999 John was to be found hunkered down against the south-facing wall of a little country church, in the shelter of the main south-pointing buttress. In the darkness the brilliant white cape was as invisible as the black Baggins. At eleven the priest arriving to open the doors and prepare for the Midnight Eucharist was startled to smell the aroma of burning tobacco. He switched off his small handtorch and grasping his trusty ash-plant more tightly began to creep in the direction from which the smoke seemed to be coming. He heard a low growl at the exact moment that he spotted the glowing tip of a cigarette and he felt the hairs on the back of his neck stiffen and rise. John spoke. 'For God's sake, Baggins, be quiet. You've given our position away.'

The vicar switched on the torch and laughed nervously with relief as John and Baggins were revealed snuggled down in the angle of the wall and buttress. They had met two days earlier when John had turned up at the vicarage, offering to cut the hornbeam hedges which were threatening to grow out of control. They had sealed the contract over tea and biscuits.

'You nearly frightened the life out of me, John. May you be for-given.'

John said, 'I'm sorry, Father. I really am. I knew it was Christmas Eve but I hadn't reckoned on you having a late service. Silly of me. I'll shift. At least you didn't need me to put the fear of God into you before frightening you to death. I think you're strong enough in that particular department already. Anyway – Happy Christmas to you when it comes!'

'Why don't you come into church with me, John? It will be warm and you will be very welcome – Baggins as well. I think you may find something inside which you don't or won't realize that you need.'

'No thanks, Father. You can spare the fatted calf. This sinner has-n't been in a church for about sixty years and I regret to have to say your God hasn't spoken to me in all that time. I gave up waiting and listening long ago.'

'Just at this moment I don't have time to sit down with you and talk it over but on one thing I am absolutely clear. My God – OUR God has carried you, probably juggled with you, since before you were born. One of these fine days you will slip through the fingers of the hands of God, as the Bible suggests in Saint Paul's letter to the Corinthians: "in a moment, in the twinkling of an eye at the last trump". In that fraction of a second you will hear his voice before he catches your soul. You can bet your life on that.'

'Whatever you say, Father. Off you go into church now and by way of possible insurance you can say a prayer for me. Every little helps. I'm not really in anyone's way here so perhaps I'll stay and listen to whatever I hear from inside the church as it floats out on the night air.'

Their brief conversation finished and the priest left the tramp with an unspoken blessing to which, even in the darkness, John in some mystical way was alert. After the communion service the priest locked the church and approached the buttress where John and Baggins had been sheltering. The space was empty and John had gone without leaving even a shred of tobacco or a dog biscuit. '*Vaya con dios,*' murmured the priest. And he meant it.

Man and dog survived the Winter and with the arrival of Spring their spirits lifted with the lengthening daylight.

It was mid-June before John found himself in the vicinity of

Skipton and he decided to check on the state of Damnit's narrow boat, the Bethdan, half in the hope that his old friend might show up if he himself cared to remain in the area even for a week or two. A Saturday afternoon found him sitting with his back to the bank by the side of the canal towpath, his knees almost tucked up under his chin, his pack leaning against the bank on his left and Ferrers, unslung, standing upright in the turf immediately to his right. Baggins was lying down stretched out in a little patch of warm sunlight with her back to Ferrers' blade and to all intents and purposes fast asleep. John's postprandial reverie was disturbed by a barely audible but ominous growl from the dog who, far from being in the Land of Nod, had been charting the approach of a gang of four young men whose demeanour suggested that canned alcoholic courage was a suitable precursor to a spot of towpath trouble. Baggins sprang to her feet when, about ten yards away from her, the leading lout drop-kicked his empty can in her direction. John was wide awake by now and said one word of command to his dog who scented the smell of danger in the offing.

'Pack, Bags.'

Baggins crossed over in front of John and went flat by the rucksack, growling no longer but with her hackles raised as stiff as a yardbrush.

'Better pick it up lad,' said John, quietly, to the can kicker. 'You've offended my dog.'

'Excuse me!' answered the leader, sarcastically, turning to his mates. 'What have we here? A smelly old tramp concerned about animal welfare. Tell him, guys. Nobody tells me what and what not to do.'

John was still sitting down with his knees under his chin.

'Old, yes. Tramp, yes. Smelly, no. I might need to break your nose for you to improve your sense of smell, little man. And I've eaten bigger rats than you for breakfast in my time. Or maybe my sight isn't what it used to be and you're nothing more than a measly worm – and I've eaten plenty of those as well. Better not to mess with me, you little runt!'

Baggins' hackles lowered as she realized that her master was beginning to enjoy himself. Something in the voice suggested a bit of water sport sooner or later.

'It's your last chance, boy. Pick it up,' said John, 'Before I decide to teach you some respect for your elders and betters.'

'You do scare me, old man. I hope you've got a decent hide 'cos I'm going to skin you alive with my knife before anyone touches that can,' said the thug and then kicked it into the canal where it remained upright, bobbing up and down like a giant float on a fishing-line.

'You kick a mean can,' observed John, 'but you shouldn't have done that without my permission. How are you skills in unarmed combat? When I get angry I reach for my beloved shovel here. He's called Ferrers and <u>he is</u> lethal. I once killed a man with a shovel who was trying to kill me with a revolver. So far I have only used Ferrers to bury bodies but that can change at any time – like now.'

The exchange of words lasted but a short time and John's increasingly truculent tone created some sense of foreboding if not mild panic amongst the supporting trio of louts. He was beginning to stiffen slightly in his cramped sitting position and stretched out his legs in front of him, prior to rising to his feet. Seeing the size of the angry man now confronting them, his right hand resting on the top of Ferrers' handle, the three hangers-on excused themselves, murmuring words about leaving their chief to deal with the situation and how they would see him in the pub shortly, before making an exit in a manner far from orderly.

John looked his remaining adversary straight in the eye and had to admire, however reluctantly, the unfrightened glare which met his gaze as the thug reached behind him for the knife in its scabbard.

'Too late by half,' said John, taking his hand away from Ferrers and stepping forward into within stabbing range of the knife, 'I've won medals for unarmed combat long before you were born. Get that can!'

'You stupid old smelly tramp, you asked for it, and now you're going to get it,' said the lout, between gritted teeth, and raised the knife to stab into John's upper body rather than attempting to drive it into his midriff.

John grinned with delight, memories of vital lessons learned long ago in the gymnasium, smell of cordite and gunsmoke, the cold steel of his bayonet came flooding back. His giant left hand snaked out to the wrist of the hand bearing the knife and his right fist, moving from left to right, smashed into the right cheek of this assailant. The knife fell into the grass beside the canal. John picked his man up as if he was a lifeless puppet and flung him into the middle of the canal. 'I said, get that can, and I meant it,' he called. 'Hurry up now.'

'Help. I can't swim,' wailed the floundering leader of the gang. 'Help. Help.'

"Oh dear," thought John with glee, "something I wasn't prepared for. He doesn't even know how shallow the water is.'

He called out, 'Fetch, Bags,' and in a black flash she was in the water swimming strongly for the sobbing, sopping wet man. 'No, no, girl. Not the man, for heaven's sake – fetch the can.'

The lout eventually found his feet and waded out of the water to the far bank of the canal. A family of rats eyed him warily – they were unaccustomed to humans on their side of the waterfront.

Apart from the main protagonists in the minor affray on such a balmy afternoon, the only witness turned out to be a retired motor engineer coming to check the status of the bottled gas on his narrow boat – the Bethdan. Daniel had arrived on the scene just as the three lesser bits of low life brushed clumsily past him in the haste of making their withdrawal. Looking along the towpath in the direction from which the three had come in such a hurry, he caught the glint in the sunlight of the knife as John's attacker attempted to bring it into play. What followed was akin to a dream sequence; it seemed to happen so fast as two men met at close quarters for what seemed like a fraction of a second before the one nearest the water suddenly flew into the air and splashed down in the middle of the canal. It was only when he heard the missile launcher call out "Fetch, Bags" did he realise he had found John after nearly seven months of silence as the wanderer, in fits and starts, had reached Skipton. The dog, clutching the aluminium can in her mouth, struggled out of the water up the short, steep bank and shook herself vigorously before approaching her master, at which point Damnit now within hailing distance shouted out, 'Baggins' in the most jocular manner he could manage. She pulled up short of John, dropped the can and bounded along the towpath to greet Damnit and share with him as much of the surplus water in her coat as she possibly could. Regardless of the moisture involved, he picked her up and carried her the final ten yards to meet John who promptly picked up both of them. 'You've no idea how much I've missed the smell of damp dog,' said Daniel as he and Baggins were again deposited on *terra firma*, 'And what was all that kerfuffle about?'

'I'm practising for the next Olympic Games', chortled John. 'You know – the Cheeky-Chappy-Chucking Championship. I understand that the current champion and world record holder is a Chinaman Chu Chin Chow from Chunking or it could be left-handed Charlie Chan from Chingford. He bowled a wicked googly as well!'

Daniel laughed. 'I can tell tramping's not done much for your sense of humour. I was sure the reigning champion was a Czech matey.'

'Anyway,' continued John, 'a few more fools like that and I will be a cert for the gold medal even if I never could pick the Chinaman when it was bowled at me. Happy Days!' And he explained what had happened in the lead up to the dunking of the drunken lout who was lucky to get away without any broken bones.

'That's a beauty of a knife,' said Daniel, having retrieved it from the rough grass. 'Judging by its mint condition, polished to perfection, I don't think its ever been unsheathed before. I'm sure its not legal but you never know – it might come in handy. Here!' And he tossed it to John. 'Tuck it into your sock.'

'I'd offer you a cup of tea, Damnit, but I've only the one cup. Baggins uses the saucer.'

'It's a nice thought though,' said Daniel. 'I only arrived a few minutes ago with the intention of checking the gas on board. So-o – – a practical test will involve me in putting the kettle on, and if you've got a drop of milk then we're in business. Let's go aboard.'

'Sorry. No can do,' replied John. 'I've got the milk all right but my self-imposed principles of tramping do not permit the comfort of living quarters. Cabin for you: deck only for me.'

'O.K.,' said Daniel, 'it's the deck for tea. But I have to point out that the Bethdan is not a floating palace – in fact she does leak in places – and if, as forecast, we have some rain overnight I shall expect you under proper cover, principles or no principles. By the way, how is the *schnapps* supply after all this time?'

'Replenished this very morning, since you ask,' replied John. 'And, by the way, as you say, Baggins enjoys a teaspoonful of *schnapps* in her tea. It helped pull us through the Winter, so she tells me.'

'You're incorrigible,' said Damnit. 'Mind you, my Ermin used to enjoy a pint or two of bitter when in her prime. Never stopped her travelling by car though. Just meant I had to drive.'

Tea was taken on deck and in the evening the two friends repaired to Daniel's favourite pub a few hundred yards from the canal basin, where in the beer garden they indulged in as square a meal as is possible to eat in Yorkshire – at Daniel's expense – and washed down with North Yorkshire's finest ale, Black Sheep Bitter. Damnit was delighted with John's display of a healthy appetite. He had not failed to notice that in spite of John's heroic manifestation of strength on the canal bank, he did not look as fit as when he had thrown his farewell party in the November of the previous year. Just before leaving the pub he bought the largest bottle of *schnapps* available and they broached it on deck upon their return. By one o'clock in the early morning the bottle was empty and the two old friends had talked themselves to a standstill.

'Come on in, John. Baggins and your backpack are safely inside. I think a good night's sleep is called for,' said Daniel, gently guiding him to the nearest berth.'God only knows about your self-imposed principles, but they're hurting me now and that is wrong.'

Very little was said over breakfast the next morning. Damnit had risen early to give Baggins her morning exercise and then went to buy the essentials for a hearty breakfast. After finishing his fourth piece of toast, John suddenly spoke up. 'You were right as usual, Daniel. I think it has been an occasion when my guardian angel has elected to intervene and declare "to hell with your principles, eat, drink and be merry before body and soul reach the parting of the ways." Thank you for providing the venue. Unconsciously, I must have been hoping, perhaps even praying that the Bethdan would call you to the canal when it was really me that needed you. After a splendid meal and a few happy hours in your company, in the words of Richard III, or rather Shakespeare, "The king's himself again!" '

'Wrong for once, John. I rather think it was Olivier who delivered that line in the film. But I know what you mean and I am glad.' Damnit smiled benignly at John and poured out another cup of coffee. The washing-up after breakfast completed, Daniel enquired of John if his principles forbade him a car trip. John contemplated for a few moments before answering and stating that such a trip was allowable only as long as he returned to the base car park.

'Right,' said Daniel, 'we'll drive out to Middinside at top end of

Yowesdale and you can buy me lunch at the Ram. Some folk say that it was a cottage in Middinside where the visiting angel left the heavenly recipe for Yorkshire Pudding and not Ilkley Moor at all. You can add that tale to your repertoire when we've had our lunch. O.K.?'

'*Jawohl, Herr Hauptmann,*' replied John, with a grin. 'Orders is orders, but it had better stay fine – my *alfresco* principles are back on track.'

As requested, Daniel returned the well-fed tramp to Skipton later that afternoon and then drove home to Tupshorne the same evening, happy in the knowledge that it had been his good fortune to inject some fine food and fresh spirit or fiery spirits into the frame of his old friend. It felt good to play the part of some sort of an earthly guardian angel.

Three months later, in early September, Daniel was walking across the market square in Tupshorne when he was suddenly startled by a voice from the past. A dog barked excitedly and he turned round to see a very large tramp sitting on a wooden bench with a gleaming black dog at his knee. John the Narrator had arrived.

'Hello Mr Greensward, Sir'. 'Let me tell you the story of the Middinside Yorkshire Pudding – fresh from the oven,' was John's first foray into Tupshorne society. Ferrers was playing second fiddle on this occasion. It was two weeks before the Festival of Saint Michael the Archangel, and sixteen days before the retirement of the vicar, the Reverend Jacob Drake, Daniel's lifetime friend.

CHAPTER XXIX

Quo Vadis?

DANIEL AMBLED OVER the short distance which separated him from John and Baggins. John got to his feet to greet him properly but the dog, to Daniel's amazement, having barked her own "hello" stayed flat as if under her master's strict order, "tum". Tum or not, John had never invented a command to prevent Baggins wagging her tail which was creating a minor dust storm.

'Well. Well. Well. You've finally made it, you old devil,' said Damnit, addressing the tramp. 'Not before time, judging by the parlous state of your footwear. We'll do something about that before you go base over apex somewhere in Yowesdale. Our rural paths can be a tramp's nightmare.'

'Now what's up with you, Baggins, not getting up to shake paws? You look in fine fettle to me: a right Glossy Flossy, as my father would have said.'

'I don't know how you've managed it, John, with so much walking but it looks to me as if she's put on a bit of weight since I last saw you at Skipton. Have you changed her diet? Maybe you've not encountered as many wild rabbits between there and Tupshorne.'

'Stand, girl!' said John, and Baggins failed to obey, rising only as far as a sitting position, and that with a rather clumsy effort.

'Oh, no,' groaned Daniel. 'I don't believe it. She's in pup. How on earth ...?' he ruffled the dog's ears and rubbed her chest vigorously. 'Didn't your master teach you the facts of life, girl? You haven't half queered his pitch.'

'How could you let it happen, John? You don't need me, I'm sure, to point out how this fairly imminent event is going to affect your plans. In nautical terms, or should I say marine engineering terms, you are already effectively in dry dock for as long as it takes to wean and dispose of the litter. Did you not think of having them aborted?' He sat down next to John on the bench and tried to put a brotherly, comforting arm round his shoulders. 'Tell me the whole sorry tale before I wake up and find it's just a bad dream.'

'First of all,' began John – 'No abortion and no drowning of puppies. I think I am more *prolife* the older I get, and I feel the most immense sadness knowing that I once had a baby brother who died at birth along with our mother. That particular tragedy I lay at the door of the SS recruiting gang which took father and me away. Thinking back now, after nearly sixty years, it is surprising that my mother didn't miscarry then instead of going the full term.

The pups will be valuable – but more of that later.

And so to the Bitch's tale! When you left me in June at Skipton canal basin to return home here, I stayed another couple of days, feeding my face as you instructed, before hitting the trail again and eventually making my way to Grassington via Bolton Abbey which enabled us to walk many a mile by – and laze by – and swim in the Wharfe. Bags had a marvellous time with so much swimming and we fished as well, when we could get away with it. So we reached Grassington a great deal fitter than when you saw us in the canal basin and I <u>was</u> aware that she had come into season. That gave me no cause for concern because, unless we were on the wilderness of the moorlands where she really could run free, I always have her under close control – on a very short leash if need be. By the end of a week in the vicinity of Grassington, without any gravedigging to be done, I had collected a fair audience of mostly young teenagers who came to listen to the tales of the tramp sitting on a bench in their Market Place. It was the middle of the evening and I looked over the youngsters lounging and loitering on the cobbles as I talked and spied a very handsome black labrador, who without doubt must have already spotted or perhaps I should say got wind of Baggins here, safely – so I thought – on the leash under my bench. I suspended my narrative to enquire if the dog belonged to anyone in the audience. 'That's our Bilbo,' chirped up a lad of about twelve or thirteen. 'My dad says he's got a pedigree as long as your arm. Do you want to be introduced? He's lovely natured – Bilbo I mean'. The kids all laughed, a sure indicator of Bilbo's appeal and popularity. 'I don't think so,' I replied. 'Just now my one dog here is all I can cope with. I presume Bilbo is named after the Hobbit, Mr Bilbo Baggins, is he? My bitch's name is Baggins because she's always ready for a snack at bagging time – a good Cheshire word for you.'

'No, it's nowt to do with the Hobbit. My name's Beaumont – Ben

Beaumont, known as Benbo. He's Bill Beaumont, answers to Bilbo, and Stupid.'

You can probably guess the rest. Bilbo vanished and so did Baggins, liberated by an unseen hand which may or may not have belonged to young Benbo – I'll never know. Bags reappeared about an hour later, covered in confusion and contrition, but wearing a smile fit to grace the *Mona Lisa* and twice as appealing. That's it. End of story and the beginning of I don't know how many wagging tails and tales to come!'

Damnit broke in at last. 'Now I know how. Tell me when. It's important.'

'The date is engraved on my memory because the next day the police suggested that the time had come for me to be moving on. That was a "first" for this particular vagrant. Apparently, Baggins had bitten Bilbo for his pains. I had not become *persona non grata*. She was *canis non grata*. Anyhow, the date of the dalliance was June 30th. Why do you ask?'

Daniel did some speedy mental arithmetic before answering the question. 'Expect her to whelp on October 1st. That's nine weeks gestation period and it's rare for it to vary. She's just sixteen days to go by my reckoning and it looks as if your trek homeward has come to a grinding halt, as they say, right here in Tupshorne. Maybe it is decreed that you should end your days here and not in Latvia. It's not a bad place, you know, and we do have some mighty comely women – that's if you need a housekeeper of course.' he grinned. 'I'll have you in church yet!'

John snorted. 'Fat chance of that, my old friend. No, I've sorted out the problem with, as yet, your unknowing assistance. My famous Isaac chapter from the SS manual has already come into play. I look around me for the nearest article to solve my dilemma and what do I see – none other than one man and no dog. Damnit man, you're the ram caught in the thicket. When Baggins whelps, I'm going on, on my own, leaving her and the pups with you. You'll love it.'

'Hold on a moment,' said Damnit, perturbed. 'This old ram might have other matters in the pipeline to take care of for all you know. Baggins and pups – and she could have as many as a dozen you know – will take up an enormous amount of time; time which for me may be at a premium in the immediate future as my vicar retires very shortly. I'm going to be very busy with church affairs. Wait 'til you meet Jake. Of course, you've heard me talk of him often – my blood brother since childhood. Aha! Pass me your Isaac, I've just had the germ of an idea; with Jake retiring he'll have time on his hands and he and Martha are coming to live at High Ash, my house, while they go househunting. They could be with me for some months. There could be a complication though – Jake's black lab, Miss Bindle, might take a dislike to Bags. I doubt that particular scenario but you never can tell with bitches. "Frailty, thy name is woman," you know.'

'That's settled then,' said John with obvious relief.

'Oh no, it isn't,' replied Daniel. 'You and I have never ever taken each other for granted so don't start now. I've not got you down as a deserter. For God's sake, you can't just abandon your dog because she's become a burden, never mind the pups. You're not thinking straight. Your precious Isaac chapter needs an update. Let's drop the subject before I get cross. At least we've got two weeks to do the right thing by your extra Baggage here.'

Baggins heard Daniel speak her name and gave his hand a friendly lick. She knew that he, at least, was on her side.

'Now, about your feet. Those boots look pretty ropey to me and I refuse to believe that the Isaac prescribed newspaper for an insole but that's what it looks like to me.'

'Right again, Daniel,' replied John. 'I've rather let that aspect of tramping slip recently, only because I've not been near the right kind of shoeshop. I don't recall if you ever mentioned one here in Tupshorne.'

'Fraid not,' said Daniel, smiling. 'Do you remember the time we were walking around Three Shires Head and we discovered we were sporting identical boots. That was when you told me about relieving your father's body of his boots at Stalingrad. Fair sent a shiver down my spine at the time! I'm not expecting to pop my clogs just yet so we'd better go shopping.' He paused. 'What's the time? Half-twelve by the church clock – means it's nearer one o'clock. It must be your turn to buy me lunch. Is Bags fed? Right then, nearest pub with an outside table for you; then I'll drive us over to Leyburn. There's a marvellous walking shop there – nothing but the best and that means the service as well. I've known the owner a long time – name of Jolyon Walker – and he calls the shop "The Jolly

Walker". I call it "The Jolly *Walkies*" because Joly knows all about man's best friend and offers a decent range of dog collars and leashes to the discerning owner. Let's go!'

The subject of the delicate state of Baggins the Beautiful was bound to arise again rather sooner than later but neither John nor Daniel intended to allow it to interfere with their lunch. It was left to two passers-by, well known in Tupshorne, to come by their open air table shortly after they had sat down with their drinks, having ordered food at the bar.

Two of Saint Michael the Archangel's church members, Timothy Welsh, Daniel's fellow Churchwarden, and his wife Muriel, approached, attracted by the new dog in town.

Tim spoke first. 'I didn't know you'd got a mature replacement for Ermintrude, Daniel.'

'She's lovely,' said Muriel sizing up the situation quicker than Tim. 'Looks like you'll have your hands full in a week or two. Presumably since you never mentioned getting another dog since you lost Ermin, this one wasn't wanted. Really! Some people make me so angry. But she really is a beauty. I suppose the whelps will be quite the opposite – poor little blighters. Mind you, all puppies make me go gooey and the sight of a bitch heavy with pups is one of the most wonderful pictures I can think of.'

'Actually,' said Daniel, introducing John and Baggins, she's not mine at all but belongs to this old tramp, a great friend in every sense and of long standing. What is more, I have it on the authority of no less a man than Benbo Beaumont of Grassington that the proud father to be has a pedigree as long as your arm. Could be an interesting litter.' Daniel sensed a possible solution to John's problem. He, unlike John, was well aware that Tim and Muriel, originally from Bolton, had been for many years puppy walkers for the Guide Dogs for the Blind Association. Their knowledge of labrador lore was encyclopaedic. Puppy love was their speciality. After a few more minutes of polite conversation – Muriel not being at all sure about Damnit's gigantic down-at-heel tramp – hot food arrived and the Welshes took their leave.

'Good people,' observed John wryly. 'I could see that Tim was dying to be introduced to Ferrers!'

'Yes,' said Daniel, 'salt of the earth, Tim and Muriel; do anything to help anyone they would, and you don't have to ask twice. Come on then. Eat up while the grub's cooling down.'

A little later, chatting lightheartedly over a cup of coffee while John indulged in one of his handrolled cigarettes, Daniel quite suddenly became serious by raising once again the subject of Baggins. 'I'll do it,' he stated.

'Do what?' asked John, puzzled.

'Take the Bilbo Baggins family off your hands, of course. I've thought it out and reckon I can see my way to resolving the awkward situation you've landed yourself in. I'll want it legally watertight – a bit like an official adoption – and I won't brook any interference in the scheme of things as I seek to arrange it.'

'That sounds more officious than official to me,' grumbled John, 'and I'm sure it's not called for. You know perfectly well I'd trust you with my life never mind Bags. Are we getting at cross-purposes here? Would you care to elucidate further?'

'All right, replied Daniel, 'just give her to me, along with the appropriate letter stating what you have done. As a brood bitch originating from Merlin Swift's pedigree kennel line, John, she's valuable, quite apart from her sentimental value as a pet. I will undertake to chase up the owner of Bilbo in Grassington and check out the dog's apparently peerless pedigree. I don't suppose for one moment that Bags' pedigree matters to you and that document from Merlin Swift will have disappeared long ago. No matter – I'll get a copy from Merlin. I'll even pay stud fees if need be to Mr Beaumont for the pleasure of getting my hands on Bilbo's pedigree. Perhaps it was fortunate that Baggins, in one mad moment of passion, bit Bilbo. Mr B. will know that such things can happen at mating. It proves that Bilbo paid for his misdeed and is surely the sire.'

'Hang on a mo,' said John. 'I don't want any money out of this forthcoming "happy event".'

'No. But I do,' said Daniel. 'I'll keep a bitch for myself, sell the remainder of the litter for the best price I can get – and I'm talking several hundreds of pounds here – any profit I'll give to the Guide Dogs for the Blind Association because Tim and Muriel used to be puppy walkers for the G. D. B. A. Meeting them earlier gave me that idea. Between us, Tim, Muriel, Jake, Martha and I will make sure that Baggins is treated like a queen for as long as it takes to sell her puppies. Then – and this is the inspired bit of my plan, though I say it myself – I will pop Baggins into Tottie and drive her over to join up with you wherever you've got to on your walk.' He dug his diary out of the inside breast pocket of his gilet, flicked swiftly to the calendar page and after hasty scrutiny pronounced that if everything went according to plan he might have his dog back in ten weeks at the very earliest.

'Trust me, John – but I need it formally agreed. Don't question my intentions or my motives. Just accept that I will do my level best for Bags and family and so help you on your way.'

John shivered, visibly, even though they were basking in the warmth of mid-September sunshine.

'Are you O.K., old lad?' asked Damnit anxiously. 'You seemed to shiver for a moment, almost as if you'd seen a ghost.'

'Not a ghost, Damnit,' replied John. 'I heard your words, "Don't question me" and they hit me like an echo from the past when I last saw Frau Eleanore Bormann nearly sixty years ago. I think now is the time to tell you a part of the true life story of Janis Kalējs, the fifteen year old SS man who killed Heino Bormann, her *Mann*. It was a pure accident that happened in a barrack-room brawl – no more, no less. I went to visit her in Hamburg to try to explain – that was some time later – but the SS had told her Heino was a battlefield hero and gave her his medal for bravery which had been awarded to him, posthumously. I couldn't tell her the truth about her "hero" husband and destroy her precious memories of him. Since I last saw her, her little girl and her then unborn son, Wolfgang, I have always sent her money. My guilt – her innocent ignorance. My final words to her were, "Ask me no questions," which you have just echoed. You probably knew when you were my director at Rolls, although you never gave the slightest indication, that a small slice of my salary went to Germany to help a lady and her little family. I never had reason to stop as the years rolled by, and then I reasoned that if I did stop, she would be unable to avoid the big question WHY.'

'I'm getting the picture,' ventured Daniel. 'She somehow learned the truth only last year, presumably by another accident of fate, and literally gave you your marching orders. I've sometimes wondered why such a warm human being as you has never married. Now I understand and now I know why she told you to go home to Latvia nearly sixty years after you left. Two cataclysmic events sixty years apart, both down to Adolf Hitler in the first place. When you told me in that letter last year that you were going to walk home I suspected something serious had upset your equilibrium if not your sanity. Now I know the why and wherefore, I must say this. You really don't have to go. Eleanore Bormann must be a very old lady by now. It seems very unfair on all concerned that she has lived so long. I'm sorry, I didn't mean that statement to sound quite as brutal as it did. Tactless of me.'

'Not really, Damnit. Just brutally honest. It is a pity she had to learn the truth and, to be frank, I would rather have died first. But for all my fancy fairy-tales, you can't put the genie of truth back in the bottle can you? Still, she was right and I am well on the way to the Newcastle-Gothenburg ferry terminal. As for Baggins – I trust you implicitly. I can't believe I contemplated deserting her in such a callous fashion. Selfishness can take some strange forms. So, as of now, I think it best she becomes your dog until the reunion. She will learn where you expect her to whelp, even if she does choose somewhere else such as a warm compost heap or your bed.'

Damnit cut in. 'No, John. You must keep her until whelping, however inconvenient it may be for you. Her bond with you will be vital over the next two or so weeks. With her pups born, she will realize you can't cope on your own and then I will come to the rescue. Just one more thing. I know she's bilingual in Latvian and English but under stress she may lapse and forget the English. So as well as providing me with an "adoption certificate", can you let me have a list of your Latvian commands, in phonetics, with their English equivalents – just in case.'

'I take your point about the bonding. I'll stick around Tupshorne until she whelps. Obviously she will see more of you over that time than she ever has before and I can teach *you* the Latvian commands which I'll write on the back of an envelope as well. Finally, I want to alter my will, in which matter perhaps you could point me in the direction of a friendly solicitor and at the same time he or she can fix you up with the Baggins "adoption certificate".'

'I'm sure my solicitor will be delighted to help you rewrite your will, once you've crossed his palm with silver or whatever passes for it these days. I must say I'm surprised you've brought a will with you,' said Daniel.

'You more or less ordered me to do it,' replied John. 'You'd be even more surprised if I emptied my backpack at your feet. Like Pandora's Box, the very bottom item packs a punch of its own but unlike its name being Hope, this one is more akin to Despair.' He laughed. 'But that's another story with which I do not intend to regale you. It goes with me to the grave.' He summoned a passing waitress and asked to pay the bill.

'Right,' said Daniel with a definite air of finality. 'And so to Walkies of Leyburn. I think it best if we walk to High Ash, leave Ferrers and your pack there – that'll save me having to put Tottie's back seat flat and Bags can have that space to stretch out. She can enjoy Ermin's best woolly blanket, and consider it her own for the foreseeable future. Are you still wearing Meindl walking boots? Of course you are. I can see the logo from here even if the uppers are a bit shot. Walkies'll have them all right – my size, your size, everybody's size. Just don't ask him for a new backpack to match your "special" – he'd have a fit! There's a thought: I know Ferrers is called after Aidan but you haven't given the bulk-carrier a name.'

'Don't laugh,' chuckled John. 'It's an "it" and "it" is called "Pregnant", being full of an unknown quantity. Come on, Mr Blacksmith. Take me to the forge and get me shoed, or should I say shod.'

At Walkies John took the opportunity to replace several items of clothing in addition to his new Meindls. With Winter not too far away special socks and warm, dry wicking vests would be top of his shopping list. Daniel thought of asking for commission for introducing a new customer to Walkies, but quite sensibly refrained which was just as well as John trotted out his favourite Yorkshire phrase, picked up on his journey, "How much for cash?"

'He's as bad as you, Damnit. Ten percent do you? And don't dream of mentioning commission,' was the answer from Joly.

'Done,' said John. 'On second thoughts though, forget the discount and throw in one of those microtorches if you'd be so kind – the sort that goes on a keyring. I had one very similar to the one on display, when I left Preston a year ago. A jolly useful accessory for a tramp, especially in the dark of Winter, and then I went and lost or rather I relinquished it in the Spring when I was holding it between my teeth as I was bleeding the fuel system on a tractor I was tinkering with. The farmer owner was watching me at work and asked me a question about the torch. Silly idiot me opened my mouth to answer and the light dropped into the jug of diesel fuel. It still shone perfectly but I didn't fancy it in my mouth again. I expect the farmer's still using it.'

'That's a cheap ten percent by my account. You must be worth at least two torches by my reckoning. Something else perhaps?' queried Joly.

Damnit jumped in. 'The Beautybags needs a new collar, John, with a dog-tag engraved with my address and 'phone number – can't risk her giving *me* the slip and trying to follow you. Not that she'd leave the pups. When she rejoins you, I'll keep the tag for whichever pup I elect to keep. How about that?'

'Good idea', replied John, 'Will the revised budget run to a new leash as well?' he addressed Jolyon.

'Just about,' said Joly. 'Would you like a red leather collar, Baggins? It's the very height of fashion at the moment so I understand.'

'On behalf of my dog let me say how pleased she will be to model one of your top of the range red collars,' said John. 'As for the existing dog-tag, I don't think I ever bothered to tell you, Daniel, but it belonged to my father. I removed it from his corpse at Stalingrad before I buried him, and for some inexplicable reason kept it until I got Baggins. Then it seemed just the right thing to do, otherwise it would have been thrown away when I die.' He laughed. 'Maybe I should not have chucked my Iron Cross away on Lüneburg Heath. It would have looked grand on a red leather collar.'

Joly Walker's jaw dropped. 'That sounds like a cue for a story. Heroic, was it?'

'Not really,' said John. 'It was an episode in my teenage years and I rarely ever mention it, never mind even think about it. Some memories are best left as cold ashes and beyond re-ignition.'

CHAPTER XXX

Miserere Mei, Deus

FOLLOWING ON THE mild admonishment he suffered from Daniel, regarding his own apparently cavalier treatment of Baggins, for the next two weeks all John's movements were geared to the well-being of his dog. Very gentle strolls were the daily norm for man and dog, with long periods spent sitting on the wooden bench in Tupshorne market place regaling the locals of all ages with an endless stream of stories. There was no call for his gravedigging expertise and Ferrers was in danger of collecting a light coating of rust until Daniel introduced the tramp to the vicarage garden and so to his great friend, Jake Drake, the vicar, and Martha, his wife. As churchwarden, Daniel, mindful of the impending retirement of the vicar, was anxious that the garden should be kept in a reasonable state of tidiness until the eventual arrival of another parish priest.

Miss Bindle, Jake and Martha's black labrador bitch, took to Baggins like a kennelmate and quite obviously elected to take on the part of a canine courtesy aunt, so solicitously did she appear to monitor Baggins' final ten days of her pregnancy, much to the amusement of the humans who witnessed her concern. When John was busy in the vicarage garden, Bags was given the free run of the vicarage itself but he never allowed himself to look for her in the house and however hard Martha tried to persuade him to share their table, she never met with anything other than a polite refusal and she never managed to find just the right moment to ask him why.

True to his promise, John tried to teach Damnit a few basic words of dog commands in Latvian and, in phonetics, committed them to the back of a brown business envelope. Damnit found it hard going!

Sunday, the first day of October was the last day of Jacob Drake's ministry in the parish of Saint Michael The Archangel, Tupshorne. After his final parish communion in the morning the parishioners laid on a magnificent farewell luncheon and presentation of parting gifts to Jake, Martha and Miss Bindle. Damnit had done his damnedest to persuade John to grace the occasion with his presence, as much in recognition of his labours at the vicarage as the strong bonds of friendship which held them together. John was not to be so seduced!

It was nearly three o'clock when the last of the diners left. Jake had insisted on staying to the very end to say a special thank you to all those who had provided and served the lunch and completed the washing up. Daniel refused to go without him and the pair were finally left alone, standing just inside the porch of the church hall. The afternoon air was warmed by bright sunlight until a dark shadow fell across the two men. The bulk of the shadow was topped by something sharper and more sinister, almost like a narrow crucifix – Ferrers was making his presence known. Out of the shadow, spoke John – agitation in every word.

' "O shrieve me, shrieve me, holy man!" '

Fast as lightning, Jake replied.

' "The hermit crossed his brow.

Say quick, quoth he, I bid thee say -

What manner of man art thou?"

'I didn't take you for an "Ancient Mariner", John.'

'No, he's my man for all seasons and in any emergency. That's right, isn't it, John?' joined in Daniel. 'What's up, old lad? Has someone rattled your cage? I'm afraid feeding time's over.'

John ignored Daniel's facetious questions, addressing the priest alone. 'I have to make my confession, Father Jacob.'

Daniel hooted with laughter. 'This I must hear. Father Jacob indeed! He's having us on, Jake.'

'Shut up, Damnit,' said Jake, quietly but firmly. 'You're out of order this time. I sense an unquiet spirit to attend to here. Let me have your church keys. I'll return them at teatime. You take Bindle and Sprottle for a walk with Martha and Lorna. I may be some time.

John remained strangely subdued, having made the initial effort to unburden his soul. Baggins lay at his feet, aware that something beyond her comprehension was taking place, and anyway the kicking of the pups in her belly was giving her cause for her own concerns.

Daniel passed the keys to Jake without further personal comment except to say that perhaps John might join them for tea and that he was sure Martha would not mind. Then, slightly mystified, he watched as Jake led John into the church, before walking to the vicarage to explain the circumstances of the vicar's early return to work.

The turmoil in John's mind was all too evident as priest and penitent reached the main door of the church.

'Is it permitted for me to bring Baggins in with me, Father?' he mumbled, only barely audible. 'She knows all my secrets and my sins already.'

'Of course you can. Our Bindle is registered as an honorary flower arranger. But you'll need to destack your backpack. Pop it in the back pew. By the way, you don't need to call me Father – Jake will do.'

'No,' said John. 'In your church here you are my Father confessor. I've not entered other than a ruined church since 1941 and that solely for purposes of shelter. In my heart I have denied the existence of God for nearly fifty years.'

'So why come to me now, John? What has brought about this sea-change?'

'Ariel's song from "The Tempest", Father. Daniel told me you were a fine actor. "Full fathom five" and all that. "Nothing of him that doth fade, but doth suffer a sea-change into something rich and strange." I had a strange, disturbing dream last night. My sea-change stems from that – it was a game of cricket.

I had batted right through the innings from the first ball, hitting more boundaries than ever before. But the fast bowlers had battered and bruised me all over in spite of my carting them all over the ground and out of it. I don't remember how many runs I had scored when finally the opposing team captain came on to bowl his slow legbreaks at me. Then he completely bamboozled me with his first googly and I was caught by the wicketkeeper after he had juggled with the ball for what seemed to me, even in a dream, like an eternity. "On your way", said the keeper. He was my uncle Zigrids. As I passed the bowler on my way to the pavilion, I looked at him more closely and was surprised to recognize my father. "Fine knock, son," he said. "Innings over. Don't forget to leave your bat in the changing room – you won't need it again. I must admit I've not seen a shovel used as a cricket bat before. Mother and I will see you at tea, after the game. It's the only cricket tea with sauerkraut as an option."

Leaving the field of play, the man holding open for me the wicket gate into the pavilion stand was you, Father. Lead me through my confession, please, before my cricket bag gets confiscated by the ultimate umpire. At long last I know where I am going. You see, my father and uncle Zigrids wouldn't have understood cricket on earth, whereas they do now. That realization speaks volumes to me. It may seem frivolous to you, Father, but to me it's obvious that angels play cricket.'

'Was that the end of the dream?' enquired Jake. 'I'm not really qualified to interpret dreams, but this one of yours doesn't seem to have reached a proper conclusion except to point you in my direction – and I am very real live flesh and blood and certainly no angel.'

'No, Father. The grand finale was all fire, smoke and such heat that I could not bear it. There were two changing rooms in the cricket pavilion and not knowing the location of that particular club, I opened the door marked "Visitors". The fiery furnace, which faced me and seared my eyeballs, burned away all memory of my heroic innings, just completed. Stumbling backwards in utter panic, I bumped into Daniel who kindly apologized for being in the way and said I was "Home", but should see you first to have my credentials checked. You could say that I got the message – loud and clear – from on high. And here I am, Father. Try me!'

With extreme care and sensitivity Jake led John to and through his confession, prompting him when he felt that he was becoming lost for words. Very quickly he understood that on John's conscience was a specific incident dating back to some time during World War II. All other misdemeanours counted for nothing. Without any respect for chronological order, John trotted out a litany of death by misadventure, deaths in mortal combat of savage warfare and finally the killing of his senior officer with an iron shovel – the imaginary burden he had carried on his mind since Stalingrad and the very real weight on his back since leaving Preston to walk back to Latvia. John poured out his heart and Jacob, the Father Confessor, listened, full of Christian compassion and some astonishment. The amazing story of John's life since he had been removed from his native land came out in his confessional conversation. Unspoken, unspeakable love and devotion; fairy stories and tales of adventure for children unknown; the self-punishment with a heavy gravedigging shovel; all became clear to Jake as John uttered his last sentence. 'I needed my Isaac chapter, Father Jacob, to deliver me from the evil

I have done and you are my Isaac in this instance – my safe and sure exit.'

Jake was puzzled. 'I understand everything you have told me, John, except for your mention of Isaac. Where does he come into the reckoning? You aren't getting confused, are you, with Jacob, son of Isaac, the son of Abraham?'

'Not me, Father,' replied John, smiling at last. 'You are the second priest I have met on my walk to whom I have had to explain the significance of the Isaac in my SS training manual.'

Jake listened carefully and when John had finished his version of Isaac's near-sacrifice he nodded in comprehension, before pronouncing his absolution with the time-honoured words of the Book of Common Prayer.

"Our Lord Jesus Christ, who hath left power to His Church to absolve all sinners who truly repent and believe in Him, of his great mercy forgive thee thine offences: And by His authority committed to me, I absolve thee, Janis, from all thy sins, In the Name of the Father, and of the Son, and of the Holy Spirit. Amen."

John gave a huge sigh of relief and gratitude. 'Thank you, Father. What a load off my mind – truly. It's time *nunc* for my *dimittis*. You know – I had come to a stage in my life when with all my fanciful stories I had nearly forgotten just who I really am. To be given absolution in my Latvian name, Janis, brought me so gently down to earth again in readiness for the rest of my journey home. I presume Damnit must have told you my Christian name. Apart from at an occasional party with my fellow "displaced persons", I've not been addressed as Janis since about 1949.'

'Yes. Obviously I have gleaned some little snippets of information about you from Damnit over the years. You yourself know that he and I have been friends from childhood and there are few secrets between us, but he's never breathed a word about anything connected with your wartime exploits. He sure kept quiet about that slice of your personal history.'

'He never knew about SS trooper Kalējs because I never told him about the blood on my hands – any of it. All my true – and many fanciful – stories of life in the mighty *Waffen SS* were those of an observer, as if my own "involvement" was more "fly on the wall" than "piggy in the middle". He does know about the Isaac, though. I won't say any more, but next time you see him do ask him about the time I had to deal with a fire in his office at Crewe. We'd only known each other a month or so and he was quite fascinated as I recall even now, how the Isaac came to the rescue.' John chuckled. 'Just think if it hadn't been for this Rolls Royce, one time SS man, the whole works could have been burned down – something the *Junkers* bombers failed to do in the blitz.'

Jake changed the subject. 'We're off the confessional record now, John, and yet I feel there is something you've left unsaid – not a crime or a sin but something of vital importance, perhaps to do with your reason for walking back to your homeland. I think you need to tell me about it and we'll share the revelation with the Lord. You did mention, very briefly, a lady – the widow of the soldier you killed accidentally.'

John gave a start and shot a startled glance at Jake. 'Your pastoral intuition has hit a nerve, Father. You ARE right and no crime is involved. What triggered off, I wonder, your use of "*cherchez la femme*"?'

'You may not know the words of the blues "Trouble in Mind" but the last verse goes "Trouble in mind, I'm blue and my poor heart's bleeding sore, Never had so much trouble in mind before". Affairs of the heart are like that – you can only bottle them up for so long and your time is up. "A trouble shared is a trouble halved", is a fine adage. If you care to tell me, I can assure you that your confidence will go no further – not even to Daniel – and your wounded heart will heal.'

'Don't worry, Father. Daniel will find out in due time everything I have told you. Eleanore Bormann is her name and I know in my heart that I have loved her since I first met her. Yet I never could tell her because ... ' John explained his undying devotion to the woman who was never meant to learn the truth of her husband's death at his hands, and Jake listened to the true story of a wartime romance destined never to blossom, blighted by the shadow of a white lie – a medal for bravery, awarded for dying in a barrack room accident.

The story finished, leaving John drained of emotion and Jake full of an extraordinary feeling of compassion which found an outlet in a quietly uttered prayer with a final blessing for John, Eleanore and her family.

John thanked the priest for his comforting words and quiet understanding and – looking at his wrist-watch – his patience. 'I'm sorry to have taken up so much of your time. Over sixty years of my life telescoped into a postprandial confession and revelation, and all within a couple of hours of your getting defrocked! Now for Baggins' meal. Hasn't she been good while we've been talking?'

'She's a lovely temperament all right,' replied Jake. 'Just like our Bindle. Of course, they're from the same breeder, aren't they. Merlin Swift.' It was Jake's turn to chuckle. 'By the way, I've only retired from my active ministry. Defrocking is only for naughty boys.'

'Just testing you,' laughed John. 'And defrocking sounds so much more serious than undressing and a lot more fun! Come on, Bags.'

Standing in the porch, adjusting his pack, John remarked how warm it had seemed to be in the church compared to the slight autumnal chill to be felt in the open air.

'It's the first time the heating system has been in action since April and it's nice to know it actually works,' said Jake. 'We should-n't be too surprised really because it is serviced regularly under contract. No doubt it'll be turned down a notch or two by next Sunday. Meanwhile there will be some residual warmth retained by the stonework from one "on" period to the next. Martha complains occasionally that the church is warmer than the vicarage to which my reply is always the same. "There's less friction at the vicarage". As an engineer, you'll know all about friction and hot air.'

As Jake was locking the church door, John hefted his massive backpack and prepared to make his way to the broken-down barn which had been his shelter for the two weeks he had been in the Tupshorne area. Jake spoke. 'I really think, Janis Kalējs, after this afternoon's confession and absolution you should reconsider your present mode of living. Stop punishing yourself. Guilt is in the past. Hang up your burdensome shovel and become human again with a roof over your head. Come and join the family for tea, for a start. I expect they'll be back from walking the dogs very shortly.'

'Maybe a bit later, thank you,' replied John 'I must feed Baggins first – she's due anytime now. And I've a lot of thinking to do – now I'm cleared for take-off, as the first Concorde test pilot said before flying off into the unknown. If I don't make it, please give my regards to Martha, Damnit and his lady friend. Thank you again for my absolution and blessing. Your first act since being debagged has made this old man very happy. Now I need a smoke!'

Jake laughed again. 'You and your language, John. Your sins may have been forgiven but you're still an incorrigible old rogue acting like a tramp under that white tent of yours. I've just remembered that I've left one of my frocks in the vestry. I'll open up again and collect it. Hope to see you later.'

John changed his mind and walked to his usual bench in the market place where he proceeded to feed the expectant mother, following close at heel.

A short time later, Jake passed by the bench as he crossed over the market place *en route* for the vicarage. John's voice reached him over the general hubbub of people and traffic. 'Father, in thy orisons be all my sins remembered.'

'Don't confuse me with Ophelia, John,' replied Jake, drawing nearer. 'And for all his confused state of mind I'm sure Hamlet could tell his frocks from his cassocks. Let me leave you with a Hamlet quotation that fits you well. '"There is no ancient gentleman but gardeners, ditchers and grave-makers; they hold up Adam's profession." See you soon.'

John watched, as Jake disappeared in the direction of the vicarage, before leaning over and murmuring into Baggins' ear. 'I have a strange feeling Beautygirl that our lives are about to change – how I don't know, but we'll both know by tomorrow morning at the latest.' Baggins wagged her tail in response to his affectionate tone, and somewhere inside her, seven little tails stirred in anticipation.

John rolled and lit his first cigarette of the day; then inhaled with deep satisfaction. He felt at peace with himself and the world. "God's in his heaven: all's right with the world", or so he thought.

CHAPTER XXXI

Amor Vincit Omnia

AFTER LEAVING Jake and John outside the church hall, Damnit had walked to the vicarage, all set to gather together Martha, Lorna, and the two dogs, Miss Bindle and Sprottle, before setting off for a vigorous walk, uphill and downdale. That was the plan but fate was to intervene to throw the next twenty-four hours into turmoil. Martha met him at the door.

'Sorry, Daniel,' she said, ruefully. 'Poor Bindle's cut a pad on a piece of glass from a broken bottle just as we were walking across the market square. Lorna and I were watching a fighter overhead – a Tornado from Leeming – otherwise we'd have spotted the danger. Actually, I'm a bit surprised Bindle didn't see it: but she didn't, so I'm afraid she's *hors de combat*. Walking's out!'

'Have you lost my husband? I thought I could at least trust you to bring him home safely after the grand farewell lunch.'

'He's been waylaid, or even sidetracked, as we were on the point of leaving the hall by a somewhat agitated John Smith in need of Jake's spiritual guidance.' He explained briefly the sudden appearance of the tramp on the hall doorstep. 'Jake could be some while because if it's confession time I suspect John will have a lot to say. Anyhow, the rest of us can go for a walk. Bindle won't mind being left behind just this once, I'm sure. We can leave a note for Jake explaining what's happened.'

'No. I think I ought to wait for Jake. After all the excitement of his final day as a parish priest, I think I should be here when he comes down to earth. The last week or two have been quite a strain for him. You take Lorna and Sprottle and we'll see you back here at teatime – about six at a guess.'

'If you're sure. O.K. It's a lovely afternoon and I know Sprot expects some kind of a daily work-out.'

Lorna joined them, with her hairy lurcher in close attendance.

'Did I hear my dog's name being mentioned?'

'That's right,' said Daniel. 'For several good reasons, it has been decided that you, I and Sprot are going walkies. Let's go and climb Penhill. We can reach the lower slopes by car in a few minutes out of Yowesdale and from Penhill Beacon, on a clear day, you can see right over to the Teesside industrial complex as well as overlook most of Wensleydale. The air up there is guaranteed to put roses into the palest of cheeks. How are you fixed?'

'Do I look as if I'm fixed, silly? This cream linen suit I'm wearing is hardly walking, never mind climbing gear,' retorted Lorna.

'I'm sure I could find you some suitable clothing from my extensive wardrobe,' offered Martha. 'Size for size, there's not much between us. Shoes may be a bit more tricky – I've got big plates as Jake is often reminding me. It'll be chilly on the Beacon but finding you something warm is no problem.'

Lorna smiled at both of them. 'Seems like I'm fixed then after all, thank you, Martha. And I think the shoes I'm wearing might just about come under the category of sensible. If they get muddied they do wipe clean with a damp cloth. You'll need to change out of your Sunday best, Daniel. Let me drive you home to change and then you can pilot me to base camp.'

Daniel looked at his wristwatch. 'There's plenty of daylight left: so let's go. We may as well use Sprottle's Volvo – no doubt her bath towel's in there in case she decides to sample one of the waterfalls *en route*. What time did you say you'd like us back, Martha?'

'I thought we'd have tea about six, not before. That should give you enough time for a decent walk.'

Two hours later the summit of Penhill had been conquered and Daniel and Lorna had descended to within easy reach of the Volvo, visible about a quarter of a mile away down the rough rocky track.

Suddenly Lorna stumbled on a loose stone and although she and Daniel had been walking together, they were separated by about three feet to enable them to negotiate the difficult terrain without for ever bumping into each other. She lurched towards him and would have fallen had he not caught her before she hit the ground. For one moment, frozen in time, he held her so closely, firmly and gently before setting her upright on her feet once more.

'What on earth did you do that for?' asked Lorna, sharply.

'Do what?' replied Daniel, equally nervous. 'I just sort of picked you up and put you down again as quickly as I could. You might have been hurt.'

'No. Not that,' said Lorna. 'You let go of me as if I had given you an electric shock.' She paused to look at him more closely. 'Are you all right, Daniel? You're shaking. You're not having another heart do?'

'No, no,' answered Daniel. 'It's your perfume which got to me as I caught and held you.'

'My perfume? It's the same one that I've always worn – "Aphrodite". It's nothing new. Just help me to that rock over there. The heel of my right shoe is broken and my ankle feels a bit twisted. I think you need a sitdown as well, judging by the state of you. I hope Sprot's O.K. – here she comes with a rabbit.'

Daniel helped her over to the rock where they perched side by side with Sprottle lying at Lorna's feet. For a full two minutes, silence prevailed before they both spoke simultaneously. Daniel deferred to her as, quite out of the blue, she asked him the sixty-four thousand dollar question dreaded by every bachelor.

'Why have you never married, Daniel?'

He prevaricated. 'Are we having a polite "question and answer" session, am I to undergo a third degree grilling or are we both in for a frank exchange of views, as they say? I'm not sure if I should be so insensitive as to ask you much the same question but perhaps I ought to, in retaliation. Why haven't you remarried? God knows, you're no less beautiful just because you're a widow.'

'Retaliatory question or not – the answer to that is simple. No one has dared or thought to come close enough to ask me! Question and answer time – cards on the table if you like. I think I need to know in terms of contract bridge which suit we're in and how many trumps you hold. Now that you've stopped trembling, you might answer my question.'

'It's very complicated,' said Daniel. 'But in a nutshell, I've never asked anyone to marry me and no one's yet suggested that a walk up the aisle together would suit both of us. I have wondered, maybe half a dozen times. But wonderment failed to develop and set like the icing on a wedding cake. I always seemed to be left with a flat tansy cake – more bitter than hyssop.'

'It's getting cooler and this rock we're sitting on is nothing but hard. Let's see if we can hobble to the car before we catch a chill. Sprot can listen to this continuing conversation in your car – if she's interested.'

'I thought perhaps you could carry me,' suggested Lorna face-tiously. 'But if "Aphrodite" is proving to be so potent perhaps you ought to fetch the Volvo – it's robust enough to stand this track. The car keys are in your pocket. Mind you don't trip before you get there. One lame old duck is quite enough – or perhaps I should say old swan!' 'The pen of Penhill.'

Twenty minutes later they were seated comfortably in Lorna's car with an hour to spare before the time appointed for tea at the vic-arage.

'Tell me more,' said Lorna. 'I'm intrigued about why or how you've remained on the shelf. Did you never look at yourself in the mirror and say, "what a waste"? I do. Every day.'

'I'm not given to such vanity,' replied Daniel with a smile. 'But maybe the absence of marital and family upheavals accounts for my full head of hair, however grey it has become. My crow's-feet are laughter lines not furrows of worry. Let me tell you a story.'

'Once upon a very long time ago there was this Cambridge undergraduate, reading General Engineering, who thought that per-haps he had fallen in love with a beautiful Arts undergraduate, who in his dreams he imagined possibly reciprocated his feelings for her. The greater part of their salad days was spent in each other's com-pany and it surprised nobody that in their final year they should attend the Masked Halloween Ball, one of the great social highlights of the academic year. The sapphire and diamonds ring in the pocket of his dinner jacket was destined to be returned to the jeweller from whom it had been purchased, the morning after the Ball, but the love poem that he had written and dedicated to his masked lady, he carried on his person for the rest of his days. She never saw it. As the witching hour approached, the young man summoned all that peculiar courage required to ask one of the vital questions of any-one's lifetime. His mouth was dry and he was aware that his racing heart had missed a beat, when she spoke to him first, so quietly that he had to ask her to repeat what she had just said. With a catch in her voice and a quiver on her lips, she told him as gently as she could that, sadly, he was not for her and that he should follow the love of his life – the motor car. She was not to be persuaded other-wise and putting on the bravest of faces they agreed to see the Ball through to the end. Nothing disguises emotional misery better than a Halloween mask.'

Lorna sat silent and stiff, staring through the car windscreen with her gaze fixed on the far horizons of Wensleydale, as if caught in a trance and hardly breathing. Daniel continued. 'The final dance announcement was made. "Gentlemen, please take your partners for the Last Waltz." In the very last twirl of the waltz, the heel of her dancing shoe broke and she would have fallen from his arms if he had not sensed the danger and swept her off her feet before she could pitch headlong. Setting her down again as the strains of the waltz died away, he was left with an aching emptiness in his heart and the scent of "Aphrodite" in his nostrils and on his jacket collar, and he felt like death.

Still staring into the distance, Lorna spoke in a little whisper. 'Show me your poem, please, Daniel. Or perhaps I should say please read it to me.'

Daniel drew a single sheet of paper, folded twice, from the recesses of his wallet. The paper was yellowed and brittle with age but he managed to open it out without it falling to pieces.

He read quietly. 'It's called, "My Life, My Love".

> You are the perfume on the breeze.
> Your fragrance tells me you are near.
> The wildflower that brings me my heartsease
> Saying that you are about to appear.
>
> I catch your whisper from afar.
> My ears are straining for the sound.
> Sifting the quiet from the roar,
> Sensing that you are near at hand.
>
>
> I taste the tears of joy on your face
> And run my fingers through your hair.
> Roses on your fingertips I trace
> Tang of raspberries with our lips we share.
>
> And when we touch, your hand is balm.
> My broken dreams are yours to mend.
> Near you, I need no magic charm,
> With you, my wanderings happily end.

To slake my thirst, I need your spring,
That bubbling fountain, bright and clear.
Your smiling eyes make my heart sing
For your heart which I hold so dear.

You are every daisy in my chain,
The gentle softness of Summer rain,
The golden glow of ripening corn,
The rippling birdsong of the dawn.

You are my shade from the sun,
My pillow, my rest when the light has gone.
Hand in hand with you, I need no glove.
These words of mine are for you, my only love.

So now, my dear, you have the answer to your question, in the last line, and I fear that my mask has finally slipped after very nearly forty-four years. It may not be the answer that you wanted to hear but if you could have put your ear to my chest you would know that my heart missed several beats in the seven verses. And now I'm wittering on, just waiting for you to interrupt my foolish chatter. I need to "catch your whisper", as the poet might say. Maybe I should simply drive back to the vicarage and we can attempt to erase this whole episode, however difficult that would be.'

Lorna remained silent still, as if struck dumb, for several seconds which to Daniel seemed like minutes. The spell was broken by Sprottle, sleeping on the back seat of the Volvo, who in the midst of a doggy-dream gave several little yelps – enough to waken any Sleeping Beauty.

Lorna spoke. 'That Arts student you mentioned never said "motor car". The term used was "the infernal combustion engine", and at that particular time she thought she was being rather clever when, in fact she was being a silly goose. On re-examining the whole scenario, it seems to me that if he had produced that passionate poem at the beginning of the Halloween Ball, the undoubted underlying magic of the occasion – masks, music, mysticism – would have worked its spell and he would have had his wicked way with her!

She turned, at last, to face Daniel: her smiling eyes brimming with tears. 'My so-called feminine intuition would appear to have vanished since you introduced me to Albert, not long before he died. The traumas of that sequence of events must have created some kind of an invisible smokescreen between me and you – certainly from my viewpoint. How dense I've been; quite put me off the scent, you'll tell me. A question. It's eight months since Albert's funeral: we've spent quite a lot of time together since then, for one reason – should I say excuse – or another, and only now, due to my own brass-necked prompting or sheer insensitivity have I tripped over the truth. Why?'

Daniel offered her his handkerchief to dry her eyes. 'Here. You're lucky it's clean. Can't take you out to tea with tear-stained cheeks and ruffled feathers, Mrs Swann! In response to your prompting, once again, I am very aware of the fact that it is more than three years since Matthew died. I see how well you cope with widowhood now, however difficult it must have been to begin with. I remember my sister Bethan telling me how that after her husband, Gerald, died she envied every other woman with a husband in tow. She tried to explain to me, obviously an uncomprehending bachelor, it was the physical presence that she missed – the happy knowledge that even if they were separated by as much as a door in their house, he was there in the flesh to touch and talk to when the door opened. You are delightfully calm and serene, like a ship in a safe haven after the storm has passed. I know I'm mixing my metaphors here, but I had a fear of upsetting your apple-cart, greater than that of being told to return to "the infernal combustion engine". As regards things infernal and having come so far in the course of a few minutes sitting here in your car, let me finish by saying that as of now, life without you will seem like purgatory.'

'Am I hearing what may be described as a disguised proposal of marriage, Daniel?'

'I suppose so,' mumbled Daniel, a trifle sheepishly. 'Any more questions?'

'Only one more. I wonder if your Cambridge jeweller ever sold that ring. Diamonds are beautiful but a sapphire is exquisite. Would my young engineer care to take a trip down Memory Lane with this happy historian to see if that jeweller is still in business? Perhaps while we're in Cambridge I might look for a temple dedicated to Aphrodite. She's a lot to answer for, or so it would appear, after all these years. Still, I suppose that's what you must expect from the Greek goddess of love – trouble with a capital T! She married the

Greek god of Fire, you know. Hot stuff the pair of them, in their different ways.'

Daniel twisted round in the driving seat as Lorna turned, at last, to face him. 'Does that mean that I get to push the apple-cart?'

'I suppose so,' laughed Lorna. 'After all, if life without me is condemning you to purgatory, what is a poor girl to do? I think you'd better kiss me before I change my mind.'

As they kissed, Sprottle, disturbed by the sudden lull in the conversation, awoke and made her own comment on the situation that had just unfolded, emitting an enormous yawn to express the ultimate in boredom. She had no way of knowing that within twenty-four hours her own carefree existence was in for an almighty upheaval. Before the Volvo reached the vicarage in time for tea, she was fast asleep once more, quite oblivious to the fact that it would also be her teatime. She awoke once more with the noise of the car tyres scrunching on the coarse gravel of the vicarage drive and Bindle limped out from the front door to greet them. Jake was sweeping up some of the fallen leaves, brilliant scarlet, which the Autumn weather had dragged off the Boston Ivy, clinging to the front wall of the house.

CHAPTER XXXII

In Limine

D ANIEL DASHED ROUND the front of the car to help Lorna out of the passenger seat. Her ankle had stiffened up and she was glad to have his arm as support while the pair of them staggered to the door, looking like the also-rans in a slow three-legged race. Jake dropped his besom in surprise and rushed forward to see if he also could be of any use in getting the battered Swann indoors. Martha appeared, wearing her kitchen apron. Chaos, in general, reigned before Lorna was comfortably seated in the vicarage dining room and Martha went to brew the tea. The second question time of the afternoon began in an atmosphere of underlying jocularity which quickly developed into a full blown celebration as Lorna and Daniel recounted the tale of the injury and subsequent events.

Jake was in his element and, divested of all his parochial responsibilities, in high, teasing good humour as he addressed the happy couple. 'I sincerely hope, Lorna, that you are aware of at least some of Damnit's major shortcomings. You'll never change him, you know. As for you, Daniel Tiltstone Greensward, I never thought I'd see the day! Have you the slightest idea what you're letting yourself in for?'

Lorna answered. 'I know all about his weakness for perfume, his knowledge of precious stones and his long hidden talent for passionate poetry. Oh! And he is a wizard when it comes to the intricacies of the infernal combustion engine. I don't care to learn about his weaknesses.'

Damnit chipped in. 'Let me remind you, Father Jacob, of a conversation we had before you and I went down to Cambridge to see Albert Prince in January this year. It was a Thursday towards the end of January. These may not be your exact words but the gist is much the same. You said, you remembered me punting on the Cam and falling in while showing off to an impressionable young lady. Reading history, you said, and a bit bright for a duffer like me. You recalled the name Laura but corrected yourself to Lorna Fairchild.

Then the punchline – of all the women I had romanced at Cambridge you said she should have become Mrs Greensward. So it's all your fault. You never realized he was a prophet when you married him, did you, Martha?'

He spoke to Lorna. 'I laughed at the time, but his prophecy seems to have come true this afternoon – quite by accident. A broken shoe-heel of an accident! Send one of your finest benedictions to the shoemaker, Jake: he or she has more than made my day.'

Martha joined in the rudery with a gentle dig. 'I did know that I was marrying something of an actor, Daniel, if not a prophet. When Jake was treading the boards as Captain Hook in his final year with the Cambridge Footlights I was responsible for his make-up for the role so I can tell stage make-up from cosmetics – at a glance. If I was a school matron I should have insisted that you wash your face as well as your hands before sitting down to tea. The trace of lipstick on your upper lip is most becoming.'

Daniel laughed as he wiped the back of his hand across his mouth. 'I seem to recall the words of a song, popular when I was a teenager – "And I ain't gonna wash for a week. Oh no! I ain't gonna wash for a week". My sentiments entirely.'

'I remember the song,' said Jake. 'Those early kisses of adolescence were a kind of qualification – a bit like earning a scout badge. Now to more serious matters. I don't for one moment expect that you've had time to plan your immediate future but if you're looking for a specialist matrimonial knot-tier I come highly recommended and comparatively cheap.'

'Cheap be blowed,' retorted Daniel. 'I want real value for my money. You can act as my Best Man as well. When you were at theological college after Cambridge, I recall telling my father, your uncle Jim, that I could see you marrying yourself to Martha with the words, "I now pronounce us man and wife".'

Lorna intervened at this point. 'No. We've had no time yet to plan anything concrete except that we don't want to delay too long. My son in Nigeria doesn't know what his mother's been and gone and done yet. I don't anticipate having a problem in persuading him to give me away, once I can get him over here on home leave. He is my key appointment. Anyhow, it will all come together quite easily, I know – that is optimism born of the experience of having done it all before.' She winked mischievously at Martha. 'Do you think Jake will appreciate having his best friend led like a lamb to the slaughter? Don't worry, Daniel dear. I will be a gentle shepherdess. Now I must think about driving back to Skipton and my berth on the Bethdan before it gets too late.'

'You're not going to drive anywhere with that wonky ankle,' stated Daniel firmly. 'You can use Bethan's quarters at High Ash for the time being – the bed is aired and, anyway, it has an electric blanket – and we'll see how the ankle is in the morning.'

'You're welcome to our guest room,' offered Martha, 'but with us moving out of the vicarage fairly shortly it looks a bit like a transit camp.'

'I think perhaps, all things considered, I should stay at High Ash, thank you Martha,' answered Lorna. 'Daniel and I will have a lot to think about together and my present lack of mobility looks like an ideal opportunity to discuss what our next moves are likely to be. So if it's O.K. with you, Daniel, Sprottle and I will avail ourselves of your hospitality once again. Sprot will need some breakfast please, Jake, if I might beg a meals-worth from Bindle – at least until tomorrow.'

'If I may speak on behalf of Miss Bindle,' said Jake, with an air of false pomposity, 'I'm sure that a few of her extra-special seaweed biscuits will not be missed. She'll want them back in due course, won't you, Bindle?'

Hearing her name being mentioned twice in the space of two sentences, in the jocular tone of voice often favoured by her master, Bindle wagged her tail in agreement. "Biscuits" was a key word in her vocabulary.

Jake continued. 'That area of moorland has always been a source of danger for Damnit, you know, Lorna – but not quite as serious as this afternoon's escapade.' He chuckled. 'When we were lads – maybe twelve or so – one school holidays, uncle Jim left the pair of us up there for a day, as an adventure in survival. Fortunately it was a warm, sunny Summer's day. Aunt Em, Damnit's marvellous mother, had provided plenty of food for us but it needed heating up in a pan, also supplied as part of the kit essential to two intrepid explorers. Uncle Jim's parting comment was, "sorry lads – no matches this time. But to save you having to rub two sticks together, there's a magnifying glass in the cooking pan – and a handful of woodshavings to make things easy". It wasn't I who set the heather alight. Need I say more? We had quite a fancy fire dance before we had it stamped out. Thinking back, I'm sure it was a risky lesson in fieldcraft, and uncle Jim had tested us both in the crucible. I can still work up a sweat at the memory of it. I imagine you're the same, Damnit.'

'Too right,' said Daniel, also remembering John's heroic implementation of the Isaac chapter to douse the waste paper basket fire back in 1974.

Not long after, with Lorna and Sprot safely on board, Daniel drove the Volvo over to High Ash, the other side of Tupshorne. The remainder of their evening was spent discussing as many aspects of getting married as they could think of. Of course, Lorna had a very good idea of what was involved even if her own experience was based on her first wedding in the 1960s. Daniel played at being secretary, making copious notes.

Approaching ten o'clock, Daniel suddenly announced that there was a problem.

'What sort of a problem?' queried Lorna, intrigued.

'Well,' said Daniel, 'this impromptu landing of yours on my doorstep means that you have no overnight clothes. I can find you a new toothbrush and that's all. No nightie. No dressing gown. No nothing. When Bethan died, keeping any of her clothes never occurred to this old bachelor. The Salvation Army had anything that I considered might be useful.'

'A pair of your pyjamas would suit me admirably,' said Lorna, sweetly. 'One of the gems that I remember my father coming out with was, "a woman is never more appealing that when wearing an outsize pair of men's pyjamas." Maybe now is the time to put his wisdom to the test. They'll need to be winter weight – I'm a bit of a sleeping iceberg, and as for my feet, maybe the extra length of your pyjama trousers will defrost them.'

'O.K. O.K.,' replied Daniel. 'I might even find a pair that's been shrunk in the wash, and I'll switch on the electric blanket – about the only item of Bethan's I had the sense to keep. Then we'll have a nightcap – I know we both appreciate Glenmorangie – crack the Telegraph crossword and then hit the sack.' He paused. 'Do you think it's gone much cooler? Time of the year, I suppose. We put the heat on in church today for the first time since Easter.'

'I think if I had brought a sweater with me, along with my invisible nightclothes etc. I might just slip it on.'

'In that case,' said Daniel, 'I'll click the heat on now. The warm air heating system works so fast it only needs a few minutes to do the trick. In the meantime, you'll look more lovely than ever in one of my sweaters. I suspect your father would have dumped large sweaters in with pyjamas.'

'I'm game for anything,' laughed Lorna, 'as long as it's not the highjump. And now for that crossword – I've not completed one for years.'

One hour later they set off for bed. The final clue in the crossword had defeated them utterly.

CHAPTER XXXIII

Ianis: Nemesis

AFTER HIS CHURCH confession and subsequent exchanges with Jake in the market place of quotations from Hamlet John remained seated on the bench, debating with himself the pros and cons of taking tea at the vicarage. Baggins was becoming visibly agitated as the minutes ticked by and as the late afternoon sun gave up its warmth she began to shiver.

John made two decisions. Although the prospect of a civilized tea at the vicarage posed a powerful temptation, it was destroyed by the thought of the warmth he had enjoyed so recently in the church of Saint Michael the Archangel. Tea was out, and comfort in for the first time since leaving the National Blacksmiths' Museum the previous November.

Very slowly and gently he led Baggins back to the church.

The previous Wednesday he had spent an hour or so sitting on a bench in the church grounds, watching and waiting for Damnit to finish mowing the grass on the south facing lawns. The two men shared a vacuum flask of tea and a handful of biscuits with Bags before eventually Damnit wheeled the mower round to the back of the church intent on mowing the northern greensward prior to stowing the machine away in the cellar. Daniel's normal routine of mowing on a Wednesday was interrupted this particular afternoon by Freda Alderwood and Muriel Welsh who had brought forward by a day their usual Thursday brass polishing services. Muriel, the labrador *aficionado*, had remarked to John that Baggins looked very fit, even if about to burst.

John had peeped into the cellar which served the purpose of a store room for a variety of church items; some of a seasonal nature such as the Christmas crib; others such as "retired" pews awaiting a recall to active backside duty. The gas fired central heating installation was the dominant feature and the heavy wooden door was secured with a padlock of uncertain age.

Arriving back at church with Bags, John quietly made his way to the cellar door, took a close look at the padlock and eased his back-pack from his shoulders before lowering it to the ground, leaning it against the stone wall to the right of the doorway. He released Ferrers from the restraining strap and pouch, and then with some delicacy of touch inserted the hardened steel tip of the mighty shovel into the tiny gap which existed between the wooden door-frame and the metal plate to which the staple was attached. From the early days of his apprenticeship he had long remembered a quo-tation which had to be explained to him at the time. It did not matter that he never knew the name of the scientist who had coined the phrase, "Give me a lever and I will move the world," but he could see that it should have been included in the Isaac. Now he applied a steady pushing pressure to the long, strong hickory handle of Ferrers the lever and with a muted deep creak, somewhere between a groan and a growl, the old screws were drawn out of their wooden bed. Baggins did not wait to be invited but pushed her way in as if she knew her way into the labour ward.

John followed the dog in, and using his mini-torch took a proper inventory of his surroundings. The stone-walled cell-like room, which housed the principal elements of the church's heating system, was dry and retained some residual warmth from the few hours of operation of the heater earlier in the day. There were two short wooden pews standing on end, leaning against what appeared to be a flight of stone steps leading up to the ceiling overhead and one particular slab there which seemed to have some kind of a pivoting device, with a complicated sprung latch attached to it.

As an engineer, he was intrigued by the metal and stone con-struction which was above his head, with no apparently useful function. He focused the tiny torch on the centre of the stone slab which bore a clearly incised inscription. He read

JOSEPH NORTH

MDCCCLXV

All unknowingly he had found the only Tiltstone to have been built into a place of worship and he could detect that it had been moved recently – What could it mean? Sometime he would ask Damnit about it.

Along with the Christmas crib, which he had glimpsed earlier in the day when Damnit was putting away the lawnmower, were two hessian potato sacks, stuffed with straw – an obvious adjunct to the scene in the stable.

'Looks like we're in for a comfy night, Bags!' said John, giving the sacks a gentle shake to disperse the filling more evenly. 'You've had your tea. Now I'll have mine and we can officially retire. My guilt is washed away and we ought to celebrate, don't you think? A quiet smoke and a stiff drink of schnapps, purely medicinal of course for these ageing bones, should see us nicely settled down for the night. And I'll tell you a special bedtime story, never heard before.'

It was after eleven o'clock when John began his last story. Lying against the straw-filled cushions, hand-rolled cigarette in his right hand, schnapps bottle in the left, and with Baggins stretched out between his knees, he smiled to himself in the darkness and in Latvian spoke quietly to his dog. The tale he told concerned a most beautiful black labrador who was so beautiful that when she walked down the street everyone who liked animals would stop to have a word with her. Had she been a human, she would have been named Princess but her master called her Baggins. When her master was little more than a boy, he was persuaded by a confidence trickster to go on a magic carpet ride with him, a long journey into the unknown. At the time he expected to return home by the same magic carpet but the driver, who had stolen the carpet in the first place, was tracked down, caught and had his head cut off by the most powerful magician who ever lived. Unfortunately, the sorcerer made a serious mistake when he burnt the carpet to ashes because he could not find the right phrase in his spell manual to make it fly. Meanwhile, the boy had disappeared, afraid of what the magician might do to him, the trainee flying carpet co-driver, and he was a very long way from home in a foreign land where the natives found it hard to understand what he was saying. Yet he prospered in the alien land where his youth and gift for friendship gained him warm acceptance. For many years he waited for another magic carpet to arrive so that he could complete his training and fly back home but none came, and when he became an old man, and foolish, he decided to walk all the way home – that was excepting crossing any oceans which might have been in the way. He knew he could not complete the long walk without the comfort of a companion – someone who could share his hardships without complaining, to whom he could impart the most intimate confidences without fear of betrayal and who would love him for what he was or would become – an innocuous old tramp, full of fairy-tales. He searched far and wide for such a travel mate and found none, until he looked down at his dog. The beauty Baggins filled every requirement and had been his best friend already four years. They set off together with high hopes and a certain jauntiness in their gaits.

Wherever possible, the master led the way, following the rivers and waterways, and certainly for the dog with webbed feet everything went swimmingly until the day she decided to get married without his permission. The princess had met her prince – Bilbo was the most handsome dog she had ever seen and for the briefest of time she deserted her master to be married in secret. When the master found out, he was only mildly displeased – he could not be angry because she looked so happy and fulfilled. Then when he realized that the princess, following the magic spell cast by Bilbo, was in the process of turning into one large and an unknown number of small copies, he contemplated abandoning her, or at least giving her away to someone who would take care of her. He knew just such a man, an old friend, living not much further down the road they were travelling. The master was very surprised, when they reached the town where his friend lived, to find that Baggins was not wanted at all, and as for any puppies – well! Serious negotiations took place before the awkward situation was resolved in a manner most agreeable to all parties, whereby the master's friend would care for Baggins for a while before giving her back and he would provide good homes for her puppies when the time was right.

Even more important than his making of proper arrangements for Baggins and family, the master's friend introduced him to another friend who was possessed of the Wisdom of King Solomon, and a magic carpet which he presented to the master, with his blessing, instructed him in its quirky ways and wished him Godspeed.

John had talked himself into the arms of Morpheus. The cigarette dropped from his fingers, his head lolled forward on to his chest and he began to dream. He was back in Stalingrad, hand to hand fighting from house to house, room by room. Smoke, dust, grit, blood, fire and the stench of cordite were in his nostrils and the fear of death was in his mind. Ghosts of comrades, long dead, were all around him, their spectral faces contorted with derision, and howling at his apparent terror. He could not remember ever being that frightened when he was in action under enemy fire. He fought on, enveloped in a cold sweat, in spite of the heat and horror of battle all round him. Suddenly he was aware of a faint stabbing pain in his left thigh and the sensation of a warm wet cloth being drawn across his nose and lips. A reverse Isaac had come into play. Man's best friend was at work.

Abruptly he awoke, coughing and spluttering and wiping the back of his sleeve over his mouth. Baggins, heavy with pups, was pawing at his thigh and licking his face as only a labrador can. The sack of straw on his right side had rolled away from him by a few inches, and as he came to, it burst into flame. The atmosphere immediately around them was full of acrid smoke, just as in his dream, and he grasped quickly the fact that he must have dropped his last cigarette as he slipped into sleep. The northerly breeze, which had sprung up during the night, had created a sharp little draught under the ill-fitting door to the cellar – enough to fan into a potentially lethal cocktail of smoke the glowing tobacco where it had come into contact with the dry straw spilling out of the open-mouthed sack.

One of Damnit's favourite sayings came into his mind. If a fundamental piece of engine research looked as if it was in danger of blowing up in their faces he would summon up his own Isaac equivalent, *"Aequam servare mentem* – Panic Ye Not, My Lads!"* Was it really twenty-six years since he had extinguished the fire in Damnit's office paper-bin? He could not go through the same procedure now – the smell would be unthinkable! Quickly he reached into his pocket for the mini-torch and switched it on. Opening the door wide to reduce the sharp draught while dissipating the smoke, he ordered Bags "Out" before systematically stamping out the fire as vigorously and thoroughly as he could. With considerable relief, he caught the gleam in the torchlight of the schnapps bottle and snatched it up before the heat could vaporize the spirit to the point of dangerous ignition or explosion. Casting the beam round the small room, he felt satisfied that he had doused the fire with little harm done, and picking up Ferrers and Pregnant backed out through the doorway. He pulled the door to and made a stab at replacing the damaged padlock fitting, pushing the old screws of the staple-plate back into the wooden doorpost.

Once outside the cellar, John found it necessary to lean against the church wall for several minutes, waiting for his racing heart to slow down, and to recover his breath before shuffling away in the darkness to the ruins of a field barn which had been his HQ for the past two weeks. Bags was free and off the leash – an extremely rare occurrence – but she kept perilously close to her master's knee. Just short of the rough shelter he was seeking, John was overcome by an immense sense of tiredness. He felt so weary that he could go no further but slumped down by the nearest wall in a corner of the field, twenty yards away from the shattered barn. Covering himself and Baggins with the white ultracape, he wished her goodnight before uttering a few words from Shakespeare: "Alack the heavy day, that I have worn so many winters out, And know not now what name to call myself!" He slept. Baggins watched and waited.

Back in the cellar of the church of Saint Michael the Archangel, a few small fragments of straw glowed red – brought to life by the wicked draught, again coming under the door. Only a few feet away from the increasingly fiery sack of straw stood the church lawn mower. Damnit had not drained its fuel tank after finishing off the mowing four days earlier. He had been distracted by a visit from John. The petrol tank exploded. Vulcan, the god of fire, was in his element and on holy ground.

CHAPTER XXXIV

Non Semper ea Sunt Quae Videntur

DANIEL, FROM HIS CHILDHOOD, had always been a prodigious dreamer of dreams yet no one would have thought of him as a dreamer or had the temerity to call him one. He had an innate ability, a genuine gift, to initiate his own dreams, conjuring them up out of nothing and never knowing how they might pan out. There were times when a dream developed into a nightmare and, ever the optimist, he did not appreciate unhappy, unpleasant endings. It was then that he discovered that he could re-script his dreams by waking up, and on going back to sleep again he would wipe out the nightmare with his own "dream" ending. It was a knack that he cherished – a talent to be kept polished. Occasionally he was able to use his dreams to solve his problems and then, occasionally, his self-entered dream world would pose him a problem, the answer to which he could find only in his real world. Daniel had few worries in life but none was greater than the fear that one day he would confuse truth with the twilight of his own sometimes dangerous imaginings. "To sleep: perchance to dream," had long been one of his pet quotations from Hamlet; even if his interpretation of it was taken completely out of its proper context. Sleep, *per se*, was such a waste of time, but sleep with a challenging dream could turn a bedroom into something approaching theatre.

All the exciting events of the day conspired together to ensure that dropping off to sleep quickly was a luxury not easily attained. The very prospect of matrimony acts as a powerful precursor to the production of adrenalin and Daniel was forced to resort to one of his own devices to find his way to the Land of Nod. Not for him the repetitive counting of sheep: he used his penchant for exploration by going on a journey to buy a country house set in its own parkland, and every estate he visited was required to have a long approach avenue of golden-leaved beech trees. Sometimes he would be asleep before the front façade of the mansion came into view. Not so on this occasion. The main door of his dream house was opened, without him needing to use the heavy wrought iron knocker, by Mrs Lorna Swann who, to judge by the smart badge that she was sporting on the left lapel of her business suit, was the representative of the estate agency responsible for the sale of this particular property. Daniel vaguely remembered meeting her before, somewhere, but not precisely where and asked her if perhaps he was mistaken. She confirmed that they had indeed met a long time ago and that it had been on the dance floor – an encounter best forgotten.

'I thought so,' said Daniel in a flirtatious manner which surprised him even as he spoke. 'I'm not one to forget a pretty face, you know.'

The flattery was not returned. 'Were it not for seeing the name, Mr Daniel Greensward, on my information clipboard, I might well not have recalled that you managed to tread on my toes more than once.'

'Sorry', said Daniel, with a rueful smile. 'It must have been one of my clumsy phases. I hope I'm forgiven.' He followed her into the well appointed hall, described in the sales brochure as "deceptively spacious", in the terminology so beloved of estate agents.

It was a most impressive property, well shown off by the charm and personality of the lady guide. Her enthusiasm for the house was infectious to the point where Daniel asked if she fancied living in it herself. "Not really", was the reply. She understood that one of the bedrooms already had a full-time resident – a ghost – and if her client had no objection she would be quite content to let him inspect the upper floors on his own.

Daniel teased her. 'Perhaps if I was to hold your hand, we could face the unknown together. I've yet to meet a ghost, but I'm quite prepared to be spooked if that's what it takes.'

'No fear,' answered Lorna. 'When we shook hands on the doorstep, I'm sure I detected motor oil on your palm. You're on your own if you're intent on confronting an apparition. My own shadow has been known to give me a bit of a turn. Off you go.'

'Can you tell me in which bedroom I am supposed to encounter a spectral chill or thrill?' enquired Daniel.

'Number seven,' replied Lorna. 'I understand that it is the only one which is not connected to the butler's pantry by a bell pull, so if you are hit by sudden panic, it's no use trying to ring me for help, and I'll be in the drawing room anyway.'

'Me, panic! That'll be the day. When you get to know me better you will realize that whereas most people are created with a "PANIC" button to press in an emergency, my button reads "IGNI-TION". I'll see you later when I've pulled all the bells.'

And with that parting shaft Daniel set off up the wide sweep of the main staircase.

He was surprised to find that the first six bedrooms were fully furnished, to such an extent that he would not have been surprised to discover that the beds were occupied. Then, approaching the seventh bedroom he met Albert Prince barring the doorway, and carrying two gleaming newly-cut keys, one in each hand.

'What on earth are you doing here, Albert?' said Daniel, puzzled. 'I could have sworn I was present at your cremation. Don't tell me that was all a dream – or have you come back to haunt me?'

Albert looked at him sternly. 'Not my style at all, my lad, as you well know. I've got just one question for you.'

'Fire away,' said Daniel, with matching mock solemnity. 'Do I win a cuddly toy if I answer correctly?'

'No. Because I don't know the answer myself – that's why you've found me here. For your information, you will always meet me outside number seven. It is our mutual lucky number and don't forget it. The question is "What's become of the ashes?"'

'What ashes? Do you mean my old prep school, High Ashes? It's still going strong so far as I know. Mind you, I haven't been back there in person for some years.'

'No, no, Daniel. The ashes that really matter.'

'Oh, <u>those</u> Ashes. I'm afraid the urn is still at the Lord's cricket ground and still wearing the famous Australian baggy cap. Some things don't change.'

'For heaven's sake, you never used to be that thick. I'm talking about <u>MY</u> ashes, you idiot. Where are they? They were supposed to be dropped into Mount Etna according to the terms of my will. Sort it out if you would, please.'

Daniel gulped in perplexity. 'I'll try, Albert, but it might take time – at least that is on your side rather than mine. Leave it with me.

Now it's my turn for a question. What's with those two keys you're holding?'

'One of them opens the door to bedroom seven. As my lock-smith's apprentice and heir to my knowledge, which key will open the door?'

Daniel examined closely the keys in Albert's hands and then threw a cursory glance at the door. 'Pull the other leg, O Master. There is no keyhole. Have I passed your examination?'

'Yes and no,' answered Albert. 'The door might not be locked but I would advise you, most strongly, not to open that door.'

'Now I get it,' said Daniel. 'I'm told seven's haunted. Is that why you're standing in my way? If you're the dreaded ghost then I'm glad I came. But tell me why I should keep out. Something's bothering you, old friend.'

'Mighty Vulcan is at work in his forge. If you put your ear to the door you will hear his hammer ringing on the anvil. If you open that door I will not be responsible for the consequences. You will be beyond my help and entirely on your own – until you choose to come back to Number Seven.'

'Stand back, Albert. I've come too far down this passage now to do an about turn. You know that I can't report to the drawing room unless I've looked into the haunted room – the only one without a bell pull.'

'God help you then,' muttered Albert, 'And I mean it,' and he disappeared like any well trained ghost through the fireproof door of the seventh bedroom, still carrying the unwanted keys.

Daniel reached for the doorknob and as his fingers touched it, the globe turned into a hasp and staple fitting secured by a combination padlock. He thought for a moment that he heard Albert's infectious chuckle at his shoulder as he applied his own little bit of sorcery to the lock. Just as when he first discovered that he could open any combination lock, that on William "Tell" Taylor's tuck box over fifty years earlier, so did his fingernails turn icy cold as he spun the dials and sensed the tumblers clicking into place. The lock fell from the staple and, as he pushed open the door, the heat hit him.

Bedroom number seven was designed, laid out and furnished exactly like the working forge that he knew so well at the National Blacksmiths' Museum. As Albert had warned him, the huge mis-shapen figure bending over the anvil surely was Vulcan. His faced was turned away from Daniel. Facing Vulcan across the anvil was his apprentice, holding in a pair of fire tongs an oblong piece of metal, laid on the anvil, and which the master was hammering out flat. Daniel recognized Aidan Ferrers.

Vulcan twisted round to look at the new arrival standing in the doorway of his forge. Through the smoke and red glow from the furnace Daniel saw the face of John Smith, running with blood and sweat. The God of Fire spoke – with the execrable accent which John always used when he wished to mock his own many-tongued foreign background.

'Damnit, man, what's kept you? You're late for the last act. This apprentice is next to useless. Be a good chap. Grab those tongs and hold this metal plate steady – I'm hammering out a shovel fit for a god. I need your safe pair of hands this very minute.' He tapped impatiently with his hammer on the anvil, making the sounds of a ringing warning bell. Daniel stepped forward as if drawn by the siren call which appealed to so many facets of his being; his great friend needed his help; this scene could have been in the smithy of his forebears; Aidan surely didn't deserve the slight on his own unquestioned skills as a blacksmith. Suddenly the fire in the red-hot furnace began to die. The tableau of the smithy dissolved into nothing, the chill of death was all around. Out of the darkness came the quiet but imperative voice of Jake, 'Get out, Damnit. You're too late for this act – only the epilogue remains for you to star in. You'll be appearing in a new drama very shortly. Out!'

Daniel had taken no more than two paces into the haunted bedroom, but he left it in one bound. Outside the bedroom, standing in the place where Albert had accosted him, was an angel dressed in an oversized pair of man's pyjamas. 'I was just coming down to the drawing room to meet you as arranged,' said Daniel. 'What are you doing here? Have you overcome your fear of the haunted room?'

'Not really, Daniel dear,' replied Lorna, visibly upset in the subdued lighting of the bedroom passageway. 'I'm frightened.'

Daniel sat up bolt upright in his bed. In the open doorway illuminated by the overhead light in the passage outside his bedroom stood Lorna, a pathetic thing clad in his spare pyjamas. 'Are you awake, Daniel?' she said, in a tremulous whisper.

'I am now,' replied Daniel. 'I've just had the be-all and end-all of a dream. I don't think I'll bother to rewrite the end. Has something happened? Couldn't you sleep? It certainly took me a while to travel to Nod. Do come in. You know I don't bite!' He switched on the bedside light. Lorna spoke as she shuffled across the carpet to stand at his bedside. 'Didn't you hear the siren on the fire engine a minute ago? I did have trouble going to sleep, largely on account of my ankle aching. Quite how long I took to drop off I've no idea but it seemed that hardly had I done so I was awakened by an alarm bell and the sound of a siren.' She trembled violently as if subjected to a sudden icy draught.

Daniel shifted slightly in the bed. This was a situation for which, at his age, he was totally unprepared. Basic commonsense prevailed.

'I think you'd better tell me the whole story in comfort. This duvet isn't called a tandem for nothing – come and share it.'

Lorna slid into bed and gathered the spare expanse of duvet round her slender form before she began to speak again. 'I'm afraid my principal fear in life is a phobia concerned with sirens. To invent a word, I suppose the Greeks would have called it *"Seirenophobia"*. It goes back to my Blackburn childhood and the blitz, when the *Luftwaffe* were targeting Preston and Blackburn in the same night air-raids. The sound of a siren terrified me then and still does to this day – even the "all-clear" failed to bring me much comfort. Being awakened from sleep is just about my worst nightmare. How's that for an oxymoron?'

'Tupshorne only suffered one stray bomb from a bomber off target who was jettisoning his load before beating his way back home to Germany,' said Daniel. 'The thing dropped in a field full of sheep and failed to explode. A good thing we never had an aircraft industry, wasn't it!'

Lorna was quiet now and relaxed, and Daniel knew that the middle of the night crisis was over. He kissed her and whispered, 'Sleep warm, my love. Sweet dreams.'

She stirred slightly once more. 'You remember the final clue of the crossword which defeated us?'

'Yes,' said Daniel. 'It was short and to the point, but we couldn't see the point. "What she says, goes!" What about it? I remember it was ten letters.'

'Well, the answer came to me just before I went to sleep. It's "dominatrix" – so off to sleep with you, my good man; we're sure to have a busy day ahead of us.' And with that, she curled herself up into a classic foetal position, turning her back to him and gently reversing her hips into his solar plexus. She went to sleep almost immediately and Daniel stretched out an arm to switch off the light.

Daniel smiled to himself in the darkness as he moved, almost imperceptibly, to cuddle the pyjama-clad bundle nestling against him. With his left arm laid along the pillow just above her head, and his right arm round her waist, he knew that Lorna had found her new home. All would be well. Drifting into his own sleepy world, it seemed to him that he had never felt so happy since scoring the winning try in the Varsity rugby match back in the heady days of his youth. At that time, as he recalled, it was only a few weeks after Lorna had chosen to reject him as an acceptable suitor. In engineering terms, the wheel of romantic fortune had at last gone full circle. Christmas had come early in the year 2000!

Down in the fields, not far from Tupshorne market place, Baggins shivered and whimpered quietly as she tried to snuggle into the hollow provided by John's splayed thighs. Both man and dog were totally oblivious to the siren call, which had so disturbed the sleep of Daniel's wounded Swann, for two completely different reasons, and Ferrers, still upright in the backpack under the giant cape, kept sentinel while John's guardian angel had deserted him.

CHAPTER XXXV

Integer Vitae Scelerisque Purus Non Eget Mauris Iaculus Neque Arcu (Horace)

Daniel awoke. He had no idea what the time was and his bedroom, furnished with a heavy dense curtain material over the window, was still in darkness. All was quiet, as for a few seconds he recalled the events of the early hours. He could hear himself breathing but could not detect any answering breath from the form he expected to find lying somewhere close to him on the other side of the bed. Tentatively he stretched out a questing arm, encountering body warmth but no body. The bird that had so recently nestled in his embrace must have left the nest shortly before he had come to. Remembering how much Bethan, when she was alive, used to enjoy her early morning cup of tea, he was quickly into his dressing gown and in the kitchen, putting on the electric kettle for a brew. As he had made his way down the passage leading from his bedroom, eventually ending up in the kitchen, he could catch the faint sound of water flowing through the pipes. Lorna must have decided to start the new day with a bath.

Hardly had the kettle begun to sing than Daniel was startled by a muffled bump, followed by a strangled cry of pain. Without bothering to switch off the kettle, he rushed out of the kitchen, as fast as his bedroom slippers would allow, down the passage to outside the *en suite* bedroom which had been part of Bethan's domain. Lorna cried out for him.

Opening the bedroom door, Daniel called out, 'Are you all right?'

'No. I am not all right, damnit!' sobbed Lorna. 'I've slipped in the shower, fallen down and I'm hurt.'

'Are you decent?' enquired Daniel, solicitously.

'What do you think, you idiot? The shower's running, I'm on the floor, starkers, wrinkled and crumpled. My modesty is compromised and I am a damsel in distress waiting for my knight in shining armour to rescue me. Don't go shy on me for heaven's sake – I think I've broken something.'

"Cometh the hour: cometh the man," said Daniel to himself, and in two wiggles of a swan's rudder had dashed into the room, switched off the shower and grasping the bath towel from the heated towel rail had gently enfolded his *fiancée* in its comforting warmth.

The next few minutes were fraught with difficulty as Daniel extricated Lorna from the tray of the shower, keeping up her spirits with a flow of inconsequential banter.

'There was me thinking you'd decided to take a bath – only to find you in the shower. At least you'd remembered to put down the non-slip shower mat as I told you last time you were here. That didn't slip, did it? No. It looks pretty well anchored to me. What were you playing at? Slip on the soap?'

'No,' replied Lorna, through gritted teeth. 'I forgot about my poorly ankle from yesterday's walk and tried to stand on that foot while I washed the other. It just buckled under me and "crash", I was down.'

'Do you think you can stand if I carefully pick you up, and lean you back against the wall?' asked Daniel. 'I can see it's your right arm that's in trouble.'

'I can but try,' replied Lorna, 'but it might be easier if you could just sit me on the laundry basket if it'll bear my weight.'

'It's strong enough, all right. Let's see how we go. Scream if I hurt you. I'll be as gentle as I can. I don't know, old girl. We go walking together and I catch you before you hit the rocks. You should have thought to ask me to share the shower. Maybe next time!'

Lorna managed a rather half-hearted smile which then developed into a cheeky grin. 'When we are married I expect you will buy me a Jacuzzi – if you really love me.'

'I'll order one today. Perhaps after this fiasco we could even try it out before the wedding. Love needn't come into the equation unless you absolutely insist!'

Ever so carefully and cautiously Daniel managed to somehow

convey her from the shower to the laundry basket where he gently patted her dry and peppered her with talcum powder fetched from her handbag. Somewhere from the past he remembered taking a ten part course in First Aid, and much to his own mild surprise and Lorna's amazement managed to apply a sling to her injured arm before, all fingers and thumbs, dressing her in her linen suit of the day before and hobbling along with her to the kitchen, where at his insistence she joined with him in a tea and toast breakfast.

'Now that the inner woman is catered for – not to mention the cook – I'll just have a shave and throw some clothes on and take you off to casualty. The Airedale's not that far away. They should have dealt with last night's drunks by now.'

'I'm not sure it's necessary, Daniel. I feel much better, thank you, now I've had something to eat. Can't we wait and see how the bruising develops? I've put you to a lot of trouble already, short of getting you to apply a touch of make-up. Swanns like me need to preen a bit, you know.'

'Don't argue with me, young lady, when I'm in my Monday masterful mode. As elegant waterfowl go, you can neither fly nor paddle in a straight line. Let's be sensible and get you checked over. I'll drive you in your Volvo – it's got a bit more leg room than Tottie.'

Daniel stopped talking abruptly. 'We've forgotten all about Sprottle in her auto-kennel. I'll deal with her before I shave. She can come with us as our security guard. You never know about car parks these days. O.K., then?'

'O.K.' said Lorna. 'I suppose you're right.' She brightened visibly. 'And we can talk weddings while we wait!'

Daniel smiled at her. 'Looks like it's going to be one of those days, doesn't it?' He glanced at his watch. 'Half eight now. Off by nine. Hospital by half nine. Back here – '

'For tea?' interjected Lorna, laughing, 'maybe today even, with luck.'

'I reckon,' said Daniel, thoughtfully, 'we'll be back here about eleven. The A & E department at the Airedale has something of a reputation for its speed of despatch – that is in terms of treatment not euthanasia, rest assured.'

'What a comfort you are,' said Lorna. 'I'm glad I'm not on my last legs just yet or I fear you might have reversed your last statement of assurance. By the way, I was most surprised that a dyed in the wool old bachelor like you, with hands like mini-shovels, was so proficient, almost deft, when it came to getting me dressed. Am I to marry a bit of a dark horse after all?'

'Good grief, no,' expostulated Daniel. 'I felt I was being terribly clumsy and fearful of harming something precious. In actual fact, I do have some experience in that particular field. When Bethan was "on her last legs", as you say, I involved myself in caring for her as much as I could, within reason. I've always been quite good with physical frailties, blood and such like – something inherited from my mother, I think.' He gave a chuckle. I'm only glad you don't wear a corset. Buttons I can manage quite well but hooks and eyes are an invention of the devil. And to think I might have been a locksmith if Albert had had his way. I'd better stop wittering on, get dressed and see to Sprot. Perhaps if she had slept in the house last night, all this wouldn't have happened.'

'So you don't think I had it all planned then?' smiled Lorna, sweetly. 'Feminine wiles come in many guises – some can be quite painful, even masochistic!'

'Stop being facetious,' said Daniel. 'Otherwise, I've a good mind to pick you up and dump you back under the shower. You can't be that masochistic. I like your plan though. It makes me feel needed. Back shortly!' And he left the kitchen to attend to Mrs Swann's hairy lurcher bitch.

As Lorna's Volvo departed the High Ash drive, with Damnit at the wheel, the telephone in the house rang. No one heard it. Five minutes later it rang again. No one answered but this time Jake chose to leave a message on the answering machine. His agitation was evident in his voice. 'There's bin trouble at t'mill, owd lad. Give us a ring *statim* when you get in.'

For a Monday morning the hospital casualty department was almost deserted. The duty doctor insisted on having x-ray investigations both on Lorna's arm and her ankle which resulted in her returning to High Ash with a pot on her arm and some fairly comprehensive strapping of the ankle.

Within minutes of leaving the hospital Daniel took control of the situation.

'Would you like me to spell out the predicament in which you find yourself, dear?' he enquired quietly.

'I don't think you need to. It's obvious that this Swann's down and grounded. Was there a music hall song "I'm only a bird with a broken wing", or something like that? That's me.'

'What a good thing I caught you yesterday when you tripped. It's obvious that I can't let go of you now. If you look at your chauffeur sitting on your right, he is your self-appointed swanherd until further notice.'

'But, Daniel, I've things to do in Cambridge – never mind finishing my current research project while in residence on the Bethdan. I must keep going regardless.'

'Can't be done!' replied Daniel, with brutal frankness. 'Be honest. Driving's out. Peeling potatoes, slicing bread, even powdering your nose will be major problems at least for a little while. When you were getting plastered in casualty I worked it all out. As long as you are able to walk down the aisle in however many months it takes to arrange our wedding, nothing else matters in between. Your research can go on the back burner – it won't spoil. In fact if you behave yourself and do as you're told I can even see myself as a research assistant – non-stipendiary! And, by the way, the bird of your song was "in a gilded cage".'

'But what about things like clothes? They're all in Cambridge.'

'I bet you've several changes of clothing on the Bethdan if it comes to the crunch. I can collect them, and anything else you may need, later in the day when I've made you comfortable at High Ash. If that's not soon enough, you know Martha would rustle up something or other for you at the drop of a hat.'

Lorna giggled. 'Strikes me you're after a trial marriage and I can be a sore trial, especially when I'm not one hundred per cent. You might change your mind.'

'Fat chance!' snorted Daniel. 'As soon as you feel up to it I'm dragging you back to Cambridge on an expedition to find the ring that got away.'

'All right. I give in this time but don't ever say I didn't warn you that I can be difficult. Just one final thing though – when you bring my spare clothes from the Bethdan don't bother with the corset!'

'Commonsense at last!' breathed Daniel with something akin to a self-satisfied smirk. 'When we reach Tupshorne I'll pick up a few items of food and then help you indoors to get that foot up. Doctor's orders if I remember.'

'By the way, when I answered your distress call in the bedroom and enquired if you were all right your reply was, "No. I am not all right, damnit". Should I have construed that as meaning "Daniel, dearest," or "Blast it"?'

'The latter, I regret to say Daniel, dearest. In the heat of the moment, it just slipped out, you understand.'

'I reckoned as much. I think, apart from my parents, you are the only person who has never called me Damnit. I hope you won't object to being known as Mrs Damnit Greensward in some circles – it does have a certain ring to it.'

'Much more attractive than Mrs Blastit, that's for sure.'

The journey back to Tupshorne was completed without incident and Daniel parked the Volvo in the market square before going into the supermarket in search of the essentials. Waiting in the queue at the check-out, he was accosted by Bert "The Bells" Alderwood.

'Terrible about the fire last night, Daniel,' said Bert.

'What fire, Bert? Where?'

'At Saint Michael's. I thought the police would have notified you first, being a churchwarden.'

'No. I've been at Airedale hospital most of the morning. You'll learn the details of that visit soon enough. I bet the police contacted Jake first, not knowing that his responsibilities to St Michael's ended yesterday. Now you've told me I'll get down there just as soon as I can when I've taken care of my patient. That's a real shock.'

A far worse shock was yet to come.

Crossing the market place on his way back to the car, Daniel was suddenly confronted by a group of ramblers. In a state of some visible distress their leader asked him the quickest path to the police station.

'Just round that right hand corner over there,' answered Daniel, pointing in the relevant direction. 'Can I be of any help?'

'Well, we've just walked down the dale from Middinside and as we made our way up from the river we were met by what I can only describe as a savage dog. It was in a corner of the last field before we reached the outlying houses in that new development of bunga-lows. There's definitely something wrong and the dog, a black lab, seems to be guarding some kind of a white sheet by a wall. It stayed quiet until we showed any slight sign of approaching and then turned nasty. I've met some vicious dogs in my time. The police will have to sort it out – it's a public footpath. It ought to be shot.'

Damnit felt a shiver of horror go down his spine. In that moment he understood that Baggins had passed into his ownership. He had no need to ask the walkers if the dog was a bitch or not. This second incident of the day had landed him in a frightful bind. John's "Isaac" was inoperational in these circumstances but if ever there was a reason for invoking his own Latin maxim from childhood, now was the time to dig it out. *"Aequam servare mentem."* Nothing was going to panic him – that much was certain.

'Hold on a moment,' said Daniel, 'and I'll come to the police station with you. Let me just put my shopping in the car. Something dreadful must have happened. I know the dog – she wouldn't harm a fly. She's guarding the white sheet and what's under it.'

'All right,' grumbled the group's leader. 'But don't hang about. We're all ravenous and we've got lunch booked at the Bread and Scrape.'

Daniel was only a matter of yards away from the Volvo and in the fewest of words explained the situation to Lorna without mentioning the implications involved. That could wait.

With his hungry walking companion in tow, Daniel was soon inside the police station, briefing the officer on duty, who was well known to him, about the ramblers' encounter with Baggins and the reason or, more likely, reasons behind her uncharacteristic behaviour. The hiker listened, incredulous, as Daniel and the sergeant, who was also well acquainted with the dog and the tramp, quickly arranged the surveillance necessary to safeguard the public and bring man and dog into care.

The officer blinked when Damnit stated that as soon as he had settled his injured fiancée at High Ash he would be down the field in question as quickly as he possibly could. Daniel relaxed for a moment and laughed. 'You'll learn all about it – or rather "her" – sooner or later. In the meantime, can you call up the vet for me? If John's dead, Baggins is my dog, and I know for sure she was due to whelp today. Lord knows how many pups she's catering for, never mind chasing passers-by away from what I fear she is really guarding. Any pups might be at risk out there in the open, with a dam that won't know which way to turn or quite where her first priorities lie. But don't go near the bitch until I get there.'

'Is there anything I can do to help?' asked the hiker, who by now had identified himself as a Mr Harold Palmer from Preston. 'I don't seem to be as hungry as I thought I was. This unaccustomed and somewhat bizarre excitement, tragic as it is, must have a depressing effect on my appetite. I feel involved.'

'No. It's O.K.' replied the policeman. 'We'll take it from here, thank you. I've got your details down and if you wish, we'll let you know the outcome.'

'Yes please. If you would. I think my fellow ramblers would quite like to know what transpires. To think I even suggested the dog should be shot. Good luck with her Mr Greensward – what a happy coincidence it was, we should have met in the market place. Perhaps the dog comes with her own guardian angel.'

The three men shook hands on parting and Daniel dashed away to transport Lorna home to High Ash. He made her as comfortable as he could in the sitting room, and while in the kitchen he quickly prepared a snack lunch for her, calling out the details, however vague, of the story unfolding in the field.

'Don't jump to conclusions too soon, Daniel,' advised Lorna. 'John doesn't *have* to be dead, does he?'

The hairs stood up on the back of Damnit's neck and for the second time within an hour he felt a shudder of apprehension travel down his back. As he placed the plateful of sandwiches on the coffee table immediately by Lorna's chair he leaned over and kissed the crown of her head. Then straightening up again, in a low voice he said, 'I know he's gone, dear. That was a part of my dream last night. But Baggins never appeared in any guise. Now I'm about to find out why. I'll take Tottie in her capacity as a mobile kennel – at least Baggins already knows the inside of my venerable Toyota, the car for all occasions. I'll be back a bit later complete with the family – all being well. But with John – no. Keep an eye on her for me, Sprot. 'Bye for now! Whoops! I nearly forgot. I must take some water.'

It was just after noon, uncommonly hot for a late September day, and Baggins was developing a raging thirst. Washing clean and feeding a young family is an uncomfortably dehydrating experience. She was well aware that there was a little beck whispering its way down the slope within fifty yards of her. She could hear it and had drunk from it several times over the last two weeks. Yet its siren song of tinkling waters was not sweet enough to lure her away from her self-appointed sentry duty. She was beginning to weaken with delirium and her eyesight seemed to become veiled in mist when suddenly the blurred figure of a man dared to approach. She bared her teeth, partly in threat but mostly in fear. The man spoke.

CHAPTER XXXVI

Exit

DAMNIT PARKED TOTTIE on the hard standing of the gateway leading into the field from the metalled road serving the little development of bungalows. An ambulance was already in attendance, awaiting his arrival.

Striding down the field, he made straight for John's brilliant white ultra-cape, unmissable in the bright sunlight. Next, between himself and his target, he spotted Baggins lying flat to the ground about twenty-five yards equidistant and she failed to recognize him by sight as, quickly, he drew nearer. Hackles raised and teeth bared, she growled at him to keep his distance both from her and from what she was defending. Daniel spoke quietly but firmly. 'Come off it, Bags. It's me, Damnit, silly. You don't frighten me, old girl. I've brought you some water.'

The dog looked at him uncomprehendingly with dull eyes, still growling murderously, before slinking back to ten yards from the cape, and lying down again.

As he slowed down his approach, Daniel tried all the English endearments and funny names that he had heard John use on his dog. Nothing would persuade her to change her attitude. She refused to budge and by the time he had crept almost to within touching distance of her she was nearly beside herself with canine rage. He suddenly realized that, under stress, she had blanked out her English vocabulary. He was never to know that the last story John had told his black princess was in Latvian. He cursed himself, such a pathetic linguist, that he couldn't for the life of him remember a single word of John's Latvian dog commands. He delved into the back pocket of his trousers, feeling for that magic envelope, inscribed with phonetic Latvian for dogs, which John had given him. He was wearing the wrong trousers. Baggins was beginning to quieten down as her strength and resolve ebbed. From out of the blue the vital word came – the word that from the earliest days of their long friendship Daniel had heard John murmur when listening to a prototype Rolls engine running on the test bed – the word that when translated meant "easy now," or "gently does it". He got down on his knees and inched his way towards her, murmuring so softly, just as John would have done, 'Lernem Bags', 'lernem black beauty, girl' over and over again. At last she knew him and he was stroking her as she made a feeble attempt to lick his hand.

'Thank God, we're in time to save her.' It was the voice of his vet, Nathan Fraser, standing behind him, at the ready with a hypodermic syringe charged with all the goodies essential to a nursing mother at risk. While concentrating all his telepathic powers on the dog, Damnit had been totally oblivious to the quiet approach of the vet on his tail.

'Pups next,' said Nathan. 'I'll put money on it, they're all right – tough little beggars usually, as long as she's cleaned them up. Try her with the water Daniel – she'll have a mouth like the bottom of a parrot's cage.'

Daniel tended to Baggins while the vet approached the puppies which were asleep in a huddle between John's knees, sheltered from the sun's heat by a chance fold of the white cape. There were seven of them, all as black as basalt.

Baggins made no attempt to move as the ambulance crew removed John's body and his belongings on two stretchers. Only Ferrers was left behind, leaning against the wall rather like a stork which having delivered the babies stops to watch the unfolding drama.

Damnit picked up Baggins very gently in his arms and carried her to Tottie where he laid her on the back seat just in time to receive a basketful of as yet, blind, squirming puppies which Nathan had scooped up. Then he went back and collected Ferrers. As he was about to drive off to High Ash, a tap came on his window. He wound down the window and wasn't entirely surprised to see Harold Palmer, the Preston ramblers' leader.

'Sorry to trouble you, Mr Greensward, at this difficult time, but it's now or never. I don't know where they're going to, but I would like one of the pups. It's a few years now since I had a dog – I always intended to get another and I think fate has just delivered one. Here's my address on an old envelope.'

'That makes you top of the list, Mr Palmer. I've just inherited the dam and her litter. You'll understand my hurry now but I'll be in touch when the dust settles. Any gender preference?'

'The biggest dog, if in doubt – but I'll drive Mrs P. over to have a look when convenient. Sorry to delay you. Cheerio for now!'

'It'll cost you. They're of very aristocratic lineage and I am honour bound to give any proceeds to Guide Dogs for the Blind.'

Harold Palmer swallowed quickly before answering. 'Money no object. It's our Silver Wedding just before Christmas. I can't think of a better joint present. Rosalind can have the head and I'll keep the wagging tail. On your way!' He tapped Tottie's roof and waved Damnit out of the field gateway.

Thoughtfully Daniel drove home, pondering on the fact that it would be difficult to come to terms with John's sudden death. It seemed obvious now that it wasn't meant to be his destiny to say a proper "goodbye" to his old friend. Just as John had tried to slip away at the end of his farewell luncheon at the Museum without a send-off, without trying he had succeeded. Daniel felt cheated.

Reliving the minutes of slow motion as he managed to retrieve Baggins from her solitary vigil, he was appalled to realize that he had never given John a second glance. Then he reassured himself that any interest he may have had in a corpse at that particular time would have been futile. He had to be concerned with the living – after all somebody very famous had once said, "let the dead bury the dead." But who was going to play the gravedigger for John's farewell scene? Ferrers?

In the short time that it took to drive from the whelping field to High Ash, Baggins' condition improved considerably in response to the vet's shot of vital nutrients for nursing bitches – so much so that Daniel hardly needed to help her climb out of the car. She waited for him to collect the puppies into the basket which the vet had used and then followed him into the house, where in the kitchen her quarters awaited her. Daniel was well prepared even if the suddenness of her arrival was unexpected. Immediately he had contracted, two weeks earlier, to cope with Baggins and her pups in his agreement with John, Daniel had arranged bed and board in case she whelped earlier than he had forecast. Nathan Fraser had provided him with comprehensive instructions on puppy care and explanatory notes with a diet sheet on the feeding of a nursing mother. The vet had pointed out the desirability of providing as quiet a corner as possible – certainly for the first few weeks while the puppies, once their eyes had opened, became accustomed to natural light – as a haven of peace for the dam. Daniel had taken the trouble to take the door off a floor-based kitchen cupboard, sited furthest away from the sink and the cooking stove, and put down a simple bedding system of clean straw on newspapers. Straw was easily obtainable anywhere in the Tupshorne area and the soiled bedding ended up on the compost heap. Once the pups had learned to walk with confidence, they would be more or less confined to the utility room next to the kitchen – there was less chance of them being trodden on there and they would have access to the garden as they became more adventurous. In the meantime, the open-fronted cupboard space, dim and calm, was an ideal environment for Baggins and her first litter.

As Daniel walked into High Ash accompanied by his eight dogs, Lorna called out to him. 'It's a good thing you left the cordless telephone next to my sandwich lunch. Jake rang.'

'Be with you in a jiffy – when I've got Bags settled. Two shakes!' shouted back Daniel. 'It'll be about the blaze at church.'

'Blaze at church?' fired back Lorna. 'When?'

'Sometime last night apparently. That's all I know.'

Five minutes later Daniel joined Lorna in the sitting-room and tried to explain that although Bert Alderwood had told him about the fire when they had met by chance in the supermarket, the predicament of Baggins and her master had taken precedence in his mind to the point that the church came a poor second, if not third, in his plans of action for the day, taking into account that his number one priority had been Lorna herself until his encounter with Harold Palmer.

'Now that you are finally home, I think you'd better give Jake a ring,' said Lorna. 'He said he'd left a message about nine but flatly refused to elaborate on his reason for phoning. We exchanged pleasantries on the matter of bodily injuries and casualty departments et cetera – no mention of fire. I suppose if I'd been a bit more "with it", I could have listened to the message on the ansaphone but since he obviously didn't intend to enlighten me on the matter, I left it at that.'

'I've only just woken up to the fact that I've not eaten since breakfast and it's now nearly two. I'm not all that hungry but I'd better rustle up a sandwich and talk to Jake while I'm chewing,' replied

Daniel. 'If he rang about nine, it would have been just as we left for the hospital. Better hear the message first on the playback.'

Jake's voice came through loud and clear. "There's bin trouble at t'mill, owd lad. Give us a ring *statim* when you get in." Daniel deleted the message before speaking again.

'Not much *statim*, I'm afraid, but he'll understand that his own worries about what was his church until only yesterday have been overtaken by events. I don't feel particularly hungry with all this excitement. A cup of tea and a bun will do me. Would you care for a cuppa?'

'Yes, please, but I need to powder the old nose first which will give me the opportunity to have a peep at your new dog and family. I hereby appoint Sprottle to the post of canine courtesy aunt. No doubt Bindle will follow suit when Jake hears the full story. Put the kettle on – it's to be a kitchen snack.' Lorna paused for a moment, then 'Can I pick a pup?'

'My goodness, you're either quick on the uptake or psychic, said Daniel. 'You couldn't have known that part of my "deal" with my late friend was that I would keep a puppy from the litter on returning Bags to her master. Of course you can have the choice. When I proposed yesterday, I realised very quickly I was taking on one woman and her dog. Matters seem to be getting out of hand. One dog to nine in the course of twenty-four hours must be a record! Do you want a hand to get out of the chair? I think we can let Sprot have a little look – I'll be surprised if Baggins objects, but you never know. By the way, I've sold one pup already, to one of the ramblers who came across John and Baggins down the field.'

CHAPTER XXXVII

Fama Malum Quo Non Aliud Velocius Ullum (Virgil's Aeneid)

DAMNIT'S TELEPHONE CONVERSATION with Jake was short and very much to the point. In the nicest possible way he told Jake that, as the newly retired vicar, no longer was there a need for him to be concerned with any of Saint Michael's problems except perhaps as an interested bystander.

Jake agreed without demur, explaining to Daniel that when the police told him about the fire in the cellar, apparently earlier that same morning, they were rather taken aback by his somewhat detached reaction to the news until they realized he had relinquished all his responsibilities within the parish the previous afternoon. Once that matter was clarified, the police were pleased to accept his offer to ring the two churchwardens. Timothy Welsh had been at home and Daniel hadn't – hence the message he had left on the answering machine. Beyond that he had decided, quite definitely, not to become involved. Daniel gave a brief report on the state of health of his newly acquired lodgers before stating his intention to go over to the church immediately and then rang off. The time was still only three o'clock in the afternoon of a day of intense drama.

On arriving at Saint Michael's Daniel walked, head bent, slowly and thoughtfully, not by his normal route to the northern elevations but taking instead the grassed track round by the southern and eastern walls. He could never explain why for the first time ever he should have changed from his accustomed approach to the cellar, the gravel which scrunched so loudly under the shoe of everyone who wanted to visit the cellar for any reason whether it might be to service the central heating boiler or as in his own case to fetch the lawnmower out of storage.

As he rounded the south-east corner of the building something agleam in the grass caught his eye. Bending over, he retrieved a highly polished bowie knife not unlike the one he had handed to John on the bank at the Skipton Canal Basin after he had witnessed the exhibition of unarmed combat, which culminated with John's assailant flying into the water after being relieved of his weapon. No doubt the thug concerned had long since discarded the sheath.

He looked more closely at the hunting knife now lying across his palms from hand to hand. About sixteen inches in overall length with an eleven inch curved blade, it vaguely reminded him of a particular German bayonet, known as "The Butcher's Knife," which fitted the Mauser 98 rifle, and which he had seen in a museum of military armaments in which seemed to him like the year dot. He wondered if Colonel Jim Bowie had ever expected his name to be associated still with such a truly lethal weapon as this nearly a hundred years after his death at the Battle of the Alamo. The knife seemed to warm to his touch as if seeking to please a new owner, a new owner who immediately understood that here was a genuine case of "finders is keepers" in the same moment that he recognized that the deadly piece of steel in his hands was illegal. Running an index finger along the sharpened side of the blade, Daniel felt its razor-edged keenness and it sent a frisson of fear and foreboding down his spine. It was as if the knife was now crying out to be hidden, in case it might be summoned to give evidence. He smiled wryly at his strange unease; the knife was obviously in mint condition and presumably unused. Nevertheless, with some care he gently inserted the knife, point first, into the left sleeve of his jacket so that the rounded pommel was barely contained within his fingertips, and then with his left arm held stiffly to his side lest the knifepoint should enter the crook of the arm, he walked on round the north-east corner of the church to the doorway which led into the cellar, where he came face to face with a fireman, a member of the local fire brigade, long known to him as Ken "Chop" Stickles, and who was checking the security of the area from a fire-fighter's point of view before reporting back to the fire station.

'Hello, Ken,' said Damnit jovially. 'I might have known I'd find you here now the fire's out.'

'Cheeky!' replied Ken. 'I'll have you know I was first in action with the squirter – it's my speciality. What brings you to the scene of the crime anyway, this late in the day? Of course! You're a church-warden.'

'Crime?' queried Daniel. 'You mean the fire was deliberate? Arson?'

'Looks very much like it, according to our investigating officer, with a bit of help from forensics. Come a bit nearer – you can still see where the staple plate of the padlock fitting appears to have been prised out of the wooden doorframe, screws and all, and then roughly replaced. It's perhaps lucky that the fire burnt inwards rather than out; otherwise the doorframe would have gone up in flames rather than being only charred. It must have been a rare sort of jemmy to lever out that plate with its two inch screws. Somebody broke in.'

'If that's the case, whoever it was didn't necessarily have to have been responsible for setting fire to the place, did he? Or she? There must be some other kind of evidence to suggest that, surely. Presumably forensics picked up on something a bit quick like for you to sound so convinced.'

'Well, yes, there was something. I don't know where you've been until now, but Timothy Welsh came round pretty smartish this morning – said the vicar had 'phoned him early. The fire was well and truly snuffed out by then and all he could do was answer a few basic questions posed by our investigators. He really wasn't much use – or should I say help – but his main contribution to the enquiry was to say that the church cellar was Damnit Greensward's domain and apart from the rather random positioning of seasonal items like straw in bags for the Christmas nativity tableau, and several redun-dant pews, you always kept the place pretty tidy. It was forensics' final question that floored Timothy when he was asked if you rolled your own cigarettes. Timothy, stunned by the very idea, just said that he didn't know you even smoked, never mind rolled your own – unless you happened to be a closet tobacco addict. "That's fine, then", was the reply. "We've raked a cigarette-rolling gadget out of the ashes." So it looks like whoever broke into the cellar fancied a quiet drag. Actually, it wasn't altogether true about raking it from the ashes – we had to budge a big stone that had fallen from the cel-lar roof and the fag-roller was under that and very flat.'

Daniel said nothing. The bowie knife, tucked up his sleeve, seemed to glow with a sudden heat, threatening to blister the hand

and forearm of its new custodian, then the steel froze to his touch as if he was hiding an icicle, not a knife. He winced visibly, unsure whether to expect to see a palm seared by hot metal or scorched by frostburn. The sensations passed off as quickly as they had arrived, but not before Chop had observed the flicker of pain across the churchwarden's face.

'You're not a secret smoker are you, Daniel? You appeared to be a bit discomfited for a moment there.'

'No, no,' said Daniel quickly, and thinking twice as fast. 'I think I know which slab fell from the ceiling. Let me have a look,' and he brushed past the fire-fighter into the cellar. There in the middle of the floor lay the Tiltstone. Joseph "Tiltstone" North's architectural masterstroke had cracked into two halves along the line of the central spindle. Vulcan had tested the invention in his furnace, and found it wanting.

CHAPTER XXXVIII

Occasionem Cognosce

K EN STOOD BEHIND Daniel and together they looked above their heads at the gaping hole in the cellar roof where the Tiltstone had rested undisturbed for one hundred and thirty-five years until Daniel had used it as his secret route into the ground floor of the church earlier in the year.

'What a stink!' said Daniel. 'Who'd have thought a few bags of straw and three or four old pine pews could create such a stench.' He looked down to see that he was standing in a pool of sloppy black ash which, still at high tide, reached to above the welts of his shoes and he fancied he could feel the mess percolating through the stitching of the uppers and creeping into his socks.

'You get used to it after you've doused your first half-dozen fires. The smell is a bit like what you get when you have to damp down a garden bonfire: a mix of steam, smoke, soot and maybe kerosene or petrol. It's the confined space here which concentrates the assault on the old olfactories.' Chop was being at his most matter of fact.

Daniel took stock of the damage in the cellar. 'The mower is a write-off, that's obvious. What a shame! I've walked literally hundreds, maybe thousands of miles behind that machine. It must have cut tons and tons of grass in that time and I thought it would see me out. It's a good job I keep the mower fuel at home.'

'Pity you didn't keep the mower there an' all,' said Ken. 'You can see where the fuel tank exploded like a can of rotten sardines. Doesn't take much blazing petrol to cause a decent conflagration. That's elementary bonfire procedure, my dear Damnit.'

Daniel gulped, remembering that for the first time in many a long year he had failed to drain the fuel tank the previous Wednesday afternoon, such had been his haste to get back to High Ash after his conversation with John just after he had finished mowing the church lawns, so that they would look at their best for the celebration of the Feast of Saint Michael the Archangel. He said nothing.

'I'll tell you something for nothing, Damnit,' continued Ken, 'you don't know how lucky you've really been. By some miracle – however fierce the heat of the blaze may have been – the gas main pipe leading to the meter never ruptured. God alone knows why it didn't.'

'I'm quite sure he does, Ken,' answered Daniel, smiling. 'There's nothing he doesn't know.'

'Maybe,' said Ken in a tone which failed to conceal any scepticism he might have felt. 'My chief fire officer reckoned that if that slab hadn't split and fallen down, leaving that hole in the ceiling, the gas pipe was bound to have fractured. The whole church could have burned down. As it happened, the hole now above us appeared and the smoke and flames went up through the gap as if they'd found a natural flue. All right – you'll need to clean and redecorate right through but there's no structural damage apart from what we can see from where we stand. I'm no architect – never will be now – but the way that stone split, you might have thought the stonemason responsible had foreseen such an incident as this.'

Daniel refrained at first from explaining to Ken the significance of the Tiltstone and his own family connection with the inventor. Then, on second thoughts, he elected to come out with the story. 'It's not just any old stone slab, Ken. It's a Tiltstone and it was invented by an absolute genius of an architect, Joseph "Tiltstone" North, my mother's great-grandfather – hence my middle name of Tiltstone. Just don't ask me what happened to the genius bit – it's not in my DNA sample, that's for sure.'

'What purpose did it serve?' queried Ken, 'That is apart from providing a flue for the fumes when it cracked in two. Presumably it tilted or swivelled somehow.'

'That's it,' replied Damnit. 'If by chance anyone got locked in the cellar with no means of getting out through the door, if he or she knew the secret of the Tiltstone set into the ceiling – even in pitch black darkness – it was possible to have access to the room above by using the very simple locking mechanism. You see those few stone steps over there, apparently leading to nowhere – they're the stairway to the stone, enabling the prisoner to reach the release catch. The clever thing is – you can't come through from above when the stone is at rest. In church all you can see is a perfectly normal stone flag like all the rest – no catch, no nothing. "Tiltstone", my three Gs father, as a child, had been locked in a cellar overnight as a punishment for a minor, accidental misdemeanour. When he became an architect, he built a reputation as a designer of fine mansions and, for one very obvious reason, every house with a cellar, or cellars, was constructed with a Tiltstone, as he called it. This is the only church he designed so we're looking at the remains of the one and only Holy Tiltstone.'

'You're not pulling my leg, by any chance, are you, Daniel? It's a bit of an unlikely tale to my way of thinking and yet you didn't seem to be making it up as you went along.'

'No. It's the gospel truth. Shine your light on those two lumps of the Tiltstone. With a bit of luck one of them will have rolled over on impact. Yes – d'you see it, Ken? The engraving "JOSEPH NORTH MDCCCLXV". My mother was Emily North before she married. Fancy doubting me!'

'Sorry,' said Ken. 'As stories go, I thought it was the stuff of dreams. What a pity after all these years to be split in two. I suppose it'll get replaced by a chunk of concrete.'

'Not on your life,' stated Damnit firmly. 'I'll make sure that stone goes back where it was stone before. The original plans or drawings will be in an archive somewhere and one of our Yowesdale stonemasons should find the job a doddle. If the locking mechanism is beyond repair, I think I still carry enough clout at the National Blacksmiths' Museum to persuade the trustees there to authorise the forging of a replacement for me. Tell me, Ken. Would granite have cracked like this limestone? I know granite was formed from molten rock – maybe the heat wouldn't have split a granite Tiltstone.'

'I'm not sure,' said Ken. 'I suspect that where the spindle ran across the stone it may have been slightly inset into a groove which would be the point of weakness when subjected to intense heat. Granite, for all its being cooled from liquid rock, might go the same way. Basalt might be a better bet. It's immaterial anyhow because, a pound to a penny, the powers that be will insist on like being replaced by like – so concrete should be ruled out as well. Whatever happens, cheap it won't be!'

'I'll need to see what our insurance policies state on the matter,' said Daniel thoughtfully. 'If there's any doubt in anyone's mind I'll foot the bill myself. The honour of us "Tiltstones" is at stake here! I think we'd better get out of here – unlike your fireman's boots, my shoes aren't meant to withstand filthy black mud. They and my socks as well are destined for the dustbin. Harking back to basalt, you sounded a bit knowledgeable on such things. Did geology crop up somewhere in your training?'

Ken laughed. By now they had left the cellar and were standing on the gravel path. 'You may have an eminent architect in your distant ancestry. My great-grandfather was a lead miner with a keen amateur interest in rocks of all kinds, not just those ones which yielded the metal that brought him nothing but an early grave. I don't believe he'd have been any happier as a gold miner. But there's no doubt that's where my rather vague interest in rocks and minerals stems from. I'll get back to HQ now. I don't see any signs of re-ignition. Nice to talk to you, Mr Tiltstone!'

'Cheerio, Chop,' said Daniel. 'No doubt we'll bump into each other again before too long. The fire may be out but this could put something of a dampener on Saint Michael's development plans. We shall see.'

The two men walked round to the front of the church before parting company, Ken returning to the fire station and Damnit entering the church to get an idea of how much of a mess had been created by the fumes. His first impression was one of surprise. Certainly there was the smell of smoke in the atmosphere but it was little more than a whiff. He had quite expected to be confronted by blackened beams, at the very least, until he realized that the burning of several pews and a few bags of loose straw, although generating heat intense enough to crack the Tiltstone, would nevertheless only produce a limited amount of soot to be dispersed in the church once it had been blasted out of the confines of the cellar. He ran his hand along the back of the pew nearest to him as he stood in the centre of the nave and looked at his smut-blackened palm. Suddenly he was hit by a vicious spasm of cramp in his left hand, drawing his attention to the bowie knife still tucked up his sleeve, and without a second thought used his sooty right hand to gently ease the weapon from the fingertip grip and draw it out into the light. The pain dissipated quickly as he carefully flexed the stiffened joints from fingers to elbow. Momentarily his grip on the pommel of the knife loosened with the slight greasiness of the soot on his palm. The heavy knife, point first, dropped and embedded itself in the wooden floor narrowly missing his right shoe. That was a close shave, thought Damnit and left it there while he inspected the chancel. The

Tupshorne Mothers' Union banner with its predominantly white background had turned a murky grey. In general, he observed that, apart from specialist cleaning which would be required for any exposed fabric items such as the altar frontal and various banners, a decent household detergent or sugar soap and hot water would probably be all that was required before essential repainting took place. The smoke must have given the spider population, resident among the rafters, cause for complaint judging by the festooned cobwebs, normally invisible in the heights of the nave, which were now looking like finest black lace.

Finally Daniel visited the ante-chapel to inspect the gap in the floor where the Tiltstone had dropped out and into the cellar. The hole appeared to be much smaller than he expected until he remembered that only the previous Wednesday he had used the Tiltstone for his final covert money drop. Now the missing slab posed a dangerous hazard. Hearing the church door creak, he moved out from the ante-chapel to meet the visitor who turned out to be Timothy Welsh, his fellow churchwarden – pipe in mouth – carrying a piece of sheet metal destined to cover the hole until proper building repairs could be carried out.

'Mind you don't trip over that hunting knife, Tim,' called out Daniel. 'It's bang in your path.'

Timothy spotted it just in time and, skirting round it, held the metal sheet to one side in the process. 'Funny place to stick a knife, Damnit! Is it yours?' enquired a slightly bemused Tim.

'Sort of,' replied Daniel. 'I found it outside in the grass. I think it is probably quite valuable, spelt <u>illegal</u>. I brought it inside a few minutes ago and it slipped out of my hand, accidentally, almost impaling my foot. There's nothing sinister about it unless you trip over it. I'll take it home with me before I decide what to do with it. It goes against my blacksmith's grain to bin anything made from high quality steel. It might be German from Solingen – the best.' He paused for a moment. 'This is a right mess, Tim – just when we've raised all that money for renovations and repairs. We'll need to have a major rethink concerning priorities.'

'Have faith, my boy,' said Timothy, somewhat irreverently, putting the metal plate down over the Tiltstone gap and taking a deep puff at his pipe. 'Have faith, if not in Almighty God, then in the Almighty Insurance Company. We might come out of all this smelling of roses. Be Christian – we are confirmed optimists after all – aren't we?'

'Supposed to be,' chuckled Damnit. 'We'd better have a meeting with Violet in the near future. It wouldn't surprise me if she knows the church insurance policy document off by heart. As church treasurer she's a miracle worker. Only yesterday, Jake told us all that there were fifty-odd thousand pounds in Saint Michael's coffers as a result of the fundraising effort. Sorry! I should have said, "ARE fifty-odd thousand." Violet can't have spent any of it yet and very soon she'll be doing battle over an insurance claim. How about popping round to see her now, if you're free? There's nothing like striking while the iron's hot, as the blacksmith said to his favourite mare.'

'No can do,' said Timothy. 'I'm due at the quack's in ten minutes but you don't need me to fill Violet in on what's happened here. You look as if you could do with a cup of tea – Vi's kettle's always on the hob.'

Daniel looked at his watch. 'Just before you rush off, Tim,' he said, 'you ought to know that I've had a quite momentous twenty-four hours. Very happily, I have acquired a fiancée – tragically, I've lost a remarkable friend, and in relation to the tragedy I've gained a bitch and seven new-born puppies – the event which you also were told to expect. All that is on top of this fire. You'd better get along to the surgery now – I'll fill you in with the details next time we meet.'

'I'm so sorry, Daniel,' replied Tim. 'Are you telling me John's dead?'

"Fraid so,' said Daniel, 'in somewhat mysterious circumstances as well, I fear. I may be wrong, but I think we could be in for a coroner's inquiry. The truth is somewhere in the smokescreen.'

CHAPTER XXXIX

Cave Quid Dicis, Quando, et Cui

D ANIEL'S FIRST QUESTION to Violet Rose when she opened the door in response to his sharp rap was, 'Are we properly covered by insurance, Vi?'

'Come in. Come in,' said Violet. 'I've just brewed up.'

She ushered him in, remarking that she was sure he wouldn't object to taking tea in her kitchen. He readily agreed, safe in the knowledge that the tin which held the award-winning Violet's Shortbread Biscuits was always to be found on the second shelf to the right of the kitchen range next to the tin labelled "HUMBUGS".

Not many folk in Tupshorne were of an age to call Damnit "lad". Now well over eighty, Violet had known him since his birth and never missed an opportunity for reminding him of his comparative youth, never mind what an ugly baby he had been. 'Sit yourself down, lad, and spill whatever beans you've managed to sweep up at church. I presume that's why you're here – and you can stop eye-ing that biscuit tin because it's empty. The next batch will be ex-oven in twenty minutes. Timothy Welsh rang to tell me about the fire but he was short on any details apart from the fact that the fire officer was playing it down as a minor incident. I wish to God it had been the wretched church hall, in which case I'd have got dressed and taken my old set of bellows to help things on.'

'Steady on, young lady,' chided Damnit with a teasing grin, 'One thing at a time. Insured are we?'

'Of course we are,' said Violet quite forcibly. 'The diocese won't let us operate otherwise. Fancy a churchwarden having to ask! We're comprehensively covered for absolutely everything. I reckon our poor church mouse could claim compensation for postnatal depression if it could read the small print on the policy. But what was your own impression of the damage – I presume you've had a good look?'

'I've seen as much as I cared to. Enough to bear out Timothy's report to you that the firefighters considered it to be a blaze of little consequence. I had quite a chat with Ken Stickles who had been detailed to keep watch on the cellar – that is apparently where the fire started – in case of any spontaneous re-ignition. Seems we've been lucky in that the fierce heat at a fairly early stage split a slab in the cellar ceiling. It dropped to the cellar floor, leaving a gap which allowed the smoke and fumes, soot and smuts, to escape into the ante-chapel directly above. Ken said that if that hadn't happened, the odds are the gas pipe to the meter would have fractured, resulting in a major explosion and really serious damage to the whole building. It'll be a "nice little earner," as they say, for a contract cleaning company, followed by a painter and decorator with his ladder.'

'What about the cellar itself?' asked Violet. 'The gas-fired central heating installation must be a write-off surely but presumably the roof will repair pretty easily.'

'You know, I hardly glanced at the heater. I was more bothered about the lawnmower. That's a goner for sure, and I suppose the heater must be as well. As for the slab that fell after cracking, that will require some real expertise to replace. It was a Tiltstone.'

'Good Lord,' said Violet. 'THE Tiltstone. I knew we'd got one somewhere, but have never been curious enough to look for such a curiosity. Never been used to my knowledge, wherever it was, but I hope its inventor would be pleased if it saved the church from destruction by way of becoming a burnt offering in the process. I repeat – it's a crying shame it wasn't the church hall. There's enough wood in that to create a really decent fire.'

Daniel laughed. 'Let me repeat, "Insured are we?" in respect of the hall. What has the poor building done that offends you so? Hiring it out provides at least some income for the church, surely?'

'It makes some profit, yes. Even after unavoidable costs such as insurance and heating are stripped out. But it's not enough. We need higher rates of occupancy or use to up the basic turnover. And to do that we have to make the premises more appealing both visually and physically, with new curtains, lighting – and maybe a new door. The stage should be modernised and as for the kitchen – well!! Of course, you already know the most serious problem. In a year or two we will be, by law, required to provide proper access and facilities for wheelchair users. That means wider doorways, no steps and a decent loo-block, all user-friendly for disabled visitors. It's a bit of a treasurer's nightmare, Daniel.'

'It shouldn't be that big a problem, should it Violet? At Jake's last service yesterday he let us know – in no uncertain terms – that the fundraising target had been achieved with nearly thirty thousand pounds to spare. That'll cover any church hall modernization and still leave us plenty to provide a decent carpark for the church. QED, it seems to me.'

'Steady on, my lad,' said Violet. 'That fund, oversubscribed as it was, is intended solely for use on the church. I'm not sure I can siphon off as much as a penny to spend on the hall. I'll have to look at the rulebook – have a quiet word with the archdeacon.'

'It's a pity that chap "Rufus" didn't insist on his twelve thousand being earmarked for our hall,' remarked Damnit casually.

'Interesting you should say that,' said Violet. 'You weren't to know, but "Rufus's" fifty pound notes were a right rough lot – well, most of them – very well used indeed. If they had been a clean sample I might have suspected they'd really been laundered. Jake had an idea who Rufus was but didn't dare to let on!'

Daniel sat up in his chair with a start. 'I've got to go Vi. I've just remembered I've an injured fiancée at High Ash who'll be wondering what's become of me.'

Violet's jaw dropped. 'A fiancée, you say? You've been hiding your light under a bushel, you dark horse you. Am I acquainted with the lucky lady? I hope her injury isn't too serious. She can't be local, otherwise I'd have known about this ere now.'

Daniel was on his feet by this time and making for the front door. 'You met her yesterday at Jake's farewell do. We actually agreed to get married later in the afternoon – must have been some rare ingredient in the sherry trifle that gave me the idea – but I've known her since our Cambridge days. Her name's Lorna Swann.

'I am so happy for you,' said Violet. 'You've been such a waste of a good man all these years. How your dear parents would rejoice. Tell your young lady I will give her the recipe for that sherry trifle of mine.'

'It was more likely to be the lovage soup,' chuckled Daniel. 'It does have that kind of reputation, so I understand. Raw celery's the same, you know.'

'Give my herb garden a grateful nod as you go,' smiled Violet. 'Your Lorna can have my lovage soup recipe as well.'

'What she really needs is a knit-bone poultice. I presume you've got a comfrey plant somewhere. She fell in the shower earlier this morning, cracked a bone in the forearm which is now in plaster. I've had quite a day myself but I'll tell you all about that another time. Thanks for the tea – see you soon.'

As he returned home Daniel remembered that he would have to drive over to Skipton to collect Lorna's clothes from the Bethdan. Perhaps if her arm and ankle were not too painful they could go together and enjoy an evening bar snack at his favourite watering hole not many yards away from the canal basin where his narrow boat was moored. They could even sleep overnight on the Bethdan, only so long as it suited Lorna, he thought – that was when a reminder of Baggins and family crossed his mind and brought him up short. Just as well, he mused. A narrow boat was not the craft most conducive for the creature comforts of anyone with a heavily-strapped ankle, never mind an arm in plaster and a temporary sling.'

On returning to High Ash, Daniel was very surprised to find Lorna still sitting in her chair as if she had never moved since he had left her a few hours earlier and yet the kitchen table was laid, as for tea. 'You've been a bit clever, haven't you?' he said to her. 'I'm sure I smell food!'

'It was absolute agony,' replied Lorna, smiling. 'Even been out and picked some flowers with Baggins' assistance. She definitely asked to go out. It was so funny, when Baggins accompanied this hobbling old lady, Sprottle just sat down in the kitchen as near to the puppies as she could get and I don't think she took her eyes off them until we came back in again. I'm sure, as Bags waddled past Sprot to return to her pups, she gave her a wink as if to say "Thanks mate." '

At that point Jake and Martha, along with Miss Bindle, appeared from the utility room where they had been hiding.'

'We've heard every word,' said Martha, with a giggle. 'Your fiancée has been coming out with more than one terminological inexactitude. Fortunately a good fib isn't one of the Seven Deadly Sins. Just to put the record straight, Jake made the casserole that you can smell. It's in the oven, ticking over. I brought the bunch of flowers, cut from the vicarage garden, to cheer Lorna up, knowing that a dry old bachelor like you was highly unlikely to think of such a romantic refinement. I don't suppose there have been flowers in this house since Bethan died. I found a lovely glass vase in a cupboard in the utility room, which looked more like a retired water jug, unless I'm mistaken. I love its shape.'

'Oh dear!' said Daniel. 'That jug is trouble with a capital T. You must have reached to the back of the shelf for it. The shape is dangerously seductive.'

'*Expliquez, s'il vous plaît,*' replied a puzzled Lorna.

'*En fait* as they are wont to say in Nice,' said Daniel, thinking his way through his reply and giving himself time to collect his thoughts on the matter, 'actually, it's been relegated to the back of the vase cupboard from the front of the crystal glassware cabinet for the very best of reasons. It is a magic water jug which was the centrepiece of a set of crystal – my wedding gift to Bethan and Gerald, and after he died and Bethan came to live here with her big brother, she insisted on me having it back. The magic bit is that if you fill it to a crucial level and put it in a sunny spot, such as on the dining table over there in the bay window, it acts like a simple magnifying glass capable of setting fire to anything combustible sitting in the path of its powerfully concentrated sunray. Bethan had hardly been here a month before that beautiful, shapely jug had melted part of a rather pretty plastic place mat and produced a nasty pungent smoke to boot. I suspected the smoke may have contained dioxin – a known carcinogen – so we replaced the table mats with a set of woven raffia mats. Two weeks later we had a repeat performance complete with flames. The raffia mats went eventually to a Guy Fawkes Bonfire, and in came good old cork like my parents used to have. It's hard to get cork to even smoulder properly as you will know, Martha, from your experience of using burnt cork in your incarnation as a theatrical make-up artist. I remember Jake complaining about his Captain Hook make-up and your excessive use of burnt cork all those years ago at Cambridge. Thinking back now, that's probably when he fell in love with you – your expertise with theatrical cosmetics improved his looks no end. As for the jug – it became a vase as Bethan reasoned that, with crowded flower stems in it, the effect of the sun's rays would be nullified. Strange though – I don't think she ever tried it out and that is why it would have migrated to the back of the cupboard.

'What a long story,' remarked Lorna. 'Strikes me, you should have put it in the bin marked "Recycled glass." Flowers or no flowers, sooner or later it will rear its beautiful head again and say to someone – maybe a future owner not of our generation – 'Here am I. I'm an exquisitely formed and elegant water jug. Fill me."'

'Point taken,' said Damnit ruefully. 'I'm sure you're right. When Martha's lovely bouquet is over, I'll dispose of the hazardous crystal pitcher, as a poet might describe it.'

Jake guffawed. 'Some poet you! "Hazardous crystal pitcher" sounds like a title for a fairy-tale. Are you sure you're not plagiarising John?'

The good-humoured atmosphere in the room died.

'I'm sorry,' said Jake. 'That was a crass remark – from me of all people. It just goes to show that I haven't come to terms with his sudden death. Bless me – it's only just over twenty-four hours since I heard his confession. Perhaps some version of the Last Rites would have been more appropriate.' He stopped abruptly – suddenly aware that Baggins had slipped into the room and placed her left paw on his knee.

'Don't read too much into that,' said Daniel calmly. 'She's not psychic. She's hungry. It's her teatime and she's confused you with me, as a likely source of *abendessen*.' He addressed his dog. 'Come on then, Bags. We'll all enjoy watching your family while you wolf your meal. There's nothing like having seven pups to feed for sharpening the appetite.'

Jake helped Lorna out of her easy chair and together with Martha they followed Baggins and Damnit out of the sitting room down the connecting passage into the kitchen.

'What a touching scene,' whispered Lorna. 'Nursemaid Sprottle is taking her appointment seriously.' Her dog was sitting, alert and erect, by the sleeping clutch of puppies, watching over them intently as if keeping vigil.

'I wonder if Bindle will eventually take the same attitude,' mused Martha. 'As a matter of interest, where is she? She's kept out of the way since the moment we arrived – being discreet perhaps. I don't know why, because for the last two weeks when John was busy in our garden you'd have thought she was Baggins' shadow. She's never had any pups.'

'Neither has Sprot,' said Lorna. 'I hope this little cameo of canine bliss doesn't give her any ideas. She's not given me the slip yet – intentionally, that is – but when she goes, she goes like the wind.'

By this time, Baggins' feeding bowl was being shoved across the kitchen floor as she cleaned out the few remaining crumbs before taking a long drink of water. Daniel was on the point of ushering her through the utility room and into the garden when a knock came on the front door. Both dogs barked as Nathan Fraser came in through the unlocked door. Baggins rushed back to her pups but Sprottle went to stand at Lorna's side as if she had received a high-frequency summons only audible to her. It was her teatime too!

'Hope I'm not interrupting anything serious – like your high tea,' chuckled the vet. 'I was passing nearby and thought it a good excuse to have another look at the family. My earlier check-up was, of necessity, rather cursory and for all my years in practice I'm still a sucker for the wonderful scent of warm, dry puppies.' Suddenly he was aware of a dog that he hadn't met before as Sprot left Lorna's shadow and loped across the carpet, greeting him with a growl. 'And I'm pleased to meet you, too – whoever you are,' said Nathan, extending a deliberately limp hand towards her, knuckles first. 'But don't bother to come to me when you need a quiet consultation and certainly not when you're due for a jab.'

'Don't worry, doc,' said Lorna, smiling. 'She's just telling you, in her politest manner, that you smell like a vet. The slightest whiff of surgical spirit upsets her normal friendly equilibrium. We haven't met before, but I'm Lorna Swann and my hairy lurcher bitch here is called Sprottle. And in case you may wonder what we are doing here, I am Daniel's very new fiancée.'

'Truly, the age of miracles is not yet past,' replied an astounded Nathan. 'No doubt you will explain yourself sooner or later, Damnit. For now, all I can do is congratulate you on your apparently excellent taste in women. I'm not so sure about the dog though. Better keep off the surgical spirit and stick to Scotch.' Ignoring the now quiet dog, he took a few paces towards Lorna and introduced himself. I expect you know what you're letting yourself in for with Damnit, dear lady,' he said jovially.

'Absolutely,' replied Lorna. 'I've known him for over forty years as it so happens. We were contemporaries at Cambridge. And my dog approves of him. Like her mistress, Sprot has an excellent taste in men. That's why she growled at you, "apparently", on first sight, as you might say.'

'*Touché, ma chérie*,' laughed the vet. 'Should she ever require my professional services I shall endeavour to remember to cover myself with one of those deodorants for chaps, guaranteed to bring the girls running.'

Lorna smiled happily. 'You can see that we have our own mutual admiration society here, as of today. Baggins and family have completed the membership. By the way, just a word of very sound advice for a man in your position. You will find in the case of Sprot that a small piece of fried liver – preferably calf's – trumps the odour of surgical spirit!'

'Point taken,' said Nathan.

'Now Baggins, old girl, let's have a more thorough look at your little lot.' He examined each pup in turn, sexing them as he went along. The dam made no attempt to hinder his inspection except to give them a quick wash when they were returned to her, as if to remove the taint of a human hand.

'Well, Damnit, whatever the strange circumstances that have lumbered you with eight dogs – it's a cracking litter, as good as any I've ever seen. 'Fraid there's a certain imbalance though – Baggins has produced a pup ratio of six to one in favour of little ladies. You might know that the dog is the biggest of them and no doubt he'll prove to be the greediest as the days go by.'

'That's all right,' said Damnit. 'He's sold already to the fellow from the group of ramblers from Preston who came across John down the field and were warned off by Bags.'

Martha joined the discussion. 'You'll have to work out a way to identify each one, Daniel, and give them a name. They all look like black peas out of the same pod and Baggins may object to you tying a piece of coloured ribbon round each one.'

'No problem,' replied Damnit. 'I've already picked up a collection of sheep marker pens. I can mark their tummies either with different colours, rainbow-like, or number them with a green, maybe pink, pen.'

'I can't wait,' remarked Jake dryly, 'to hear what weird names you come up with. Knowing the story of their parentage, will you be consulting J. R. R. Tolkien for ideas?'

'Good grief, no,' expostulated Damnit. 'I have given thought to the matter already, which will no doubt surprise you, and decided that with Baggins for a mother, the pups will be named in relation to her. You can all put your thinking caps on and come up with nouns which mean, or can be linked to, baggin time. I'll jot them down as you suggest them and then decide which ones I like. To start the bidding, I offer Tiffin.'

A few minutes later, between the five of them, they had produced enough words to cover two litters worth:

Tiffin.
Snack.
Elevenses.
Tea Break.
Snap.
Break.
Minin.
Piece.
Sandwich.
Nibbles.
Snackerooley.
Butty.
Collation.
Beans.
Nosh.

Other words were mentioned only to be laughed out of contention. Daniel thanked the others for their contributions before stating that the final selection would be down to himself with perhaps a small input from Lorna. Then suddenly he surprised them by announcing that the puppy which he would keep, in addition to inheriting Baggins from John, would be called Rauch.

'That's not right – not right at all,' said Jake. 'It's got nothing to do with food, or has it? You can't just change the rules to suit yourself.'

Daniel stroked his chin with his left hand before replying with a mock-stony face. 'My game – my own rules, if you please, Father Jacob. No arguing with this referee or you'll be off to the sin bin.' The frown disappeared as he smiled and began to explain, not before Lorna had intervened to suggest that the name sounded like the German for "smoke."

'Smart girl,' said Daniel. 'I should have remembered that you read History with German. You're right, of course. When I first encountered John in the Rolls Research Department he had already been working there for several years. All his colleagues from before my arrival were quite accustomed to the fact that their coffee or tea break was to John his *Rauchenpause* – literally his pause for a smoke – a lifelong habit he had acquired during his wartime service with the SS. He must have smoked from the age of fifteen – I make that nigh on sixty years. Add all those *Rauchenpausen* together and it's a wonder smoking didn't kill him.' He paused, himself, for a brief moment as if a flash of intuition had illuminated or penetrated a smokescreen, and then spoke again. 'Maybe the habit did catch up with him in the end. Better not to know maybe.'

'So there's the explanation for you. It'll be a good name for calling her by. Not many words rhyme with "ouch", the "ch" to be pronounced as in "loch" – right guttural like!'

The meeting broke up shortly after, when Nathan decided that his tea was probably on the table as he got wind of Jake's casserole of lamb which was ticking over in the oven, quietly but aromatically.'

'Right,' said Jake, confidently, and raising his voice a few decibels called out, 'Grub up.'

He might have uttered the word "abracadabra" and waved a magic wand as within seconds Bindle materialized from wherever she had been hiding.

'I've brought a meal for Sprot as well. It's all a matter of priorities. Animals before humans as the book of Genesis informs us.'

'That was the <u>Creation</u>,' murmured Lorna, 'Unless I'm mistaken – not the <u>Cateration</u>, for want of a more fitting word! Sprot understands "Grub up" as well, so on her behalf let me say "thank you".'

Damnit chimed in. 'You've just jogged my memory, Jake. When John set off to walk home to Latvia last November, I hinted, subtly so I thought, that Bags would need proper care and every consideration. My words, addressed to her at the time, were that she should look out for him but he understood that they were directed at him and he was not amused. His reply sticks in my mind until now. "There will be times on our trek when we will share the same dish, but she will always have the first helping. She comes first." He'd have known about Genesis and he always got his priorities right – always!'

The dogs were fed without further delay while Daniel set the dining table. Hardly had Miss Bindle and Sprottle finished their meal than Baggins left her pups momentarily and went over to Bindle in a move which, if interpreted in anthropomorphic terms, would have meant, "Come on, Bindle – there's no need to be shy. They can't bite yet." Bindle took a brief peek at the wriggling seven, followed by a lingering sniff, before backing away as if retreating from a royal presence, and returning to settle close to Jake as he began to dish up the early evening meal.

Halfway through the main course, Daniel, speaking with his mouth full, suddenly asked Jake what he'd done for pudding.

'Lorna, have you noticed,' enquired Jake with a chuckle, 'how like a camel is your fiancé when talking with his mouth full?'

'Bactrian or Arabian? answered Lorna, quick as a flash. 'I suppose it has to be the latter single-humper. Mind you,' she smiled sweetly at Daniel, 'he's so good-tempered that I can't imagine him taking humprage when taken to task by such an ancient friend.'

'Don't fret, Daniel,' ventured Martha. 'I elected to take care of puds. I do hope you like ice cream, Lorna, because the High Ash deep-freeze testifies to his weakness for the stuff. He must have taken you to the Brymor Ice Cream Parlour at some stage, when you've been up here. He takes all his lady friends there, you know, to impress them. In fact, I think he has acquired "privileged customer" status to the point where, if they're trying out a new flavour, he gets first lick. You're marrying a gelatiholic who keeps at least ten different varieties in his freezer.'

'Suits me,' said Lorna. 'I have to admire his sense of taste – after all he's always been highly selective in his choice of women. So why not ice cream?'

'When you two have quite finished taking my name in vain, you might notice that your food is going cold. All this repartee is more than a man can stand. The only reason I enquired about pudding was that when we've eaten it – and I'd be perfectly happy with ice cream, surprise, surprise – I'm going to dash off to Skipton and fetch Lorna's clothes from the Bethdan. Don't worry about the washing up. I promise to do it when I get back. Now there's a happy thought – by getting married, not only shall I be acquiring a bride, there is her dishwasher to take into consideration.'

'And there was I,' said Lorna, 'thinking I was marrying a

dishwasher. Mine clapped out ten days ago. Does that rule me out of the marriage stakes? I can't bear the idea of your having chapped hands, dear – I'll treat you to a pair of rubber gloves as a wedding present.'

Eventually, the meal finished, the table was cleared and after thanking Jake and Martha for their several kindnesses, Daniel set off for the Bethdan leaving Lorna in their care until they felt like going home to the vicarage.

Daniel was just about to close the door behind him when Martha fired a parting shot. 'Oh Daniel,' she said, 'we should have told you earlier, but with all this excitement today we never got round to it. We think we've found a cottage at Middinside – vacant possession and all that. Something else for you to ponder as you drive over the moors to Skipton. You won't need to put up with us for very long after all.'

'*Deo gratias*,' sang out Jake as the front door closed.

'I'm by no means certain what I should be thanking God for,' said Daniel to himself as he set off along the road to Skipton. 'In the words of a song that comes to mind, "What a difference a day makes – only twenty-four hours!" I'd better write it all down in the diary, in strict chronological order, before I forget what a roller-coaster of a ride I seem to have hitched.'

Somewhere between Tupshorne and Skipton, on the cross-moorland road near to where he had come off Moll the motorbike in the middle of one night the previous February, he pulled off and proceeded to log the events of his last twenty-four hours, both waking and sleeping.

Beginning with Jake's farewell lunch, he realized immediately that he would run out of diary space long before he could record, even in the briefest detail, all the events that had occurred. The solution to the problem was to be found in Tottie's glove locker – an old exercise book which he used to record fuel stops, trip mileages between fill-ups and distances covered from Tupshorne to various destinations in Great Britain.

He began again.

1) Jake's Farewell Lunch.
2) John insists on making his confession to "Father" Jacob.

3) Walk with Lorna ends in bethrothal. Surely not L's perfume. How trite my poem sounded after such an interval since written. A sprained ankle threw us together.
4) Much ribbing on return to vicarage for tea.
5) Lorna's damaged ankle prevents her driving back to Bethdan. Bethan's room brought into use again.
6) A disturbed night. Vivid dreams involving Albert. Lorna distressed by sound of siren.
7) L slips in shower, hurts arm and needs hospital check.
8) Bert Alderwood tells me about fire at Saint M's.
9) John is found dead, and Bags with pups beside him. Take her home.
10) Inspect church fire damage. Secrete a bowie knife.
11) Visit Violet. She wishes Church Hall had been burnt down.
12) Jake produces casserole for tea. Martha brings flowers for L and uses Bethan's crystal water jug to display them.
13) Amusing antics of three dogs and seven pups.
14) Fetch L's clothes from Bethdan.

His log was up to date in the matter of the bare bones only and certain of the entries would need fleshing out. Life was becoming very complicated and he could as yet detect no simple outcome to a bright future.

Damnit's personal crystal ball was aswirl with clouds of many colours.

CHAPTER XL

Ignipotens: Scintillae

THE TASK OF STUFFING Lorna's clothes and other personal belongings into the single, highly capacious suitcase which he located on the top berth of the main cabin took no longer than ten minutes and Damnit found himself back at High Ash just before ten o'clock.

The washing-up was done and dried.

'You've been quick,' said Lorna. 'Am I to presume that you just threw everything into the case, sat on it and then drove home as fast as Tottie would go?'

'Sort of,' replied Daniel, 'except that I was quite surprised that you travelled so light. I was always under the impression that, for starters, women liked to pack everything. Shows how much I know about such things, but then, as a bachelor, I might be excused my ignorance. I hope I haven't missed anything in my haste but I did make an effort to keep the clothing flat. I'll go and hang up what needs hanging up before I come and sit down. Can I get you anything while I'm on my feet?'

'A nightcap would be nice. I'll be off to bed very shortly. The day's happenings have caught up with me.'

'Your usual dram of Glenmorangie suit?' asked Daniel.

'A double would suit better,' said Lorna. 'My aches and pains require the anodyne element – one tot for the ankle and t'other for the arm. Please!'

'I'll bring you the bottle – then you can say, "when",' chuckled Daniel as he left the sitting room.

A short time later they were discussing the various merits of malt whiskies in general and Glenmorangie in particular, when Lorna raised the subject of the crystal water jug masquerading as a flower vase. 'Your story reminded me of the time that Matthew and I took Douglas, our lad, – I suppose he was about thirteen – to a wildlife park. We'd done the rounds, to the point of near exhaustion, on a really hot sunny day, when on making our way back to the carpark, as we spotted our car the one parked next to it burst into flames. I'd never seen Matthew move so fast. We were only about thirty or so yards away and as he leapt, or should I say sprinted, into action he shouted to me and Douglas to shelter behind the nearest tree. To coin a phrase, he'd sized up the situation in a flash. Ignition key already in hand, he opened our car door, flung himself inside and within moments had driven clear of the burning car before it exploded, showering lighted fuel and debris all over the place. In hindsight, he admitted later that he had been stupid but lucky. I agreed, but secretly I knew that fortune truly had favoured the brave. Douglas obviously thought his dad a hero, in marked contrast to what the fire brigade and police had to say when we made our statement. "Jammy so-and-so," was the mildest epithet I heard. Fortunately nobody was hurt, and with our car out of the way the one in flames was isolated to the extent that the burning fuel fell short of any other on the carpark. The police told us the opinion of the chief fire officer was that it was almost certain that the cause of the initial fire which first caught our attention was a bottle of lemonade resting on the fascia. The sun had done the rest. Matthew had managed to get clear before the fuel tank went up.'

'What a drama for a teenage witness,' said Daniel. 'When Martha's flowers are over I think I'd better scrap that jug. After the second occasion on which it set fire to the placemat I took the trouble to take a file and carefully score a mark in the glass at the vital water level at which the sun appeared to trigger off ignition. I should have chucked it then instead of wasting my time scratching the wretched thing. Maybe I should paint it black. No! It's a pity, but it's got to go. Playing with fire is not in my regulation bag of tricks and I'm not renowned for my sentimentality.'

'Don't be too hasty, dear!' ventured Lorna. 'Sleep on it, – and I don't mean the jug. You might think differently in the morning.'

Lorna was right. By breakfast time the next day Daniel had changed his mind but not in the manner that she might have expected. It was to be Albert Prince who put him straight.

As Daniel spread marmalade on his slice of buttered toast, he already knew that dangerously secreted away at the bottom of his so called bag of tricks was a latent flicker of flame, courtesy of mighty Vulcan, the god of fire and forge.

CHAPTER XLI

Vis Somnii

Once he had shepherded Lorna safely to bed Daniel had attended to the dogs' overnight needs before settling down himself with a final dram and pondering on the dramas of the day. Time after time, without any prompting of which he was aware, his thoughts returned to his chat with Violet and her vehemently expressed wish that the church hall should have burned down – not the church. He trusted her instincts as much as her acumen as treasurer when dealing with the financial affairs of the church of Saint Michael the Archangel, Tupshorne.

He took Violet's problem of the antiquated church hall to bed with him and, light out, head on the pillow, he applied his mind to solving it. Which direction should he take he asked himself. What would Albert Prince have made of it all? Albert. As he recalled his dream of yesternight when Albert had said that if needed he would always be found outside the seventh bedroom, he retraced his steps to that country house at which Lorna had been acting as the property guide. No sign of her. The front door was exactly as he remembered it except that, unlike the previous day, there was no trace of the massive knocker and in its place was an inscription, crudely carved into the oak, which read, "Knock. It shall be opened unto you. Abandon hope, all ye who enter." Do I detect the hand of my joker in the pack, Albert, thought Daniel with a wry smile as he clenched his fist to hammer on the door. The door anticipated the blow and opened noiselessly as if loath to bruise the knuckles of any potential buyer. He stepped inside, strode across the parquet floor of the hall and ran up the broad staircase two steps at a time as if he was fifty years younger.

Outside bedroom seven there was no sign of Albert – only a bunch of newly-cut keys lying on the carpet of the passage, shining in a shaft of sunlight. The master locksmith could not be far away.

Damnit called out. 'Albert, where art thou?' in as jocular a manner as he could muster. 'I'm not here to play hide and seek. Let's be having you!'

One of the keys from the bunch resting on the floor at his feet suddenly detached itself from the ring and, like an arrow, flew through the air to embed itself in the keyhole of the doorlock of bedroom seven. The remaining keys seemed to melt away and disappear into the carpet as if sucked up by a sponge. That is strange, thought Damnit; the last time I was here meeting Albert that door was fitted with a combination padlock that required my little bit of personal magic to unravel; now it's a normal rimlock. The key flashed on and off like a neon sign, suggestive of red for danger and tempting him to unlock the door. As he stretched out his hand towards the glowing key, it turned of its own accord and simultaneously the doorknob also turned as if gripped by an unknown hand. The door opened wide to reveal Albert who was walking away from the anvil, still positioned where it had been previously, and approaching him through the smoke emanating from a process not connected with the furnace. Daniel could make out the misshapen form of Vulcan who was intent on watching another figure at work close to the anvil. It was obvious that the new shadowy being was giving a demonstration to the God of Fire and Forge. John Smith looked up over Vulcan's shoulder and, with the broadest of grins, called out, 'Just giving my old friend here a tutorial on arc welding, Damnit. Put your goggles on – you might learn something as well.'

He backed out through the doorway followed by the advancing Albert who, once they were both safely in the passage outside the bedroom, slammed the door shut with such force that Daniel feared for the hinges. In confrontational mode Albert addressed him. 'What about my ashes, Daniel? You've done sweet nothing so far.'

'Steady on, Albert,' replied Daniel in a reproachful tone. 'If you know that, then you must know why and you must know what kind of day I've had. Pretty hellish.'

'Just trying your patience, Daniel. Perhaps my sense of humour has altered or your perception of it, at least. Of course I know what you've been up to – a knowledge confirmed by my conversation with John since he arrived in bedroom seven. Vulcan's tickled pink, I can tell you, with the opportunity to catch up with some state of the art technology. If you call back again in a month or two, I reckon

John will have built a tractor for his godship.' He paused for thought. 'You've lost no time coming to see me again, lad. Is there a little problem to be sorted out? Are you thinking of robbing the Bank of England, for instance? I can help, you know, if that's what you're planning – but only if the cash goes to charity.'

'No, no,' laughed Damnit. 'I'm not that daft! Our church treasurer thinks our old church hall is a liability, so much so that she would like to rebuild it to modern standards of safety and hygiene. I suspect she had demolition in mind. Any ideas, O Master?'

It was Albert's turn to laugh. 'You already have the answer, Daniel – in triplicate.' He began to fade away even as he was speaking. 'I'm running out of time right now.' His voice started to break up like the sound of a mobile phone out of area and his final audible words were but a whisper. 'Look to Job. Chapter five. Verse seven.'

The air in the passage suddenly became chilly and Daniel gave a shiver of discomfort as he recognized that his interview with Albert had been terminated. He shivered again as he turned round, intent on quitting the mansion as quickly as he could.

In his sleep Daniel shivered and turned over in his bed. The cool night air of late September was playing on the small of his back where the duvet which covered him had slipped off, revealing a vulnerable gap of skin between pyjama top and bottom. He awoke with a start, gathered the duvet round him again and promptly returned to the Land of Nod, without any plan to visit a potential change of address.

Waking up bright and early next morning Daniel recalled Albert's final words of dismissal and before putting the kettle on for Lorna's cup of tea he took his tattered old bible from the bookcase, finding his way to Job. The pages of Job were not as well thumbed as many of the other books in his bible, largely because he found no pleasure in gloating over Job's afflictions even if he did end up with umpteen thousand head of sheep, camels, oxen and she-asses. Turning up Job, chapter five, he was astounded to discover that the seventh verse had already been highlighted in red by a hand unknown. There's something supernatural going on here – I'm getting out of my depth, he thought. The words leapt off the page and burned their way into his consciousness. He read what Albert wanted him to read. "Yet man is born unto trouble, as the sparks fly upwards." "In triplicate," had been Albert's words, when asked for an answer to the poser of how to deal with the question of the church hall. He looked again at the verse under his gaze. The red highlighting was gone and as he inwardly cursed the stupidity of his own over-worked imagination verse seven disappeared also. As he blinked in sheer disbelief so did chapter five vanish altogether. The book in his hand was becoming heavier by the second, and hot. He snapped it shut for fear of searing his hands and, as if breaking a spell, it dropped to the floor. Ignoring the disturbing beat of his heart, with a supreme effort to return to reality he bent down to retrieve the Bible and was relieved to find it cool to his touch; its weight was restored to normality and turning to Job, chapter five, verse seven, the printed page was perfect. With a sigh of satisfaction he sat down in an easy chair and tapped the Bible several times with his finger-tips as if congratulating it on coming up with the answer to his problem. He was suddenly reminded of the wisdom of his first school headmaster, the Reverend Samuel Bone. Sambo never tired of telling all his boys that the Holy Bible held the answer to everything if only they would take the trouble to look into it – with due dili-gence. Sambo was right. Albert was right. Job was right, even if it meant trouble.

Daniel chuckled to himself. Three wise men – a conspiracy to pro-vide an answer in triplicate. He put the kettle on, attended to Sprottle, Baggins and her pups, and took a cup of tea to Lorna.

'Would your ladyship care for me to run a bath for her?' enquired Daniel mischievously.

'I think not,' replied Lorna with mock *hauteur*. 'Breakfast in bed takes precedence. Fresh ground coffee, two and a half pieces of toast, English butter and Scottish marmalade. Oh! And a selection of the daily newspapers.' She collapsed in a fit of giggles at her own effron-tery, almost spilling the cup of tea which Daniel had handed to her.

He smiled at her indulgently. 'You'll have to be satisfied with the Telegraph, old girl. But seriously now – would you like your break-fast in bed?'

'Certainly not! My aches and pains seem much easier this morn-ing. I'll see you at table in twenty minutes. O.K.?'

'O.K. We can breakfast in the kitchen. By the way – I'm sure the pups have doubled in size overnight. You must have a look at them after we've eaten and we can settle on their names. It's early yet, but

I have a feeling I'm in for a busy day, one way or another. Let's hope it won't be quite as dramatic as yesterday. Top of my list of priorities has to be the not inconsiderable figure of John. It seems dreadful that I've hardly given him a second thought since the ambulance men removed his body from the field. Of one thing I am sure – his passing must be classed as having taken place in suspicious circumstances because, a pound to a penny, the bowie knife that I picked up – out of the long grass round the quiet end of the church – belonged to him.'

Over breakfast he explained to Lorna how John had come into possession of the potentially lethal, certainly illegal knife. Furthermore, he told her that he would not be handing it to the police. In the same way that John had taken the heavy clasp-knife from his father's corpse at the Siege of Stalingrad – a true story that Damnit was privy to – so did the bowie knife pass into his ownership. The covert sign of Daniel's deviousness was not lost on Lorna, causing a flicker of apprehension concerning the secretive nature of the man she was taking as a second husband. Perhaps she did not know him as well as she thought she did. She pushed the disturbing idea to the back of her mind as being unworthy of her, a self-confessed excellent judge of a man. Paramount in her thinking was the conviction, warmly comforting in every way, that the man she was going to marry had loved her longer than any other she had ever known.

After washing the few items of breakfast crockery, Daniel left them to air-dry in the rack on the draining board. Then he enquired of Lorna if she would be comfortable, left to her own devices for the morning while he set about getting some semblance of order into the pattern of his everyday life, so fundamentally disrupted by the arrival and now the departure of Big John. She assured him that she was perfectly capable of tending to all the dogs' needs since it was clear that they ranked ahead of her although he couldn't say so to her face.

Daniel leant over to kiss her, as she sat in her chair, murmuring important sweet nothings in her ear such as "I shall return at one o'clock, fish and chips in hand." The telephone rang. The caller was Martha, inviting herself to lunch with Jake in tow carrying a picnic hamper filled with vicarage goodies.

CHAPTER XLII

Vir Sapit qui Pauca Loquitur

TUESDAY, THE THIRD of October, had dawned clear in Tupshorne but with a heavy blanket of mist overlaying the river Yowe in the dale below the town as Damnit departed High Ash for his first destination of the day – his local police station. He wanted to know what the law had to say about the manner of John's passing, hoping against hope that the whole issue might be cut, dried and simplified because some spark of insight or intuition was warning him that the final act in the drama "Janis Kalējs – His Life and Times," would need a suitable epilogue, with a part for him.

The only information he could glean from the duty officer was that since the death had occurred in suspicious circumstances there was certain to be a coroner's inquest involving forensic testing to determine the cause. The results should be known by the end of the week, when, if nothing too dreadful had been revealed, the body would be released for disposal – presumed to be a simple cremation.

Daniel asked the officer if it would be in order for him to use the police station telephone to contact Henry Stint, his solicitor, whom he knew to be in possession of the will which John had drafted shortly after his arrival in Tupshorne just over a fortnight earlier. Permission granted, it was only a matter of minutes before Damnit found himself in Henry's office facing the solicitor across his broad-topped desk.

Having ascertained over the telephone Daniel's reason for visiting – Henry knew already of John's sudden death – he greeted him with a statement that brought him to a halt with a jolt. 'John Smith left you a letter, Daniel, with his last will and testament which is lodged with me. I haven't the faintest idea what he has written except to say that it constitutes quite a bulky envelope. Would you like it now?'

'I'd rather know what's in the will first, if that is possible or
permissible before an inquest, which appears to be inevitable from
my earlier visit this morning to the police station. It's not that I have
any expectations by way of being a beneficiary – I doubt I'm even
mentioned and that's how I would prefer it – but there may be a
veiled message there which only I can interpret. Nobody could tell
a tale like John could, and I would not be surprised if he had used
his will as an excuse to introduce a little fantasy into a dry document!'

'I'm sorry to disappoint you, Daniel. You're letting your imagination run away with you. Regardless of any law or protocol
regarding the release of the terms of a will ahead of a coroner's
inquest, I can tell you that this particular dry document as you call
it, is one of the shortest, most cut and dried I've ever prepared.'
Henry smiled. 'It's that dry, you might say it's as dull as ditch-water
and in it there is no mention of one Daniel Greensward of this
parish. As a fishing man, I would say that you are off the hook without having to wriggle. So, if you are looking for a story to occupy
your leisure time, methinks it is in the envelope. At this stage I can't
be of any further help to you unless John mentions me in his letter
to you, in which case I am at your service. I repeat, "Would you like
it now?"'

'I have a horrible feeling that I would be wise to say "No",'
replied Daniel, with a sigh of resignation. 'But if I refuse to accept
the letter, I won't be able to look Baggins in the eye ever again. She's
– was – John's dog and it looks as if while he was dying she was
whelping. Ironic, isn't it? I've inherited Bags and seven little black
beauties. A sweet legacy from one of the greatest men I've ever
known. Yes. I'm ready to read what I must.'

The solicitor rang his personal secretary and asked her to bring
John's letter through to his office.

As Henry Stint handed the letter over to Daniel he made an
important observation. 'Just a few words of warning, Daniel. In my
experience – and you know I can, in all modesty, lay claim to
nearly fifty years of it – when a man makes a brief will and leaves
a letter with it then that letter can be a revelation not always welcome to its recipient. Read it very carefully as you would the small
print on the bottom of a contract. There is no copy anywhere in our
files and I personally have no idea as to its content; yet as the will

is so tersely brief, the letter in your hand is, judging by its weight alone, the longest of its kind – that is in my experience! So that's that, except to reiterate if there's anything legal to unravel that's beyond a simple mechanic's comprehension I'm no more than a phone call away.'

'Thanks, Henry. Whatever happens, I'll keep you in the picture. No doubt this letter will provide more than one topic of conversation suitable for the dining table. And on the subject of food, after I'm married you'd better bring Susan for a bite of supper sometime.'

'You! Married?' snorted Henry. 'Pigs might fly!'

'They will. They will,' beamed Damnit, 'Probably in June next year. I don't know where just yet but Jake's laid on for the ceremony, and consider yourself and Susan to be invited as of now.'

'Well, I'm lost for words – unusual for a man in my profession. Congratulations to you and ...'

'Lorna.' Daniel completed Henry's sentence. 'We've known each other since our Cambridge days. But more of this anon. I must dash now and study this missive you've kept for me. Thanks again.' He took his leave of Henry and, once in Tottie drove down to the banks of the Yowe where a wooden bench occupied a spot overlooking a bend in the river as it flowed by. Apart from his church of Saint Michael the Archangel in Tupshorne, the old riverside seat was his favourite place for serene contemplation. The early morning mist had lifted as the sun strengthened.

He sat down and thought for a few moments before opening John's final letter to him. He was not disappointed. As Henry had suggested, it may not have been written by Saint John the Divine, but as representing John Smith's last words to a friend the letter was truly the revelation he had prayed for. As in John's confession to the Reverend Jacob Drake, he lifted the curtain shrouding every important detail of his life previously unknown to the reader. It was significant that the personal letter predated the confession by nearly two weeks and in the space of those few days in John's long life he had changed.

Damnit read out loud. There was nobody near to hear him as John's opening salutation recalled immediately the manner in which when a little boy of eight he had earned his nickname of Damnit.

John must have smiled as he began to write, knowing that with just two words as so spoken, he would grab Daniel's attention:

"Damnit Man!

If this letter of mine ever reaches you, then I will be beyond your reach, having travelled from my cradle to my grave. If you never receive it, then I will have seen you to your grave. Yet, in my own mind, I am confident that you have it in your hand right now.

I have a premonition that my destiny precludes my ever setting foot on continental Europe again. I may be wrong – in which case you may cheerfully disregard this letter, John's last epistle! In a nutshell, if I make it over the North Sea and die somewhere there, – say my own country or one I have yet to walk across – then I will be its problem, not yours. That leaves just Baggins the Beautiful to be considered. If this letter takes a long time to reach you, Bags may have been assigned to a new master and be happily settled with him, (or her) or she may have been put down, God forbid! In which case, Amen. However, should you be reading this shortly after I have died, Bags is yours if you want her but you will have to take the necessary steps to claim her, quarantine her and bring her to High Ash. I know she would be happy in Tupshorne with her Uncle Damnit. As for me – I couldn't care less! Perhaps I should say, I'll be past caring!

In some sort of a more perfect world I would like to be buried alongside my father outside Stalingrad where I dug his grave. Even after almost sixty years, I know I could find the exact spot, so vividly does the memory live on. Perhaps the farmstead there has been built on by now and his remains scattered to the four winds. Who knows? And no one would have been able to identify his body anyway because, as you know, I kept his personal effects and his dog tags, one of which adorns Baggins' dog collar. So Stalingrad is out and if the authorities that find me wish to feed me to the lions in the nearest zoo, again I say AMEN.

However ... my dear friend for so much of my life – if my premonition is correct, things are different and Baggins will still be this side of the North Sea. I leave her, Ferrers my super shovel, my Pregnant, my giant backpack and its contents, AND ME to you to dispose of as you wish. I shall be in no position to argue. Our mutual solicitor, Mr Stint, will take care of the arrangements concerning the disposal of my estate. Consult with him if necessary – I know you value his friendship as well as his legal expertise.

It seems odd, after all these years, we have never discussed a life here-after. Maybe we recognized that our beliefs on such matters were diametrically opposed and so not open to argument. I wonder. It must be as a result of my experiences of war in all its vicious horror and brutality that I cannot discern the hand of a good and loving God at work in my life since the SS took away my innocence. It seems to me that there is a case to be made for the existence of two Gods and one is called the Devil, perhaps referred to in Trinidadian parlance as De Evil One, responsible for the pain and terror which Creation endures. So make no effort please to hand over my remains to the tender mercy of any God, lest I end up in the ever-lasting arms of the wrong one. If I have a soul, set it free of my human frame by letting me be consumed by fire. That done, I ask of you one last favour. I lay on you the duty of strewing my ashes under the chestnut tree we planted at the National Blacksmiths' Museum. I'm sure that will put a smile on the portrait of Vulcan, hanging in the foyer. No doubt you can remember people's reaction when the Museum opened – the question, open-mouthed, Who is that? when first seeing the God of Fire and Forge. After you've scattered what puff of dust I'm reduced to, the visitors will look at the painting and say, Whoever that chap is in the picture, I wish he'd share the joke with me. It should make a good pub sign for The Jolly Blacksmith. Don't ask anyone – just do it."

The mood of the letter changed at this point as John chose to discard his mixture of facts and facetiousness.

"Since we first met, Daniel, we have shared some hairy, scary moments and more than a few secrets. Now that my mortal coil has been shuffled off, as the Prince of Denmark might have said, I think it right that you should know why I decided to walk home to Latvia toting Pregnant, the biggest pack you ever saw, topped with Ferrers, the massive shovel, and spurning the shelter of anything better than a roofless, ruined barn. (Except for the time you lured me onto the Bethdan when I was at a physical low ebb without any resistance to the dreaded drink you plied me with!) You know that it was Eleanore Bormann who suggested that I should go home. I'm not sure that I ever told you why I had been so devoted to her and her family since my early months in the SS. If not, then it was because it was my guilty secret, established in the most bizarre circumstances. To be brief, I killed her husband Heino during a routine bit of harmless barrack-room horseplay. He hurt me, quite accidentally of course, so I picked him up and threw him through a window. Death must have been instantaneous and,

on my part, absolutely unintentional. No SS man ever messed with me after that – I had earned my nickname, Janis der Jähzorn, or in your language, John, The Fiery Temper. (I'd rather have been called Damnit.) The incident went down in SS records as an "accident in training" but I, in my own chivalrous, naïve mind – I was, after all, only in my mid-teens at the time – decided to call on the man's widow in an attempt to explain how the tragedy had come about and to express my personal remorse. I was quite prepared to face any verbal or physical abuse which Eleanore might have thrown at me. However unlucky had been the accident to Heino, the guilt I felt was unbearable – it is, even today. Ready as I was for an onslaught, I was totally undone by the beauty who opened the door to me, listened to my pathetic self-introduction as a comrade of her late husband and then, without an opportunity for me to say why I was there, led me across her sitting room to a low table on which was displayed the citation for valour awarded on the battlefield where he lost his life. The SS had lied to her and so the truth was locked away in my heart for ever – or so I thought. I stayed with her for several days and, like a foolish youth, fell in love with her, her little girl and the unborn son she was carrying. War can make a man so cruelly vulnerable in so many ways. I'm sure you will understand that along with the guilt I carried, so my love would have to remain buried. But we remained truly loving friends from that time, corresponding over the years more like brother and sister than lover and lass with a heigh and a ho and heigh nonny no. Shakespeare would have made a fine tragedy out of such an unlikely plot. You already know that from that impossible, implausible start I had always sent her gifts of money to help with her family finances – no questions asked. Somehow the arrangement worked and in some small way my conscience was salved until, after fifty-eight years, FIFTY-EIGHT, (can you believe it?) the inevitable happened when she encountered another SS man who had been party to the rough-house brawl in which Heino had died. He remembered Janis der Jähzorn, that giant Latvian, all too vividly. Our friendship was smashed in a flash of enlightenment and, although she understood why I had done what I had done for her and her family for so long, I should think of her as dead. Then she told me it was time I went back to Latvia, on foot. She was never to know how hard the SS tried to frustrate my search for her. Yet I'm still glad I found her.

If this letter ever gets to you, you will know how far I have travelled to my journey's end.

But I carry a double burden of guilt on my shoulders like a heavy yoke.

Once again, you already know my rather unlikely tale of how I buried my father in the countryside outside Stalingrad. That story was gospel. In short, I fell over his body and then buried it. In an artist's terms, what I told you was only a part of a much bigger picture altogether, which I will now endeavour to reveal to you – a picture tucked away in the cellars of my mind since I uttered a brief prayer over my father's grave. Those were the days, I suppose, when there must have been a good God looking out for me, guarding my every step.

Going back further in the story of my life, again you know how I was forcibly conscripted into the SS after witnessing the cold-blooded murder of my Uncle Zigrids by a Scharfschütze, a sniper, while we were all lined up in the village street. The senior officer of the conscription unit was, I still think even now, appalled by the target practice perpetrated by his sniper comrade whom he named as Lutz, and promised that in due course he would be disciplined for his crime. Some hope, or fat chance you might say nowadays! The officer was trained to play by the rules, however unfair they may have been: whereas Lutz, a trigger-happy, sadistic sniper crack-shot recognized no rule book and considered himself to be above the law and untouchable. He was never punished."

At this point in his letter John tried to explain rather than excuse the strange manner in which he himself took to life in the SS as a fifteen year old conscript – how he gloried in the iron discipline and power of the brotherhood. He had been adopted into the SS family when at an age ready to respond to the challenge of men already in the prime of manhood. When the SS hierarchy told him that he was part of the most fearsomely efficient warrior force the world had ever known, he believed it. It had taken a few years for him to understand that the Death's Head emblem of the SS was no fancy insignia. The letters D E A T H on an SS officer's cap would have said it all. The murderous activities of the Allgemeine SS were the antithesis of any imaginary crusading zeal exhibited by the Waffen SS. A brutal war may have produced an untold number of heroes, yet the idea of war itself was an invention of the devil – unheroic in the extreme.

The letter continued:

"I made it my business to find out the name of the murderer of Uncle Zigrids – not so much out of any desire for revenge, although there must have been that element present in my thinking. No, part of my intention

was concerned with self-preservation in that I would not want to cross the path of such an undoubted psychopath if I could avoid it. He was called Ludwig Kaltmann – a small, insignificant man with the kind of beady eye one might expect of the holder of medals for shooting at the Berlin Olympic Games of 1936. I was to meet him once again at Stalingrad in the guise of my senior officer, still a small man but now dedicated to discipline – you might say he had become a "proper little Hitler!"

What follows now, as I look back, reminds me of the grand tale of David and Goliath except that in this case I was the giant, armed with a humble shovel, while little Kaltmann had the drop on me with a Luger revolver. He knew that I was a Latvian and I knew that he hated having to look up to me when issuing orders. His record relating to service in Latvia was never open to inspection and I chose to follow my own wise counsel, not disclosing the name of my home village and certainly never mentioning how my uncle was picked off by some sniper just known as Lutz. The one and only time he managed to talk down to me was when he found me standing in the trench which I was digging out to provide a grave for my father's body using a heavy iron shovel I had found in the ruined buildings of the farmstead nearby. Hard at work, about four feet down, I was unaware of Kaltmann's stealthy approach until he spoke. He asked precisely what was I doing. The ensuing conversation seems surrealistic even now. I was at his mercy if he wished to dispose of me in a classic case of 'He dug his own grave.'

I replied that I was digging a grave for the soldier's body which he could see lying the other side of the pile of earth which I had dug out already.

He pointed out that I was going against orders. After the removal of any identification all our dead were to be left for the Russians to bury. It was demeaning for the mighty SS to bother about corpses. Then he enquired, with a steely note of sarcasm, why I had chosen to disobey strict orders.

At that point I was beginning to get emotionally upset, searching for the right German words to express the mental turmoil in which I had become embroiled. I tried to explain that the corpse was that of my father whom I had not seen since the two of us had been "grabbed" from our little village in Latvia and conscripted into the SS. Surely he could understand that I could not leave my father's body for the Russians to abuse – as they most surely would have done.

He didn't understand. In chilling tones he ordered me to fill the hole again – immediately.

I reminded him of my nickname, Janis der Jähzorn, first of all, before suggesting that it might be unwise to try to stop me in my sad task – "a matter of family honour" were my precise words.

Kaltmann still appeared to be oblivious to my increasing agitation because he responded by pouring scorn on my supposed reputation and then coolly informed me that the SS was my family. Was I threatening him, he asked.

In the brief time we had been confronting each other – perhaps I should say talking up and down, me in the grave, he above me – I was becoming chilled after my digging exertions. To defy an officer in the SS, I well knew, was asking for instant execution. Nevertheless, I invited him to try to force me to fill in the hole.

As I recall now, Kaltmann smiled – almost gleefully. He was actually beginning to enjoy himself. He pointed to the Luger at his belt, indicating without any question that he had me at his mercy but this would not be a moment for such a nicety. His smile hid the murderous intent behind his sniper's eyes.

I was now in a mood to give genuine substance to the myth of just how I earned my nickname. My skin was cold and clammy, my mind was stone-cold but in my heart I was incandescent with rage, (one of my favourite English phrases – a supercliché). "Furious" doesn't begin to describe how I felt.

I'm sorry to be so longwinded about this, but I have a compunction to dredge up the details of such a climactic, definitive event in my early life which has been a burden of guilt ever since. I think I will feel purged when I have finished the outpouring of my secret to somebody after all these years. They say that's what friends are for!!

So, – slowly lifting the iron shovel up and out of the grave, I insulted him, pooh-poohing his pathetic show of strength with the revolver and calmly telling him I'd pull him to pieces with my bare hands and, being kind, I'd save him (or the bits of him!) from the busy Russian gravediggers by dropping him in with my father.

Even in the gloom, at last I detected a flicker of fear in those killer's eyes. But I had driven him too far already. I tried to suggest we should forget what had transpired; he could let me bury my dead and no more said. He could even join me in prayer over the grave. Then I made a mistake, revealing my own weakness; – I said (again my exact words, so clear to this day) "I take no pleasure in killing."

There was to be no going back. The fear in his eyes gave way to blind rage as he made his move. The Luger was hardly clear of its holster before that massive heavy shovel scythed through the gap between us as I swung it with all my furious might. It nearly cut Kaltmann off at the knees and he pitched forward into the grave beside me. A wild shot from the revolver passed through the material of my right trouser leg, furrowing the calf muscle but in all the excitement I scarcely felt it. My Uncle Zigrid's murderer lay crippled at my feet and his Luger had gone flying. I finished him off. My rage died with him as I buried him with father but it was only the dying light which intervened to prevent me from tearing him limb from limb as I had promised. Pragmatism finally won the day.

And so, my friend, you will now understand why I undertook my last walk home the hard way, carrying my heavy shovel on my back and with a Luger revolver at the bottom of my pack. I didn't mean to kill either Heinrich Bormann or Ludwig Kaltmann. Heino's death was purely accidental; the assassin got what he deserved only because he aroused my fury in self-defence. But still I am confused, knowing now that by attempting to punish myself I have not succeeded in washing away the blood guilt which has stained my life since my teens. I am beyond redemption.

Now I am gone, it matters not who knows what I have told you in this letter and perhaps Max Herrick, who has a collection of my stories to publish sometime, should be aware of its contents. He could never tell the difference between fact and fiction when he was recording my tales, so you can safely tell him now, that Eleanore is still alive, (I think) and Scharfschütze Lutz is very dead.

On re-reading what I have written so far, I appear to be going round in circles. Old age I suppose!

In summary, perhaps Ferrers should return to Aidan who made most of the implement under my instruction.

Pregnant can go back to the makers for archive material if they would like it.

Keep the Luger if you can – it is not licensed and the safety catch is OFF – and isn't it lucky for you that my boots are your size!

As for Baggins – brush up your Latvian dog commands! She never appreciated having to learn English. She's a remarkable dog and now she's yours.

Given one wish, it would be for an after-life where we would meet again, tune our beautiful engines, play the glorious Summer game, and together with our dogs walk the high hills of the Lake District. That's five wishes –

five slices of pie in the sky. I'm getting maudlin, damnit! My innings is over. Is there a God somewhere to catch me?

P.S. If you feel I may have missed mentioning something of importance in this letter of explanation – use your imagination. See you in your dreams. J.

P.P.S. Of course, I knew who Lutz Kaltman was when I killed him – even if in my own self-defence. For preference, I should like him to have known that this son of Arvids had avenged the cold-blooded murder of Zigrids, his uncle, the brother of Arvids. But he never was to know. At least I did see fear of me present there in his killer's eyes before my Russian Ferrers cut him down. In bullfighting terms, it was a clean kill – more than he derserved.

Now you will understand the importance of Ferrers in my life. If I live to write my life story, it will be titled 'Shovel on my Back'. J."

CHAPTER XLIII

Tempus Omnia Revelat

D ANIEL LOOKED AT HIS wrist-watch. Lunchtime was not far away. He had never found reading John's handwriting an easy task and this final epistle was no different from the usual but, as he approached the final page, increasing familiarity with the script brought about a greater degree of fluency. His second sight-reading though took only a fraction of the time his first struggle had taken, leaving him some time to ponder the content of the letter and decide how to interpret the information unveiled. His first notion was to destroy the letter and tell Henry Stint that it was of no significance despite its bulk.

It was the postscript that brought him back to reality. John actually <u>knew</u> that he would see him in his dreams and, sure enough, last night he had appeared in Vulcan's forge along with Albert Prince. Albert wanted his ashes dropped into the volcano that is Mount Etna and now John wanted his ashes to be spread like fertilizer under the chestnut tree at the N.B.M., a commission he could not ignore. John's last wishes would be carried out to the best of his ability and to the letter. Any arrangements he might have to make would be simple.

Cremate, spread ashes, disperse personal effects to nominated people and take care of Baggins.

A cloud passed over the sun, the sudden chill breaking his reverie. He rose to his feet from his seat and strolled over to Tottie. Five minutes later he walked in through the front doorway of High Ash to be greeted by Sprottle, full of exuberant enthusiasm at the sight of him.

'Steady on, girl,' were his first words to her as he bent over to fondle her ears. Next came Bindle with a rather more sedate welcome but still vying with Sprot for his close attention. Daniel luxuriated in the sensation of warm fur running between his fingers and smiled with pleasure at the thought that in a few weeks' time he would be welcomed by a rushing, tumbling septet of boisterous black pups, probably piddling all over the parquet floor in the excitement of seeing him.

'Thank goodness you've arrived at last,' said Martha, coming out of the kitchen wearing one of his rather fetching aprons depicting Adam clad in nothing other than a fig leaf – a last Christmas gift from Bethan before her death. 'We thought either we'd have to start lunch without you or share out your portion between us. Better get sat down and explain what you've been up to!'

Over lunch Daniel recounted his doings of the morning from his initial visit to the police station to the reading of John's farewell letter. Acknowledging that the missing chapters of John's life were now to enter the public domain, he summarized the paragraphs as he told their story, eliciting various sharp comments from the two women particularly with regard to the part played by Eleanore. Jake said nothing until Daniel read a sentence of four words, "I am beyond redemption," at which point he exploded.

'What arrant nonsense, Damnit. Redemption is for everyone, and John was no exception. He achieved that state of grace with his confession and my pronouncement of absolution, Sunday afternoon, two days ago. One hears about "secrets of the confessional" being sacrosanct – absolutely right – but his letter to you, so obviously meant for public consumption, was echoed almost verbatim in his confession, so you have come out with nothing I didn't already know. However,' and at this point Jake paused for dramatic effect before repeating, 'however, he went to meet his Maker, a confessed Christian and not an agnostic. As his final priest-confessor, I feel it incumbent upon me to insist on a proper Christian burial for him.'

'O.K. O.K.' said Daniel hastily. 'Simmer down, as we used to say. John didn't ask to be buried, but to be "consumed by fire." His own words – so clear it is almost as if he was asking me to light the fire under him. So a cremation it will have to be. As his final confessor, Father Jacob, I think you'd better be forthcoming rather than retiring and we'll give him a proper Christian send-off. I suppose you'll need to ask the bishop before getting your robes out of pawn.'

'Oh really, Daniel,' said Martha. 'His robes are at the dry-cleaners right now. Jake's already preparing himself for the celebrity circuit, being a visiting preacher or a dogsbody with dog-collar. They say the money's good! I mean, just because my husband has retired is no excuse for a reduction in my dress allowance.'

'And there was I, thinking I'd get his services for free,' smiled Daniel. 'Don't worry. If I'm to be in charge, I'll make sure he's on double time and then we'll pass the hat round at the close of play when the curtain comes down or across as it does at the crem. Can't have Martha driving round Tupshorne playing Lady Godiva.'

'I've no objection to that,' said Jake, 'In this day and age. She's still a fine specimen of womanhood!'

'I've always admired your imagination, dear,' commented Martha, 'and it's so much more vivid when the light is poor.'

Lorna joined in the hilarity. 'It reminds me of my last year at school. The drama mistress wrote a comic sketch entitled "Lady Godiva – Learner Driver" which included a starring role for a pantomime horse, which was permanently out of control and doubly incontinent. The horse was of a Trojan breed – a wood frame on wheels, pushed around the stage by the two sturdy lads hidden by the caparison. I suppose, for its time, and in a school scenario, it was distinctly *avant-garde*. The core of the plot, as I rather vaguely recall it now, was that, if any poor burgher of Coventry was short of fuel or food or water, Lady G was despatched by her hard-hearted husband to deliver the goods on his behalf on her horse. You can imagine what it was like inside the horse – shelves of packets of tea, lumps of coal, bottles of water, bread rolls, china eggs and, of course, the obligatory black puddings. No prizes for guessing the item that brought the house down but rest assured that Lady Godiva, dressed in her body-stocking, was no match for a clutch of award-winning Bury black puddings, even if she was played by little me!'

'You never acted at Cambridge,' said Jake. 'If you had, I'd have known about it. That sketch would have gone down a bomb in a Footlights Revue.'

'It was no more than a bit of farce, really. Great fun, but not likely to cause me to wonder if I was Lady Macbeth material. Singing was more in my line.'

'You used to give a fair rendition of Edith Piaf,' chipped in Daniel. ' "*Non, je ne regrette rien*" was a favourite of mine – that was until we split up. Then it became just so much *eau sous le pont* as they say in Avignon.' He paused, then 'How have we managed to get from the crem to the stage in a few sentences?'

'It was your snide remark about my clerical robes being in pawn,' replied Jake. 'As a matter of fact, I thought I ought to clean up my act in case you seriously expected me to officiate at your wedding, whenever that might be.' He addressed Lorna. 'Don't make him wait too long, Lorna. He's past his "sell by" date.'

She looked at Daniel. 'I wondered if June would suit you, dear. June – honeymoon – and all that jazz.'

Damnit's brain switched into overdrive even as he spoke. The way ahead was becoming clearer by the moment. 'I don't suppose you have spoken to Douglas in Nigeria yet to tell him of your momentous decision to marry this not so young man.'

'I'm plucking up the courage before I give him such a pleasant surprise,' said Lorna. 'As a matter of fact, I meant to do it sooner but I missed the time-slot yesterday. When it's two o'clock here, it's the same in Nigeria so I'll wait for the next window in his working day. He'll enjoy giving me away – I think! Hold on! I've suddenly remembered. He's in Brunei for two weeks, on business, and I don't have a contact telephone number for him because he usually phones me on a Sunday evening anyway. There's probably a message waiting for me on my answering machine. He'll find out sometime.'

'I've a phone call to make as well,' Damnit said. 'All this talk of disposal of human ashes reminds me I've got to ring Albert's solicitor.'

'What on earth for?' asked Jake. 'I thought your obligations in that direction finished when you arranged the acquisition of Albert's locksmith's collection by the National Museum of Engineering. So what now?'

'It's just that I had a dream about Albert in which he stated that his ashes hadn't been dealt with. I think you knew he wanted his ashes dropped into Mount Etna. That task was down to his solicitor, Kevin Orison, to arrange. Don't laugh. I had a second dream, the night after the first one, and Albert asked me why I'd done nothing about it. So you see – I must check it out before he haunts me again.'

'Steady on, lad,' said Jake, as Lorna and Martha looked on with some measure of disbelief at what they were hearing. 'I suspect you're in danger of playing with fire here – supernatural fire. Best leave well alone!'

'You know I can't do that,' replied Daniel. 'After two dreams on successive nights, both starring Albert, I have no alternative open to me, other than to find out if there has been a dereliction of duty on the part of Orison and Company.'

'Don't hang about then if your mind's made up,' retorted Jake. 'Ring Orisons now and put an end to this nonsense. I think you've been either taking too many of your vitamin supplements or the distillers have altered the formula of your usual nightcap.'

'Most kind of you,' observed Daniel acidly. 'Perhaps you would care to place the call. After all, you do deal with the supernatural all the time.'

'Now you two,' interjected Martha with a hint of exasperation, 'I'm not used to hearing you being so sharp with each other. Stop it! Before Lorna thinks she's making a mistake.' The last remark was uttered with a warning glance directed at Daniel.

'Kiss and make up,' suggested Lorna, quietly, 'Before a superior force knocks your heads together. As they say in Avignon, *pas devant les chiens, mes enfants*.'

The tension dissipated immediately as Daniel and Jake looked at each other slightly sheepishly before breaking into laughter.

Lorna and Martha smiled at their men and each other. With a few gentle words they had made them feel foolish but not stupid. Even so, the die was cast – what had been said could not be unsaid and there was a telephone call waiting to be made.

It took Daniel less than two minutes to find the telephone number of Orisons solicitors amongst his papers concerning the arrangements for Albert's funeral the previous February. He rang the Cambridge number to be answered by the Orisons' receptionist who in reply to his request to speak to Kevin Orison put him through to Kevin's secretary without querying the nature of his business. Could he possibly speak to Mr Orison? asked Daniel.

'I'm very sorry, Mr Greensward,' answered Kevin's secretary, 'Mr Orison is still on sick leave after his operation. Can I be of any assistance or perhaps one of the partners ...?'

'I had no idea,' said Daniel. 'I do hope he's making a good recovery and will soon be back at his desk.'

'I understand he's making good progress now, thank you, and all being well we expect him back by Christmas. It's been a long haul for him, and not always easy for us to maintain "business as usual." But perhaps I can answer your enquiry.'

'I think you very probably can,' replied Daniel and posed his question about the whereabouts of Albert's ashes.

'That's easily answered, Mr Greensward. The tiny casket reached us shortly after the cremation and has been in our vault ever since. It had been Mr Kevin's intention to take the casket to Sicily himself and I feel sure he will in due course.'

Daniel paused before his next statement. 'Leave that to me, if you please. I expect to be visiting Sicily sometime next year and I would be privileged to carry out Albert Prince's last instructions. He regarded me as the son he never had. Could you arrange such a transfer for me with authorization from one of the other partners? I'm coming down to Cambridge in a week or two and could collect the casket and a letter of permission. It would be one item less for Mr Kevin to worry about when he returns.'

'Do you want an answer now, Mr Greensward?'

'Well, if it's not too much trouble.'

'If you could hold for a minute, I'll put your offer to one of Mr Kevin's associates here.'

'That's fine,' replied Daniel. 'I'll wait. There's no rush.' It seemed within two shakes of a cat's tail, the secretary was back on the line with a spoken approval for his plans, and the promise of a letter of confirmation in the post within forty-eight hours.

'Thank you so much,' said Daniel. 'Mine will not be the only mind to be put at rest. I'm much obliged. Please give my best wishes to Mr Kevin for his speedy recovery.' And he replaced the handset in its cradle. Jake was the first of Daniel's three listeners to break silence by asking, not without a note of cynicism, a very pointed question. 'So how are you going to notify Albert of your cosy little arrangement? Don't tell me you're going to consult a medium. It's not your scene. Churchwardens do not play such games.'

'Worry not, my old friend. Until this moment you were not to know that I can control my dreams – it has to be a kind of self-hypnosis, a skill only recently acquired. Occasionally I need to interpret what goes on as best I can – and I can make mistakes. I will say no more on the subject except that I know I'll find Albert outside bedroom number seven. You, as a sometime actor of good repute, will appreciate Hamlet's words, "There are more things in heaven and earth, Horatio, than are dreamt of in your philosophy."'

Lorna spoke next. 'I know we're supposed to be going to Cambridge in search of a ring but I wasn't aware that you were off to Sicily next year. Did you just make that up?'

'On the spur of the moment, my dear! I'm told that Sicily in June can be delightfully warm and sunny – and, as you mentioned a few minutes ago, in the words of the well known song, honeymoon rhymes. So your suggestion of June for our nuptials seems ideal and if Sicily appeals we can deal with Albert's ashes at the same time. Two birds – one stone.'

Martha spluttered with restrained indignation. 'Daniel, you're a romantic dead loss. Surely you don't expect your bride to help you with that kind of chore while on honeymoon? It seems a bit morbid to me.'

'No. It's quite all right by me, Martha. I suggested June originally so maybe the choice of honeymoon destination should be the groom's. In fact, it might be appropriate, in a strange way, for us both to be involved. No doubt you knew that Daniel and I had to break into Albert's cottage where we found his body. I had only met him comparatively recently – long enough in my acquaintanceship to put him on my list of "lovely men I have known." So, if June's O.K. by you, Daniel, I'm quite happy with Sicily – or maybe you would like to bring our wedding forward and placate Albert's shade a bit sooner.'

There was a sudden hush in the room as Lorna, Jake and Martha waited on Daniel's reply. He appeared to be pondering over the matter of timing with inordinate concentration before he came out with his answer.

'June will be perfect for my plans, thank you. Just perfect.' For a moment, his mask had slipped.

Jake swallowed as if he had a pill stuck in his throat. Puzzled, he asked Damnit which plans he was talking about.

'Naughty, naughty,' chuckled Damnit not very convincingly. 'I always thought that bridegrooms had plans which were ever so secret and not to be divulged – at least not until the honeymoon. Nice try, Jake.'

Now it was Lorna's turn to look pensive. 'Be careful, Daniel,' warned Martha. 'Don't try to be too clever. As you know, we married in a January. Our honeymoon destination was Jake's secret. Even you didn't share it. All he would tell me was to pack some smart, warm clothes. We had a wonderful holiday in northern Scotland – that was once I had recovered from the disappointment of missing out on the skiing I had been looking forward to. We're still married. Just one more miracle you can believe in!'

Thoughtfully Jake stroked his chin between the thumb and fore-finger of his left hand. He was well aware that Damnit had answered his question about tentative plans for a June wedding with a highly questionable reason. The words from the bidding-prayer before the general confession at matins came to mind. "Dearly beloved brethren, the Scripture moveth us in sundry places to acknowledge and confess our manifold sins and wickedness; and that we should not dissemble nor cloke them before the face of Almighty God." Daniel Tiltstone Greensward was both dissembling and cloaking something or other but Jake had not the foggiest idea what that something was, and he opted to let the matter drop. Sooner or later, he thought, Damnit's mask would slip again and, if his wedding plans were designed to obscure a hidden agenda, a few careless words might reveal what his devious friend was up to. Time would tell.

CHAPTER XLIV

Nec Scire Fas Est Omnia

TWO WEEKS TO THE DAY following John's death the coroner produced his report. It was timed to coincide with the publication
of the results of the enquiry by the Fire Service into the fire at the
church of Saint Michael the Archangel.

The cause of John's death was stated to be heart failure, exacer-
bated by smoke inhalation. The task of the investigating forensic
scientist was simplified greatly when, secreted away in a pocket of
Pregnant, John's enormous rucksack, the police found a sealed letter addressed to John's general practitioner in Preston from a certain
consultant physician, one Mr Nathaniel Ross. On enquiry from the
coroner as to how an unopened letter addressed to his GP had been
found in John's personal effects, the doctor explained how it had
been seized from under his nose while he was writing up the case
notes of a previous patient by John himself. The situation had its
comic aspect, wrote the doctor. As I was completing my notes, he
spied the letter on my desk, asked if it was the report on his health
from Mr Ross and, when I said it was, he grabbed it, saying he
couldn't stop to discuss its contents, he didn't want to know what
was in it and didn't want to waste any more of my time. His last
word as he went out of my surgery was "shalom". I fancy he had
learnt it from Mr Ross. The doctor's final paragraph gave his authorization to the coroner to open Mr Ross's letter and, as a postscript,
added that John Smith was possibly the most incredible man he had
ever met.

The coroner studied most carefully Mr Ross's medical report on
the health of Mr John Smith before submitting a précis to forensics.
In brief, the medical examination revealed that, for his age, John was
in excellent health in all respects bar one. Cardiac investigations had
thrown up an indication of a minor heart flaw which was only
barely detectable by the most state of the art equipment. The condition was almost certainly congenital but considering the size of
John's frame and the fact that he had reached his then age of

seventy-three there seemed to be no reason why he shouldn't live to be a hundred. Such longevity, however, could not be guaranteed in the body of a regular smoker and if put under unusual stress the heart might decide to burn out without triggering an alarm. Death would be rapid.

The report from the Fire Department stated that the cellar of the church had been broken into by the use of a levering implement which had forcibly dragged out the screws of the plate which secured the staple to the door jamb. The fire had been started by the intruder, a smoker, who very conveniently had relinquished his little gadget for handrolling his own cigarettes. There appeared to be a chance that, whoever the culprit was, he or she had attempted to stamp out the fire, which in all probability was purely accidental, before leaving the scene. It would have been simple for a small draught entering under the door, which had been dragged to, to re-ignite even the tiniest live ember. If such had been the case, then the person who tried to stamp out the burning straw would have shoes and trousers covered with soot and smuts.

John's almost new boots, boots which would fit Damnit's feet, bore witness to the accuracy of the fire investigator's report. They were smothered in smuts and the rest of his clothing stank of smoke. The bowie knife that Daniel had hidden away from prying eyes was not needed to establish the fact that John had been there, so close to the church cellar that night.

Thus did the story of John's passing speak for itself and the sole witness was safely cocooned in her own world of silence as she suckled her litter of seven demanding puppies. If it hadn't been for Baggins alertness, they would all have been burned alive – and she knew it!

PART 2

CHAPTER XLV

Laudate Dominum

DANIEL TILTSTONE GREENSWARD, churchwarden of the church of Saint Michael the Archangel in Tupshorne, reviewed the current situation in his parish and after further consultation with Timothy Welsh summoned the parochial church council to an emergency meeting to discuss the fire in the cellar – the only item on the agenda.

The meeting took place in the church hall a week after the publication of the coroner's report. Earlier the same day, Monday the 23rd of October, Daniel, Jake, Martha and Lorna had attended John's cremation at the Darlington crematorium. Daniel, as requested in John's farewell letter, made all the necessary arrangements, with the help of the Tupshorne Funeral Services Company and Jake officiated in his capacity as John's final father confessor.

Timothy Welsh, as chairman in the absence of any priest-in-charge, called the meeting to order and, after a short prayer asking for God's blessing on their deliberations, asked Violet to brief them all on the financial situation with regard to the fire damage in the church.

During the three weeks which had elapsed since the fire Violet had taken the opportunity to study in depth the relationship between Saint Michael the Archangel and Matthew, patron saint of tax collectors, and Saint Benedict, patron saint of speleologists. The A.I.C. recognized that Saint Benedict was the saint most likely to help you should you, as the insured, find yourself in a hole. Violet was delighted to be able to report that Michael, Matthew and Benedict were "in cahoots" – so much so that, barring a reasonable excess clause in the insurance policy, the A.I.C. would foot the bill for repairs.

Hardly had the PCC uttered a collective sigh of relief before Violet, choosing to ignore the fact that there was no provision for widening the agenda, startled all except Daniel by saying how she wished that the fire had occurred in the church hall cellar, below where they were seated. Uninterrupted, she pressed on. 'This dump needs gutting and rebuilding with all mod. cons. to satisfy the welter of new regulations coming out of the Health and Safety Executive. A sort of Gunpowder Plot ought to do the trick quite nicely and there's much more timber in the construction here, where we are convening, than in the church. I'm rather sorry that your lovely friend picked the wrong cellar, Daniel.'

Freda Alderwood chimed in. 'You've made me feel uneasy, Violet. I hope there's no one in the cellar right now, listening to you and chuckling as he lights the touch paper. But surely we raised enough money from Jake Drake's Appeal, over and above what was needed for the church improvements, toilets et cetera, to make a decent job of the hall as well.'

'Sorry. It's not on,' replied Violet. 'I've checked out all options for the spending of the Appeal money and the powers that be at diocesan HQ stated, quite categorically as they say nowadays, it must be reserved for the fabric of the church. "Non-negotiable," was the term used. Gold-plated taps in the new church loos – yes. New loos in the hall – no.'

Daniel entered the discussion. 'Freda, as church hall co-ordinator, do you know off-hand what bookings you might already have for next June? It's just that when I come back from my honeymoon I'll need a project to get my teeth into – at least to keep me out of my bride's hair for a day or two while she settles in as chatelaine at High Ash. Even a decent lick of paint would work wonders in sprucing up the sparkling welcome we aspire to give those clubs which frequent the hall on a regular basis. It would be a statement of our intent to update the facilities, and paint isn't expensive. Provide me with a set of brushes and a roller and I'll guarantee to liven up the décor. Doubtless, I'll have help.' The final remark was made with an obvious nod at Bert Alderwood and Timothy Welsh.

'As a matter of fact,' said Freda, 'June is always a quiet month in the Church Hall year – what with folk on holiday and so much open air activity in the evenings. I'm confident that we have no midday bookings and if the Circle Dancing Club meet on a fine evening they will go through their paces *al fresco* in the church grounds.'

'If the place is empty for most of June,' said Bert, 'maybe you should hold your wedding bun fight here, Daniel; in which case we'll paint it in May, specially for the happy couple. I'm sure Freda would negotiate a special hire rate for a churchwarden.'

'Not a bad idea, Bert,' replied Daniel, 'but I quite expect that Lorna will wish to be married at her own local church in Cambridge. I can ask her, of course. The question of where we will live after our wedding has yet to be faced. We have some difficult choices to make. I do, however, promise to paint the hall sometime in late June, if you all agree. And, what is more, I'll buy the paint. The whole job will take a few gallons, working on the premise that two coats are better than one.'

'Thank you,' said Timothy. 'That all sounds pretty straightforward to me and I know you won't be short of help.' He paused. 'Can we just backtrack to the sole item on the agenda? We have been most fortunate, to say the least, that the fire only caused minimum structural damage. Our own attempts at clearing up the mess, so much of which was superficial, have been very successful. The hole in the cellar ceiling has been temporarily secured with a heavy iron plate, a brand new boiler for the central heating system will be in place by the end of next week and will have a facility for providing hot water. In discussion with the heating engineer Daniel and I were taken with the idea that the new boiler would be far more efficient and economical if the four inch cast iron piping was to be replaced by a small bore system which would, together with a modern circulating pump, provide a "rapid response" when extra warmth is needed. We would need to check with the diocesan authority but I don't believe we would have to apply for a faculty to replace like for like. In which case, next year we can change the piping and pay for it out of our appeal fund – that is if we are all agreed on the matter.'

It was agreed.

Daniel has something to say before we close this meeting,' said Bert. 'It's personal!'

'That's right,' said Damnit. 'I've located a stonemason in Wensleydale who is up to recreating or rather rebuilding my great-great-grandfather's brainchild, the Tiltstone. He reckons that because the stone block split into two simple chunks of rock he can drill holes in each piece and pin them together again, using steel rods and a modern adhesive. He made it sound quite easy – that was when he'd discovered that the locking mechanism had survived intact. Something of a miracle, I think. The second personal item on my plate is that I, or I should say Saint Michael's, will be acquiring a new lawnmower. The dirty black cloud in the cellar has turned out to have a silver lining. One final piece of information. The fire officer's report was, as expected, submitted to the Almighty Insurance Company who now state, in an updated clause of the policy document, that no fuel of any kind – be it coal, wood, kerosene, petrol et cetera may be stored in the church cellar. They insist that the lawnmower, when not in use, should be kept in the church hall cellar and be drained of petrol. This will mean that I shall have to keep the petrol at High Ash – but that's no problem to me. Up until this unhappy incident, I've always, without fail, drained the petrol tank and taken the fuel home. It must have been written in the stars that the only time I haven't drained the tank, it was John who provided the distraction. If I had carried out my regular routine, perhaps all this mess might not have happened.'

Daniel gave an involuntary shudder before looking at the mystified faces of his fellow PCC members. Then he spoke again, visibly emotionally upset.

'I've only this moment realized that because of my failure to empty that fuel tank I've brought fire and death on my own head. God forgive me!'

Time seemed to stand still and the silence in the room was palpable for a few moments, before the PCC drew a collective breath. Timothy Welsh broke the spell by removing his tobacco pipe from his mouth, where it had rested, unlit, since his opening remarks, and slapping it down on the table in front of him, he began quite grandiloquently, 'My dear Damnit, don't talk nonsense. I'm the pipesmoker, not you; and it was neither you nor I having a peaceful puff in the cellar – it was John with his hand-rolled cigarettes; and the autopsy revealed that it was his heart defect, aggravated by smoke inhalation, which caused his death. So let's have no more of this blaming yourself.' And without allowing any further discussion he brought the meeting to a close with a brief valedictory prayer. Until he reached out a hand to pick up his pipe, he was unaware that in slamming it down on the table he had broken the stem in two.

Daniel watched as Timothy gathered up the pieces before remarking, 'Looks as if Muriel will need to buy you a new dummy for Christmas, Timothy.'

Timothy smiled. 'It's my birthday Tuesday, next week – who needs Christmas? That was my favourite pipe as well, but if smashing it knocked a bit of commonsense into your thick skull, then so be it.'

'Amen to that,' replied Daniel. 'Leave the choice of pipe to me. See you on your birthday.'

CHAPTER XLVI

Tredecim. Septem. Novem.
Tres Numeri Optimi

AFTER BREAKFAST the next day, the 24th of October, Damnit consulted his next year's diary for 2001. He never considered himself to be superstitious and looked upon thirteen as a prime lucky number. After all, he reasoned, a baker's dozen has to be a blessing and he recalled somebody, in his schooldays, assuring him that thirteen was a fisherman's lucky number. Of a naturally optimistic bent, he didn't bother to ask why. Seven, he regarded as a lucky number in all respects – only trumped by number nine. Being on cloud nine meant happiness and nine months was the miraculous period of human gestation. The plan which was forming and firming up in his mind would reach fruition nine months from the date of the fire – and he would be enjoying his honeymoon if everything went according to plan. The portents were good. After all, it had taken just about nine months for Saint Michael's to raise the remarkable sum of fifty-three thousand pounds.

By the beginning of June 2001 Damnit's diary was very full. The written word told a story of a church repaired, restored and improved, a romance being pursued to the altar, a growing legend of the giant tramp and the dog that he left behind. Yet the real thread of Damnit's life went deliberately unrecorded – there was never a mention of the Church Hall until the last day of May when "Buy paint for C.H." was the only entry.

CHAPTER XLVII

Aurum

LORNA RECOVERED FROM her injuries more quickly than the hospital doctors had given her to expect and, together with Daniel, returned to her Cambridge home whence a visit to that selfsame jeweller's shop, which had sold him the first engagement ring so many years earlier now yielded a ring of Lorna's choice. It fitted perfectly!

'While we are here,' said Daniel, pursing his lips, 'why don't we buy the wedding ring as well. As a Yorkshireman I'm always on the lookout for a discounted bargain. "Two for the price of one," always appeals to me.'

'I don't come that cheap, Daniel,' retorted Lorna. 'I'm more of a valuable antique than a moulting old bird.' Then she laughed. 'How about me buying a wedding ring for you and we can try for "buy two and get one free?"'

'Being serious for a moment,' said Daniel, 'I seem to recall that you used to be a trifle superstitious once upon a time. Is there anything in the realms of superstition that says "Thou shalt not purchase thy wedding ring until one lunar month before the marriage – or marital strife shall befall thee?'

'Not that I am aware of,' said Lorna. 'But it would not surprise me in the least if there was. May I suggest that we get round such an idea by selecting two rings and asking our favourite jeweller here to reserve them until next June. Even if a small deposit is requested, I feel sure any possible superstition would not be disturbed.' Then, as with one voice, they said, 'And bang goes any hope of "buy two and get ..."' Their words tailed off as they recognized a remarkable piece of unplanned synchronization and they broke into laughter.

The jeweller, a soul of discretion in such an intimate discussion, had failed to catch the humorous banter concerning bargain deals but picked up on the subject of superstition. He assured the pair that a seventy-five percent deposit would guarantee the reservation of any purchase for as long as they wanted, without infringing any superstitious beliefs.

Daniel was too happy to quibble and half an hour later two gold rings had disappeared from the limelight of the counter to be hidden in the darkness of the jeweller's strong-room. The jeweller guaranteed a full refund in the event that the rings might not be required. Daniel of the White Rose was impressed.

That same evening of the day they had settled the business of the wedding rings Daniel entertained Lorna to dinner at Fenlanders. In the candlelight, seated at the sequestered corner table in the restaurant, he reminded Lorna of the times they had dined together at the same table over forty years earlier. 'Regardless of our different paths followed in those intervening years, I am so glad to have lived long enough to be able to say "Darling Lorna, marry me."'

Lorna smiled at him across the little gap that separated them and proffered her left hand across the tablecloth to allow Daniel to slip the engagement ring on the appropriate finger. 'As a motor engineer, Daniel, you will understand what I mean when I say that your timing is perfect. Of course, taking into account your first intended but never uttered proposal when a student, this is your third appeal to my better nature. You know I love you. Third time lucky! I'm yours.'

Once home at Lorna's house, they talked long into the night. Somehow, during her convalescence at High Ash with many an opportunity for working out their wedding plans, the right moment never seemed to present itself. Daniel put it down to his concerns over John's death rather than the firesplit Tiltstone and his new acquired family of black labradors. By the time they were ready and tired enough to go to bed they had settled all the wedding details except for the recipe for the wedding cake.

Daniel kept notes in tabular form as they went along for fear they might forget a single important fact. Lorna led the way, comfortable in the knowledge that she had travelled the same road with another man.

The list read: WEDDING

1) When? *11 o'clock. Saturday 2nd June 2001.*
2) Where? *Lorna's church of the Holy Cross, Cambridge.*
3) Who to officiate? *Jake together with the vicar of H.C.*
4) To give the bride away? *Douglas (back from Nigeria, we hope.)*

5) Bridesmaids? *No.*
6) Best Man? *Jake.*
7) Reception? *If available, the Wheatear Hotel at Gorrington, close to Albert Prince's old cottage. Failing that try Fenlanders.*
8) Honeymoon? *Two weeks on Sicily. (Remember to take A.P.'s ashes.)*

Breakfasting late after their discussions of the previous night, Daniel, in all innocence, accidentally upset Lorna's emotional apple-cart. Recalling the humorous angle of buying three rings at one go, he was quite suddenly moved to ask, in a quiet aside, what Lorna had done with the rings relating to her marriage to Matthew.

Lorna nearly let her coffee cup slip from her fingers – caught in the act of raising it to her lips. Angry in an instant, she calmly replaced the cup in its saucer before answering the question. Quite innocently Daniel had touched her on the raw but even such an affable character as he was unprepared for the sheer bitterness of her reply, delivered in a classic sentence of four words.

'Mind your own business.'

Daniel recoiled as if bitten or stung, and for a few moments the atmosphere at the breakfast table was supercharged with a chill silence. "What have I done?" he asked of himself, before *"Aequam servare mentem"* swam into his consciousness. "Panic not," was ever his favourite maxim. In all the years of their long acquaintance, even at the time of their broken student romance, they had never once exchanged harsh words. At some point in the intervening years between then and now Lorna must have been wounded, quite how he knew not, but the residual scar must have been formed comparatively recently and was still tender. This was no time to be confrontational for fear of aggravating the situation. He elected to take a hurt, slightly humorous approach in an attempt to defuse a potential explosion. Taking a deep breath, he spoke almost in a whisper as if talking to the angry Baggins guarding her pups.

'Steady on, Old Girl. It's Daniel at your breakfast table – not a stranger. I really didn't mean to pry, you know. To upset you was never in my mind. The loving memories that you have of Matthew have never come between us – that is, until now. If something has changed, please tell me. I'm the world's best listener.'

Lorna's heightened colour had receded in the short space of time since her flare-up. Yet there was still more than a hint of defiance in her tone as she replied. She spoke quickly. 'If you must know – I sold them! What's more, I cleared everything of Matthew's out of this house that reminded me of him within days of his death. Everything except articles in which Douglas might have had an interest – and I would have scrapped those as well if I could. Fortunately, he intervened before I had completed the job. The only item I kept was my favourite wedding photograph which sits on my bedside table. So now you know.'

She laid her forearms on the table and buried her face there. Her shoulders began to shudder and Daniel realized that she was sobbing. Rising from his chair, he walked the few feet round the table which separated them, knelt down on her right and putting an arm round her shoulders drew her head into the hollow space between his left shoulder and the upper part of his chest, close to his heart.

'Carry on, my love. I know there's more to tell.'

'You would not understand, Daniel. I felt so crushed and so utterly bereft. Nobody and nothing appeared to ease the pain I was going through! In some strange kind of way, Matthew's spirit was around still but unable to comfort me. It was as if I had to go it alone, without his help. That was when I decided to erase all evidence of his previous physical existence and depend on the happy memories in my head to keep me sane. I was wrong and I had made a catastrophic mistake. Yet no one, except Douglas, either thought or perhaps dared to question my actions. A grief-stricken woman is difficult to deal with – I see that now. It took nine months to regain my equilibrium and until now to acknowledge to another human what a fool I had been.'

Lorna paused for a moment before turning her head to look at Daniel. Until then, she had been talking into his chest. 'I don't expect you to understand – you're a man, after all.' She reached out a hand for her table napkin and used it to dry her tears. She smiled shyly. 'The rings had lost all meaning and most of their value. They didn't fetch much either. Served me right. It never occurred to me I was creating space for another ring or two.'

Daniel sensed that she had unburdened herself with as honest an explanation as he would ever hear and he chose his next words with care.

'This may surprise you, but I do understand – and perfectly. My sister, Bethan, went through precisely the same experience after her husband, Gerald, died in 1990, with the exception that they had no "Douglas," and I, still taking things easy after my heart attack, was in no position to be of much help in that, what you might call, property department. She too kept just the one wedding photograph which you will have seen when using her old quarters at High Ash. That photo also features my parents which may explain why it wasn't burnt with the rest. Apparently she had quite some bonfire at the time. Gerald was a gifted amateur artist, revelling in oils, and selling quite a number over the years – mostly commissioned by pet owners wishing to have a permanent reminder of their pet in its prime. The point is, after Gerald's death she burned all his artists materials, his easel and every painting he had left in the house, hung and unhung. The lot. Sheer vandalism of course! Nine months later she was wondering if she could work up the courage to approach even one of Gerald's pet-painting owners with a view to buying back a puss or pooch picture. By that time I was in a strong enough frame of mind to dissuade her. As I sit here with you at your kitchen table, so did Bethan sit with me at my kitchen table at High Ash ten years ago. I suppose there's a lesson in all this for me. Perhaps it's "Don't bother with wedding photos." And while we are on the subject, please don't do anything silly with that photo of you with Matthew. I'm sure we can find a place of honour for it at High Ash after our wedding.'

Lorna's customary good humour had returned and with a quizzical tilt of one eyebrow she enquired mischievously, 'Who, may I ask, has decreed that I should leave Cambridge for Yowesdale?'

'Oh dear,' said Daniel. 'I think I may be guilty of presumption or taking something for granted. It never occurred to me that you might want to stay on here while I carry on at High Ash.'

Lorna gave a chuckle. 'As a matter of fact, I've not given it a thought until now. You know how I love Cambridge – it is such a vibrant city – and yet Yowesdale, as I have come to know it with you, is also very lively in its own different but special way. How about tossing a coin to decide? That's what my father would have done.'

'I'm not for tossing a coin – I always lose,' said Daniel. 'What if we opt to live in Cambridge half the year, and Tupshorne the other half? That would mean keeping both houses which is a needless expense even if we could afford it. Maybe we should live here and treat High Ash as a holiday home – rent it out in between times.'

'No, no,' said Lorna. 'I've solved the problem. I'll sell this house as soon as I can find a buyer and live with you if you'll have me. Alter our plans to a Tupshorne wedding, still involving my vicar here, and then – a masterstroke – we can buy a small flat in Cambridge, or nearby – a *pied-à-terre* – that will hold just us and our dogs, and we can revisit our salad days whenever we like. A flat with two bedrooms is all we need, then Jake and Martha can join us if and when it suits them.'

'Absolutely, blooming brilliant!' said Daniel, with a huge sigh of relief. 'Ring the estate agent now.'

CHAPTER XLVIII

Commemoratio

L ORNA'S DECISION TO SELL her Cambridge house and move in
with Daniel at High Ash so far ahead of their proposed wedding day simplified many of the niggling little problems often
associated with preparations for the happy event. The reduction in
the frequency and the duration of telephone calls between
Cambridge and Tupshorne was only one of the benefits of getting
together as soon as possible. Lorna was aware of Daniel's intention
to paint Saint Michael's Church Hall once they had returned from
honeymoon and suggested that as she would be resident at High
Ash sooner rather than later, presuming that her house would sell
reasonably quickly, he would have plenty of time to complete the
job before the wedding. He rejected her suggestion out of hand and
was adamant that his late June appointment with the paintpot was
not up for rescheduling. She was bemused by his obduracy. All her
previous experience of his attitude to life in general had indicated
that here was a man who never put off until the morrow that which
could be done today.

Hardly had Damnit returned home from Lorna's, when he had a
telephone call from Max Herrick, the one-time schoolteacher who
had tapped John Smith's genius as a storyteller and used it as an
inspiration to his pupils via the English classroom. Damnit knew
already of Max's undertaking to produce a collection of John's stories.

Max weighed in without preamble. 'Max Herrick here, Damnit.
John Smith's favourite schoolmaster! I have a compulsion to have a
proper chat with you about him. So much has happened since we
last met at the famous farewell do.'

'Good to hear you, Max,' said Damnit. 'What can I do for you?
Do you require a foreword for the book?' He halted abruptly as if
stopped in full flow. 'Hold on, Max,' he continued, 'you must know
of John's sudden death but not necessarily of the strange circumstances in which he died.'

'That's right,' said Max. 'I'm not sure how the news reached me eventually, but I'd been on holiday – and then it took a while to track you down at home.'

'I'm glad you did,' replied Daniel. 'You've saved me the task of finding out your whereabouts. In John's last letter to me, enclosed with his will, he asked me to tell you the true story of his life – the details of which will fill in all the puzzling gaps which you must have often wondered about. When can we meet?'

'That wasn't exactly what I had in mind when I rang, but it has to happen sometime. No! How would you feel about taking part in some kind of a celebration of our friend's life?'

'Are you suggesting an opera or just a musical?' enquired Damnit with a chuckle, at his end of the telephone.

'No, no,' replied Max, echoing Damnit's shaft of humour. 'There's no star large enough to fill John's boots – never mind his character. No, I thought some kind of a thanksgiving get together – certainly not a church service, because I don't think he recognized any God. An opportunity to meet somewhere and talk about him, tell some of his tales – both tall and true – and I never could tell the difference – and remember a most remarkable man. What do you reckon?'

'I reckon,' said Daniel, slowly, 'I wish I had thought of such a tribute. It only seems like yesterday that I told him I would follow him into battle, using him as a shield. He had worked under my direction for seven years by then and was about to leave Rolls for Agri-Presto. I've never known a man like him. Oh, before I forget, he was reconciled with his God shortly before he died. He made his final confession in my church here to my great friend, Jake Drake, just a few hours after Jake had preached his last sermon before retirement. He didn't know he was about to die so soon but had come to the realization that the Christian God of his childhood had never deserted him.' Daniel paused. 'You and I have a lot to talk about and we can't do it all over the 'phone. If you've nothing better to do, how about coming up to Yowesdale and staying with me for a day or two? I may have more than one tale, personal to me, to add to your catalogue as well as explaining his reasons for returning to Latvia.'

'How about you coming here instead? You'd be very welcome. I could even show you my English Department where John had such an impact. I may be retired but there are several teachers still at the school who would remember the gentle giant.'

'Sorry, Max. No can do. John's little legacy to me includes eight dogs. Baggins, whom you would have seen at the farewell luncheon, produced seven pups the same night John died and I inherited the lot. I've just been down in Cambridge for a few days and left two friends, Timothy and Muriel, real doggy folk, in charge of my family. I can't ask them again so soon. The puppies should be off my hands in a few weeks but if sales are slow I might be tied down here well into January. It would be better if you could come here – and do bring Ro Rose Rosemary ...'

Max cut in. 'Nice try, Damnit. Rowena, I'm sure, would love to come. She's a Darley Dale girl and her father was a Crufts judge for some years – in the Gundog Section. She may well outstay her welcome if I say the words "labrador puppies".'

Max Herrick had set the ball rolling and between the pair of them he and Daniel assembled a team of players who would do justice to the conception of paying suitable tribute to John Smith of Latvia. Max and Rowena spent three days at High Ash with Daniel, thrashing out some kind of a programme of celebration. That was the easy part. Finding out who might attend was the most difficult part and Daniel solved that poser by decreeing that the National Blacksmiths' Museum should be the venue for the function, using the same marquee hire firm and catering department who had dealt with John's famous leaving luncheon. The catering side of the Museum decided to make no charge for providing tea and sandwiches after the event and Daniel persuaded Merlin Swift of Agri-Presto to share with him the hire cost of the marquee. The trump card which Daniel thought the Museum held – and he was right – was a list of the names and addresses of all those who had, at John's instigation, made donations to the Museum Endowment Fund. They would make ideal invitees, and who knows, surmised Daniel, they might even think to help the Museum once more, although it was an idea that he breathed to no-one.

Jake dropped in when Max and Damnit were talking of invitations and made a suggestion of his own, to the effect that there might be a number of people who had encountered John on his route from Preston. Some of them might wish to pay their respects – young Ben Beaumont for example and his dog, Bilbo.

'You know, Damnit,' said Jake, 'when John was walking from

parish to parish offering to dig graves and such, the various vicars gave notice to the next parish priest down the line when the giant tramp was on his way. I can reverse that system by phoning the vicar who let me know and eventually pass the info back to his Preston starting point, parish by parish. A vicars' grapevine, if you like.'

'That'll do nicely,' said Daniel. 'The vicars could let me or Max know if any of their flock might wish to join the throng. They wouldn't need to be invited officially but it would give us some rough idea of how many seats we'll need.'

Despite the efforts of Max and Damnit to drum up an attendance worthy of John's reputation, they were to be disappointed in the end that only two hundred and five people expressed an intention to put in an appearance. There was to be no Latvian presence such as there had been at John's farewell luncheon and it was too late before Damnit realized that the list of donors which he was counting on to provide numbers was limited to those whose donations were not anonymous. The majority of the benefactors were unknown. The marquee which was erected on the Museum car park was large enough to seat two hundred and twenty people.

The reunion, for such it was, of those whose lives John had touched took place on the last Friday of November, the 24th. Lorna came up from Cambridge for the weekend and with Daniel at the wheel of her Volvo and Jake with Martha sitting in the back they motored over the Pennines to the Museum. There had been a serious accident on the M6, not far from Junction 32 resulting in the Volvo arriving at the Museum only ten minutes before the scheduled start of the thanksgiving celebration. The overflow car park was close to overflowing and a crowd was milling around outside the marquee which was bursting at the seams.

It transpired that the day before the event television news had latched on to the fact that John Smith was about to be honoured in remembrance. The weather was fine and dry. The marquee was too small and every sandwich was cut into two. Teacups were in short supply but everyone was smiling.

The principal speakers were Damnit, Max, Aidan Ferrers and John's first Lincolnshire pal, Young Tom Howard. The side curtains of the marquee had been drawn back to allow everyone, inside and out, to be included in the action.

Warm good humour ruled and the light was beginning to fail before Jake sent the crowd home with a prayer of thanks for the life of John Smith, and a brief classic blessing "The Lord bless you and keep you."

On the journey back from the Museum the main topic of conversation related to the various people who had made the effort to attend the celebration of John's life. Jake was amazed to meet almost every vicar of every parish between Preston and Tupshorne.

'John must have made a huge impression on them,' said Jake. 'To hear them talk about him was as if they were telling of a visit from a prophet. At least one vicar brought his Mrs and his three "vicarage kids". He told a lovely story about John's flat refusal to eat with them in the vicarage so they took to eating occasional meals with him in the dangerously dilapidated greenhouse. He said it was well worth risking injury from falling glass to see the wonder in the children's eyes as he talked. Another chap told me a hilarious tale of how John, with Baggins, I should add, nearly frightened him to death on Christmas Eve. Apparently, he was about to open up his church and prepare for the Midnight Eucharist when, in the blackness, he got a whiff of tobacco smoke. Of course, it was John, settled for the night in the shelter of a buttress, having a last fag. The vicar invited him into the warmth of the church, together with Bags, but John wouldn't have it and had vanished without trace by the time the priest was locking up.'

'Something that struck me,' said Damnit, 'was that everybody who met John and listened to him and his stories, seemed to have a story to tell about him. Max had the brilliant idea of giving everybody in the marquee a sheet of paper inviting them, if they had an anecdote about John, to send it to him. It will go a long way to doubling the length of Max's proposed book, "John Smith – Storymaster-Supreme." By the way, I was buttonholed by Mr Beaumont, the owner of Bilbo, the dog that fathered Baggins' pups. He brought his lad, Benbo, with him. I'd been in touch with him early on about Bilbo's pedigree and such, to try and establish a sale value for the pups. There was an unwritten agreement between us that he would have the pick of the litter in lieu of any stud fee. Today he waived that right, knowing that any proceeds from the sale of the pups would be donated to the Guide Dogs for the Blind Association. Next time he threatened to charge double stud fees.

Mind you, I don't expect Bilbo will fancy a second encounter with my Baggins. She bit him for his trouble!'

Martha introduced a new note into the conversation. 'The greatest or most important thread in John's life had to be his constant devotion to Eleanore. If only the Fates had enabled him to tell her about how her husband died. I wonder if she knows of John's death.'

'I wrote to tell her,' said Daniel. 'Her final letter of "dismissal" was amongst his papers at the bottom of his rucksack when it was passed on to me after the coroner had concluded his report. So I had her address. Maybe she's moved – after all, it is eighteen months since she wrote that fateful letter. Perhaps it would be best if she doesn't find out. I don't know and in some ways I don't care. Maybe she's dead. To echo your "if only", Martha – if only she had died before learning the truth of her *mann's* death, John might still be with us. We'll never know.'

Back at High Ash in the evening, it was Lorna who picked up the only letter to arrive by the second post and it was Lorna who was able to translate. Wolfgang Bormann had written to inform Daniel that Frau Eleanore Else Bormann had gone to meet her Maker in the early hours of the second day of October. She had died in her sleep.

Daniel felt the colour drain from his face as the hair rose on the back of his neck. Then Baggins brought the puppies tumbling to greet him and Lorna. The spell was broken.

CHAPTER XLIX

Nunc Lux: Mox Nox

NEXT MORNING DAMNIT picked the infamous glass water jug off the shelf in the vase cupboard and took it to the cellar beneath the Church Hall. Built into a south facing slope, the ground floor of the hall was approached via a main entrance door in the northern elevation, while the cellar beneath had a door which faced south, downhill to the Yowe, running some six hundred yards away. The hall itself had been designed and built several years after the death of Joseph "Tiltstone" North, otherwise it might have included an example of his trademark. A trapdoor in a corner of the main room on the ground floor opened to reveal a flight of wooden stairs leading to the cellar.

Damnit's principal concern in the cellar was the external door, subject to the prevailing weather – wind, rain and the warmth of the sun. The lower two-thirds of the door were made of solid oak but the top third was glazed with six small panes of glass which at some time had been painted black on the inside surface. When the door was closed the cellar was like a black cave, unless illuminated by the single electric light bulb which dangled from a fitting in the ceiling. The light bulbs never seemed to last long before the filament broke – something Damnit put down to the heavy footfall of certain dancers when there was a knees-up in the hall overhead. The cellar was empty, essentially, except for a couple of rickety tables and three or four old wooden chairs awaiting the attention of a joiner who would have mended them if invited to do so. Tidiness was not in evidence.

Quite the ideal place to store the new lawnmower, thought Daniel. I'll use it as my maintenance department. By lunchtime the cellar was ready for an admiral's inspection, shipshape and Bristol fashion. He fetched from High Ash a selection of his superfluous gardening tools that he could keep in the cellar ready for use in the church grounds. Up until then he had always brought tools from home, carrying out any necessary work on the flowerbeds and lawns before returning the tools to the High Ash toolshed.

Damnit's tummy rumbled – a timely reminder that he should have something to eat. His final act before exiting the cellar was to pick up his Dutch hoe and, using the tip of the wooden handle, smash the top central pane of glass in the door.

An impatient Lorna was waiting for him and his lunch was on the dining table. 'You've been very busy, Daniel,' she said tartly in a tone which voiced her displeasure at his tardiness. 'Have you finished what you set out to do?'

'I'm sorry, dear. I got carried away and forgot the time. Another couple of hours should suffice. I've a small pane of glass to replace and two old tables to stabilize for want of a better term. As yet, there's no shelving in the cellar so I want to use the tables to stack stuff on when it suits me. Pity about the glass – I just happened to clout it with a hoe handle as I was leaving for lunch – in a bit of a hurry, you'll understand.'

Lorna was concerned. 'You haven't cut yourself, have you?'

'Thankfully, no. I'm more likely to do that when I cut a new pane with my glasscutter. I'll be extra careful.'

'Don't be too long please,' begged Lorna. 'You haven't forgotten that Jake and Martha are coming for an evening meal, I hope. I need you to set the table.' She paused for a moment. 'I'm glad you've got rid of that glass jug. I noticed its absence only after you'd left this morning and I had cause to go to the cupboard for a vase to display some chrysanths in. It was such a dangerously beautiful shape too.'

'Just like a woman,' said Daniel with a chuckle.

It was that same evening, having enjoyed a leisurely meal, the four friends were playing a game of Scrabble which included, inevitably, a great deal of harmless banter. Jake, unusually for him, had been having a quiet time until suddenly he cleared all his tiles in one go. On his tile rack were the letters S N E R G U M.

Jake let out a snort of delight and triumphantly laid out all seven tiles on the end of an existing word, INTER.

'How's that for sheer brilliance?' he enquired as the other three looked at his twelve-letter effort.

'Oh really, Jake. You of all people should know the plural of your word ends in an A,' said Lorna gleefully. 'We can't allow that, can we, folks?'

'Just because it's the highest score of the evening. Do I detect a challenge here to my encyclopaedic knowledge of etymology?' said Jake confidently.

'Certainly,' replied the other three, as one.

'Right,' said Jake. 'If you would care to back your challenge with a pound bet each, then I will have recourse to your Chambers dictionary, Damnit. My money says the plural of INTERREGNUM, can be either NA or NUMS.' He grinned. 'I will accept I.O.U.s!'

'All bets off!' stated Martha with a sigh. 'He obviously knows he's right and he's insufferable with it. There's no need to ask Mr Chambers.'

Jake, however, insisted on consulting the dictionary in order to reinforce his confident assertion. He would have won three pounds. The game was over.

It seemed an opportune moment for Martha to enquire of Daniel how the interregnum was going at Saint Michael's.

'We're managing all right so far,' replied Daniel. 'Christmas celebrations are all in place with one retired priest – you'll know him, Jake, Arthur Wren – taking all the services. Of course, it's far too early yet to expect any news of a possible successor to Jake. As you might expect we're all praying like mad that we don't have to wait too long.'

Jake chipped in. 'You have to realize that, where there is a hard act to follow, the bishop needs more time to find the right man.'

'Or woman,' said Lorna as she began to gather the Scrabble tiles and scoop them into their storage bag. 'By the way, I was very taken with your final sermon, Jake. Particularly the bit about the need to be wary of replacing one old devil with seven new ones. You were so right.'

'Jake's always right, dear,' said Daniel. 'He sees a devil when he shaves each morning.'

'May I continue?' said Lorna, a trifle acidly. 'My Matthew had a great friend, sadly no longer with us, who was a churchwarden in a Devon parish. A little bit of heaven on earth. After an interregnum of about a year the parish's interviewing panel settled on an Essex man whose credentials, testimonials and references proclaimed him to be so perfect that he could have written them himself. He had! He just stopped short of claiming to be able to walk on water. What is more, he was an actor who, at interview, was highly impressive. It took him less than a year to ruin that parish; it became hell on earth. They couldn't get shut of him and he knew it. Matthew's friend took a holiday in Colchester where he learned the truth. I needn't say more except to point out the wisdom of on the spot investigation. The man was a rogue elephant wearing a dog-collar. He had fooled everybody.'

'That can't be the end of the story,' queried Martha.

'What became of him? It's difficult to lift a curse.'

'I'm not sure you want to know,' said Lorna. 'It was all rather cleverly hushed up at the time but his regnum lasted a further year by which time the church was empty and broke. Thankfully, he had no immediate family. Strange thing, it was his own church that broke him. Nobody knew what reason he might have had for being up the church tower except that a camera, presumed to be his, was found there afterwards. Whatever. It appeared he had been leaning on or over the parapet when it must have crumbled. They buried him not far from where he fell. It was a nasty death for a thoroughly nasty piece of work. Apparently, one PCC member with a black sense of humour remarked that at least he jumped before he was pushed. The poor Bishop was so appalled at the callous way in which the shepherd, whom he had appointed to tend the flock, had nearly destroyed the parish – and the suspicious manner of his passing – that without waiting for a request of any kind from the PCC he insisted on re-consecrating the church and the grounds on which it was built. Believe it or not – and personally I don't – but local legend had it that, consecrated ground or not, grass never grew on that man's grave. He'd poisoned everything!'

Jake cleared his throat before speaking.

'I vaguely recall the incident being mentioned in the Church Times – a very low-key report which avoided any attempt at sensationalism. The lesson has to be, Damnit, that anyone seeking to occupy my recently vacated pew ought to be investigated by secret agents from Saint Michael's, answerable to you. If you get an interesting application from a priest in, say, Bermuda or Mauritius, you should go yourself – a holiday would do you good.'

Daniel looked serious. 'I find your story immensely sad,' he said to Lorna. 'Sad for the parish and sad for such a flawed priest. What saddens me most of all is this. Right down the line, he was, it seems, a good enough actor to hoodwink any selection panel when seeking to enter the lists of those training for the priesthood. On a lighter note, Jake – I don't think you ever climbed our church tower. Next time I'm up there, I'd better check the parapet, just in case the army missed pointing a section before they used the tower for their abseiling courses that raised all that cash for your appeal.'

'Don't bother,' said Jake. 'Your church of Saint Michael the Archangel has enough money in the bank to implement all repairs, large and small, thanks to that impassioned plea for funds by the last incumbent. And don't forget – he was something of an actor when in his prime.'

'Big 'ead,' said Daniel amicably. 'Now you've vacated our pulpit, you'll be able to join the MADS.'

'The MADS?' said Lorna, raising a quizzical eyebrow.

'It's sort of self-explanatory,' laughed Martha.

'They're a bunch of harmless lunatics – the strolling players of the Middinside Amateur Dramatic Society, specializing in farce.'

'If you fancy playing the tragedian, Jake,' Lorna enquired with a grin, 'Is there an ADS at Skipton?'

The evening was over.

CHAPTER L

Domus et Dominium

A T THE TIME OF Jake's retirement from his last parish – that of
Saint Michael the Archangel in Tupshorne – he and Martha, at
Daniel's invitation, had made arrangements to vacate the vicarage
and live at High Ash until such time as a suitable property came on
the market. Knowing how strongly Church of England tradition
demanded that a priest, on his retirement, should not remain within
his last parish, Daniel offered the Bethdan to the Drakes if they felt
they were outstaying their welcome for any reason at all. Daniel considered such strictures to be a nonsense but respected Jake's wish to
abide by the existing code.

Originally Jake and Martha expected to quit the vicarage one
week after his Farewell service, put their furniture into storage and
possibly lodge with Damnit for up to three weeks before taking to
the water on the Bethdan. They had been property hunting without
success all Summer and were becoming despondent at the prospect
of spending a Winter on a narrowboat. Then on the day of John
Smith's death they went to look over a cottage at Middinside and
their quest was at an end. The property was for sale with vacant possession and in a fine state of repair even if not all the colour schemes
were to Martha's taste.

Jake explained to the diocesan authority that completion could
take up to four weeks and requested approval or understanding of
his wish to stay in the vicarage during that period. Four weeks at
the beginning of an interregnum was neither here nor there, and
without any need to order Jake to keep a low profile he was given
a diocesan blessing to stay in the vicarage even until Christmas if
such an indulgence was needed.

Daniel was very relieved that the Drake's property situation had
been resolved so fortuitously. The High Ash accommodation would
have been bursting at the seams with four adult humans, three adult
dogs and seven fast-growing puppies. With Jake still at the vicarage
and Tim and Muriel Welsh roped in for puppy-watch duties if and

when required, he had no qualms about taking Lorna home to Cambridge when her injuries had healed.

While Lorna was resident at High Ash, Martha took every opportunity to get to know her. Daniel's culinary skills were never in the same league as those of Jake though both were tutored by Aunt Em, Daniel's mother, and while Lorna was banned from the cooking stove Martha and Jake enjoyed the run of Daniel's kitchen.

For her part, Lorna wasted no time in putting her house on the market even before she had recovered full mobility after her accident in Daniel's shower cubicle. Daniel's reputation as a man of action was matched by the manipulative skills of his bride-to-be and he revelled in the manner in which she set both of their homes in order. Initially Daniel had expected her to sell up, house and contents, bank the cash and move into his bachelor establishment. It fell to Jake to put him straight about the place of a woman in the home.

'Just tell Lorna, Damnit, that High Ash is hers to do whatever she likes with. Don't open your mouth except to say "Yes, dear – No, dear – Three bags full, dear." You'll live to thank me for my words of wisdom. Let her get on with it.'

Lorna was all discretion, gentleness and reason once she grasped that Daniel was giving her carte blanche in the property field. She asked him which pieces of High Ash furniture he held in sentimental affection – for whatever reason, and then, with his good-natured acquiescence, replaced most of the rest with her choice of furniture out of her Cambridge home. Any item surplus to requirement was sold at auction and the proceeds donated to the Daniel-Prince Bursary fund which Albert Prince had instituted at Daniel's old Cambridge college.

Lorna's house had sold by Christmas, by which time she had been resident at High Ash for over a month. The six of Baggins' pups which Daniel had decided to part with all went to "approved" homes. As agreed from the day that Baggins whelped in the shelter of John's thighs, the only dog pup went to Harold Palmer, the rambler who encountered the savage Bags guarding her pups as well as John's dead body. Daniel stipulated that the Palmers call the dog Nosh because from the very start he was always first in the puppy food-trough. Merlin Swift, as a noted breeder of labradors, was highly instrumental in finding homes for the remaining bitch pups and they were sold without recourse to any advertising. Lorna wept over each puppy as it was being collected by its new owners. Daniel had asked her to name the little bitches from the list they had compiled with the help of Martha and Jake. Butty was the first to go, quickly followed by Tiffin, Collation and Snackerooley. Coll and Snack went to the same home. But the puppy which Lorna had named Elevenses – Lev for short – went to a lady owner who insisted that Lev would be called Baggins. Daniel smiled at her as she picked Lev up and said, 'I'm sorry, but that is not good enough. For you, she will be Beautybaggins. That is what Bags' original master would have called her. Agreed?'

'Agreed,' stated Beautybaggins' new owner and Lorna shed a few extra tears over the last puppy to go. The sale of six labrador retrievers of peerless pedigree realized over three thousand pounds for the Guide Dogs for the Blind charity.

Hardly had Elevenses disappeared with her new owner before Daniel donned his thinking-cap. Perhaps, he reasoned, there was now no necessity for him to keep Rauch because, with John dead, Baggins was his dog and Lorna had her Sprottle. He put to Lorna the idea that Rauch would be one dog too many. Her answer blew his thinking cap off and away.

'Rauch is your wedding present to me, Daniel dear. I haven't had the chance to tell you – we've been so preoccupied with seeing Lev off – but the 'phone call I answered just before her new owner arrived was from Miladdo in Nigeria. His oil company have decided to bring him back to head office in London. It means that when he comes to walk me down the aisle and pass me over to you, he will already have been working in the U. K. as from next Easter. I will miss Sprot but I always knew she would return to Douglas sooner or later.'

'Oh dear,' said Daniel. 'Sprot will be awfully confused, I'm afraid. You'll need to let her down as lightly as you can. Douglas had better come and stay with us for at least a week before he takes up his new post. That way they'll reconnect quite seamlessly. So Rauch is yours, with my love. Shall I gift wrap her now?'

Lorna laughed. 'I don't think she'd appreciate it now or at wedding time. She'll be only a month off fully grown by then, if my arithmetic is right.'

Daniel looked at her thoughtfully. 'There's something more to that 'phone call. Am I right?'

She laughed again. 'You can read me like a book. This is a year for Swanns, it seems. Douglas will be bringing a new mistress for Sprottle home with him. He didn't say when he plans to marry.'

'I hope he doesn't, like me, have a forty-odd year wait to get wed. But that's marvellous news. You must have wondered occasionally if he'd ever meet the right girl.

I say – do you think she's actually Nigerian?'

'No,' said Lorna. 'She's not. Douglas didn't say very much except that she is a Lagos hospital doctor, originally from Preston, trained at Tommy's. Her father is a consultant physician called Ross. She answers to Rachel Rosenbaum, her original family name.'

'What does that mean?' asked Daniel.

'It means, dear, that you will be acquiring a stepdaughter-in-law of German extraction. No doubt you'll call her your little rose tree now I've translated for you.'

'R. R.,' mused Daniel quietly. 'You can't get better class initials than those. I can hardly wait to meet the happy pair.'

For a few moments a wall of silence materialized between them. Lorna breached it first.

'Penny for your thoughts, dear. Your brow is more ploughed than furrowed.'

'Maybe I'm jumping to conclusions or looking for a strange coincidence. I almost feel as if I already know Doctor Rachel Rosenbaum. You see, the evening I managed to lure John into spending a night on the Bethdan – I used the dreaded drink, I'm afraid, but there was no real alternative in his world and he was at a low ebb – he'd told me all about the medical examination he'd undergone before leaving on his walk home. It was one of his great tales at that time, and in his cups John could be truly unbelievable.'

And he told her of John's encounter with Mr Nathaniel Ross, born Rosenbaum, a baby not destined to be a victim of the Holocaust.

'I took it with a pinch of salt at the time. I know now that *in vino* was *veritas*. At the bottom of John's rucksack were the result and report on his health from Mr Nathaniel Ross of Preston. John never opened the sealed envelope, so he was never to know that Mr Ross had found the minute heart abnormality that eventually took him.'

'Well,' said Lorna, 'If it's true, you'll be meeting Rachel's *Vater* sometime in 2001. I hope so. By the way, talking of holocausts, what did you do with John's ashes?'

'I wondered when you might ask me that question. You know that he wished them to be scattered at the N. B. M. under the chestnut tree. It was a task he laid on me alone so I dealt with it in my own solitary way. At his memorial thanksgiving you may, at one stage, have missed me for a few minutes. I was obeying orders while there was nobody near the tree. I had mixed the ashes with the remains of John's last packet of tobacco – everything in his rucksack came to me – and took "the fertilizer", if anyone was to query my strange movements, in a paper bag. A week earlier I had asked the current museum curator to tidy up round the tree and make sure the commemorative stone plaque was free of weeds *et cetera*. All I needed to do was raise the plaque at one end and stow the paper bag with its "fertilizer" under, before releasing. The worms will have taken it all down by now. Expect large conkers next year!'

Lorna was unamused. Not for the first time, since she had agreed to marry Daniel, she was aware of a sense of unease on her part which she put down to his ability to keep or hide from her matters in which she might have had more than a passing interest. She felt the need to air her misgivings.

'I do wish you had told me at the time,' she said. 'Maybe you've been a die-hard bachelor for too long to place confidences in somebody else. I have a feeling of being excluded from your innermost thought processes and I don't like it. I hold nothing back from you and would be much happier if we could achieve a "reciprocal agreement", as they say. I deserve it.'

Daniel was somewhat taken aback at the disappointment in Lorna's tone and apologized immediately. 'I've been so used to keeping my own counsel as a crusty old bachelor. You'll have to forgive such shortcomings and I will try to amend my ways even before I end my bachelor days.'

I won't try too hard, even so, thought Damnit. A man must have some kind of a still private life. Certain items on his personal agenda were not for sharing with anyone – least of all his nearest and dearest. He vowed to tell Baggins instead.

CHAPTER LI

Somniorum Homo. Somnium!

DANIEL BEGAN TO HAVE second thoughts – very disturbing second thoughts. With the exception of Jake, he had never made a habit of confiding in anyone on the earthly side of heaven, content to be a self-contained individual without being self-centred. Was such contentment the end-product of such a long bachelorhood, he wondered? His present state of mind was not one which he could discuss with Jake. His personal problem was too close to home to involve his *alter ego*, as the Reverend Samuel Bone had referred to him when they were both little lads at High Ashes Preparatory School. That was Lent term, 1945 he mused – just a few months after Jake's mother had died in a road accident. Daniel cursed his own insularity. To approach Lorna in these circumstances and ask for <u>her</u> help was out of the question. There had to be somebody, somewhere to whom he could take his gnawing anxieties. Then, most unusually for him, he did not, as Jake surely would have done, turn to his God. He turned instead to Albert Prince – his mentor since his Varsity days who, months ago, had informed him that he could be found in bedroom number seven of Daniel's chosen country mansion.

Albert would be the one to set his mind at rest and point him in the right direction. He would pose the leading question to Albert – "Should he marry the girl of his dreams next June?"

It took all of seven days before Daniel decided to look for Albert.

The country house of his dreamland had altered since his last visit shortly after the death of John Smith, when Albert had proffered some advice to do with the future of the Saint Michael's Church Hall. The house had grown into a mansion, set in many acres of parkland. The number of rooms had remained the same; only the size of them had trebled.

Estate workers seemed to be everywhere. Gardeners were

gardening, cowmen were herding, and all doffed their caps as he arrived at the front door, to be helped out of his Rolls Royce by his chauffeur who very much resembled Colin Blunden.

It became obvious immediately that he was expected. The butler who opened the door, even before he could knock or use the bell-pull, greeted him with warm respect. 'Welcome home, sir. We have all missed you so much over the past months. Madam is waiting for you in the drawing room and afternoon tea will be only a matter of minutes. May I take your coat?'

'Thank you, Ferrers,' answered Damnit courteously as the butler eased his coat from his shoulders. 'Before I take tea, I have a strong desire to visit bedroom seven – on my own, you understand.'

'Certainly sir. I will tell Madam that you will be with her shortly. I must say, sir, what a marvellous job the builder and the decorator have done on number seven. You would not know we'd had a fire there at all. They never found the precise cause of the fire, did they, sir?'

'Apparently not, Ferrers. Act of God was the term used in the final outcome. God alone knows which god. Thank God for the Almighty Insurance Company, I say.'

Both men laughed and Daniel climbed the main staircase on his way to number seven. There was no sign of Albert in the passage outside the bedroom so Daniel stretched out a hand towards the door handle in case Albert was hiding inside. The doorway bricked up before his eyes and he found himself staring at a message, writ large in white chalk. The message said "TRY THE STABLE-YARD."

Returning to the entrance hall, he asked a mystified Ferrers to direct him to the stables. 'They are where they were when you had them built, sir,' replied Ferrers solemnly. 'The quickest route would be to go through the kitchen, out of the back door and you will see the stable-block about three hundred yards away, directly ahead of you. Should I accompany you, sir?'

'No. It's all right Ferrers, thank you. If you point me towards the kitchen, I'll be fine. Put a cosy on the teapot and assure Madam that I'll not be long.'

The butler led him to the outside kitchen door and scratching his head in puzzlement watched him set off for the stables.

Entering the stable-yard, Daniel was amazed to be confronted by three djellaba-clad men mounted on camels. He stood rooted to the spot as the camels circled slowly around him, drawing ever closer before coming to a halt. In spite of feeling intimidated by the height of the animals towering above him, he asked the riders to explain their presence in the yard.

'We are three wise bachelors from the East, arriving in response to the invitation to your wedding,' stated the nearest rider, pushing back the hood of his djellaba which until that moment had obscured his face. Albert had spoken. 'You seek my advice, as usual, Daniel. To be brief – to realize your full potential and know true happiness you <u>will</u> marry. You <u>will</u> honeymoon in Sicily where I expect you to dispose of my ashes in Mount Etna. No ifs or buts – just get on with it.'

The rider of the second camel commanded the animal to kneel, allowing him to dismount. There was no disguising the colossus that towered over Damnit as he took a step backwards as much in alarm as to avoid the camel reaching out to bite his thigh. The voice of John Smith with all its gloriously grating gutturals issued from the hooded rider. 'Don't be a fool, Damnit. Your wait for her is over, after so long. In the end, I failed Eleanore. You never broke a promise before. You will not now.'

The third hooded figure spoke with the mellifluous yet gravel-gruff bass of the Reverend Samuel Bone, M. A. (Cantab), who in a wonderful move of sleight-of-hand produced a rugby ball from within the folds of his djellaba and tossed it in Daniel's direction.

'Catch it, Damnit,' he chortled. 'You of the safe pair of hands since childhood. Must I remind you of your first school shield and school motto? The shield pictured two pairs of hands, firmly clasped. The hands were feminine and masculine you will recall – the two smaller ones well manicured, the larger ones callous, with barely clean fingernails. You were brought up to recognize that these hands represented lifelong commitment, protection and affection – regardless of class or gender. I would now add race and colour to that latter pair of abstracts. And your school motto? *Meum verbum mea vita*, of course. My word – my life on it. You have given your word to a lady and you will not break it. Her life is in your hands now, Daniel – and *vice-versa*.

I have to go now and I leave you with three little words of eternal truth. *Amor vincit omnia.*'

The stable-block, the camels and the three wise bachelors faded away before his eyes. Daniel found himself standing in the centre of a maze, designed with the use of box bushes which reached only to the height of his shoulders. He could see over the complicated labyrinth to the point of entry, to where Lorna was standing and calling out to him.

'I've brought you an early morning cup of tea, dear. Don't let it get cold.'

'Don't leave me alone, Lorna,' pleaded Daniel. 'I need you to guide me out of this tangled web. Your heart is just my cup of tea. Keep it warm for me. This may take some time. Thank God *amor vincit omnia*.'

He woke with a start.

Lorna was standing at his bedside, bearing a tray of tea. 'I've just had a 'phone call. Aidan Ferrers is coming to see us later today. I hope the idea of lunch at the Sandpiper, Leyburn, appeals.'

CHAPTER LII

Magnum Nomen Habere

A UTUMN TURNED INTO WINTER. Christmas came and went. With obvious grounds for gossip, Tupshorne tongues wagged once the news was out that churchwarden Damnit Greensward had a permanent lady guest happily ensconced at High Ash. Yet never was heard a malicious word. Terms of admiration and even envy were used when the chattering class, referring to Daniel, could state that there was life in the old dog and he appeared to be getting more lively by the day. For her part, Lorna charmed everyone she met. Many of the good folk of Tupshorne, normally reticent with their personal praise of others, could be overheard to say "That Lorna's lovely." Once in a while, on the Christmas party circuit, where there was a chance that they would find themselves among strangers, Daniel was asked to introduce his wife. Whereupon she would answer very quickly and with her most dazzling smile, "I'm Daniel's Lorna," leaving him speechless, but in no mind to contradict her.

The Christmas period saw High Ash turn into a bed and breakfast establishment. Douglas came home to England for a holiday break combined with house-hunting in advance of his permanent move to his London head office at Easter 2001. He brought with him Doctor Rachel Rosenbaum, a raven-haired, blue-eyed beauty, intent on finding a suitable post in medicine within reasonable distance of her fiancé's office.

Early in the New Year, at Lorna's insistence, Rachel drove the Volvo over to Preston to collect Nathaniel Ross, her father, and bring him back to Yowesdale. She knew that Daniel would be intrigued to meet the man who had discovered John Smith's minimal heart defect. The two generations got along famously even before Daniel produced the Glenmorangie.

Damnit was mildly amused when, from their first introduction by Lorna, Douglas displayed a certain coolness of attitude towards him which persisted until Jake and Martha invited Rosenbaums, Swanns and himself on a mid-morning visit to the Brymor Ice

Cream Parlour. The day was bitterly cold but Jake was on his most extrovert and irrepressible form, teasing both engaged couples as if they were love-struck teenagers.

'You do realise, Douglas,' said Jake seriously, 'that this is where your stepfather-to-be, Damnit here, brings all his lady friends. It's a kind of tasting test that they have to undergo to merit his approval. Apparently your dear mama passed *summa cum laude*.'

'You great fibber,' said Lorna. 'As a matter of fact, I really came to look at the beautiful herd of Guernseys – ice cream on the hoof. The superb ice cream is a secondary consideration.'

Rachel joined in the banter. 'Douglas and I first met at an ice cream party in Lagos. It was a case of lick at first sight. There's more to a real ice cream than meets the eye, and in the heat of Nigeria you only get one look!'

'Well,' said Douglas, with a throaty chuckle, 'If this old boy likes his ice cream in weather as chilly as today and my dear mama, as you say, Jake, goes along with the idea then who am I to withhold my own seal of approval? Now I have to decide what to call him.'

'Your mother never calls me anything other than Daniel but you may call me Damnit. Then when somebody says to you "Who's this fellow with you?", pointing at me, you can say in all honesty, "He's my stepfather, Damnit."'

Nathaniel Ross brought the name-calling to an end with a brief comment. 'Rachel doesn't know this – but if she had been a boy, he would have been Daniel, which has the meaning, God is my Judge. Before anyone asks me the obvious question, Rachel means Ewe.'

Lorna surprised everyone, but Douglas most of all. 'You ought to have been named Esther Sarah, Rachel dear, which being interpreted for those who are ignorant of the meaning of names would have you as Star Princess.'

'And I love you too,' laughed Rachel happily. 'I trust that as your stepdaughter-in-law, Daniel, I have passed the ice cream test so where are you taking <u>me</u> to lunch today?'

Daniel looked at the group sitting round the table and wiped his mouth with a paper napkin before replying. 'As God is my judge, you've had enough ice cream to seriously worry the herd. However, my little black-fleeced ewe, when we've all enjoyed a brisk walk round the Marfield Bird Reserve and recovered our appetites, where else can I take you except the bistro at the Black Sheep Brewery? I think they might allow you in without a preliminary sheep-dip at this time of year.'

'Just thank God that your mother changed her mind at the last moment, Rachel,' chipped in her father. 'Originally she wanted to call you Leah. May I assume, Lorna, that your knowledge of Hebrew extends that far?'

'You certainly may,' giggled Lorna. 'You may also safely assume that Daniel, with Jake's help, knows of a Black Cow pub somewhere within striking distance of Tupshorne but not necessarily in Yowesdale. Come on, Princess – the dogs need their baggin.'

At the coffee stage Jake tilted back his chair and looked around the bistro before he spoke. 'Do you recall, Damnit, after my final service and farewell luncheon at Saint Michael's I suggested that you ought to write to book about your escapades? Well, it seems to me that this would be an ideal venue for a book launch. It's a great place for a party – as if you need an excuse!'

Damnit gave Jake his finest knowing smile. 'Tell you what, Jake – I'll call up Albert. He'd make a cracking ghost writer.'

CHAPTER LIII

Dulcedo et Dulcedo

IT WAS INEVITABLE that Winter gave way to Spring that year of two thousand and one, and by the time Easter Sunday arrived Daniel, with a new spring in his step, had become well accustomed to living *à deux* with a woman other than his late sister, Bethan.

High Ash, from the moment of Lorna's installation as mistress of house, even if not as yet married to its master, acquired a certain new buzz. A hive of activity was Martha's term for the new regime. Daniel's queen bee was, like all queen bees, a highly social animal, always busy and never happier than when surrounded by friends of a similar nature.

Always bearing in mind Jake's advice, *vis-à-vis* Lorna's reign, that he should do as he was told without any argument, Daniel found his bachelor world turning upside down. And how he enjoyed it! High Ash, the beehive with its own queen bee, had just one resident drone named Daniel Tiltstone Greensward.

Lorna's many friends in the Cambridge area all wanted to come and visit her new domain in glorious Yowesdale, regardless of the time of year and the occasional spell of inclement weather. Daniel's favourite visitor, by a long chalk, was her lady vicar who needed no second invitation when asked to conduct their wedding. At the outset, Daniel had wanted Jake to officiate and tie the wedding knot, as well as acting as his Best Man if that were possible. On being asked to adjudicate in the matter, Jake's bishop intimated that, while he could see no reason for not combining the two rôles, perhaps it might be kinder not to lumber an old friend in case he had an attack of stage-fright. The bishop's humorous dig at his thespian past was not lost on Jake and they both laughed at such a prospect. Whereupon, Jake took himself out of the equation by declaring that having been Damnit's best man since childhood, he was too old to change. Daniel, in his capacity as churchwarden, could visualize Lorna's delightful vicar sitting in the pew that Jake had vacated the previous October and sounded her out accordingly. Professing to be both flattered and tempted by the suggestion, she dismissed the idea citing the best of all reasons. She felt that she still had much to accomplish in her present post. In the meantime, she said, Daniel would have to be satisfied when she came to conduct his marriage with Lorna.

During the first three days of Holy Week, Damnit was to be seen hard at work in Saint Michael's church gardens making sure that everything was neat and tidy for Easter. Late in the afternoon of the Wednesday that week he was wiping clean the tools he had used, prior to hanging them up in the cellar of the Church Hall, when he noticed the small pane of clear glass, which he had replaced in the door, after smashing it with the hoe handle at the time he was tidying up the previous year. Then on the morning of Maundy Thursday he returned to the cellar and effectively blacked out the pane, using several strips of opaque vinyl tape. Damnit was starting to set out his stall.

Lorna and Daniel were enjoying a post-lunch cup of coffee on Maundy Thursday when the telephone rang. Lorna picked up the cordless which was on the small table at her right elbow. Her ensuing conversation gave Daniel cause to double check the sequence of events which he had planned in the lead-up to his wedding. One of his early schooldays skeletons was about to be brought out of the cupboard and subjected to Lorna's scrutiny.

'Hello,' said Lorna in her best warm telephone answering mode.

'Sweetie! How lovely to hear you. Where are you?

At home?

So to what do we owe the pleasure of this call?

When?

Next week? That's rather short notice.

No. There's no need to apologise. We'll cope. As it so happens we were expecting Douglas and his fiancée but they've had to cry off. Let me just check with Daniel.'

Covering the mouthpiece, she spoke to Daniel.

'It's Sweetie – William Taylor. He and Bronwen will be coming up to Skipton next week and wonder if they could spend a couple of nights here. I couldn't really refuse, so is it O.K. with you? Do you think you'll recognize him? We can get Jake here to meet him as well. Three little boys from school!'

She laughed.

'Of course you couldn't say no,' lied Daniel. 'Let me have a word. I've not seen him for – it must be about fifty years.'

As Lorna passed the telephone to him, Daniel indicated that he would take their empty coffee cups to the kitchen while speaking to William.

'Hello, Tell. Damnit here. We look forward to your arrival. You'll recognize Lorna even if I'm past recognition.'

By this time Damnit had reached the kitchen and switched from banter to serious manner.

'One little thing, Tell. Kindly make no mention of my episode with your tuck-box and its wretched lock. Lorna knows nothing about it and I'd rather keep it that way.'

Lorna entered the kitchen quietly.

'What is it now that you are trying to hide from me?' she asked suspiciously.

'It's nothing to worry your pretty head about, my love.' He spoke very clearly to make sure that Tell could hear. 'William was just reminding me of my career as the High Ashes card-sharp before the headmaster caught up with me.' 'We'll see the pair of you next week then, Tell. I'll hand you back to Lorna to clarify your E.T.A.'

Telephone call over, Lorna said, 'I can't wait to see your face when Sweetie arrives with Bronwen, known as Bel because she's so beautiful. Actually, Belinda is her middle name. By the way, what punishment did my little card-sharp suffer? Something painful, I hope.' She gave him her finest Mona Lisa impression of a smile. A real fish-face!

'Sambo was a marvellously subtle H. M. He dug out from God knows where, in his study, a grubby old book of fifty card tricks and ordered me to learn five of them to be performed at the school Christmas party. You know how much I enjoy a decent game of cards. Now you will understand why I find card tricks such an anathema! Sambo was a great one for making the punishment fit the crime. He once told me a nice tale of a lad, before my time at High Ashes, who was responsible for a harmless but humorous bit of *graffito* on a lavatory door. His punishment was to design a set of half a dozen Christmas cards which could be printed, and sold for school funds. He went on to become a famous cartoonist, but what is even more remarkable, he never forgot to send Sambo a Christmas card – hand-painted – every year. So now for <u>my</u> next trick ...'

'With your ability to hide your feelings, Daniel, you would have made a world-class poker player, I'm sure, but I think I prefer you as a grease-monkey.'

Lorna paused for a moment before continuing.

'It will be a good excuse to visit Brymor once more. You'll be happy – Sweetie has a sweet tooth, as you might remember – as a farmer's daughter Bel will appreciate the Guernseys – and as for Jake, I can't wait to learn from William and him together, just what you were like at High Ashes. Coals are going to be raked over, my good man!'

Daniel smiled wanly as he replied. 'Revelation can be a two-edged sword. I don't think William "Tell" Taylor will drop his ice cream or spill the beans about my murky pre-teen days for fear that I might retaliate by explaining to Belinda why we used to call him "Tell". It had nothing to do with the Swiss patriot and everything to do with telling tales. He grew out of the habit very quickly when eventually Sambo took him on one side and explained, man to man as it were, that sneaks were loathsome creatures and even a plenti-ful supply of sweets would not buy true friendship. After that we all got on like the proverbial house on fire and "Tell", like "Damnit", became terms of affection. You have to laugh now because it all sounds so ludicrous, but it was Tell who said to Sambo, "Greensward swored sir. He said DAMNIT." Thank goodness I didn't say anything worse.'

Lorna hooted with laughter. 'I knew why you were called Damnit when we were at Cambridge but you never named William as the boy. I wonder what Bel will say when <u>I</u> spill the beans, as you say.'

'Don't you dare,' said Daniel with mock severity. 'You wouldn't betray a confidence. It's definitely "not cricket" and Tell <u>was</u> a good cricketer and a fine sport.'

'Only teasing,' said Lorna and then with a wicked little grin remarked, 'I'm counting on Jake to lift the lid on this particular can of worms.'

Six days later, Wednesday in Easter Week, it was indeed Jake, who, while investigating his knickerbocker glory at the Brymor Ice

Cream Parlour, recalled how William had played such an important part in Daniel's nicknaming. On being introduced by Lorna to Bel, Jake – once the niceties had been observed – informed her that her husband, when a lad in the early 1940s was already famous for the size of his tuck-box and the high quality of its contents – when he could remember how to open it without outside help.

'You might not believe this, Bel, but he came back to High Ashes one term with a brand new combination lock on that tuck-box and promptly forgot the number code that would open it. It was dear old Damnit here – and I can see him even now, coming in to the tuck-room in a right sweat after a training run – who cracked the combination in two shakes of a cat's tail. It cost Tell two bars of chocolate, as I recall. I've witnessed a few miracles in my time but Damnit performed the first of them.'

William looked at Daniel, a smile playing across his features. Jake had just put him in to bat.

'I'd totally forgotten the episode, Jake, but now that you remind me I tried to palm him off with only one bar of chocolate. So he locked the box again until I honoured my two bars offer. Then he repeated the fluke. I don't believe in miracles.'

Jake threw a sharp, shrewd look at Daniel before opening his mouth again.

'I wonder if Gary Brickshaw ever owned a tuck-box.'

'Was he at High Ashes? I don't remember the name.' said William.

'No,' said Jake, 'he's a Tupshorne estate agent who had his safe rifled last year by someone who cracked its combination. Only money was taken, the thief locked up after himself and never left a trace except for a packet of kipper fillets skewered to a desk. The security alarm never went off so there was a suspicion it was an inside job. Gary pooh-poohed that idea saying it certainly looked (and smelt) fishy but nobody in his office had that mischievous sense of humour. Actually it's more Damnit's style, I reckon.'

'I have to confess,' said Daniel, it made me chuckle when I heard about the kippers. I'd have been proud to be the perpetrator of such a slick job. Perhaps it's a good thing I was on the Bethdan all that weekend when it happened and went straight from the canal basin to Lorna's.'

Jake wasn't finished and probed a bit deeper.

'Just suppose you drove back to Tupshorne in the middle of the night, Damnit. You could have done it, you know. Albert, at one time, must have taught you most of what he knew about locks.'

'And who was Albert?' asked Bel, somewhat perplexed by all the cross-chat between the men.

Lorna answered the question.

'Albert was Daniel's mentor since his early days in engineering at Cambridge. He was a master locksmith – and a lovely man. He died last year.'

Daniel produced a bombshell for his five eager listeners. He spoke quietly.

'Jake's right.' He paused for maximum effect.

'I could have nipped back in Tottie, in the middle of the night, and done the job. Unfortunately for your supposition, Jake, Tottie never left the canal basin that night. Her owner couldn't even walk straight after a long evening at his favourite pub not many yards from the Bethdan. Mine host there will bear me out. I was sozzled.'

At last Jake smiled indulgently at his friend.

'Just testing, me old mate. As Sambo would have said, it appears that your *tabula* is *rasa* after all. *Deo gratias.*'

'I remember that,' chimed in Tell. 'Your slate is clean. Thank God.'

Non semper ea sunt quae videntur, thought Lorna. Things are not always what they seem to be. Tottie certainly knew the road from Skipton to Tupshorne and back. Moll, Daniel's Honda C90, lived on the Bethdan. Did she know that road? Jake had told her once that he had never met anyone who could hold his drink like Daniel. Had her leopard changed his spots?

CHAPTER LIV

Vir Novus: Currus Novus

TELL AND BEL TAYLOR enjoyed greatly their brief stay at High Ash and while in Yowesdale took the opportunity to motor over the hill into Wensleydale and book bed and breakfast accommodation for the duration of the Swann-Greensward wedding weekend. Lorna and Daniel had arranged their wedding reception at the Sandpiper Inn in Leyburn and it seemed sensible, if a room was available, to make use of the opportunity. Tell reasoned that if the wedding breakfast involved an overactive toastmaster, then he might need a divan within easy staggering distance. Too much vintage champagne never failed to make him sleepy – a fact that Bel discovered only in the evening of their own wedding.

After waving off their guests down the High Ash drive, Daniel turned to Lorna and delivered his personal assessment of the couple. 'Well, my dear, Bel is the real Sweetie Taylor and William Tell is maturing nicely, rather like a ripe cheese, a bit crumbly and crusty around the edges. I think Sambo would have approved.'

'I like to think that he would have approved of all three of you,' replied Lorna. 'You've probably forgotten that I met him once, just fleetingly, after that Varsity match when you scored the winning try.'

'I'm not sure I ever knew. The mood after that match was one of such euphoria we didn't really know if we were coming or going, and, of course, you and I had parted company a few weeks earlier. I'm glad that you remember though.'

'How could I forget that deep bass voice – like dark treacle and chocolate? I've a memory for voices or vocal timbres. I suppose it's something to do with my singing. I will need to sing in a choir other than your Saint Michael's church choir after we're married. Martha's Ladies' Choir might have a spare copy for an ageing soprano next September when the Autumn season starts.'

'They're always on the look-out for new talent. I reckon you and Martha would make a fair duet for next year's Wensleydale Tournament of Song.'

'Here comes my favourite black duo,' said Lorna as Baggins came charging through the open doorway being chased by Rauch, now nearly seven months old.

'Poor Bags! I'm afraid my pup is making your life a misery now that Sprottle's returned to her master.'

'She loves it,' laughed Daniel. 'It's a good thing that Rauch understands it's "game over" when Bags snarls that little bit louder.

To change the subject – seeing the Taylors leaving in their shiny new car leads me to thinking it's time we changed your trusty chariot.'

'Over my dead ...,' Lorna broke off. 'I thought it would see me out after you last serviced it for me. Are you now saying that my Volvo estate is about to become defunct before me?'

'Not necessarily,' said Daniel, 'but ...'

'But nothing,' replied Lorna tartly. 'It was good enough for me and Sprottle so it will do for Rauch and Baggins – with space to spare. It's Tottie you need to trade in.'

She changed tack, enquiring sweetly what sort of car Daniel had in mind for her anyway.

'No, no,' replied Daniel. 'Sorry I spoke. It's just that I thought the moment opportune to swap one of our cars for something higher off the ground. Almost without exception, our visitors complain about not being able to see over the dry stone walls of the Dales when we give them the tourist bit. When I collected a new tail-pipe for Tottie from the Toyota centre at Knaresborough last month I was rather taken with the various RAVs on display. Actually, the idea struck a wedding bell but maybe I've dropped a clanger as Lord Idiom might say.'

'But Rauch is the wedding present I wanted – anything else would be ..., well not unwanted – a trifle unnecessary perhaps. What if we go the other way? Will your RAV take our dogs and us in reasonable comfort? You're always telling me dogs have priority.'

'No bother,' said Daniel. Are you suggesting we have three cars?'

'No, silly,' replied Lorna. 'Let me buy you a RAV as my present to you. As the advertisement would have it, "Because you're worth it"! And, having sold my house, I can afford it.'

'Hold on,' said Daniel, 'that means Tottie has to go.'

He thought carefully for a few moments, recalling Jake's instruction to do whatever Lorna fancied.

'I give in. You're right as usual. I am worth it, of course, but it won't be easy breaking the news to Tottie. I'll explain about the wedding present angle. So thank you very much, dear. I accept with all possible grace and gratitude. The RAV is a four-wheel drive vehicle – if we get a bad winter, and it can happen here – then it could prove to be invaluable.'

Lorna looked at him with a gleam in her eye and then raised an eyebrow. 'Although it is a present, I will let you choose the colour – subject to my approval – but the choice of name on this occasion shall be my prerogative. I know all your cars are required to have suggestive names, so how does *Leman* sound to you?'

'Deliciously derogatory,' guffawed Daniel. 'I wonder if the Toyota colour chart includes a suitable "saucy red," as in tomato ketchup. We can check that out tomorrow. I'll ring Knaresborough now – they're a most obliging car firm but it's always a courtesy to call by appointment.'

Two weeks later a red Toyota RAV4 was delivered to High Ash, by which time Lorna had altered the name to Trollop, and Daniel had decided to change his Best Man.

Damnit came straight to the point with Jake by telling him that it had always been his wish from student days that, if he ever married, Jake should officiate before the altar.

Jake, for his part, was not surprised by Damnit's change of heart. Their ties of brotherhood almost demanded that when the time came he would be honour bound to pronounce Daniel and his chosen bride to "be man and wife together, In the Name of the Father, and of the Son, and of the Holy Ghost. Amen."

Damnit further explained his decision by saying that Jake the Rake would always be his *alter ego*, but on this occasion Colin Blunden, the Rolls Royce colleague who had saved his life when he had a heart attack, would be geared up to be Best Man. After all, without Colin's timely arrival at the scene of his collapse, there would have been no Damnit Tiltstone Greensward to be entered in the marital stakes.

The arrangements for the wedding were falling into place. Lorna's lady vicar was in no way put out by Daniel's request for Jake to tie the knot – most of the remainder of the church service was "in her hands". Colin Blunden was delighted to act as Best Man – he had many a tale to tell of Daniel's days at Rolls; some involved

John Smith, the raconteur supreme.

Lorna had second thoughts about the subject of bridesmaids. If Daniel could have a Best Man, then why shouldn't she have an aide as well? Rachel, her future daughter-in-law, would be the perfect choice and it might not be a bad idea to have a doctor on hand. Such excitement ...

CHAPTER LV

Ecce! Venit Pictor

ONCE LORNA HAD ASCERTAINED that Rachel was happy to be her sole bridesmaid, she and Daniel sat down to examine the list of essentials appertaining to their wedding on 2nd of June. Baggins and Rauch were with them.

It was a warm, almost balmy May evening, heavy with the scent of lilac and roses. They sat on an old teak garden bench under the tall, golden ash which had been planted there as a young tree by the original owner of the house, a man of vision who could foresee the tree in its maturity, golden in leaf and golden of twig. It was to be Daniel who called the bungalow High Ash, recalling his early schooldays at High Ashes Preparatory School.

'Wonderful things happen under high ash trees,' said Daniel wistfully, looking up to the sky through the tracery of branches. 'Here we are, sitting on a now rather wobbly bench, discussing our future, very much in the Autumn of our years. And I know it to be true that all too many years ago when Jake was at Cambridge and in despair about his damaged eyesight, he was sitting in his college garden on just such a bench under a massive ash tree when he recognized his call to the priesthood. The omens are good for those who contemplate under the shade of an English relative of the olive tree. Perhaps it has something to do with olive branches carried by doves. Serenity.'

'Coming from you, Daniel,' murmured Lorna, 'that is almost romantic verging on the poetic. And it's time you wrote another poem for me – I've just about recovered from the shock of the first one. When we are married I intend to frame it and hang it in the hall.'

'Let's get wed first,' chuckled Daniel, 'then we'll see. Now back to our arrangements. Where's our list?'

The list was self-explanatory and as they considered each item Lorna "ticked the box".

Wedding. *L & D. (Douglas to give me away! L)*
When? *11am Saturday 2nd June* ☑
Where? *St M. the Archangel, Tupshorne* ☑
Bridesmaid? *Rachel* ☑
Best Man? *Colin* ☑
Celebrants? *Jake and Julia* ☑
Church Bells? *Yes* ☑
Church Choir? *Yes* ☑
Church Flowers? *St M's Floral Team* ☑
Bouquets + Buttonholes? *Tupshorne Florashow* ☑
Wedding Cars? *Ewes-R-Cars, Tupshorne* ☑
Wedding Cakes? *Jake (& Brymor I.C. Parlour)* ☑
Reception? *Sandpiper Inn, Leyburn* ☑
Airflights? *4th June and 18th June* ☑
Order of Service Sheets? *Yowesprint* ☑
Weather? *Pot luck!* ☑
Care of dogs while away? *Jake and Martha* ☑

I've an awful feeling there's something missing,' said Daniel. 'We know that guests at the reception will number forty-nine.'

'Got it!' said Lorna. 'No photographer.'

'Oh no,' replied Daniel. 'I had pushed that item to the back of my mind because I think, or thought, that Timothy Welsh could take care of it. He's an award-winning amateur photographer. I'll give him a ring now. It's getting cooler so we may as well go indoors.'

Daniel's fellow churchwarden was quite overcome when asked to take on the appointment of wedding photographer – a branch of his art as yet unexplored. 'I'd be honoured,' was his reply, 'just so long as you recognize that I make no claims to being a professional.'

'All you need, Timothy, is to keep your pipe-stem between your teeth and you'll do a grand job, I know,' Daniel reassured him and went on to say, 'I'm not looking for something for nothing, Timothy. A handsome going rate is negotiable now I've found the right man, amateur or not.'

'You can forget about that, Damnit,' expostulated Timothy indignantly. 'It'll be a labour of love as Herakles said when asked to steal Hippolyte's girdle. His ninth labour.'

'Tut tut,' said Damnit. 'That sounds a bit saucy. Who was Hippolyte?'

'Queen of the Amazons.'

'Of course she was,' said Damnit, 'now you remind me. A pity Herakles had to kill her to get the girdle. No matter. I'll find a way of saying thank you to you after the wedding, even if its only something to stuff in your pipe and smoke. "Old Walnut" plug, I think, for a kick-off.'

'That would be lovely, thank you,' said Timothy and rang off.

Daniel looked into his pocket diary and scanned the date calendar. Only four weeks to go to the great day. His eye caught an entry for the 31st of May which stated, "Buy paint for C.H." That's two weeks too late he thought – only two days before the wedding – and moved the entry to the 17th. That would give him adequate time to calculate the physics required.

By the time the 17th of May arrived, Damnit had measured the area of the surfaces to be painted in the Church Hall and calculated how many litres of gloss and emulsion paint would be required to apply two coats. Then, quite deliberately, he reduced the quantities by three-quarters before buying the cheapest brand he could find, together with a large bottle of turpentine substitute for cleaning paintbrushes. By nature a thrifty son of Yowesdale, he elected to use all of his old brushes and a collection of dustsheets from High Ash. All the painting materials and paraphernalia were then taken to the cellar of the Church Hall and positioned with meticulous precision on the two old wooden tables which he had repaired the previous Autumn. They were only just strong enough to bear the weight of the paint.

On the fourth day after the setting of the cans of paint on the tables the sun shone in all his glory and as the church clock struck twelve Daniel had made it his top priority, even if at very short notice, to find a vital little job to do in the cellar. It did not take long. He filled up with water the glass jug, discarded from High Ash, to the mark he had scored when Bethan was alive and placed it at the front of the first table visible on entering the cellar. Taking a torch which he had brought from home, he switched it on before turning off the ceiling light and retreating to the entry door. The opaque vinyl tape was so easy to remove from the small pane of glass allowing a powerful beam of sunlight to illuminate the table nearest the door. Daniel switched off the torch and shifted the glass jug to catch the centre of the sunbeam which came to focus on a dustsheet covered by a newspaper. On the paper stood the bottle of turpentine substitute surrounded by several cans of paint. Daniel moved quickly to the door and masked the glass pane once more with the vinyl tape. Ten minutes later he was back at High Ash, in good time for his lunch, and in excellent humour.

Lorna called out to him from the kitchen. 'That was quick, Daniel. Whatever the little problem was, it must have been easily solved.'

'That's right,' replied Daniel. 'I managed to cast light on the matter in question.'

'What matter in question?' asked Lorna.

'How to make the best use of sunshine to heat and light our church hall without resorting to solar panels. What's for lunch? I'm proper peckish.'

CHAPTER LVI

Habendum et Tenendum

TEN DAYS BEFORE THE wedding Lorna, out of the blue, suddenly announced to Daniel that he had omitted one special event from their pre-nuptial arrangements.

Daniel was mystified. 'What on earth do you mean?' he asked. 'I feel as if I've been eating and sleeping nuptials for months. Tell me!'

'No stag do,' said Lorna.

'And no hen party either,' retorted Daniel.

They both burst out laughing before he calmed down and admitted that he wasn't all that keen to relive the days when he would be the last one standing at the bar when the rest of the team had gone home to bed.

'I remember an occasion when Jake told me, with some admiration I may say, that he never met anyone who could hold their liquor quite like you. Old age must have caught up with you last February when you thought you were unfit to drive Tottie.'

'It looks that way,' said Daniel, 'but if you fancy throwing a hen party, don't let me stop you.'

'I'm not that bothered,' said Lorna. 'If you were to ask me, I think I would opt for a light quiet meal out somewhere with a few friends the evening before.'

Daniel stroked his chin, thinking. 'That,' he said, 'is a lovely idea. A sort of extended supper party for our favourite local yokels who all know you by now, and add in those near and dear who will have come from away. Perhaps we could arrange to meet at the Black Sheep Brewery Bistro at Masham. A Black Sheep Party has an appealing baa to it.'

'That sounds fine to me. Early evening meal and not too late to bed, at least as far as I am concerned. Remember, you're spending your last night of freedom at Jake and Martha's. How many takers do you reckon for the bistro?'

They put their heads together and came up with a figure of twenty-eight, including vicars, relatives, local and Cambridge friends, together with a few "wild cards" such as Colin Blunden, Aidan Ferrers, Tell and Bel, and Max Herrick.

The bistro supper made a delightful entrée for the wedding breakfast the following day and the diners parted company, making their separate ways to various hostelries for the night.

Lorna had a restful night, untroubled by dreams, at High Ash.

Daniel was restless, trying to go to sleep in a strange bed at Martha and Jake's cottage. Eventually he resorted to visiting dreamland and his imaginary country mansion to catch up with Albert. Bedroom number seven was empty and bare – devoid of furniture, carpet and curtains, except for one large wall mirror. Damnit looked at himself in the mirror only to see, standing behind him, his three bachelor sages.

Albert spoke. 'Daniel. Hear the word of the master locksmith. Tomorrow, you will gain the key of happiness. It is fragile. Guard it with loving care.' He vanished.

Janis Kalējs spoke. 'Damnit, man. Hear the word of him who would have been a blacksmith. You will find a lucky horseshoe under a stone by the front gate where you rest this night. Nail it above your own front door.'

Janis' reflection in the mirror faded and Daniel turned to face the Reverend Samuel Bone. Sambo smiled before addressing him. 'Greensward. Translate. *Bono animo esse. Dominus tecum. Dominus vobiscum.*'

'Yes, sir,' answered Daniel. 'Be happy. God be with you – singular. God be with you – plural.'

'Well done, Daniel. Now look in the mirror again.'

Daniel turned to the mirror once more, only to see the reflection of Sambo break up into a myriad of stars to be replaced by a message, written as if with a fiery red lipstick and in Albert's hand. He read *"NOTA BENE: NOTA AQUAM IN.* He slept.

At breakfast, Daniel enquired of Jake, the real classics scholar, if *"Nota bene: nota aquam in"* meant anything to him.

'No,' stated Jake firmly. 'It sounds like something contrived to mean <u>something</u> though. Roughly translated, it says "mark well: mark the water," but what it actually means ... your guess is as good as mine.' He looked sharply at his friend.

'Been dreaming again, have we?' he enquired.

'It's time you put away childish things, as Saint Paul might have said. Anybody might think you'd been looking through a glass darkly – Paul again. I do hope you're not playing with fire, old friend. I'd hate to see you burn your fingers unnecessarily.'

'Don't fret,' said Daniel. 'It's only my wild imagination running riot in a more puzzling way than usual.'

After breakfast Daniel walked the few paces to Jake's front gate and, with something of an effort, rolled to one side a medium sized rock which looked as if it had lain undisturbed for many a year. The horseshoe of his dream lay there, pressed into the earth.

'Oh, My God. My God, what have I done?' croaked Daniel in horror as he picked up the horseshoe. Then he went indoors and told Jake the whole story of his dream. 'What on earth can it all mean, Jake? I'm at a loss.'

'That makes two of us,' said Jake grimly. 'You really have burnt your fingers. But rest assured – whatever it does mean – it will all come right when you attain wedded bliss in a few hours time. Meanwhile, you can leave that rusty old horseshoe with me. I will undertake to have it sanded, cleaned and lacquered. Then I will ask the bishop to consecrate it before I hang it above your front door by the time you and Lorna return from your Sicilian honeymoon. Maybe then your wretched visits to another world of dreams might come to an end, lest you go out of your mind. As for getting yourself off to sleep at times of stress, why not try my chosen path? I don't go looking for country properties or pie in the sky; I pray myself to sleep, without fail.'

Back on an even keel now, Daniel responded with a chuckle. 'Not nearly so exciting as my dream world, but I might give your method a try. There is, I think, a Chinese curse which runs, "May you live in exciting times". Thanks for the offer to attend to my horseshoe dilemma. You have to admit, it's a quite extraordinary episode. What would you have to say if John had told me of a pot of gold lying under that rock? You would be entitled to half.'

Now it was Jake's turn to laugh. 'Next time you decide to consult Albert, can I tag along?'

'Only if you ask nicely,' replied Damnit. 'Do you remember our English master at Rockcliffe? What a stickler! I hear him even now, saying "You most surely <u>can</u> Greensward. Whether or not you <u>may</u> is an entirely different matter."' He looked at his wristwatch. 'It's high time we were getting changed.'

And off they went to dress for the single most important event in Daniel's life.

It was as he was brushing his teeth that Daniel grasped the significance of "*Nota bene: nota aquam in*". His shirt sleeve brushed against the glass tumbler standing on the little shelf where the Drake toothbrushes and toothpaste were kept. With a speed of reaction which astounded even himself, he left the toothbrush lodged in his mouth and caught the tumbler before it crashed into the wash hand basin. The lipsticked writing on the mirror was incomplete. A vital word was missing and the closing inverted commas were absent. In full, it ought to have read, "*NOTA BENE: NOTA AQUAM IN VITRO*". So simple – "Mark well: watch the water in the glass".

The key to the church hall cellar was ever present on his car keyring, and there was always a small plastic bottle of drinking water to be found in every car he had ever owned.

Arriving early at the church with Colin Blunden, Damnit parked Trollop round the back of the building by the cellar door which gave access to the Tiltstone and the central heating installation. Under the pretext of going to use the loo, he crossed over the road to the church hall, let himself into the cellar and switched on the light. Just as he expected, some of the *Aqua in vitro* had evaporated since he had filled the glass jug up to the mark two weeks earlier. Using the water from his little bottle he raised the water level to the magic line, before peeling the vinyl tape off the small window pane in the door. Then, light switched off and door locked, he re-crossed the road, replaced the plastic bottle in Trollop and with Colin at his right marched down the central aisle of the church to take his seat at the front. Twenty minutes to zero hour.

The church bells rang and rang and rang until, twenty minutes past the hour appointed, Daniel despatched his Best Man to fetch the bride. Something very serious must have happened to Lorna for her to be so late and Daniel felt more than a flicker of apprehension as Jake, until then waiting in the chancel, came forward to have a word with him.

Jake smiled and placed a firm and reassuring hand on Daniel's shoulder. 'Sambo says this. "*Aequam servare mentem et bono animo esse.*" Get it, Damnit?'

'Got it,' replied Damnit, quick as a flash. 'Panic not and be of good cheer.' His sigh was one of relief.

'Good,' finished Jake. 'Sit down and pray – now!'

Hardly had Daniel begun to pray for Lorna's safe arrival before he was aware of a flushed Colin Blunden sitting beside him breathing heavily, as the organ began to play Bach's "Sheep may safely graze", adopted long ago as the Yowesdale anthem. Lorna was on her way.

Daniel stood to greet her, amazed at her apparent poise considering she was nearly half an hour late.

A quick whispering match ensued.

'What kept you?'

'Rauch ran away.'

'What, for twenty minutes?'

'No. Ten.'

'What next?'

'The wedding car died.'

'And?'

'I tried the Volvo.'

'And?'

'Flat battery!'

'So?'

'I nearly walked until Tottie coughed. Don't ask me how or why, but what a good thing you had kept her *'pro tem'*.

'Er hum,' coughed Julia. 'May we proceed with the marriage?'

Fifty minutes later the bells again rang and rang.

Miss Spotty Potts set sail on the organ, full steam ahead, with her powerful rendition of Bach's Toccata and Fugue in D minor. She played it so beautifully. Such a pity the happy couple, on their own cloud nine, were oblivious to the sublime sound of Bach, mighty Bach.

CHAPTER LVII

Ignis at Sulphur. Calor et Fumus

TAORMINA IN JUNE is a wellnigh perfect holiday resort. Soft and gentle sunlight, allied to the natural warmth of the Mediterranean found on the Strait of Messina, provided the ideal atmosphere for a relaxing honeymoon. Perched high above the sea, from the town's selected viewpoints a traveller has a stunning panorama, incorporating the magnificent coastline stretching northwards to Messina and due south to Siracusa. Across the Strait to the East lies the rugged mountainous beauty that is Calabria while to the West is the dominating mass of Mount Etna, looming over and controlling the lives and way of life of all that lives under its mighty footprint.

Yet in high season, Taormina falls far short of perfection for those seeking the quiet life. Traffic density on the road and population density on the beaches in high Summer militate against a truly restful break. Some years the heat bothers even the locals.

Daniel was well aware of the congestion which might have blighted their honeymoon, knowing that April would have been so much more pleasant with a cooler atmosphere and freedom from crowds. In discussion with Lorna about their honeymoon destination he made no secret of the fact that it was the sunshine in the month of June which drew him to Sicily. She was quite content to follow his wishes, knowing how important had become the intention to drop Albert's ashes in the crater of mighty Etna. Daniel also made it clear that their next holiday would be "his lady's" choice.

On Wednesday, the 6th of June, Daniel decided to make their ascent of the largest active volcano in Europe. He reasoned that once Albert's mortal dust had been consigned to the care of Vulcan, the remainder of the honeymoon would take place in an atmosphere of untroubled calm – so long as Etna kept quiet about his ash disposal actions. Etna is unpredictable, capable of upping the force of volcanic activity at any time, without warning.

To reach the summit of Etna is an experience never to be forgotten. For certain travellers the journey entails passing through a floral heaven to get a view of Hell. Soil of volcanic provenance is rich, and leaving by car from Taormina one passes through orchards of various citrus fruits, vineyards and olive groves on the lower slopes. Higher up are vast woods of oak, pine and eucalyptus before reaching the barren lava and ash near to the summit.

Daniel and Lorna took a car to the end of the road at Rifugio Sapienza where at a height of over two thousand feet they transferred to a cable car which carried them up to the top terminus. The final approach to the rim of the crater was only a short distance to be accomplished on foot.

The travel agent through whom Daniel had booked all their arrangements recommended that diligent study of a modern guidebook concerned solely with Sicily would pay a handsome dividend. Apart from offering considerable help with the language and the nature of the native Sicilians, the guide featured a special section on clothing. With prior warning, he and Lorna could be seen nearing the brink of the main crater dressed in warm clothes and stout footwear. Regardless of the heat emanating from the lava, bubbling away in the crater, the top of Mount Etna experiences a chill wind even in Summer when the summit is not crowned with snow, and the sharp rocky terrain, rich in brimstone, rules out the wearing of holiday sandals. The air is full of sulphur fumes.

At precisely one o'clock, Sicilian time, Daniel stepped forward to the brink of the crater and looked down, with a shudder, into the mouth of Hell. Nobody, except Lorna, standing near him took the slightest notice as he retrieved from his coat pocket a strong, twin-walled, paper bag which weighed surprisingly little and tossed it into the glowing furnace. They never saw the bag burn or the mineral remains of Albert blow away, obscured by the fiery smoke. For a moment Etna quivered before emitting a sound more akin to a grumble than a rumble. Lorna and Daniel stayed standing on the rim of the volcano as the other onlookers stepped back in alarm. Then, after about thirty seconds, they too turned away not in fright but in astonishment.

'Did I imagine it,' said Daniel, 'that I heard Albert's voice?'

'No,' replied Lorna. 'I heard him too.'

'What did you hear?'

'Albert said "thank you for coming," as if we were here by invitation.'

'Yes, yes,' said Daniel. 'Then there was something else about "See you sometime – not bedroom seven – but in the Prince Collection." What can that mean?'

'It's no use asking me,' replied Lorna. 'We don't have more than four bedrooms at High Ash. As for the Prince Collection, you'll need to contact your friend "Prof" Tobias – he's the man responsible for Albert's collection of locks at the National Museum of Engineering.'

'You're a bright lass,' said Daniel cheerily, and giving her a kiss. 'It means, my love, that Albert has not signed off yet. I just wish he'd have said "Under that portrait of Vulcan at the N.B.M." It's much nearer than the N.M.E.'

Returning to Taormina, Lorna once again had cause to wonder to what manner of a man she now found herself married, and she vowed to find out somehow in such a way that Daniel would never know. For the time being, all she knew was that he loved and adored her. That had to suffice – for the time being!

CHAPTER LVIII

Igniculus Alibi

I T WAS NOON, PRECISELY, in British Summer Time as at one o'clock in Sicily, Daniel relinquished Albert's ashes into the care of Vulcan, working away in his smithy under Mount Etna.

At that same moment, in the room which housed the Prince Collection of the locksmith's art at the National Museum of Engineering all the light bulbs exploded and the room was plunged into darkness. Later the strange phenomenon was explained away as being due to a sudden surge of power from the national grid. "Prof" Tobias could never understand why only the Prince Collection took the hit.

A coachload of engineering students were on an educational visit to the National Blacksmiths' Museum. On entering the foyer, their tour guide for the day, Mr Aidan Ferrers, brimming over with infectious enthusiasm, as part of his introductory *spiel* brought the students to admire Athene Hope's magnificent painting "VULCAN, ANCIENT ROMAN GOD OF FIRE AND FORGE, CREATES THE FIRST WOMAN, PANDORA, OUT OF SOIL." As they were all gazing in some awe at the huge picture, one student remarked, 'How in Hades did the artist know that Vulcan was such an ugly bru ...?' The smoke and sweat-grimed face of the Divine Smith in the portrait broke into a grin, followed by a knowing wink. None of the students saw the facial changes – after all, to them it was a grand day out away from run of the mill lectures. But Aidan Ferrers saw what had happened and marvelled. After fifteen years, the portrait of Vulcan, the God of Metalworkers, had come to life. Wonders never cease.

Tupshorne in Yowesdale was luxuriating in the traditional flaming June sunshine beloved of the tourism industry. This day the heat was tempered by the gentle southwesterly breeze sauntering in from over the Pennines and down the dale.

The mid-Summer sun beamed down on the Church Hall of Saint Michael the Archangel, seeking out the clear glass chink of a pane in the cellar door and so unlocking the latent power hidden in the crystal water jug which Damnit had given to Bethan and Gerald on the occasion of their wedding. The heat was on.

A faint blue tendril of smoke arose from the newspaper on the old table.

Vulcan, Ancient Roman God of Fire and Forge, was at work – with a grin and a wink.

Daniel Tiltstone Greensward stood on the summit of Mount Etna – two missions accomplished.

Donovan Caldwell Leaman Scripsit
VIII – XII – MMIV

Chapter I from

Part Three of
THE TILTSTONE TRILOGY

TILTSTONE, GEM AND
TOMBSTONE

Audivi Illum Canentem
(I heard him sing)

CHAPTER I

Audivi Illum Canentem (I heard him sing)

IT WAS MID JANUARY 1947 and the beginning of the Lent term at High Ashes Preparatory School in Derbyshire. The Headmaster, The Reverend Samuel Bone, MA (Cantab), an outstanding sportsman when in his prime with 1st Class Honours in the Classical Tripos, did not include in his list of attainments the title of Weather Prophet. The Lent term was destined to go down in meteorological records as one of the most bitter Winter periods of the twentieth century. Snowdrifts as high as telegraph poles were the norm in the neighbourhood of High Ashes and for some weeks it was necessary to collect essential food supplies by toboggan from the nearest town.

Ten days after the start of term a rather unusual new boy arrived who spoke little English, and that, only when spoken to. Yet his command of French, especially his accent, was so good that if the French teacher was indisposed then the latecomer, even allowing for his limited vocabulary of a typical eight-year-old, was quite capable of taking a French class – provided the class, with pointed juvenile humour, was prepared to listen to *le petit pain* in the neck. Schoolboys of a certain age can sometimes be capable of tactless cruelty. Silas Kinnon Beaune was the only son of an English mother, Katharine Kinnon, and a French father, Marcel Beaune, a Commissioner with the International Refugee Organization, working under the auspices of the United Nations.

One of the several peculiarities associated with the residents of High Ashes was the high incidence of nicknames. It was an affliction common to staff and pupils alike, starting at the very top with Sambo, the Headmaster, and eventually reaching down to the latest arriving new boy. Silas, in name only, disappeared within days, replaced by "Skinandbone" which quickly gave way to "Skinny". It mattered not a jot that "Skinny" was a roly-poly pudding of a boy, fair-haired and blue-eyed. He looked like a cherub, sang like a little angel, yet for all the overall impression of chubbiness visible to an observer he had inherited from his mother the long slender hands of an artist. To the staff he was for ever Beau and never to be confused with their revered Headmaster.

For a boy of only eight years old Silas was nobody's fool. Born on New Year's Day 1938, a Paris suburb was his home until late May 1940 when Marcel Beaune, anticipating the fall of France to Nazi Germany, fled the country to Switzerland with his wife and young son before enlisting in the Free French Army led by General Charles de Gaulle. For the next five years, at times living in considerable deprivation, Katharine Beaune reared her son in the absence of his father, always mentioning his name as if he was expected to come home on the morrow. Doubt never entered her mind, and her unfailing optimism was mirrored in Silas's attitude to life. Living on her wits for a few years called for some base cunning at times and Silas, even as a little boy, was well aware that his mother had a talent for being manipulative when it suited her to be so. As a well qualified linguist fluent in several European languages, it was as a teacher of English that Katharine survived the War years, and the one child who received true one-to-one tuition was her son, Silas. Katharine was also an accomplished musician, both a pianist and a soprano singer, which all went to explain why her son, at eight years old, spoke and understood English perfectly well and could sing folk songs in three languages. He was clever enough to notice that, when his mother needed time to think before answering a question, she would either ask for the question to be repeated or pretend that her knowledge of the language was not secure enough to grasp the question. Silas imitated his mother, developing a fine impression of total puzzlement as and when it suited his plans. He could be devious.

The final week of the Lent term at High Ashes was one which featured two highlights of the school year. On the last evening before leaving for the Easter holidays the drama department staged a performance of a show titled, "Hyperhistrionics". This theatrical vehicle was a means of allowing any boy in the school to appear solo on stage to speak a "party piece" of his own choosing. Histrionic behaviour to the nth degree was positively encouraged in an attempt to give the youngsters an opportunity to release their pent up emotions. In such a way did Mrs Askey, the drama teacher, identify many a promising actor or orator.

Two days prior to "Hyperhistrionics" saw the culmination of the term's athletics events, the Age Cross Country Championships. This was a handicap race over a roughly oval shaped three-mile course running through the fields of the four farms that were contiguous with the High Ashes estate. The handicapping system resulted in those boys who were in their final year being required to cover the full distance, while those in their first year started the course with only two miles to run. The boys of the intermediate years were handicapped at levels between two and three miles. The 1946 Championship had been won by an outstanding schoolboy athlete, who was confidently expected to beat his own course record in his final year. If betting on the outcome of the Championship had been permitted at High Ashes, any wise bookie would have been on holiday quoting the weather as an excuse for his absence.

On the day, however bright the sunshine, the snow-melt threatened to turn the form book upside down. Mud, slush and the remains of snowdrifts in north-facing hedgecops negated all thought of a new record time. The reigning champion appeared to be oblivious to the conditions underfoot, picking his sure-footed way, shod in his seemingly magical spikes, through all the hazards until having left behind all his contemporary competitors, as he clambered over an elevated stile, he caught sight of HIS Championship Trophy glinting in the sunshine, standing on the trestle table by the finishing tape. He had a half-mile to go and he exulted in the knowledge that he could easily run down the few junior stragglers left in his sights. Then, approaching an open gateway he became aware of a fat eight-year-old French boy snared in a bramble bush. Skinny Beaune had slipped in the mudslick by the gatestump and landed on his back in the prickly thicket. Between his sobs of pain and frustration Silas displayed a remarkable command of the English language. Overcoming his surprise at Skinny's vocabulary – hidden until now – the Champion, a boy known for a "safe pair of hands" whatever the circumstances, stripped off his running singlet and, binding it round his hands, used it to free the little French canary. As the sun slipped behind a cloud, the shine on the Championship

Trophy died away. The Champion donned his vest again and gently shepherded Silas to the finish, uncaring now if he was to come in last. The incident went down in High Ashes history. The Champion's course record of 1946 was to last another fifty years but he himself chose to forget the Age Cross Country of 1947. Silas Kinnon Beaune never forgot the day that a bramble bush loosed his English tongue or the Champion who, in his innate compassion, threw away his Championship.